W9-BRI-291

"I ALWAYS COLLECT WHAT'S COMING TO ME."

"Your brother gave me a message to give to you. He said to tell you that everything was going along fine."

Raven slammed her fist on the table. "Didn't you think that was important enough to tell me?"

"Well, yes." Chance still refused to look at her. "Like I said, I forgot about it."

"I can understand that," Raven jeered. "You had other things on your mind."

Chance's head jerked around at Raven's thinly veiled meaning. "Yes, I did." His eyes bored into hers. "And you might as well know I still have the same thing on my mind."

Her eyes snapping, Raven leaned forward and shot at him, "You might as well know that I'm advising you to get it out of your mind."

"Oh no, lady." Chance glared back at her. "I always collect what's coming to me."

Raven

Norah Hess

LEISURE BOOKS   NEW YORK CITY

With love to sister June.

A LEISURE BOOK®

October 1999

Published by

Dorchester Publishing Co., Inc.
276 Fifth Avenue
New York, NY 10001

ISBN 0-8439-4611-3

Raven

Through the uncurtained window of a log cabin a shrill scream pierced the night. And in the dark of midnight a baby girl with pitch-black hair was born.
She was named Raven.

Chapter One

Nineteen-year-old Raven McCloud Spencer knelt at her husband's side, watching his life's blood spill out onto the dirty floor of the saloon.

Her green eyes shed no tears. Her only emotion was relief. At last she was free of him. Never again would she be forced to sit beside him at a gambling table, exposed to the penetrating eyes of the rabble that gathered at Milo Spencer's table to ogle the firm tops of breasts revealed by her low-cut dress.

She had objected strongly the first week after they were married when Milo ordered her to wear the revealing gown. She had exclaimed in disgust, "It practically shows my entire breasts!"

He had only laughed and drawled. "That's the idea, honey. Just keep the nipples covered. I want the men so busy trying to see down the front of your dress, they won't be paying any attention to what my fingers are doing."

She had not given in at first, but when he backed up his verbal threats with his fists, she had no choice.

So it had continued, the men ogling her bare-bosomed beauty, lust stabbing out of their bold, hungry eyes. Milo was often urged to use her as his ante. He had always refused . . . until last night.

He had been losing heavily, despite his slick manipulation of the cards. She could tell he was becoming desperate by the sheen of sweat on his brow.

Of the five men who had been playing, three had dropped out and there remained only her husband and a man whose dusty clothes and unshaven face said that he had been on a cattle drive for some time.

Unlike the other men, who looked at her with leering eyes, this one hadn't seemed to pay any attention to her since he joined the game.

She had been startled and shocked when the cowboy said, "There's close to a thousand dollars lying there on the table. You can have it all in exchange for letting me spend one night with your wife."

She had looked at Milo and gasped softly when she saw indecision in his eyes. He was actually considering the man's offer. In the hush that came over the table and bystanders, she had jumped to her feet and run from the saloon. . . .

*   *   *

As the patrons and saloon women stood in a circle around Raven and her dead husband, she felt the bartender gently lift her to her feet. Milo had been caught cheating at cards.

"Let me take you back to your room, Raven. A couple of the men will carry Milo over to the funeral home. You can make arrangements with the director in the morning."

Funeral arrangements, Raven thought bitterly. Well, at least money would be no problem.

When they arrived at her room and she unlocked the door, the big saloon owner said awkwardly, "If you're short of money, Raven, to see Milo properly buried, I can lend you what you need."

"That's awfully kind of you, Tom, but it's not necessary," she said automatically, unable to believe that any of this was real.

The big man shrugged. "I thought I'd offer. If you change your mind, you know where I am."

Raven stepped into her room and after locking the door behind her she flung herself onto the bed and let her hopeless tears flow. As of tonight, her whole life had changed. How could she live with herself after what her husband had forced her to do?

"Damn you, Tory," she sobbed, "where were you when I needed you so desperately?"

She hadn't seen her brother, twelve years her elder, for over a year. He had been working as a ranch hand on a big spread in Nevada and had seemed content for the time being.

But she knew her brother well, his restlessness,

his inability to settle down in one place for long. He could have moved on twice since she'd last seen him.

Tory was thirty-one years old, and ever since she could remember, his dream had been to own his own ranch some day. "I want to be my own boss, Raven," he'd say. "I want to do things the way I think they should be done, not have to listen to orders that I know are wrong."

Twelve-year-old Tory and Grandpa McCloud had raised her since the night she was born. Her prolonged birth had been too much for her frail little mother, and sighing gently, she had joined her husband, dead from an Indian arrow only three months before.

Raven's rearing had been a haphazard affair, but full of love. She had learned from her grandfather honesty and the ability to look life in the face.

She could still hear him say, "Take all you can from life, Raven. If you don't, it will take from you."

"How do you stop it taking, Grandpa?" she had asked.

"You gotta stand up to it and not let it get the best of you. If what you want is worth havin', fight tooh and nail for it. But if it's of small importance, don't waste your wits on it. And always remember this, honey: The young fool will die an old fool if he don't pay heed to his mistakes as he goes along the trail of life."

The golden, happy time had lasted seventeen years, spent on the small farm in South Dakota.

Then one summer day her life was shattered. Claude McCloud had been struck down by a lightning bolt during a fierce electrical storm.

Overwhelmed by their grandfather's death, she and Tory had tried to carry on for a year, working the farm. But with the mainstay of their lives gone, their hearts weren't in it. It was the old man's gentle encouragement that had made them go on when the hot sun had sweat pouring off their face. He would remind them that when winter set in, all they'd have to do was sit in front of the fireplace and toast their feet.

One late September day, a day she would never forget, she and Tory had taken their meager supply of wheat to the miller in the nearby town of Crestwood. Their business concluded, they had started to return home when a man barreling out of a saloon almost knocked her down. He grabbed her by the arms just in time to keep her from hitting the wooden sidewalk. She looked up into the face of the most handsome man she had ever seen.

He wasn't from around Crestwood, she knew. His black suit was too nice, his boots too shiny.

It was obvious that the stranger was just as taken with her as she was with him. His white teeth flashed her an apologetic smile. "Pardon my clumsiness, miss," he said, his hands still on her arms. "My name is Milo Spencer. It would please me greatly if you would join me in a cup of tea in the hotel dining room. I must do something to show you how sorry I am for almost knocking you down."

She had looked at Tory for guidance. Should she

go with the stranger or not? His answer had been a firm shake of the head. She looked back into the handsome face, and for the first time in her life didn't heed an order from one of her menfolk.

Milo had courted her for a week, bringing her chocolates, and once a small, fancy fan. She ignored her brother's frowning face every time her suitor came riding up to the farm. The day Milo asked her to be his wife, she again ignored her brother's warning not to marry the man who would take her away from the back-breaking work the farm demanded.

"He's a gambler, Raven," Tory had tried to warn her. "He wants to use you. He wants to use your beauty to draw men to his gambling table."

She had not listened to her brother and had married the flashy gambler the following day. Before she left her sad-faced relative, she asked, "What will you do now, Tory? Will you stay on at the farm?"

"No." Tory stared out over the land where he had worked so hard all his life. "I'll sell the farm and go to Montana. I've always had a secret dream of being a cowboy, maybe a rancher someday." He turned his worried eyes back to his sister. "Do you know where he's taking you? I'd like to keep in touch, know if you're well, if maybe you need me."

"We're going to Montana, too." Raven smiled. "We'll be staying at the Crown Hotel in Clayton. Maybe you can visit me before you take off for some ranch."

"You can be sure I'll do that." Tory's eyes were

wet when he gave her a fierce hug. "Take care, little sister. I'll miss you."

Tears pooling in her own eyes, she had blindly made her way to where Milo waited with the saddled horses. He helped her to mount, and as they rode away, she didn't look back. She didn't want to take with her the picture of the old homestead that had sheltered her all her life, the brother who stood watching her ride away, the distant view of the cemetery where her parents and grandfather rested.

I'm a married woman now, she told herself, *and I must look forward to a new life with my husband.*

It had taken but a short time to realize that Tory had been right about Milo. She didn't tell Tory this, though, on the day he spent with her before riding off to look for work at some ranch. She wanted him to think that she was the happiest woman in the world.

There had been a sparsity of letters from her brother over the past two years. Usually he wrote to notify her that he was moving on to a different ranch.

Where he was now, she had no idea. She hadn't heard from him in months. She wondered if she could bear to look him in the face after what she'd done.

Raven scooted off the bed, wiped her eyes, and tried to compose herself. She had to make some kind of plan. *But how can I make plans when I feel as if my life is over?* she wailed inwardly.

She walked over to the window, pulled aside the drapes which sagged with an accumulation of dirt and dust. She yanked the window up and propped it open with a stick that lay on the sill for that purpose.

The street below was almost empty. It was long past midnight and the married men had gone home to bed. A couple of drunken cowboys staggered down the boardwalk.

She had been sitting in this same spot when Milo had burst into the room earlier that evening.

"Put on that red dress I fancy," he'd ordered. She could tell he'd been drinking, and from the fury on his face she guessed he'd been losing all afternoon.

"Do you want me to go over to the saloon with you?" she'd asked nervously.

"No, you're going to that hotel across the street—to earn a thousand dollars." Striding to the battered wardrobe, he pulled out a red satin dress with a daring neckline and thrust it at her

"A thousand—?" she gasped "No, Milo, you can't—"

One look at his clenched fists told her there was no point in refusing. She did not doubt that he would force her to do what he wanted.

"I've lost all our money, every penny. Now you're going to get me a new stake from that cowboy. He's so hot to bed you, it probably won't take more than three minutes." Milo laughed. "Go on, honey. I've arranged everything. He'll meet you in the hotel dining room."

Raven put her head in her hands and sobbed. She wished she could wipe out the memory of what had happened next.

The clinking of silverware and the hum of conversation had directed Raven to the hotel dining room. She'd stood in the archway, her eyes looking over the diners, searching for the cowboy. He wasn't there. As if in a daze, she'd made her way to a table in the corner of the room.

As she settled herself, removing her shawl and draping it over her chair back, she sensed the many eyes upon her. The gazes of the men were hungry; the wives and single women were full of scorn, yet envious of her beauty. She was that gambler's woman.

Raven was used to those looks. Relying on habit, she swept the room with a haughty look, then turned her attention to the menu lying on the table.

She had barely begun to read the menu when she sensed that the man she waited to meet had arrived. Her heart racing, she lifted her head, her eyes drawn to the arch where he stood.

There was little resemblance between the man who stood there and the the one she had seen in the saloon the night before. His strong face was clean-shaven now, and his black hair, parted in the middle and hanging in loose waves a little past his shoulders, had recently been washed.

She could not see the color of his eyes, but his lips were firm, yet somehow soft-looking. His long, lean body was clad in a gray shirt and black trousers that came to the toes of his well-polished boots.

He was not handsome like Milo, but there was a hard attractiveness about him that stirred her in a way Milo's good looks never had. And this man would never back away from anything. His very stance said so. If he loved a woman, he would cherish and protect her. The last thing he would do would be to offer her to another man for his own benefit.

He, too, scanned the room, and she knew when he recognized her by the slight widening of his eyes. When a waitress would have directed him to a section she served, he shook his head and said, "The young lady over there is waiting for me."

With easy grace he sat down across from her. A wicked glint in his deep gray eyes acknowledged the illicit reason for their meeting.

Raven found herself blushing. This was wrong, so very wrong. But despite that knowledge, she found herself attracted to him in a way she'd never imagined.

"Shall we order, Raven?" He smiled at her as he opened the menu. "I'm starved."

"So am I. . . . I'm afraid I don't know your name."

"The name is Chance. Chance McGruder."

"I'm pleased to meet you, Chance McGruder." Raven stretched a soft white hand out to him and realized she spoke the truth.

"Not nearly as pleased as I am to meet you." He looked into her eyes as he held her hand and stroked a thumb across the inner side of her wrist.

The sensual feel of his flesh on hers sent a flood of sensations such as she had never known tingling through her body. In a state of confusion, she freed her hand and pretended to read her menu. From the corner of her eye, however, she saw a small smile twitch the corner of his lips. Damn Chance McGruder, he knew that she had been affected by his touch. The hand-printed listing of dishes blurred together, and when Chance ordered the fried chicken, she said she would have the same.

"And we'll have a glass of wine while we wait," Chance said, lifting a questioning eyebrow at her.

Raven nodded agreement. She would welcome alchohol to blur her memory of what was to come.

The wine was delivered to their table, and as they sipped it, Raven asked, "Have you been on a cattle drive?"

"Yes. The men and I have been on the trail for a month." His lips twisted wryly. "Those crazy cowpokes are out there going from saloon to saloon, to the bawdy houses. They won't be happy until they've spent their hard-earned wages. They'll hit the trail home then, their heads pounding and their stomachs on fire from the raw whiskey they've poured into it."

Desperate for something to say, she asked, "Have you joined them in any of their carousing?"

"I had a few drinks with them last night, but before I got around to visiting the red light district, I saw a beauty that banished all desire for any other woman."

Raven looked at him through her long lashes. "Even though that woman comes at a high price?"

His eyes smoldered a moment, then he answered, "I would have paid double the price to get what I want."

To hide from the raw hunger staring out of his gray eyes, Raven lowered her glance to the wine. She admitted to herself, though, that she also wanted to hide the fact that she felt the same hunger.

The girl brought their dinner, and Raven turned her head away from Chance to hide the relief she felt. Little conversation went on between them as they ate the fried chicken, mashed potatoes and gravy, and green beans. They refused dessert, and a strained silence grew between them as they drank their coffee. Each wondered if the other was also nervous about leaving the dining room and climbing the stairs to Chance's room.

When Raven set her empty cup back in its saucer, Chance rose and walked around the table to assist her to her feet. He draped the shawl around her shoulders, laid some bills on the table, then crooked his arm for her to lay her hand on.

Raven felt the eyes of the diners boring into her back as she and Chance left the dining room, and unconsciously her fingers tightened on his arm.

"Don't pay any attention to them, Raven." Chance patted her hand as he guided her up the flight of stairs.

Raven made no answer. Speech was beyond her. She was gripped with a sudden attack of panic. What lay ahead of her on the other side of that door Chance was unlocking? Would he be a tender lover, or a brutal one? He was a stranger, after all, and she knew nothing about him. What might he demand of her for his thousand dollars?

She felt sure of one thing now. Milo had been

wrong. It wouldn't be a three-minute affair. This cowboy would take a long time satisfying his hunger.

When she entered his room and Chance closed the door behind them, she wondered how she could ever go through with this. Then she remembered the look in Milo's eyes and knew he'd kill her if she didn't bring him the money.

Chance had laid a roll of bills on the bedside table and removed her shawl, saying, "Don't tremble so, Raven. I won't hurt you." When he began to expertly undo the glass buttons of her low-cut bodice, he said softly, "I just want to make long, slow love to you."

He freed her arms of the bodice and pushed it down past her waist until it lay on the floor, her petticoat and bloomers with it. He knelt then and removed her slippers, kissing the instep of each foot. As he rose to his feet, his hands slowly skimmed the sides of her thighs and waist. He pulled her into his arms then, and his lips, hot and urgent, claimed hers. Raven grasped his waist and leaned into him. Never had Milo kissed her like this, so caring, yet so demanding.

Feeling her response, Chance deepened his kiss until she was breathless. He slid his mouth off hers then and slipped the strap of her camisole—the only article of clothing she still wore—over her shoulder. He pulled it down until one throbbing breast stood proudly free.

"Beautiful," he whispered, stroking a thumb across the pink, hard nipple. "I knew it would be," he sighed harshly before lowering his head and drawing it into his mouth.

Raven thought she would surely swoon as he took turns laving the nub, then gently nibbling on it. Without being fully aware of it, she slid the other strap off her shoulder, baring the matching pink-tipped mound.

Chance's mouth was on it immediately, his tongue swirling, his mouth drawing on the nipple. Raven moaned the pleasure that rose from her woman's core when he began a slow sucking on first one and then the other breast.

All the time his hands had been busy sliding the camisole down to join the rest of her clothing. When she stood bare before him, he left her breasts to trail little sucking kisses down her body, stopping only when he came to the thatch of black curls at the vee of her hips.

"Open to me, Raven," he whispered, his eyes glazed over with hot passion.

Raven wasn't sure what he meant, what he intended to do to her. She tentatively shifted her feet several inches apart and almost jumped out of her skin as Chance buried his head between her legs and his tongue darted inside her. When his teeth found the core of her femininity and began to nibble, she felt she was going up in flames. Never had she dreamed of a man doing this to a woman, never had she dreamed something could feel so wonderful. Nor had she ever felt so helpless when a few minutes later she was lifted on a crest of unbelievable pleasure.

When her body stopped shuddering, Chance

rose to his feet and whispered, "You undress me now."

He had to help her weak fingers undo his shirt and belt buckle. But when she had pulled the shirt off him, he left it up to her to get the rest of his clothes off.

He had to sit down on the bed in order for her to pull off his boots. When they lay on the floor, she lifted her eyes to the spot she'd been avoiding and gave a small gasp. In her innocence she had imagined that all men looked like her husband down there. It was a shock to discover that wasn't true. Chance McGruder was half again longer than Milo and also in girth.

Raven continued to kneel and dared to slide her palms up Chance's inner thighs. When she came to where his hard shaft throbbed against his belly, he reached down and unpinned her hair. When it had fallen down about her shoulders, his hands grasped the soft tresses and stroked them back and forth across his hardness.

"Ever since I saw you, your beautiful hair, I've wanted to do this," he whispered.

"Do you do this to all your women?" Raven asked as he continued to toy with her hair.

"No, never. Nor have I ever done all the other things I did to you."

"Truly, Chance?"

"Truly, Raven." Releasing her hair, he leaned back on his elbows and coaxed softly, "Kiss me, Raven."

When she made a motion as though to join him

on the bed to kiss his lips, he said huskily, "I didn't mean that kind of kiss, honey."

She looked at him with wide, startled eyes. "You mean . . . ?"

"Please."

With her hands resting on his knees, Raven gazed up at Chance. "I've never . . . I don't know how to do . . ."

Chance looked at the appeal in her lovely eyes and lifted her up to lie in his arms. "You don't know how much that pleases me, my little innocent. You will do it on your own when you are ready. I can wait."

Together they scooted up in the bed to lie lengthwise on it. As Chance positioned himself between her legs, he said softly, "There's so much I want to teach you."

He entered her then, slowly, gently, until they were one.

"Oh, God," he moaned, gathering Raven close. "I knew it would feel good, but never like this. You are as smooth as velvet."

Raven looked at him with wonder in her eyes. "I had no idea . . ." She wound her arms around his shoulder and whispered, "It feels so good."

With a husky laugh, Chance said, "It's going to feel better yet. Hold on, honey, while I take you to heaven."

The moment Chance started to move rhythmically inside her, Raven clutched his shoulders and began to toss her head back and forth. She was sure that she was going to die in his arms. There was no way she could live through the waves of intense pleasure the stroking of his maleness was building inside her.

"Chance, hold me. Something strange is happening to me."

His hips pumping faster, Chance gathered her closer in his arms. "Let yourself go, honey. Hang on to me and together we will climb that mountain."

There was no outcry from either one when they reached that crest of little death. Their release was too strong, too satisfying to waste a moment of it to make a sound. Both wanted to hang on to the earth-shattering experience, to stretch it out as long as possible.

Finally, it could last no longer. Chance braced his hands on either side of Raven's head, taking some of the weight of his body off her. However, his manhood kept them fastened together. Looking down at her with awe in his eyes, he said, "I have had more women than I can remember in my adult years, but if they were all put together, they couldn't come near to what we have just shared."

Completely spent, Chance kissed Raven tenderly on the lips and rolled over on his back. Within seconds his even breathing told Raven that he was in a deep sleep.

She sat up and leaned over him, taking a last look at the lover she knew she would never forget. She slid off the bed and as she got dressed she wondered what Chance's reaction would be when he awoke and found her gone. Would he care? Probably not. After all, she was only a well-paid whore. Most likely he'd expect her to be gone. Men never slept with the women whose bodies they had paid for.

With one last lingering look at the man who had made her feel cherished for a few hours, she picked up the money on the nightstand, slipped it into her reticule, blew out the lamp, and quietly left the room. Milo would be waiting.

Chapter Two

Raven stood to one side of the worn drapes, looking out on the silent street.

She had returned to her and Milo's hotel room after leaving Chance, knowing Milo would be eager to begin gambling. He'd taken 100 dollars from her, hidden the rest, and dragged her over to the saloon. Her husband had never realized he was hurrying to meet death, that this was the night his cheating would be ended forever.

The sun was just beginning to rise now. Chance had mentioned that he and the other ranch hands would be heading home early this morning. She wanted one last look at the man who had taught her the pleasure of true lovemaking. She longed to go to him now, to tell him she was no longer married, but she knew it was no use. He must think her no better than a whore. A woman like her could have no place in his future plans.

What her own plans were, she had no definite idea. She had retrieved the money from Milo's hiding place. After she paid the funeral home, she would give deep thought to what she was going to do with the rest of her life.

She wasn't going to leave her room until she was sure Chance had left town. She didn't think she could bear it if he looked at her with scorn this morning.

Five minutes passed, and her eyes remained riveted on the hotel. She stiffened suddenly. A tall, slim man, his hat pulled low on his forehead, had just stepped through the door. Her heart pounded, her pulses raced. She was remembering lying in his arms, his strong body moving on hers, bringing her a delight she had never known existed.

She leaned closer, peering through the window, trying to get a closer look at Chance's lean, hard face as he joined four mounted men at the bottom of the steps. She saw him speak briefly to the men before mounting a horse one of the cowhands held. As she watched, he kneed the stallion around and headed out of town, the others trailing along behind him.

Unshed tears glistened in Raven's eyes when they rode out of sight. Chance McGruder's short chapter in her life would be long remembered.

As she crossed the room to check the time on her watch, her lower body protested. Especially her thighs. They weren't used to being spread so wide.

Forcing herself to get on with her life, Raven

went down to order a bath. A few minutes later, pails of warm water were carried into her room and poured into the tin hip-bath tub.

Tossing some bath salts and a washcloth in the tub, Raven finally undressed and stepped into the warm, soothing water. She scooted down as far as she could so that the steaming warmth covered her sore breasts. The nipples were swollen from the attention Chance had given them.

As she slid the washcloth down her body, it encountered many little love-bites scattered in its path. She remembered with a weakening of her lower body when every one had been put on her flesh.

Raven didn't linger long in her bath. She wanted to get to the funeral home before too many people were out and about. She wasn't up to facing the women who would snub her, or the leers she would encounter from the men. She had been dealing with that for two years and she was tired of it.

Toweling herself off, she donned clean underclothing, then chose a dark dress from the battered wardrobe. She had coiled her hair in a roll at her nape and picked up a black hat to set on top of her head when a knock on the door made her lay it back on top of the dresser. She stood frozen in place. Who was on the other side of the door? Could it be Chance? Had he returned and ferreted out where she lived?

When the rapping came a second time, this time a little louder, she called weakly, "Who is it?"

"Open up and find out," a laughing voice answered.

"Tory! Is that you?"

"None other, little sister."

Raven raced across the floor, jerked open the door, and flung herself at the big, blond man grinning at her. As his arms came around her and held her tight, she burst into tears.

Finally, Tory held her away from him. "Why all the tears, Raven?" He studied her face, a frown creasing his forehead.

She swiped the back of a hand across her wet eyes, sat down on the edge of the bed, and motioned her brother to sit on the only chair in the room. "Milo is dead, Tory. He was caught cheating at cards yesterday and was shot."

"Ah, I'm sorry, little sister." Tory leaned forward and took her hands in his. "I guess you're feeling pretty low."

"I feel bad that Milo was struck down at such an early age. And I feel bad for the reason he was killed. I had warned him many times that one day he would be found out, but"—she sighed—"he was always sure that he wouldn't."

Raven paused, then said in a small voice, "You were right. He did use me to lure men to his table. I hated it so much, Tory, thĕ scandalous dresses he made me wear, the way the men leered at me, and—" She couldn't go on.

Tory's hands knotted into fists. "I wish I'd come sooner and put an end to what he was putting you through."

"But thank God you're here now. What has brought you here at this time?"

"I'm on my way to another ranch," Tory's lips spread in a wide smile. "I've been corresponding with an old man who lives there. I read his ad in a magazine, and just for the heck of it, I wrote to him. He's seventy-five years old and lost his wife last year. He wrote that ranch life was getting too hard for him and that he wanted to move into town.

"I've been saving as much money as I can doing cowboy work. I have enough to put down on the place and I plan to pay Mr. Chadwick more money every time I sell some cattle. His last letter said he wanted to meet me before he decided on my offer."

"I can understand that he would want to meet you, decide if you looked honest, trustworthy. But won't it cost a lot of money to buy stock, to get you started on a herd?"

Tory shook his head. "That's the beauty of the deal, if Mr. Chadwick agrees to it. A hundred head of cattle comes with the ranch."

"You've given this a lot of thought, haven't you, Tory?"

"I've thought about running a little spread for years. It started a way back when I was chopping weeds under the blazing sun at the farm."

Tory gave Raven's hands a shake. "You're so quiet suddenly. What are you thinking? Do you think it's a bad idea that I want to venture into ranching?"

"Oh no, Tory, I think it's a grand idea. I was just

wondering if you would take me with you."

Tory gave her a stern look. "Of course you'll go with me. Do you think I'd leave you here alone in this hell-hole?"

Raven leaned forward and threw her arms around her brother's neck. "Oh, Tory, it will be so good, being with you again."

Tory hugged her back, and when she straightened up, he cautioned, "It won't be no pleasure trip, though. It will be a long ride, sleeping out at night, cooking our meals on an open fire.

"I want you to understand that I haven't got much money beyond what I've put aside for the ranch, so we won't be eating high on the hog as we travel. For that matter"—he grinned wryly—"even if I strike a deal with the old man, it will be slim pickings for a while."

"Not necessarily, brother," Raven said as she reached over and pulled out the shallow drawer of her nightstand. "I think this will help us." She took out the roll of bills Chance had paid her, and while Tory's eyes goggled at the greenbacks she told her first lie, ever.

"Every time Milo had a lucky streak at cards, we put some of his winnings aside. There's almost a thousand dollars here." She held the money out. "Take it and use it however you see fit."

"Good Lord, Raven." Tory unfolded the roll of money and stared at it in awe. "We'll be able to pay the old man the entire amount he's asking for the ranch." He looked up at her, tears of happiness glistening in his eyes. "How soon can you get ready to leave?"

"There are a few things that have to be attended to first. Would you go down the street to the funeral home and pay them their fee for Milo's burial and all?" When Tory nodded that he would, she said, "And we'll have to buy a packhorse. Then I'll need proper clothes to wear on the trail."

"And more trail grub." Tory jumped to his feet, excitement vibrating through his body. "My supply sack is pretty slim."

"Your clothes don't look in all that good shape either," Raven grinned at him, eyeing his trousers which were worn thin at the knees, and his dusty, scuffed boots. "I bet your boots have holes in the soles."

"That they do. I didn't want to spend any more money than I had to."

"Well, give me some of that money now and I'll go to a mercantile and purchase what I need while you're gone. You can buy the trail grub, and some new clothes for yourself. Oh, and don't forget to buy a horse for me to ride."

Raven looked at her brother hopefully. "Do you think we can be ready to leave in a couple hours?"

"Maybe less." Tory folded the bills she had given him and shoved them into his shirt pocket, buttoning down its flap. After taking several bills from his own savings and handing them to Raven, he slapped his stained and battered hat on his head and left the room humming under his breath. Raven smiled. She had never seen her brother so happy.

It didn't take Raven long to do her shopping. Before she stepped into the mercantile two blocks down from the hotel, she knew what she wanted to purchase. On entering the large room whose shelves were stocked with most anything a person could want, she walked straight to the boys' and teenagers' section. After sorting through a stack of woolen trousers, holding a few up to her waist for size, she settled on what she thought would fit her best. In a matter of ten minutes she had folded over her arm three pairs of pants and five flannel shirts, all in different colors.

When she had laid them on the counter, she walked over to the women's department and tried on jackets. She chose a lightweight one for the fall weather and a sheepskin-lined one for winter. She had no way of knowing if there would be a store nearby the ranch where she could purchase what she might need.

Next, she tried on boots, finally deciding on a sturdy pair that she figured she would need for ranch life.

From the display of boots she walked over to the wall where hats hung from pegs. After setting a few on her head, she decided on a black Stetson. She added heavy socks and four neckerchiefs to her pile of clothing. Two young clerks argued so heatedly over who would total her bill, the owner took over and added it up himself. He allowed both young men to carry her packages to her hotel room, however. When she offered to tip them, they shook their heads, stammering it was pay enough just to help her.

An hour later when Tory knocked on the door,

she was wearing one of her new outfits as she let him in.

"Well, look at you." Tory grinned as his eyes skimmed over her. "You're gonna knock eyes out in that shirt and britches."

"I guess the trousers are too tight," Raven said uneasily. "I didn't think I'd fill them out so. I thought they'd fit me the same way they do the teenagers."

"They don't have your little butt to take up the slack," Tory teased. "And as for that, they don't have nothing up front to fill their shirts so nicely."

"I shouldn't have bought them," Raven wailed, plopping down on the edge of the bed. "I thought they would be more practical than a long skirt swirling around my legs, tangling me up."

"Don't cry, sis," Tory coaxed. "Your reasoning was right." His lips twitched in a grin as he continued, "You can't help it if you have all those curves."

Raven grabbed up a pillow and heaved it at Tory, knocking a new hat off his head. "Hey, watch it," he laughed, picking the black Stetson off the floor and brushing it off. "I paid good money for that. It's the first new hat I've had in years."

"Did you buy anything else to go with it?" Raven gave him a doubtful look.

"Yes I did, Miss Smarty," Tory answered and motioned to the flat package he had laid on the chair. "I outfitted myself real good. I brought along a change of clothes to put on before we head out. If you'll turn your back, I'll get into them."

As Tory exchanged his rags for the new clothes

he had purchased, he told Raven what he had bought for them to eat while on the trail. "And after seeing all your packages, it's a good thing I bought a pack mule to carry everything."

"Did you buy me a horse?"

"I sure did. I bought you a handsome gelding. He's a deep rich chestnut with a black tail and mane. I didn't think it would be wise to buy you a mare or a stallion because of Drago. You know how he is."

"I know that stallion of yours is the meanest horse that ever lived."

"You shouldn't say that, sis. He was always nice to you,"

"I guess so," Raven agreed, "but he's still a devil."

"That meanness of his has saved my life a couple of times. I wouldn't have him any other way. Now, are you ready to leave this hell-hole?"

"More than ready, brother." Raven turned around and nodded her approval at Tory's changed appearance. She settled her hat on her head and picked up half her packages, leaving the rest for Tory to carry.

It was a beautiful day as they left Clayton. Raven and Tory rode side by side, the mule, George, bringing up the rear. Bittersweet memories filled Raven's mind. Bitter memories of her unscrupulous husband with whom she had become completely disenchanted in so short a time. Then there were the sweet memories of the hours spent with the cowboy. If she lived to be a hundred she would never forget him.

With determination Raven put the past out of

36

her mind and concentrated on the reason she and Tory were on the trail to Montana. What did the future hold for them? Would the small ranch live up to her brother's expectations? What if Mr. Chadwick had made his ranch sound more valuable than it was? What if the buildings were run-down, in need of repair? What if there wasn't a hundred head of cattle?

None of her worries seemed to be on Tory's mind, Raven thought. She hadn't seen him look so carefree and at ease since he was a young teenager, long before he had to work himself half to death on the dirt-poor farm. For his sake, she prayed that what the old man had written was the truth.

Chapter Three

Chance stared broodingly into the flames of the campfire, anger and frustration in his cloud-gray eyes.

When he had awakened this morning, eager to make love to Raven again, he'd found her gone. He had at first thought that she had gone to use the facilities at the end of the hall. He hoped she wouldn't be gone long, for he was hard with morning desire.

Besides, he wanted to ask her to go with him when he left Clayton. He knew she was a married woman, but what kind of a man would sell his own wife? He would have no qualms at all taking her away from the gambler.

As he'd lain waiting, he visualized them together on the trail. They would be wrapped in each other's arms in the same bedroll, making slow, quiet love so that his men wouldn't hear them. That dream had burst when some fifteen minutes passed and Raven hadn't returned. He became suspicious of her lengthy absence and looked at the bedside table.

A savage oath ripped from his throat. The roll of money was no longer there. Raven wouldn't be coming back ever. She was gone.

But gone where? He swore again. He had no idea where she lived. In his heated rush to possess her, he hadn't taken the time to know her, to converse with her before tumbling her into bed.

He untangled himself from the bedcovers and stood up, telling himself to calm down and to think back. What else should he have expected? He had offered to buy her services and she had served him well. It wasn't her fault that there had been no plans made beyond last night. It was only logical that she would take the money and leave.

As Chance pulled on his clothes and stamped his feet into his boots, he cursed himself for being all kinds of a fool. When he'd made love to her he had known that he would want her for a long time. Why hadn't he said that he wanted her to go with him to his ranch?

He looked at his pocket watch and grunted. Eight o'clock. By now his men would have been waiting an hour for him to join them. He strapped on the holster of his Colt, then settled his hat on his head. Pulling it low on his forehead, he left the room in which he had found the perfect lover and went downstairs to meet his men.

The four cowboys looked at each other with

raised eyebrows when he only grunted in response to their "Good morning, boss." As they rode out of town, the last two riders said to each other sotto voce, "He's gonna be a mean bastard to be around today."

"Yeah, I'm gonna stay out of his way as much as possible."

Chance's dark mood hadn't changed when they made night camp, and it was a silent group that ate the meal of fried salt pork and heated beans. By now they knew that something had upset the man who usually laughed and joked with the rest of them. Privately, they wondered if a woman had anything to do with his unusual behavior. They dismissed that thought. Chance McGruder would never be affected by a woman. He never had been before, and certainly a whore wouldn't get under his skin.

The men turned in early. Besides not wanting to be around their morose boss, they all suffered headaches and upset stomachs from trying to drink the town dry.

Staring broodingly into the campfire, Chance knew he should turn in also. After heaping on the fire a huge pile of wood that would last all night, he rolled up in his blankets. His body ached for Raven, and he was a long time falling asleep.

Raven and Tory had been three weeks on the trail when they spotted a cluster of buildings in the distance. Tory's eyes blazed with hope. "Maybe that's Bitter Creek," he exclaimed, "the small town where Mr. Chadwick's letters were postmarked."

The animals were set at a gallop, and in ten minutes they learned from a sign on a post that they had reached Bitter Creek, Montana. Grinning at each other, they entered the frontier town and rode down its single dusty, rutted street. On one side there was a mercantile whose painted sign read BITTER CREEK MERCHANDISER. Several yards later there was a barber shop where a Dr. James Enlow had his office upstairs. After another few yards open space there was a livery stable. Across the street was a restaurant with a sign over the door proclaiming Nellie's Home Cookin'. Next came a saloon named High Country.

It was open prairie from then on except away in the distance where the dim outlines of what looked like houses were scattered about.

When they came to the end of the street, Tory kneed Drago around and he said, "Let's step in that restaurant and have us a beef steak for lunch. I don't know about you, but I've had enough trail grub and wild game to last me for a while. At the same time we can make inquiries as to where we can find the Chadwick ranch."

As they dismounted in front of Nellie's establishment, Raven worried that they might be turned away because of their scruffy appearance. But when they walked into the room, no one paid any attention to their attire. A hurried glance over the tables showed Raven that the men there didn't look any better than Tory did.

But as usual she was getting interested looks from the men, mostly cowboys, she thought. That made her think of Chance, and a sadness came into her eyes.

Evidently Tory had noticed the amorous attention directed at her. When a balding, beanpole-thin man came to take their order, Tory spoke in a voice that carried through the room.

"Me and my wife will have a steak and all the the trimmings."

After that announcement, she received only careful sidelong glances from the men. She imagined that they were hesitant to tangle with a man as large and dangerous-looking as her brother.

As they waited to be served, Raven became aware that Tory was getting some female attention. Especially from a red-headed woman who had an avaricious look in her green eyes. Raven glanced at her brother and saw that he was returning the woman's inspection with interest.

She kicked him in the ankle and hissed, "Get that wolfish look off your face. We're supposed to be married, remember?"

Their meal was delivered shortly after that. Raven's mouth watered as she looked at the large piece of meat, lean and crisp at the edges.

Later, when they were being served their dessert of apple pie, Tory asked the thin man if he knew where the Chadwick ranch was located.

"Everyone knows where ole Cal's spread is," the waiter answered. "He's got it up for sale. He's gonna retire and move into town. Says ranchin' is too hard on him these days."

Raven sensed by the quietness that had fallen in the room that everyone was listening as Tory said,

"I know all about that. I'm probably gonna be the new owner of the place. I just rode in from Clayton. We're pretty beat and hope we don't have to ride much farther to find the place."

"You won't have to. Cal's ranch is about fifteen miles due east from here. You can't miss it."

There was a look of relief and satisfaction on Tory's face as he said, "Eat up, Raven. I want to get there before darkness sets in. I can't wait to look over the land, see the cattle."

As Raven gulped down the last of her coffee, she was thinking that she couldn't wait to inspect the ranch house. And sleep in a bed again.

Chapter Four

Later that afternoon, four cowboys heaved sighs of relief as they drew rein on a flat stretch of land above a river and looked down on the many buildings of the McGruder holdings. It would be a relief to get to their bunkhouse and away from the scowling face of their boss.

Chance McGruder, their boss, looked down and prayed that Jadine wouldn't be inside waiting for him.

His prayer was answered. Only Mary Penny, his cook and housekeeper, was in the kitchen when he opened the door and stepped inside. She flashed him a wide, welcoming smile.

"I've been expecting you for two days," she said, pulling a chair away from the table. "You look beat and hungry. Sit down and I'll give you a bowl of beef stew and some sourdough I baked fresh this morning."

"I am tired, and I'm famished. If I never have to eat prairie chicken or hardtack again, it will suit me to a tee."

"I expect you'll want a bath after you've eaten." Mary placed a bowl of steaming, savory meat and vegetables before Chance. "If you don't mind my saying so, you smell a little overripe."

Chance grinned. "I expect I do. It's been too cold to bathe in the creeks," he said, picking up his fork.

When his appetite was sated and Mary was pouring him a cup of coffee, he asked, "Anything new happen while I was gone?"

"No, not that I can think of offhand . . . well, yes, come to think about it, I guess it's pretty sure that old Cal will sell his ranch to a young man who's supposed to show up any day."

"I hate to see the old fellow leave his spread. He's been a good neighbor."

"The new owner will probably be as good."

"I hope so. I need to water my cattle in the river that runs through his property. If he denies me access to it, I'll be in a bad spot. My herd would have to travel ten miles before the river turns and runs on my land."

"Now don't go borrowing trouble," the plump, middle-aged housekeeper scolded. Then she added, "These kettles of water are hot now. You can take your bath whenever you're ready. I'm going to ride into town to get some supplies I'm running short of."

Chance finished his coffee and put his dirty bowl and spoon in the dry-sink. It took but a minute for him to bring the wooden tub from the porch and fill it with the steaming water.

He had shed his clothes down to his underwear when the outside door opened and a red-headed woman stepped into the kitchen.

"Oh, Chance," she said with delight. "I've missed you. You've been gone for two months."

"I know how long I've been gone, Jadine," Chance said testily, pulling her eager fingers away from his crotch, "and I don't want to go to bed with you."

"Why not?" Green eyes flashed fire at him. "You've never missed a chance to crawl between my legs before."

"Look, woman, I'm dead tired. All I want to do is take my bath, get into bed, and sleep the clock around."

"I guess I can understand that." Jadine pouted. "I'll ride over tomorrow, alright?"

Chance didn't answer yes or no. When the door slapped behind his neighbor, he removed his underwear and stepped into the tub. As he lathered his body, he thought back over the years to when he was sixteen and his uncle George McGruder married for the second time after losing his first wife to a snake bite.

Uncle George's new wife was a widow with a daughter, seventeen-year-old Jadine.

The day he and his father rode over to meet the

new wife and her daughter, Jadine had invited him to go to the stables to see her horse.

It was a beautiful animal, a roan with a white star on its forehead. As they looked at the roan, Jadine laughed and said, "He sure is hung, isn't he?"

Chance remembered how he had blushed. He had never heard a female talk like that. His embarrassment had grown threefold when she reached down between his legs and laughingly asked, "How are you hung, Chance? You're a big fellow. I bet you're big down there, too."

His face crimson, and his body frozen in place, he stood helplessly while she unbuttoned his fly and freed his young manhood. Still unable to move or speak, he watched her fondle him. He was more ashamed than aroused.

"Well," she said finally, disappointment in her voice, "you've got the right equipment, but it doesn't have any lead in it yet." She gave him an impish grin. "I'll keep working on it."

Which she had done every time they were alone together. And as those hot summer days passed, he had begun to lose his awe of her fingers on him. Still he didn't feel it was right. After all, she was family, wasn't she?

He had turned seventeen the day Jadine suggested they take a walk along the river. "It's cool down there underneath the willows."

Once they hit the river road and were out of sight of the house, Jadine said, "The water looks so inviting, let's take a little swim."

In seconds they were out of their clothes and

47

into the river. While he swam around, Jadine dived under the water. A second later he felt her fingers on his untried manhood and suddenly there was an explosion in his loins. He didn't care that Jadine was almost his cousin. All he cared about now was burying his hard shaft inside her. Jadine's head popped up out of the water, a wide, pleased smile on her freckled face.

"At last you're ready, Bucko," she exclaimed, and grabbing his hand, hurried him onto the bank. She flung herself onto a patch of grass and, opening her legs wide, urged, "Come on, bury that hard thing inside me."

He did, and turned into a young animal, taking her again and again until dusk settled in and they heard his father calling to him.

"Same place, same time tomorrow?" Jadine asked when they had gotten dressed and turned toward the house.

"You damn betcha," he had answered, strutting alongside her.

They had met every day the rest of the summer and into the fall until it got too cold to lie naked on the grass. That last fall day after they had exhausted themselves, they agreed that this must be the last day they would meet at the river.

"What will you do about getting your pleasuring now?" Jadine asked. "You're used to getting it regular."

He shrugged. He knew what he would do, but didn't want to tell her. He would visit the whorehouse. He had heard the cowboys talking about what the whores would do to a man for a couple dollars. "I guess I'll do without," he answered. "What will you do?"

"Oh, I won't have any problem in that department. I'll still have Juan."

"Who's Juan?"

"You know, that young Mexican who takes care of Mr. McGruder's remuda. I started pleasuring him a week after me and Ma moved to the ranch. We meet in the stables every morning."

"And you'd still meet me in the afternoon?" Chance asked in disbelief.

"That's right, I just can't seem to get enough. By the way, he knows nothing about us. He's very jealous." She laughingly snorted, "He claims he loves me."

"Maybe he does."

When Jadine only gave a careless shrug of her shoulders, he had realized how cold she was. He decided then that he didn't care if he ever lay with her again.

In their early and mid-twenties Jadine had caught him a couple times before he could hide. Against his will, she had managed to arouse him. The second time they were together he had asked her, "Why do you continue to chase after me when you have half the men in the area who you could go to bed with anytime you wanted to? Besides, don't you still have Juan?"

She had answered with a salacious smile, "You're hung bigger than him, and all the rest."

He had made no response to her remark. She'd probably had enough men to compare him with.

He had slipped once more in his determination

never to bed Jadine again. It had happened the night before he and his men started the drive to Clayton. He had gone to bed early because he and his men would be up at the crack of dawn to head the longhorns out. He had been in a deep sleep when he was awakened, his hard erection in Jadine's hand. Half asleep, he had taken her, achieving his release in less than a minute. He hardly remembered it the next morning.

Pulling on clean underwear, Chance stretched out in bed, knowing with certainty that neither Jadine nor the whores in Bitter Creek would ever stir him again. Black-haired, blue-eyed Raven Spencer would stand in the way. And suddenly, Chance knew what he had to do to get his life back on track. Tomorrow morning he was going to ride back to Clayton and tear the town apart until he found the woman who would not leave his mind alone.

Chapter Five

"There it is," Tory exclaimed, pulling Drago in sharply.

Raven kneed her gelding Sam up alongside him and smiled. Nestled in a hollow were a house and several outbuildings. They were weathered gray but sturdy-looking.

"What do you think, sis?" Tory's eyes glittered with excitement. "It's just how I dreamed it would be."

"It needs to be painted, and there's no grass in the yard."

"Those are minor things that can be taken care of in no time. Next spring I'll scatter some grass seed around. I see smoke coming out of the chimney, so somebody is there. Let's ride on down."

When they pulled the horses up in front of the wide porch, an elderly man with a wrinkled face shoved himself to his feet, a friendly smile wreathing his face.

"I reckon you be Tory McCloud," he said. "I been expectin' you."

"You're right. I'm Tory McCloud," Tory said, returning the genial smile. "And this is Raven, my sister," he added as he helped her to dismount.

Tory mounted the steps and shook the calloused hand held out to him. When Raven offered her hand, the old man's eyes sparkled with gentle humor. "The young men around here ain't gonna give you a minute's peace, they'll be hangin' round so much."

Raven smiled, but the image that came to mind was Chance McGruder's handsome face.

"The two of you look saddle weary," the old man said. "Come on in and we'll have some coffee and a piece of apple pie my neighbor's housekeeper brought me yesterday."

"That's the best offer I've had in three weeks," Raven said, grinning at the old man. She took off her hat, and her black curls fell around her shoulders and down her back.

"You sure got beautiful hair," Mr. Chadwick said admiringly. "It's the color of the bird you must have been named after. How come you're so dark and your brother is so fair? You don't even look related, let alone like brother and sister."

"I took after our Irish father and Tory took after our English mother," Raven said, following the old man into the house.

"Have a seat and I'll pour us some coffee. And

call me Cal. Try not to mind the dirt. I'm not the housekeeper my Emma was."

Raven put her hat back on when she saw the condition of the floor. She knew her Stetson was dusty, but it wasn't greasy. She glanced around and mentally agreed that the old man wasn't much of a housekeeper. The stove and the area around it were covered with a long-time accumulation of grease. Clods of dirt, big and small, littered the floor.

Of course, hot water, soap and elbow grease could take care of that, Raven thought. But would she be able to eat and drink at this unwashed table?

To her relief the cups Cal placed on the table and filled with coffee were as clean as the ones she had used on the farm in Nebraska. The flatware and the plate that held their pie were in the same pristine condition.

When Mr. Chadwick placed a small jar of milk and a sugar bowl on the table, Raven asked, "Do you have a milch cow, Cal?"

"Yeah, her name is Sweetie," Cal answered with a sheepish grin. "Isn't that a hell of a name to give to a critter? But Emma, God love her, treated the cow like she was a pet. Raised her from a calf."

A sadness came into the old man's eyes. "We never had any young'uns and Emma never liked dogs, so Sweetie got all her affection. I do believe that cow misses her."

But not as much as you do, Raven thought when Cal and Tory began to talk cows and ranch size.

"I own five hundred acres outright, and there's

the open range that all the ranchers use. But the real worth of my spread is its source of water. The Old Missouri river runs through the middle of my holdings. My cattle will always have fresh, clear water to drink when other ranchers' creeks have run dry. I allow my neighbor's cows to use the river."

"What about in the winter when snow covers everything, how do the cattle manage to stay alive?" Raven was curious.

"Usually the cattle can search out windswept spots and find enough dry grass to survive on. But to be on the safe side, I have a hay waddy to help the critters out."

"What's a hay waddy?"

"An extra hand on the ranch who cuts hay for winter feed. Anyway"—Cal looked at Tory—"if we strike a deal, there won't be that many head to worry about, 'cause you'll be drivin' most of the critters into Clayton to sell.

"You'll be a little late with your fall roundup, but if you get started within the week, you should get there and back before the first snowfall. But you're gonna have to hustle. I feel it in my bones, the cold is comin' early this year."

"Is Bitter Creek the nearest town where I can get supplies?" Raven switched to a subject more important to her. "It will be a long, cold ride to go there every time I need something."

"Bitter Creek is the nearest town, but you won't have to go there too often. There's a peddler who comes by every week, drivin' a wagon that's loaded with staples, tobacco, and most anything a woman might need."

"This neighbor of yours, how old is he and does he have a wife?" Raven asked, hoping that there would be a young woman nearby that she could strike up a friendship with.

"That hellion?" Cal snorted. "He ain't got no wife. He could have if he wanted to, though. Women flock around him like chickens around a June bug. I think that's the problem. He's got too many to choose from."

"Other than that, what kind of man is he?" Tory asked. "How old is he?"

"I think he's around thirty. He's pretty hard and he drinks too much. When he's mad he's a man to be left alone. But he's a good neighbor and his men all like him. He don't set around on his butt while they work their rears off. He's right out there with them in all kinds of weather."

"I guess I'll have to hire a couple men to help me with my drive."

"Not necessarily. I've got a couple hired hands. They're good men and will appreciate it if you keep them on. They ain't never rode a grub line and don't hanker to do so now."

"That's settled then." Tory shoved away from the table. "Can we take a ride now, look over what I may be buying?"

"I'm tellin' you no blazer when I say you're gettin' a nice little spread." Cal stood up and reached for his jacket, which hung on a peg next to the kitchen door.

"Are you coming with us, Raven?" Tory asked, looking at her.

"No, I think I'll stay here and look over the house," Raven answered.

"Don't let the dirt scare you," Mr. Chadwick said earnestly. "A good cleanin' will show you sturdy and reasonably good furniture. If I'd known that Tory was bringin' you with him, I'd have asked Chance McGruder to send his housekeeper over to give the place a good cleanin'."

Chance McGruder? When the door closed behind the two men, Raven stared down at her tightly clasped, white-knuckled fingers. In her mind ran the refrain. *Chance McGruder is not a cowboy, Chance McGruder is not a cowboy.* He's the owner of a ranch only a few miles away. Of all the places in Montana Territory, why did Tory have to choose this area to buy a ranch?

What would be Chance's reaction when he saw and recognized her? Would he be angry or amused? Would he try to buy her again?

Raven felt that her heart had stopped beating for a moment. Never mind his trying to buy her, she thought, what if he decided to blackmail her back into his bed? And if she refused, what then? Would he spread the word that she was a high-priced whore?

Her shoulders drooped. People would believe him. After all, he had probably lived here all his life, while she was a stranger. "Please, God," she whispered, "don't let Tory be hurt. He thinks so highly of his little sister. It would break his heart to learn that I was forced to sell my body and that the money I received for doing so enabled him to buy this ranch."

Could she talk Tory out of buying the place? Raven wondered. She could say that she felt it was too isolated from everything, that she would get lonesome for the city life she had known for the past two years.

Raven shook her head. Tory wouldn't believe that part about her missing the city. She had said too often, too vehemently, how she had hated living in Clayton. And they weren't all that far away from other people. She gave a small, hysterical laugh. Only a few miles away lived a handsome rancher.

Another ragged sigh escaped her. Worse than all the other things that had passed through her mind was the realization that she loved the man who could cause her so much anguish if he wanted to.

Chance McGruder was an angry, bitter man when he left Clayton. Three weeks later. Angry that he had a long, cold ride ahead of him, bitter that his trip to Clayton had been a fruitless one. Black-haired Raven with the blue eyes that smoldered when she made love to him had, it seemed, left town the same day he had.

According to the owner of the mercantile, she'd been widowed the very night he had made love to her. Then the next day she and a large blond man had purchased a big supply of trail grub and winter clothes before they rode out of town.

"She knew the man real good," the store owner had added. "They were laughing and carrying on, calling each other by name. It made me wonder if Miz Spencer had been puttin' the horns on her gambler husband for some time, she and the big man being so friendly to each other and all."

"Did they say where they were going?" Chance asked tightly, his fingers clenched in fists.

"No, they didn't, and I didn't ask. That big blond man had a cold look in his eyes that warned me not to ask any questions."

"That whoring little bitch," Chance swore savagely now as the stallion cantered along. "How many others did she take to her bed?"

Damn, he thought, she had duped him good. The way her soft arms had held him, the way she had wrapped her long legs around his waist, purring her pleasure at his thrusting hips, he had thought she was feeling the same way he was: for the first time in his life, love had entered into mating. If he hadn't fallen asleep, he would have asked her to leave with him.

But she hadn't felt those strong emotions. She couldn't wait for him to fall asleep so that she could take the money and run.

His eyes blazing, Chance wished he could get his hands on the little witch now. He would take her again, but it wouldn't be with gentleness and caring. He'd ride the hell out of her.

Damn. Just thinking about her slender body moving beneath his had set fire to his loins. He had an erection that threatened to pop the buttons on his fly.

Chapter Six

Raven wrung the dirty, soapy water out of the mop rag, drew an arm across her sweaty face and stood up. Finally the parlor floor was done, the last one in the house to be scrubbed.

For the past four days since Tory had left on the cattle drive, she had worked at bringing the neglected house back to the pristine state in which Emma Chadwick had kept it. She had swept, dusted, polished furniture, washed towels and bed linens and spent half a day scouring the big black range in the kitchen.

This morning after breakfast, she had tackled all the windows in the place and they now sparkled like sheets of clear ice. Later, when she had eaten lunch, she would heat the irons on the stove and press the curtains she had washed yesterday.

Raven picked up the scrub pail and stepped out

onto the back porch. As she tilted the wooden bucket to let the dirty water drain down the steps, she smiled. Old Cal was wielding a broom, whacking away at several scatter rugs thrown over the clothesline. For someone who claimed he wanted to live in town, he was taking his time to move there.

His excuse for staying on was to look after her while Tory was away. She appreciated that. The old man was good company, and she imagined that without him the evenings would be long and lonely.

During their evening chats by the fireplace she had learned a lot about her neighbors. She knew, for instance, which of the husbands sneaked into Bitter Creek to visit the bawdy house, as well as which wives had secret rendezvous with lovers. And of the teenage girls in the area, she now knew which ones gave the young men privileges and which did not.

She heard a lot about the bachelors in the vicinity, the ones that Cal declared would come courting her, and she had heard more than she wanted about Chance McGruder. According to the old man, every single female from fifteen to fifty wanted to rope Chance and drag him in front of a preacher.

"But that Chance ain't gonna be easy to break to the halter. He's not one to court a woman, so he stays clear of his neighbor's daughters. When he feels the need of female company he rides into town . . . if you know what I mean."

"I get your meaning. He pays the woman for

what he wants, then goes on his way, free of any obligation," Raven said, her voice sharp.

"Yeah, that's about the size of it," Cal agreed with a grin. "All the mothers who want him for a son-in-law tell him to his face that they hope some day he falls for a young woman who won't have nothin' to do with him."

"What does he have to say about that?"

"He just laughs and says that's not likely to happen, that he ain't seen a woman yet that could put a ring in his nose and that he don't expect to see one in the future."

The old man had given her a sly grin and said, "I got a hunch he's gonna get his comeuppance once he sets eyes on you."

She had laughed and changed the subject, thinking how foolish she had been to think that Chance might have tender feelings for her. He wasn't interested in marriage, and certainly not to a woman whom he must look on as a whore.

Raven pushed her neighbor from her mind and upended the empty pail to dry out. She walked to the edge of the porch and called, "Lunch time, Cal." The old man threw down the broom and walked toward her with a wide grin on his face.

"You've got this place as spic and span as my Emma used to have it," Cal said as he washed his hands at the dry-sink, being careful not to splash water on Raven's clean floor.

"Thank you, Cal." Raven smiled at him as she set out cold roast beef and sliced a loaf of sourdough for sandwiches. "I like taking care of a house. I started doing housework at a very young age."

"You did?" Cal looked surprised. "I don't mean you no insult, but you don't look like you'd know which end of a broom to use, you look so ladylike."

Raven gave a wry laugh. "I'm far from being a lady."

They dug into their lunch then and didn't speak any more until Raven poured their coffee. Cal said, "Let's drink the java out on the porch. We ain't gonna have many more warm sunny days like this. In a couple more weeks we could have snow on the ground."

"I expect once winter comes, a person is pretty much snowed in," Raven said, following Cal out onto the porch.

"Yeah, kind of. For a few days, at least, after a fresh snowfall. A person learns then whether or not he likes his own company. Them who don't sometimes go a little loco for a spell. Like some cowpokes who have to spend an entire winter in a line shack, spreading hay ever day for the cattle."

"Goodness, that must be awful. Alone day and night, week after week," Raven exclaimed.

"Yeah. Some don't mind it. The ones who do, though, usually have themselves a klooch."

"What's a klooch?"

"An Indian woman. Usually a young maid."

"Does she go with the cowboy willingly?" Raven frowned. "He doesn't force her, does he?"

"Oh no. The klooch is quite willin' to go. Sometimes they even ask the feller to take them in for the winter. They know they'll have plenty to eat and a warm bed to sleep in durin' the freezin' weather. Believe me, it's not like that in the Indian village. They durn near starve to death. Chance sends them over a steer ever once in a while during the winter."

"That's very thoughtful of him," Raven said, surprised.

"Chance is like that. His pa before him was the same way, always ready to help someone who was down."

With the warm sun bathing their faces, Cal and Raven were about to nod off when Cal saw a cloud of dust rolling their way. "Looks like we're gonna have company." He stood up and shielded his eyes with his hand. After a moment he grunted and sat back down.

"Do you know who it is?" Raven asked when he didn't say anything.

"It's Jadine Walker. She's Chance's uncle's stepdaughter. The two ranches run alongside each other. No doubt she's heard about your goodlookin' brother and is ridin' over to check him out. If ever there was a man-crazy female, she's it. She's just about used up half the men around here. That includes married men. She'll be eager to get her claws on some fresh meat."

She's not very pretty, Raven thought as her neighbor drew rein and slid out of the saddle. She looks almost masculine, flat-chested and almost hipless.

But Jadine's plainness was forgotten as she stepped up on the porch and gave Raven a smile that lit up her face. "Won't you come in the house and have some coffee and a piece of cake?" Raven invited.

"Thank you, but I can't stay long." Jadine sat down on the edge of the porch and leaned her back on a supporting post. "My mare is horsin' and I want to get her down to Chance's stallion."

When Raven gave her a quizzical look, Jadine laughed and explained, "She wants to breed. She wants a stallion to ride her."

"Oh, I see." Raven colored a bit. "I've never heard that expression before. In Nebraska we always described a female animal as being in heat."

Jadine looked at Cal with an amused twist of her lips and remarked, "It looks like our new neighbor is a lady."

Cal made no response, but the warning look he gave Jadine said plainly, *And don't you forget it.*

Jadine shrugged her shoulders indifferently and looked back at Raven. "What do you think of Montana and your new ranch? Do you think you'll like living here?"

"I've fallen in love with the territory, and so far I like ranch life."

"Ranchin' is a good life if you can stand the loneliness of it."

"I don't think I'll mind that. I have my brother Tory to keep me company in the evenings."

"Where is your brother?"

"He left on a cattle drive four days ago. He'll be gone for a while, and in the meantime Cal is staying with me."

After a short silence, Jadine asked, "Have you met your neighbor Chance McGruder yet?"

"Chance has gone to Clayton on business," Cal answered for Raven.

Both women looked surprised. Why had he gone to Clayton? Raven wondered. Surely not to look for her.

"I wasn't aware of that." Jadine frowned. "When did he leave?"

"A few weeks ago, accordin' to Mary." The look the old man slid Jadine held dislike and mockery. "You're slippin', Jadine. I thought you knew everything that went on around here. I guess you've been too busy lately to keep up on things."

Jadine sent him a killing look and stood up. "If you ever get lonesome, Raven, come out to the ranch and we'll visit."

"Thank you, Jadine, and you must come visit me again."

As Jadine mounted the mare and sent her away at a gallop, Cal snorted, "She'll be back, you can depend on that, but not before Tory returns. You'll see plenty of her after that."

"I got the feeling she doesn't care much for women's company, although she was friendly enough."

"Don't be taken in by that, Raven. She was only tryin' to get on the good side of you so's she can get to know Tory. That woman don't have one woman friend. Never did have, even as a teenager. She always hung around men."

"She's to be pitied then. I'd give anything to have women friends again."

"You will, honey. Most of us ranchers live some distance apart, but we do get together sometimes.

65

If you ride into Bitter Creek on a Saturday you'll meet most of the womenfolk."

"I'll look forward to that."

"What do you say to us goin' into town this comin' Saturday, day after tomorrow?" Cal said.

"Sounds fine. I need to purchase a few things anyway."

After a companionable silence Cal said, "I wonder how Tory and the men are doin'."

"I'm sure everything is going well. Tory has made cattle drives lots of times."

"He does seem to know his way around a ranch and cattle."

"Well," Raven said briskly, rising and picking up their empty cups, "I want to get some ironing done this afternoon."

"I think I'll get my fishin' pole and mosey on down to the river. Maybe we can have fried fish for supper."

Chapter Seven

When Chance and Tory met on the trail, going in opposite directions, Chance was a quarter of the way home and Tory was three-quarters of the way from his destination.

Tory and his men had left the cattle to graze while they ate a lunch of beans and sourdough and hot coffee. They were squatted around a small fire when Chance rode up. "Step down and help yourself to beans and coffee," Tory invited.

"I recognize the Chadwick brand on the cattle," Chance said, dismounting. "You must be the fellow who bought old Cal's spread."

"Yes, I am." Tory stood up. "I'm Tory McCloud."

As they shook hands, Chance gave his name, then added, "I'm your nearest neighbor." When Chance had helped himself to beans and coffee, he hunkered down beside Tory and said, "You're making a late drive, McCloud."

Tory nodded. "I hope we can get home before the snow flies."

"You might make it if everything goes alright. To hear the old folks tell it, there's going to be an early winter."

"They have a way of being right." Tory laughed lightly. "My grandfather used to predict the weather, and most times he was right."

"I heard you and your wife passed through Bitter Creek when I stopped there a few weeks ago on my way to Clayton," Chance said, polishing off his plate of beans.

"That was my sister with me. I'm not married."

"I'm not either and I'm not planning on getting married in the near future," Chance said with a grin.

"Neither am I. I haven't seen a woman yet that interests me enough to settle down with her for the rest of my life. Have you ever come near making that fatal mistake?"

"No . . . well, once I did," Chance answered, a slight bitterness in his voice. "Luckily I came to my senses in time."

"Are there any bawdy houses in Bitter Creek, or any loose women in the area?"

"Yes to both questions. There's Hattie's pleasure house. She has four girls working for her, and we have one very loose lady." Chance grinned. "You'll know her quick enough. She'll come visiting you."

"Well now, I'm looking forward to that."

"You'll need stamina. She takes a lot of pleasuring."

"I take it you know from experience." Tory's lips tilted in a grin.

"I sure as hell do. She took my virginity when I was only sixteen. I must have lost twenty pounds that summer. I made a real hog out of myself. We'd meet down by the river every afternoon."

"That's the kind of female I like." Tory grinned as he made himself a smoke. "It's been a long time since I've had a woman."

"You can catch up on that once you've gotten rid of your cattle."

Tory shook his head. "I can't waste any time wallowing around with some whore. I want to get back to my sister before it snows. Cal is with her now, but if I should get held up somewhere for a couple weeks because of a blizzard, she'd worry herself sick."

"Do you want me to ride over to your place and tell her I've seen you and that everything is going well with the drive?"

"I'd appreciate that, McGruder. She'd be happy to hear news of me." A soberness came into Tory's voice. "She worries a lot about her wild brother. We haven't got any other relatives and I guess she's afraid of losing me. My pa was already dead when Ma gave birth to my sister and it was up to me and Grandpa to raise her. She managed to survive our care somehow. The only way we knew how to take care of her was the same way you would a very young calf that's lost its mother. Anyhow, I'm awfully proud of her. She grew into a fine young woman.

"I'm anxious to meet her," Chance said respectfully.

"I want you to, but"—Tory's eyes grew hard—"don't try any funny business with her."

"I never mess around with decent women," Chance said, standing up and brushing off the seat of his pants. "Thanks for the grub, and good luck with your drive. I'll see you when you get home. We'll ride into Bitter Creek, have a few drinks. Then I'll introduce you to Hattie's girls."

"I'll look forward to it." Tory grinned. He watched Chance mount his stallion, and as the big animal moved out, he called out, "My sister's name is Raven."

Raven! Chance stiffened and very nearly reined Brutus in. Surely Tory's sister and the little witch he had made love to weren't the same woman. It had to be a coincidence. It was just too far-fetched that she would turn up in Bitter Creek.

That night he was still thinking of the Raven he knew while he sat in front of a campfire eating the prairie chicken he had shot. As usual, he was rehashing every moment of the time he had spent with her. Could it be that she had left Clayton with her brother, not a lover? Later, rolled up in his blankets, with a distant pack of wolves serenading him, he fell asleep to dream of soft arms embracing him and a silken body responding to his.

A week later Chance rode Brutus to the top of a knoll and looked down into a shallow valley. In the distance were his ranch buildings, and closer, to his right, was Tory McCloud's spread. Although he was tired and hungry and longed for a hot bath and clean clothes, Chance decided that since Tory's place was so near, he'd ride there first and relay Tory's message to his sister.

When he approached the ranch house, the first thing that caught his attention was a feminine shape in tight-fitting trousers walking away from him, going in the direction of the barn.

If the rest of her looks like her rear end, she's a beaut, he thought as he called out, "Miss Mc-Cloud?"

Raven spun around. An observer would have been hard-pressed to decide which of the two was more astounded, Chance or Raven.

"You!" they exclaimed in unison.

Raven forgot to breathe as she stared up at Chance in open-mouthed disbelief. His face dark and brooding, Chance leaned from the saddle and snatched her up to sit across his lap. Before she could make an outcry, his lips descended on hers in an angry, hungry kiss.

But the hardness of his lips gentled as Raven responded with equal heat. The kiss went on, their lips clinging, neither wanting to pull away.

Chance gained possession of his senses first. He jerked his mouth away and held Raven away from him, saying in a voice that dripped acid, "I've ridden all over hell looking for you. We've got some unfinished business, lady."

"I don't know what you're talking about." Raven struggled to get off the horse. "As far as I'm concerned, our business was finished once you fell asleep."

"It wasn't, not by a long shot." Chances's hands tightened on her arms. "As far as *I'm* concerned, it would have been over after I'd sated myself with you."

"But you had fallen asleep."

"So what? Any whore knows a man has to get a little rest before riding her again."

Hurt and humiliated, Raven could only stare at him, asking herself how she could have ever had tender feelings for this crude man. Why had she thought of him so often, wishing that things could have been different between them?

She couldn't believe him when he said, "You owe me, lady. Shall we go to the house, or in the barn on a pile of hay—"

"You're out of your mind," Raven gasped. "I'm not going anywhere with you." She glared at him, her eyes shooting defiance.

"Oh yes, you are," Chance said savagely, and swung out of the saddle, then jerked her to the ground. Grasping her arm, he grated out, "We'll use the barn."

"Please, Chance," Raven begged, her voice thick with tears. "You'll hate yourself if you do this."

"I'd hate myself if I didn't," Chance grated, jerking her toward the barn door.

They were inside the barn, Raven still pulling away from Chance, trying to pry his fingers off her arm, when he suddenly released her with a savage oath.

They could hear the sound of a horse coming up the ranch's gravel road.

"We'll settle this another time," Chance promised in a tight voice and pushed her outside again.

Raven had barely composed herself when Cal called out a greeting to Chance. When the old man climbed off his horse, garrulous as usual, Raven took the opportunity to escape to the house. She hurried to her room and burst into tears as she threw herself onto the bed. "How could I have been so mistaken about a man?" she sobbed. "If Cal hadn't arrived home when he did, Chance would have raped me."

Raped her? she questioned when her heartbeat slowed. It wouldn't have been rape. Once he held her in his arms, kissed and caressed her, she would have become his willing love slave just like before.

Raven also knew that there would come a day when they wouldn't be interrupted and Chance would extract from her what he believed he still had coming to him.

"Oh, Tory," she cried in the pillow, "please get home soon. I desperately need your protection. Chance McGruder has the power to turn me into his private whore."

Tory stepped out of the First National Bank, a wide smile on his face and a roll of money buttoned down in his vest pocket. At last his long-time dream had come true. He was an honest-to-God rancher who had completed his first cattle drive.

He stepped off the boardwalk and crossed the

street to the saloon straight ahead. His two cowboys waited for him there. He would pay them, have a drink with them, then head for home. They could return to the ranch whenever they wanted to. Probably when they were broke, he thought wryly.

Tory had a drink at the saloon and went to get his horse. He had ridden a couple hours when gathering clouds began to hide the sun. "Damn," he swore under his breath, "Am I gonna get caught in a blizzard a million miles from nowhere?"

Tory heaved a sigh of resignation. There wasn't anything he could do but pray that he could find some kind of shelter if Mother Nature decided to raise hell.

It began to snow an hour later, big, heavy flakes that clung to everything they landed on. In no time the snowfall became so dense Tory couldn't see a foot in front of him. His forehead creased in a worried frown. What if he got turned around, became lost?

An hour passed, and in the dead calm of the snow-covered land there was no sound or movement, only the soft thud of the horse's hooves plodding in snow up past his fetlocks.

Daylight had long since faded when the wind came up, bitterly cold, blowing from the north. Tory jerked the collar of his mackinaw up around his ears, pulled his Stetson low on his forehead and prayed that he was keeping his horse in a straight line.

He was growing numb from the rapidly falling temperature and the horse had slowed down even more. How much longer could they go on?

"But we must go on," Tory whispered between cold, chapped lips. "If we go down in this snow, we won't be found until next spring."

Tory was weaving back and forth on the sturdy little horse, clutching the saddle horn to keep from falling, when he smelled wood smoke. His heart beating a little faster, he lifted his chin off his chest. There was a house or a camp nearby. He blinked the snow off his lashes and peered through the white curtain. He could see nothing but the huge white flakes blowing around in a frenzy.

A silent laugh shook his body. It didn't matter anyway. He wasn't cold anymore. He was only tired and needed to sleep. The horse stopped of its own volition, and Tory slid out of the saddle onto the ground.

As he curled himself into a ball, he mumbled, "I'm sorry, Raven. I've got to sleep awhile before I can get home to you."

Chapter Eight

The cold, snow-laden wind whipped across the girl's face, stinging her cheeks, pinching her nose. She was nearly ten miles from home when the blizzard hit. She was thankful that the storm was at her back. Its fierceness would drive her cattle forward, in the direction of the ranch.

Amy Mitchel had been in the saddle for the greater portion of two days and one night. Her old friend Ike Blocker had predicted that within the week they were in for a blue norther, and since the old mountaineer was usually right about such things, she had hurried to ride out to find her small herd and drive the cattle close to the ranch. She would be able to scatter hay for them then, keep them alive.

It was important not to lose a single one. The sale of her herd later would permit her to pay her taxes, and give her the money she needed to carry on.

She had started her herd by mavericking, taking possession of unbranded cattle. Her herd had grown when bosses of cattle drives gave her calves that were too young to keep up with the herd. For the past three years, every spring and fall she kept watch for dust clouds that told her a cattle drive was coming through. She would mount her pinto and ride the mile or so to hunt out the boss of the drive, ask him if he had any calves he wanted to get rid of. She never failed to get additions to her growing herd.

A smile creased the corners of her green eyes. Next spring she would make her first real cattle drive. From the sale of a hundred or so head she would be able to pay her back taxes and buy some much-needed new clothes. She knew that she looked like a scarecrow in her rags.

Amy had been fourteen when the old-maid aunt who had raised her passed away from heart failure. She'd had a choice then: go to an orphanage, or to an uncle she had never seen. The lawyer who was handling her aunt's affairs tried to dissuade her from choosing her uncle. "He's a rough fur trader, Amy," he said. "He and his ilk are as tough as the rawhide they lace their boots with. You'd never be happy with him. You wouldn't fit in with his kind of life."

But she had opted for the uncle. After all, he was blood kin, and Aunt Emma had loved him.

A letter had been sent off to her uncle, and three

weeks later he and three of his friends had met the coach that pulled into Bitter Creek.

She had been tired and hungry, and half afraid of meeting the uncle who was a stranger to her. But one look into the twinkling eyes above his bushy beard had laid to rest all her fears.

With a roaring laugh, Jacob Mitchel had gathered her in a bear hug that almost knocked the breath out of her. He had held her away then and said in a voice that was a little husky, "I'd have knowed you anywhere from them green eyes. You're the spittin' image of sister Emma, God rest her soul."

Amy had been introduced to her uncle's friends then. Ike Blocker, Henry Sipes, and Isaac Hunt. Although the three were not related, they looked much the same with their bushy faces and rough clothing. They shyly shook her hand with beaming smiles.

"Are you hungry?" Jacob asked. "We can go to the cafe and get something to eat before we start out."

Before she could answer, Ike Blocker said, "I think you ought to eat somethin'. We've got a long ride ahead of us."

The little restaurant they entered was offering fried chicken that day. As the five of them crowded around a table and waited for their meal to be served, Amy was told the history of her uncle and her new friends.

All four had been mountain men from their teenage years. Along with Jedediah Smith, the five Sublitte brothers, Jim Bridger, Mike Fink, Robert

Campbell and Jim Beckwourth, they had marked trails, eastablishing landmarks and posts for the wagon trains of settlers who followed.

When the four friends had grown tired of that, they built themselves a cabin and settled down to fur-trading. "But, Amy girl," Uncle Jacob had said, "I don't expect you to live with us in our boars' nest. I've bought you and me a little cattle ranch."

Ike Blocker gave a snort of laughter. "He calls it a cattle ranch. I bet it ain't got a dozen longhorns on the place."

"Don't forget there's one bull," Isaac Hunt interjected with a grin.

"Both of you go to hell," Jacob said, growing tired of their razzing. "It's a start, and me and Amy will turn the place into a fine little spread, see if we don't."

"We was just funnin' you, Jacob," Ike said. "You and Amy will do fine. The house and buildin's are built strong and tight. And I believe I saw some chickens scratchin' round the barn. You'll be able to have eggs for breakfast ever mornin' and that's somethin' you ain't had in many a year."

Jacob had been mollified, and when the chicken arrived, he ate with as much gusto as his friends. They finished off their meal with peach cobbler, then left Bitter Creek behind. Amy rode the little pinto her uncle had brought along for her.

It had been near sunset when they spotted a ranch house with a shed and a barn and a corral to one side of it.

"There she is, Amy girl, your new home," he'd said, his voice full of pride that he could provide for his niece. She was the first human being he had ever been responsible for.

And the rough old mountain man had taken that responsibility seriously. He was ever watchful over her, doing all that he could to keep her happy and content. And he had been successful. She had loved running wild, racing her little mount over the range, doing pretty much as she pleased as long as it wasn't dangerous to her well-being. Uncle Jacob hadn't put many restrictions on her.

But it was plain to her that he wasn't as content as she was. She knew by the way he sometimes stood and gazed for long minutes toward the mountains where his friends were. She could also see his discontent in the way he became excited when they came down to the ranch to visit. It was easy to see that he missed trapping; he wanted to know every little detail of where his friends laid their lines, whether the beaver were plentiful this year.

She had grown to dearly love her uncle during the six months she had him. It was one spring morning while he was sitting outside staring up at the mountain that his heart stopped beating.

The events of that morning were clear to her, but she vaguely remembered an old Indian coming along, shaking his head in sympathy for her tears, then announcing that he would go up the mountain and tell Jacob's friends.

Ike and the others were there almost immediately. And after trying to console her in their awkward way, they had asked permission to take their friend to the mountains to bury him. She had agreed. It was only proper that the old man's last resting place should be where his heart had always been.

"I'll stop by every week to see how you are, Amy girl," Ike had said before they rode away, with her uncle's body strapped on a travois pulled by his old gray horse.

Twice a year she went up the mountain to visit his grave, to sit beside it and tell him all that she had been doing and that everything was coming along fine.

Since her uncle's death when she was fifteen she had more or less been on her own. As she matured and outgrew her dresses, she sent Ike to Bitter Creek to purchase her some Levi's and men's shirts. As the years passed and she worked hard at building her herd, the only remaining feminine things about her were her curly reddish hair and the rose-scented soap she bathed in every night. The people in the area weren't even aware that a nineteen-year-old female lived in the foothills of the mountain.

The wind died down suddenly and Amy pulled the little pinto in to let it blow. As she sat waiting, her chin tucked in her collar, there came to her the sound of stamping feet and the jingle of a bit. She lifted her head and listened intently. There was a horse nearby. Did he have a rider? Was that rider alright, or was he down?

She reined her pinto in the direction from which she had heard the sound. In a short time she almost rode into a horse. It had an empty saddle on its back, and the reins were dangling. A quick glance around showed her the body of a man curled up in the drifting snow. She quickly dismounted and floundered her way to the still form. Kneeling beside him, she brushed the snow off his face. Then removing her gloves, she laid two fingers on his throat, feeling for a pulse.

She found it almost immediately. It was weak, but steady. Now, how was she to get him to the house? He was too big for her to handle. She wondered if by some miracle Ike had come down from the mountain to check on her and was at the house right now. She hadn't seen him all week.

With a prayer on her lips, she pulled her Colt from its holster and shot three times in the air— a signal Ike had said would tell him she was in trouble.

She was rubbing the man's hands and massaging his arms and legs through his clothing when she saw a bobbing light coming in her direction. She cupped her hands around her mouth and yelled, "Over here!"

Amy could hardly distinguish Ike's face through the swirling snow as his big horse tried to gallop through the snowdrifts. She only recognized his large, bulky figure.

"What's wrong, Amy girl?" Ike asked anxiously, reining in and sliding to the ground.

"It's this man. I think he's half frozen. He must have fallen off his horse."

"Probably a stranger that got lost." Ike knelt down beside Amy and held up the lantern to shine on the still face. "We'd better get him up to the house and warm him up."

It was a struggle for Ike to lift the big body over his horse, then climb up behind him, but with Amy's help it was finally done. They headed for the house, Ike leading and Amy following, holding the reins of the man's quarter horse.

She breathed a sigh of relief when she saw the lamplight spilling out of her kitchen window. Would it be too much to hope that Ike had built a fire in the fireplace?

The scent of wood smoke told her that he had. When they reached the house and she opened the door for Ike to stagger through with his limp burden, the warmth of the room comforted her like being wrapped up in a warm blanket.

Amy led the way to her uncle's bedroom and threw back the covers. When Ike had eased the man onto the mattress, he stood a moment, catching his breath, then said, "Warm up all the quilts you can find while I get him out of these wet clothes. And add more wood to the fireplace. We've got to get some heat flowing in here."

Amy hurried to her room, lifted the lid off a trunk and took out three folded patchwork quilts, then at a half run went into the other room to spread them out on the hearth. She piled wood on the fire until flames were licking up the chimney.

She was closing the heavy curtians across the windows to shut out the cold air when Ike called, "You can bring in the covers now."

Ike had stripped her unexpected guest down to his two-piece longjohns when Amy hurried into the room. Together, she and Ike wrapped the warmed quilts around the shivering body.

"He's danged near froze," Ike said, drawing the rest of the bedding up around their patient. "But he's not in as bad a way as I feared. I don't think he lay in the snow very long before you found him."

Ike shook his head and grinned. "He's gonna yell bloody murder when he begins to warm up. He'll think there's a million needles stickin' him all over.

"He's a good-lookin' cuss, ain't he?"

Amy didn't agree out loud, but she silently thought that she had never seen a more handsome man, even with the light-colored stubble on his chin and jaw.

"I wonder who he is, where he came from and where he was headed," she said.

"He's no grub liner, I can tell you that. His boots and clothes are in too good condition. Accordin' to his horse, I think he may be a rancher that got turned around in the storm and got lost. He keeps mutterin' to a woman called Raven, sayin' how sorry he is that he couldn't get home to her. His wife, I guess."

Amy felt a pang of disappointment at Ike's last words, then said to herself, *I should have known a handsome man like that would be snapped up by some woman. Not that he'd pay any attention to a scraggly thing like me.*

"Why don't you go put on a pot of coffee, honey, and warm up that pot of stew I saw sittin' on the stove?" Ike suggested. "I ain't et nothin' since this mornin', and I bet you ain't either."

Ike walked toward the door, saying, "While you're doin' that, I'll take the animals down to the barn and give them somethin' to eat too."

Amy put on a pot of coffee and pulled the big black pot of stew to the front of the stove where it could heat. She stood a moment in indecision, then, squaring her shoulders, walked into her uncle's bedroom to check on her patient.

He had stopped shivering, but was still muttering to the woman Raven. Amy sighed and picked up his wet clothing and boots and carried them into the other room and spread them on the hearth to dry out.

Tory came to in acute agony. He felt as though someone was sticking his entire body with red-hot needles. He groaned aloud his pain, and almost immediately a big, bushy-faced man and a green-eyed girl hovered over him. While he stared in confusion into the most beautiful eyes he'd ever seen, the bearded one said, "I reckon you're in a lot of pain. You was near froze to death when Amy found you." He nudged the girl. "Go get him a cup of coffee, Amy girl, and lace it good with some of Jacob's whiskey."

While Amy was out of the room, Ike learned Tory's name, that he owned a ranch in the vicinity.

"I want to get started first thing tomorrow morning," Tory said as the pain left his limbs. "I've got to get home as soon as possible. I should have been home a week ago. Raven's probably sick with worrying about me."

"It will depend on the storm, whether or not you can leave in the mornin'," Ike said as he walked to the bedroom door and took the cup of coffee Amy held toward him.

When Ike put the cup on the table, Tory pushed himself up in bed and reached for it. When he had drunk the coffee in three long swallows, Ike asked, "Do you feel like gettin' up and havin' a bowl of stew with us, or do you want Amy to bring it to you?"

"I'd like to get up, if you have a pair of pants I can borrow."

"I do, but they're up at my place. I don't live here." He looked at Amy hovering in the doorway. "I expect he could wear a pair of Jacob's while his duds are dryin'. They'll be too short and too big around the waist, but they'll keep him covered."

Amy nodded, and walked over to a dresser where she pulled out a bottom drawer and removed a pair of woolen trousers, a heavy shirt and a pair of socks.

"Thank you, Amy," Tory said as she laid the articles of clothing on the foot of the bed.

Feeling herself blush, Amy hurried from the room. Not for the world would she let the big blond man see how he affected her.

As she dished up the steaming stew, she wished that her hands were smoother, her palms free of calluses, and that she wore a dress so that she would look more feminine.

What difference does it make how I look to him, she thought. *He's got a wife.*

But despite that knowledge, by the time she called the men to the table she had scrubbed her hands and nails and spent a couple minutes in her room brushing her curls until they lay smoothly around her shoulders.

When the men came in Amy suppressed a giggle at the comic figure Tory made in her uncle's clothing. The legs of the trousers were at least a foot too short, and the belt cinching his waist formed many gathers. But the red flannel shirt fit his broad shoulders to perfection.

Tory caught the glimmer in her eyes, and his own sparkled. "I don't look much like a fashion plate, do I?" he questioned.

Amy didn't know what a fashion plate was, but she shook her head anyway. She felt sure it had something to do with his appearance.

"I'd like to wash my hands before I eat," Tory said. "They haven't seen soap for a while."

"The washbasin is here on the dry-sink," Amy said as she walked to the stove. "I'll fill it with warm water from the reservoir." Tory stood close behind her, watching as she dipped the water into the basin. She could feel the heat of his body, and her heart raced and her hands trembled. When he said, "You sure smell good," she almost dropped the dipper.

She managed to say a shy, "Thank you," before turning away to pick up a pan of biscuits, which she placed on the table.

All three ate with ravenous appetites, and little

was said during the meal. When they were sated and leaned back in their chairs to drink their coffee, Tory complimented Amy on her tasty stew. When he said, "I believe it's better than Raven's," she blushed with pleasure.

"Whereabouts is your ranch, McCloud?" Ike asked.

"It's about fifteen miles east of Bitter Creek."

"You're almost home then. Me and the fellers make a trip down there three or four times a year. When we run out of supplies, or when we bring in our furs."

"Speaking of furs, you won't be able to run your line tomorrow, will you?" Amy said.

"I'll be able to do it. This snow is so wet, it'll have an icy crust on it tomorrow. I'll strap on my snowshoes and not have a speck of trouble gettin' through the snow."

"I'll be headin' out early in the mornin'," Ike said at the end of a yawn, "so I'm gonna get some shuteye." He grinned at Tory. "I hope you don't snore or hog most of the bed."

"I've never been told that I snore"—Tory grinned back at him—"but I don't know about hogging the bed. You'll just have to wait and see."

Ike stood up and shoved his chair back under the table. "I'm gonna turn in now. I'll see you in the morning. And, Amy girl"—he touched her shoulder—"you won't be up when I leave. You know the signal if you need anything."

"Do you live here alone?" Tory asked Amy disapprovingly when Ike had left.

"Yes, I do." Amy nodded. "What's wrong with that?"

"But that's crazy, dangerous. How can a youngster be expected to take care of herself?"

"I'm not a youngster," Amy said sharply.

"Oh?" Tory raised an amused eyebrow. "How old are you? Fourteen?"

Amy gave him a cool look and said stiffly, "I'm nineteen years old."

Tory stared at her, stunned. "You sure don't look it. You're joshing me, aren't you?"

"Why would I do that?" Amy demanded, anger in her voice.

"I don't know. Most young girls are so anxious to grow up, they sometimes add years to their age. But maybe in your case it's the clothes you wear. If it wasn't for your long hair, I'd think you were a boy."

Green fire shot out of Amy's eyes. It was bad enough that he'd said she only looked fourteen, but adding that she looked like a boy was too much. She shot to her feet and in a voice near tears said, "Good night, Mr. McCloud."

Tory jumped to his feet and caught her arm before she could run to her bedroom. "Ah, honey." He looked into her green eyes swimming with tears. "I was only funnin' you. Couldn't you tell? One look at your little rear in those tight Levi's told me plainly that you are female. It's just that you don't look that old."

But up close as he gazed down at her red lips, Amy suddenly looked every bit her age. And her soft body felt very much like that of a woman's. He lifted his hand, threaded his fingers through her silky hair, then cupping her face in his hands he lowered his head and captured her trembling lips with his.

At first Amy tried to move her head, to dislodge his mouth, but he only moved his head with hers. When he released her arms and pulled her up against his hard body, a smoldering heat moved through Amy's body. She leaned into him, her fingers clutching his forearms to keep herself from falling.

Encouraged, Tory slid a hand up her shirt, and his manhood jerked when it encountered a bare, satin-smooth breast. She wasn't wearing a camisole.

He had fit both hands on her small rear, drawn her between his legs and was pressing his hardness into her when he realized how far things had gone. Another minute and he would have her in bed making love to her. That would be a hell of a way to repay her for saving his life. Especially since he would probably never see her again.

Although it was the hardest thing he had ever done, he broke the kiss, removed his hand and dropped his arms from around her. "Sweet, Amy"—he looked into her confused eyes—"don't let any man, other than your husband, do to you what I just did."

He dropped a light kiss on her brow, whispered good night, then went into the bedroom where Ike lay snoring.

Amy stared after him, her fingers on her swollen lips. She had never felt so unfeminine in her life. She was so unattractive, Tory couldn't bring himself to make love to her.

She numbly stacked the dirty dishes in the dry-sink, then went to bed. Even as tears of shame seeped from the corners of her eyes, soaking the pillow, her body still throbbed from Tory's kiss and caressing hands.

When Amy awakened the next morning, the man she had dreamed of all night was gone. She would probably never see him again, she sighed, but she would never forget him.

Chapter Nine

Raven swiped her hand across the vapor her breath had put on the windowpane and peered out at the white-blanketed landscape. The first snowfall of the year, she thought.

Where was Tory? she fretted. He should have been home days ago. Had he run into trouble during the cattle drive? So many things could have happened on the trail—getting run down in a stampede, drowning in a river crossing, getting shot by cattle rustlers. Or maybe he had been caught in the blizzard and was right now lying in some snowdrift.

The kitchen door opened, then snapped shut. "It's bitter cold out there, Raven," Cal said, coming in from shoveling a path to the door. He walked over to the stove and picked up the coffee pot. As he filled a cup he continued, "That was a real blue norther."

Raven turned from the window. "I'm worried about Tory. He should have been home days ago, Cal. You know that. Something must have happened to him."

"Now don't go gettin' yourself all fussed up. He ran into the blizzard he's holed up somewhere."

"But where? Tory and I rode that cattle trail on the way here and we didn't see one ranch house."

"That don't mean there ain't any there. There's all kinds of valleys hidden away with ranches and homesteads in them."

"I don't even know if he got to his destination," Raven wailed. "I'm worried about him, Cal."

"Now calm yourself," Cal soothed as he stood up and eased her down in a chair. "Let me get you a cup of coffee and things will look better to you."

Raven gave him a look that told him what a foolish remark he had just made. But she remained at the table, telling herself that it wouldn't help matters to pace the floor, it wouldn't bring Tory home any faster.

As Cal poured her coffee, he looked out the window, then exclaimed, "We've got company. Chance is ridin' our way."

The flutter of excitement that ran through Raven was quickly suppressed. "What does he want?" she said crossly.

Cal looked at her, surprised. "He probably doesn't want anything. He's just makin' a neighborly call. The ranchers around here look in on each other ever once in a while, to see if ever'thing is alright. Especially when the snow is up to your rump. We're so far away from civilization, we have to look out for each other."

Raven didn't voice her opinion of why Chance McGruder was coming to visit them. He wanted to remind her that she still owed him. Her eyes took on a hard glint. As far as she was concerned he had been paid in full.

As Chance dismounted, he marveled at his desire for Raven. She seldom left his mind. He had welcomed the snowfall that gave him a reason to check up on her.

He was ashamed of how he had lost control with Raven the last time he saw her, and regretted the things he had said. He felt he must apologize to her if she was ever to trust him again. The one thing that gave him hope was that she hadn't gone off with a lover when she left Clayton.

Old Cal opened the door to Chance's knock. "Come in, Chance," he said warmly. "Me and Raven was just having some coffee. You're in time to have some with us."

Chance removed his hat and gave Raven a wary look. "How are you, Raven?" he said.

"I'm fine, thank you," she answered coolly.

"No, she's not," Cal said as Chance removed his jacket and hung it on the back of the chair where he sat down.

"Oh? Are you ailing?" He looked at Raven as Cal poured him a cup of coffee.

"She ain't ailin'," Cal said before Raven could answer. "She's worried about her brother. He's a few days late gettin' home, and with this storm, she's thinkin' that all kinds of things have happened to him."

Chance was thinking that Tory, like most men was probably celebrating the end of the trip. That he was having a few drinks and catching up on some sheet-shaking. But he knew better than to voice that opinion to Raven. Such a possibility wouldn't enter her mind, and she wouldn't thank him for putting it there.

"You're worrying unnecessarily, Raven," he said. "It takes time to have your cattle counted, then you have to dicker with a buyer for the best price you can get. And after that, if the banks aren't closed, you go to one and get your check cashed. But by then it's dark and you don't want to start home then; besides, your men want to celebrate a little. If you're a good boss, you go to a saloon with them. You have a few drinks, play a few hands of poker. The next day you have a headache and a sour stomach from the whiskey you've had and you lie around all day recovering. It will be night again, so you'll wait until the next day to start home."

"But I don't even know if he arrived in Clayton," Raven pointed out.

"I'm sure he did. I met him when I was coming home. He was almost there then." Chance paused and, averting his face from Raven, said, "I forgot to tell you when I was here before. He gave me a message to give to you. He said to tell you that everything was going along fine."

Raven slammed her fist on the table. "Didn't you

think that was important enough to tell me?"

"Well, yes." Chance still refused to look at her. "Like I said, I forgot about it."

"I can understand that," Raven jeered. "You had other things on your mind."

Chance's head jerked around at Raven's thinly veiled meaning. "Yes, I did." His eyes bored into hers. "And you might as well know I still have the same thing on my mind."

Her eyes snapping, Raven leaned forward and shot at him, "You might as well know that I'm advising you to get it out of your mind."

"Oh no, lady." Chance glared back at her. "I always collect what's coming to me."

The air was so thick with animosity, old Cal grew uneasy as he tried to figure out what was going on between Chance and Raven, and how had it come on so quickly. He jumped to his feet and grabbed his jacket off the wall. "I'm gonna ride into town and get some kerosene," he said.

The combatants didn't hear him, didn't even know when he left. They were locked in a silent battle of wills.

Then Chance leaned across the table, only inches separating their faces. Forgetting the promise he had made to himself, he lost control. He forgot his intention to apologize for his previous behavior, that he wasn't going to pressure her again. All he knew and felt now was that he had to have her. He had to experience again the ecstasy, the bliss, that only she could give him.

He jumped to his feet, tipping his chair backwards. As he came around the table he grated out to the startled Raven, "I won't leave you alone until I feel that I'm amply paid for what you still owe me."

Swooping her into his arms, he continued, "And there's no better time than now to collect a little of it."

As Chance strode to her room, kicking the door open, Raven pounded him on the back, the chest, calling him names she hadn't realized she knew.

The fire burning in Chance's loins at having her so close to him made him immune to her small fists. He had an aim that consumed him, drove everything else from his mind. He felt that if he didn't make love to her in the next few minutes, he would drop dead.

He laid her on the bed and came down with her. As his hands went straight to the buttons on her shirt, she raked her nails down his cheek. Chance swore under his breath, and capturing her wrists in one hand, he quickly undid her shirt and pushed her camisole down around her waist.

And while she lay helpless to stop him, he stroked her breasts, then lifted one to his mouth.

Raven tried to ignore the warmth gathering in her lower regions as his lips began to draw on her hardened nipple, but when he drew it between his teeth and nibbled gently, she moaned and arched her back to get her breasts closer to him.

A satisfied smile curved the corners of Chance's lips and he released her wrists. She was his now.

Raven's hands came down, one burying itself in his hair, the other moving his head to her other breast. He gently nibbled and sucked at the new mound while his fingers kneaded and fondled the wet one, all the time knowing that he was sending Raven into a frenzy of desire.

A moment later she was bucking her body against his, whispering, "Now, Chance, now. I'm on fire. I need you inside me."

"I want to be there, honey," Chance rasped, tearing at her clothes, then his own. They were both bare then and Raven was lifting her arms to him as he crawled between her open legs.

"Ah, God," he whispered as he slid himself into her. "You feel so good. Just like hot velvet wrapped around me." He stretched himself out on top of her, then lay still. Before he bent his head to draw a puckered nipple into his mouth, he begged, "Work your muscles around me, Raven. Like you did the first time we made love."

Raven wrapped her arms around his shoulders and started to make the walls of her woman's core constrict around his thickness, to draw at the manhood that filled her so completely. He moaned his pleasure, and in just a short time his lean body was shuddering and she felt him emptying himself inside her as he bucked his hips rapidly against her.

As she knew it would be, Chance's manhood was still hard and wanting. Raven sighed softly when he raised himself up, slid his hands under her rear and started pumping in and out of her in slow, easy strokes. She leaned up on her elbows to watch his largeness slide in and out of her, making her pleasure all the more intense as it grew inside her.

Chance felt the tightening of her body, knew what it meant, and began to thrust deeper and faster. Raven threw herself back on the bed and began to buck her hips against the strong drives of his body. A moment later she gave herself over to the waves of overpowering rapture that were flooding through her. She clung to Chance's shoulders as he too, climaxed, her name on his lips.

Their breathing had returned to normal and Chance, taking most of his weight off Raven by propping himself on his elbows, gazed down at her flushed face. He opened his mouth to speak, then closed it. Hoofbeats were coming toward the house.

Alarm jumped into Raven's eyes. "It can't be Cal." She pushed Chance away. "He hasn't had time to get to town and back."

"Dammit!" Chance swore when he looked out the window. "It's Jadine Walker."

"What are we going to do?" Raven looked panic-stricken.

"Hurry and get dressed," Chance said pulling on his own clothes, "I'll answer the door and tell her that you"—he looked wildly around the room—"are getting some salve for my housekeeper's chest congestion." The excuse came to him when his eyes fell on the bottles and jars on Raven's dresser top.

Chance was out the door as Raven finished buttoning up her shirt. She swiftly brushed her hair, then looked through the articles on her dresser. There was only one jar that looked large enough to hold salve and it had belonged to her grandfather. He had used it to put on his face when he cut himself shaving.

She heard Jadine's knock on the door, then Chance greeting her. She checked her hair again, peered closely at her face to see if there were any whisker burns on it, then with a nervous sigh picked up the jar and walked into the kitchen.

A fast glance at Chance told her that he had put on his jacket and hat and had put the dirty cups in the dry-sink. It looked as if he had just arrived. There was no sign that he had just finished making wild love to her.

She smiled at Jadine and said, "I'm so glad that you have come to visit. I was wondering this morning how I was going to pass the day."

"Isn't your brother home yet?" Jadine asked, and Chance had to look away to hide his amusement at Jadine's disappointment.

"No, he's not, and I'm quite concerned," Raven answered, then handed the jar to Chance. "Tell your housekeeper to rub the salve on her chest two or three times a day. It always helped my grandfather."

"Thank you, Raven." Chance stood up and put the jar in his pocket. "You girls have a nice visit," he said as he opened the door and stepped outside.

"How do you like your handsome neighbor?" Jadine asked as Raven took two cups from the cupboard and placed them on the table.

"He seems very nice," she said, taking the coffee pot from the stove and filling the cups.

"Nice." Jadine gave a little laugh. "Be careful of his niceness. Chance McGruder is only nice when he wants something. When he gets whatever it is, he can change in the blink of an eye."

"Really?" Raven pretended surprise as she sat down at the table.

"Yes. For one thing, when he sees a woman he wants, he chases her until he gets her. After he's lain with her a few times, gets his fill of her, he drops her like she was a total stranger to him." Jadine took a sip of her coffee, then added, "He's broken many a heart around here."

As Raven sipped her coffee, she wondered how much she could believe of what Jadine said. Was the older woman in love with Chance herself? Did she suspect that something was going on between her and Chance?

Chance had certainly chased after her, Raven thought. Of course, in her case he was looking for his money's worth.

"Have you known Chance long?" she asked Jadine, setting her cup back down.

"Oh yes. Ages. Since I was seventeen and he was sixteen. We're cousins like. His uncle married my mother." Jadine finished her coffee then and stood up. "I'd better be getting home. It looks like it might snow again. I certainly don't want to get caught in a blizzard."

Raven walked her to the door, and as Jadine mounted her horse she thought, Jadine doesn't like women, or at least she doesn't like their company. An unexpected chill ran up her spine. She knew she shouldn't trust this woman. She felt that someday Jadine would try to harm her.

Chapter Ten

Chance argued with himself all the way home.

He knew he would make love to Raven every chance he got. She was a fire in his blood, a cronic ailment that would never go away, but obviously she wanted nothing to do with him.

"Damn the beautiful little bitch," he grated out. "Why can't I get her out of my mind?"

A blast of icy wind in his face brought Chance out of his thoughts and he kicked Brutus into a gallop.

A dark frown creased Chance's forehead when he stepped into the kitchen and saw Jadine sitting at the table. "How in the hell did you get here before me? And why didn't you ride on home while you could? It's getting dark now," he said as he took off his jacket and hat.

"I beat you here because I took the short cut

over the rocky pass. And as for the dark, I can ride home when the moon comes up. I wanted to see how Mary was doing."

Chance looked at Mary, and the look she exchanged with him was one of confusion. He ventured to ask, "How is your chest?"

With relief in her eyes Mary took the line he fed her and said, "It's not much better." She coughed then to give credibility to her lie.

Chance took the jar from his pocket and placed it on the table. "Here's the salve you wanted me to get from Raven. She said to rub it on your chest three or four times a day."

He slid a sideways glance at Jadine, but couldn't tell by her face whether or not she she believed his and Mary's exchange. He didn't want her spreading rumors about Raven.

"I guess you're stuck with me until it stops snowing." Jadine gave Chance a wide smile.

He ignored her remark, then asked Mary, "Do you know if the men have come in from town?"

"Yes, they came in just before it started snowing."

"Good. We're gonna have to haul hay out to the cattle in the morning."

"Supper will be ready at five," Mary said, sifting flour in a bowl. "You can set the table, Jadine."

Chance kicked off his boots and went into the main room to stretch out on the leather couch. With an arm lying across his eyes, he began to relive the hour spent with Raven.

He was remembering the feel of her hands stroking his manhood when he felt fingers doing the same thing to him now. His eyes flew open and he knocked Jadine's hand away from him.

"What's wrong with you?" His eyes were furious. "What if Mary should walk in here and catch you doing that?"

"She wouldn't. She's got her hands in biscuit dough."

"No matter. Go back to the kitchen, or go sit down in that rocker beside the fire. I don't want you pawing me."

Jadine glared at him from her kneeling position. "I bet you'd let Raven paw you right under Mary's nose."

Chance shrugged his shoulders, and decided to bait Jadine. "I probably would. The thing is, Raven is not the pawing kind. She's a lady."

"Hah!" Jadine's face was an angry red as she jumped to her feet. "I bet money she pawed you this afternoon, just before I got to her house. Come to think of it, you did look all flushed."

Chance laughed and turned his back on her. Jadine stood a moment in frustration, then wheeled and stamped back into the kitchen. She wore a pouty face all through supper, which Chance ignored.

After the meal she disappeared, and Chance went into the kitchen to ask Mary where Jadine had gone. "She just now went down to the bunkhouse," the housekeeper said in disgust.

"I'm not surprised," Chance said, unconcerned. He'd had a pretty good idea Jadine would do that.

Mary shook her head. "I don't know what's going to become of that one."

"Some drunken man will kill her one of these days."

"Or some man's jealous wife," Mary said.

"That's a possibility too," Chance agreed. "She's been beaten up a couple times by irate wives."

"I feel sorry for your uncle. He's had his hands full with Jadine since her mother died. She doesn't pay any attention to anything he tells her."

"Uncle George gave up on her some time ago. He doesn't care what she does," Chance said. "He's not leaving his ranch to her, though. She's gonna be madder than a castrated bull when she finds out he left it to me."

"What will become of her then, Chance?" Mary asked a little anxiously. "Will you turn her out?"

"Of course not. She can live in the house as long as she needs to, out of respect to her mother. She was a nice, decent woman."

Mary agreed, then asked, "What was that all about, my needing salve for my chest?"

"I made a neighborly visit to Cal and the new owner of his ranch to see how they were getting along. Tory McCloud, the brother, has gone on a cattle drive." He paused to take a long swallow of his coffee, deciding how to go on with his story. When he continued he didn't mention the argument that he and Raven had become involved in, or that it had chased Cal out of the house. He only said, "Cal had gone to town and I was alone with the sister, Raven, when Jadine came calling. That's when I made up the story about you ailing. You know Jadine. If I didn't have a good reason for being there, she would spread all kinds of rumors about Miss McCloud."

"She's not a miss, is she? I heard she was recently widowed."

"Yes, I believe she was."

"I heard she's a real beauty."

"Yes, I'd say she is."

Mary realized by Chance's short answers that he didn't want to talk about the new neighbor woman. Had he finally met the woman who could tame him? she wondered. She hoped so. His wild, reckless ways were going to put him in an early grave otherwise.

She dropped the subject of Raven, and Chance pushed away from the table, saying with a grin, "I'll get on down to the bunkhouse to play a few hands of poker with the men, spoil Jadine's fun."

Raven had spent most of the afternoon staring out at the white landscape, alternating between worrying about her brother and remembering the hour spent with Chance in her bedroom. Besides the lust it was obvious he had for her, did he feel anything else? she asked herself. He was never rough in their lovemaking. He always made sure that she found release as well as he. He always made her feel loved, that she was very important to him.

But then maybe that was his way of getting from a woman all that she had to offer. He had done that to her. He had gotten her into such a state with his lovemaking, she did everything he asked of her.

Raven hated her weakness where Chance was concerned. He had only to touch her and she lost all control.

She wondered if he now felt he'd gotten his money's worth. Perhaps he would no longer want to make love to her. She hoped so. She hoped not. It was insulting to be used as a whore, but on the other hand it was pure bliss to lie in his arms, his big body bringing her a pleasure she had never experienced before.

When the sun had sunk behind the distant mountains and it grew dark, Raven had given up her vigil with a deep sigh. She would ask Cal to begin a search for Tory tomorrow. She'd lit the kitchen lamp and halfheartedly begun preparing supper. The moon had risen when she heard Cal step up on the porch and stamp the snow off his boots before opening the door and stepping inside.

"You can start out looking for Tory in the morning," she said, not looking up from the stew she had started cooking an hour ago.

"Now, why would you want to go looking for me when I'm standing right behind you?" a deep voice teased her.

The knife and potato fell into the bowl as with a glad cry, Raven spun around and threw herself at the big man smiling at her.

"Oh, Tory," she cried, "I've been so worried about you. What took you so long to get home?" She hugged him so tight he grunted.

"I'd have been home yesterday if I hadn't got caught in the blizzard and almost froze to death."

"Did you really, Tory?" Raven gazed up at him with wide, alarmed eyes. "How did you survive?"

"A young girl found me unconscious in a snowdrift. She and her friend, an old mountain man, got me to her house. They saved my life, Raven. I owe them such a debt of gratitude."

"I should say you do. I'd like to meet them, thank them for helping you."

"You know," Tory said, "I'm not sure I could find their place. It's tucked away in one of those valleys in the foothills. When I became lost I wandered miles from the cattle trail. And it wasn't quite dawn this morning when the old man pointed me in the direction of home. I rode for an hour before I could make out any landmarks that looked familiar."

"Somebody around here must know of them, where they live."

"Maybe Cal will know. Where is he, by the way?"

"He went to Bitter Creek to buy some kerosene. He must have stopped for a few beers. He should be coming home soon." Amusement curved Raven's lips. "He never misses a meal."

"Did Chance McGruder stop by to give you my message?" Tory asked as he took down a cup and poured himself a cup of coffee.

"Yes, he did."

Tory gave Raven a searching look at her short answer. "He seems like a nice fellow, don't you think?"

"I suppose so. I didn't pay that much attention to him."

You little liar, Tory said to himself, *I bet you paid*

a lot of attention to him and it made you angry that you did.

The subject of Chance was dropped when they heard footsteps on the porch. The door opened and Cal stuck his head in with a big grin on his face. "Sure am glad you made it in, Tory. Your sister has been drivin' me crazy."

"I'm glad to be home, Cal. There was a time when I wasn't sure I'd ever be home again."

"You can tell me all about it later. I'm gonna stable our horses now."

When their late supper had been eaten and Raven and Tory and Cal sat in the parlor, their stockinged feet stretched out to the warmth of the fireplace, Tory retold his story to Cal. At the end of it he asked, "Do you know where the Mitchel ranch is, Cal?"

After Cal thought for a moment, he said, "I've heard of a Jacob Mitchel, but I believe he's a mountain man, a trapper. Come to think of it, though, I heard he died."

"What about Ike Blocker? Have you ever heard of him?"

Cal nodded. "I'm noddin' acquainted with him. He's a mountain man, too. Him and Henry Sipes and Isaac Hunt. The three of them live together up in the mountains. Mitchel used to live with them."

"I don't suppose you've ever heard of a girl named Amy Mitchel?"

"No, can't say as I have. Is she the girl that found you?"

"Yes. I'd like to bring her a couple of my cows

in thanks for saving my life. Ike told me her herd is small, and I think she would appreciate a couple more."

"That's a good thought, Tory. Why don't you do that?"

"I don't know if I can find the place. It's in one of those valleys that's tucked away. I thought maybe come spring you'd help me look for it."

"Sure. Thing is, it might take a week to find it. Them valleys are scattered all over that area."

Cal went to bed shortly after that, leaving Raven and Tory sitting alone before the fire. Tory laid another small log on the fire, and as he sat back down, he looked at Raven and said, "When I was in Clayton, I met this rancher from Idaho. He runs a new kind of cattle on his spread. They're called Herefords, a breed of cattle that orginated in Herefordshire, England. Some years back this rancher got hold of some breeding stock of these Herefords and has upgraded his longhorns with them. They are a shorter animal, but real stocky, outweighing the longhorns. The rancher claims their meat is much more tender than other steers."

"I don't suppose you'd like to get your hands on any of these cattle?" Raven asked, her eyes twinkling.

"You know I would," Tory laughed. "That is, if it's alright with you. They don't come cheap. Four bulls would cost half of what we made from the cattle drive."

"Would we have enough money left to live on until you make another drive?"

"Yes, we'll be able to eat," Tory laughed. "And

maybe have enough left over to buy paint for the house. What do you think about white with green trim?"

"And you could build a picket fence around the yard and I'll plant flower seeds all around the house."

Tory nodded, his eyes shining. "And you can plant a garden. Having fresh vegetables is one thing I miss from the old farm."

Brother and sister sat on, speaking aloud the dreams they had for their ranch. It was after ten when Raven began to yawn, and got up to tell Tory good night.

As the flames cast shadows on the ceiling, Tory's thoughts drifted from cattle to a slender, long-legged girl named Amy.

Chapter Eleven

The roan lunged up a coulee and was brought to a halt on the plateau above. The tired stallion stood, his breath pale clouds of vapor rising from his nostrils. He had fought his way through snowdrifts the better part of the day.

The rider, hungry and weary from lack of sleep, rubbed his whiskered jaw as he stared down at the valley below, studying a ranch house and its outbuildings. When he saw no activity anywhere, he lifted the reins and started the roan downward.

"I'll soon see what kind of welcome I'll get from my dear stepfather," he muttered.

Jadine, dressed for the icy weather, stepped from the ranch house and walked toward the barn. She had not gone far when she glimpsed a rider coming down a knoll behind the barn.

A grub-liner, she thought with a curl of her lips.

He must be awfully hungry to force his mount through such heavy snow.

As the rider drew closer, Jadine could see that he wasn't too old and was rather good-looking, even with the stubble on his face. Her interest was piqued. She would feed him, and before he rode away they could spend some time in her bedroom. George, her stepfather, had gone into Bitter Creek and wouldn't be home for another two hours.

When the man drew rein a few feet away and looked down at her she thought he looked a little familiar. She flashed him an inviting smile and said in a low, sultry voice, "Hello, cowboy. You look hungry."

The man made no answer right away, only sat studying her face. Then with a mocking smile curving his lips, he said, "Sorry, Jadine, but where I come from brother and sister don't lie together."

Jadine stared at him in disbelief. Could this be Carlin, the black-sheep brother who had never been talked about since her mother married George McGruden thirteen years ago?

"Is it really you, Carlin?" She stepped closer to the horse and stared up at the smiling face.

"It's me, sis. The brother you probably thought was dead."

Jadine smiled back at him. "I've thought about you a lot, but I never thought you were dead. Even the devil wouldn't want you," she teased.

"That's about the size of it, I guess," Carlin Walker agreed, then said, "Since you haven't invited me to dismount, I take it I'm not welcome here."

"Oh, Carlin, no such thing. I'm so excited and

surprised to see you, I forgot my manners. Come on in the house and I'll fix you something to eat."

When Jadine noticed how stiffly her brother was holding his body as he dismounted, she asked in worried tones, "Are you alright?"

"I've got a slug in me," he said in a tense voice, leaning on the saddle.

"Oh my God!" Jadine stared at the patch of blood staining the back of his jacket. "Who put the bullet in you?" she asked as she put her arm around his waist and helped him up the snow-trodden path and into the house.

"One of the men in the posse that was following us. He snuck up on me. I never heard a sound. I only felt the bullet strike me. I killed the bastard, though," he panted as he eased himself onto a chair and breathed a sigh of relief.

Anxiety in her voice, Jadine said, "The law will hunt you down for killing him."

"Look, Jadine, it was me or him. He was aiming his gun at me a second time before I shot him. Anyway, it took place up in the mountains. I dropped the body off the ledge of a deep ravine. No one but the buzzards will find him in the rocky chasm below."

"That's a relief," Jadine said before it occurred to her that maybe Carlin had been followed. It would be easy to track him in the snow.

Carlin shook his head when she put the question to him. "I didn't leave our hide out until we saw the sheriff and his men ride north."

"Let's get your jacket off so I can take care of your wound. Then I'll get you something to eat."

When she had eased the mackinaw off him, then stripped him to the waist, she said in relief, "It's not too bad. The bullet went through the fleshy part underneath your shoulder blade. It stopped bleeding some time ago. The cold air did that, I imagine. When did it happen?"

"Early this morning." Carlin winced as she cleansed his wound.

"You said 'us' before. Do you have a gang of outlaws with you?"

"Not a gang. We're four altogether. We held up a bank on the Utah border and had lost the posse until it started snowing. We ran for the mountains then and took refuge in an old deserted cabin. We thought sure we had lost them, but the snow had grown deep enough for them to follow us. It was the blizzard that saved our bacon. They had to turn back and get home while they could still see a little."

"You're going to be snowed in up there for some time. You know that, don't you?" Jadine said as she went to the door to fling the bloody water outside.

Carlin nodded. "We're short on rations and blankets. We can kill deer and such for meat, but we need the staples to make a meal. I was wondering if you could help us out."

"I can get you what you need out of the cook's storage shack. But how did you know it was our place you were riding to?"

Carlin eased back in the chair. "I've kept track of you and Mom over the years. I knew when she died. I visited her grave the night of her burial."

His eyes shining wickedly, he said, "Me and my men have helped ourselves to our stepfather's cattle a few times."

"Was that you?" Jadine laughed. "George raved and ranted about that for a month."

"Hell, the old bastard could afford losing a few head."

"A few head!" Jadine exclaimed, still laughing. "You always took at least a hundred head every time."

"He could afford it. Anyhow, he never did anything for me after he married our mother."

"In all honesty, Carlin, you were nineteen, a grown man and the wildest hellion in the area. You and your friends were always on the wrong side of the law. Besides, you could have come with us to Montana if you'd straightened up and behaved yourself."

"I wasn't about to come to his ranch and let him boss me around." Carlin leaned forward so that Jadine could smooth salve on his wound. "Where is he, by the way?"

"He's gone into Bitter Creek. He won't be home for an hour or so." Jadine capped the tin of boric acid and placed it back in the cupboard. Then she said that she would be back shortly, she was going to get some bandages for his wound.

When she returned she had several wide strips of cloth which she had torn from a sheet, folded over her arm. In her hand she carried one of her stepfather's undershirts and a flannel shirt one of her lovers had left behind in a hurry when his irate wife came looking for him. Jadine still laughed to herself every time she remembered seeing the fat, bald-headed neighbor scrambling through the window.

Jadine deftly wound the cloth beneath Carlin's armpits and midway down his back. He had begun to shiver, and she took the undershirt and pulled it over his head and arms. She then held the shirt for him to slip his arms into it. While he buttoned it up, she cut two thick slices of ham from a shank and laid them in a skillet to fry. As she tended the meat, she asked, "Where will you go when the weather warms up and the snow has melted some?"

"I'm not sure. Me and the men were headed for Texas before the posse made us hole up in the mountains. I'm thinking of making different plans now."

"What kind of plans? Will you stay around here?"

"Maybe."

"Are you afraid to tell me? I would never tell anything you confided in me."

"I know that, Jadine, and I'll tell you when the time comes."

Jadine had to be satisfied with that. She remembered how stubborn her brother could be.

Later, as Carlin was wolfing down the ham and cold cornbread, he asked, "How come you're not married? Don't you fancy any of the men around here?"

Jadine gave a short, bitter laugh. "The one I fancy doesn't fancy me back."

"Do you know why?"

117

Jadine shrugged and looked away from the inquiring eyes. "I'm afraid I've got myself a bad reputation around here, and he holds that against me. I was making a little progress with him until this widow moved into the area. She's young and beautiful and I think he's quite taken with her. At any rate, he's turned cold to me again."

"Hmm," Carlin said as he pushed away from the table and began to roll a cigarette, "I'll have to shave my face and clean myself up and go drop in on the lady. Maybe I can steal her right from under this fellow's nose. You didn't give me his name or where he lives."

"His name is Chance McGruder. He is a nephew of George's, and his ranch abuts ours."

"And the lady, what's her name and where does she live?"

"Her name is Raven Spencer. She's a widow, and she lives on the other side of the McGruder place."

Jadine stood up. "I'm going to take care of your horse now, give him some oats. Then I'll see what I can find for you in the cook's storage shack."

Jadine had filled a grain sack with flour, sugar, salt, coffee, beans and some canned goods and had just tied it to the horse's saddle when she saw George riding toward the house about a quarter mile away. She quickly untied the sack and hid it beneath a pile of hay.

"George is coming!" she exclaimed, out of breath, as she burst into the kitchen. "What should we do?"

"We won't do nothing," Carlin said calmly. "You

just follow my lead, go along with whatever I say."

When several minutes later an elderly man, somewhere in his seventies, stepped into the kitchen, two smiling face looked at him. He looked curiously at Carlin.

Jadine, with a nervous laugh, said, "It's my brother, Carlin, George."

"Well, howdy, Carlin." George greeted him cordially, but a little stiffly. "I didn't recognize you under all them whiskers."

Carlin grinned and said, "I'm growing a beard to keep my face warm while I run my traps."

Jadine's eyes widened slightly at his lie, but she kept her mouth shut.

"So you're a trapper," George said, taking off his jacket and hat, then sitting down at the table.

"Yes. I have been for four years now. I only recently came to the Montana mountains. I was on my way to Bitter Creek to buy some extra traps when I recognized Jadine going to the barn. You can imagine my surprise at seeing her."

"I expect so." George nodded. "It's been a long time since you've seen her. I expect she told you about your ma."

"Yes." Carlin looked genuinely sorry. He had always loved his mother; probably she was the only person in the world he'd ever loved. He had a careless fondness for his sister, but if he should never see her again, he wouldn't notice it.

Carlin and George had a polite conversation for a few minutes; then Carlin said he'd better get going. When he stood up, Jadine held his mackinaw for him, knowing it would be difficult for him to pull it on because of his wound. If putting on the jacket pained him, he didn't let George see it.

"I'll walk you to the barn," Jadine said, taking down her own short coat.

When George and Carlin said goodbye, Jadine noticed that the older man didn't invite him to come visiting again.

Angered at the slight, Carlin said darkly as he and Jadine walked to the barn, "I'll get that old bastard if it's the last thing I do."

Jadine smiled slyly at him and said, "You know, don't you, that when he's gone the ranch will be mine?"

Carlin was suddenly all interest, his eyes narrowed in a calculating look. "Now, how could I have forgotten that," he said as though to himself. He swung into the saddle and smiled down at Jadine. "You've given me something to think about, sister."

"When will I see you again?" Jadine asked eagerly as she retied the grub sack to the saddle.

"I'll drop in when I'm sure he's gone to town. I want him to think that I'm too busy running my nonexistent traps to come visiting."

Jadine stood in the barnyard watching the stallion carry her brother over the path he had broken through the snow on his way to the house earlier. When horse and rider moved out of sight behind a knoll, her lips twisted in a mirthless smile.

She had planted the seeds that would soon make her the owner of the second largest ranch in Montana Territory.

*　*　*

Chance had just finished currying Brutus and was closing the barn door behind him when he heard his name called. He looked up and saw coming toward him a large horse with a large rider astride him.

A warm smile curved his lips. "Howdy, Uncle George," he said as his relative reined in beside him. "You're up and about early."

"Yeah, I reckon. I got something on my mind that I want to talk to you about."

Chance reopened the barn door. "Put your horse inside and we'll go up to the house and talk about it over a cup of coffee, or a glass of whiskey if you'd rather."

"What I have to say I want kept quiet. Can you trust your housekeeper to keep her mouth shut about anything she might overhear?"

Chance knew he could trust Mary not to repeat a word she heard in his house. She had been the housekeeper on the ranch as far back as he could remember, but to assure the old man that their talk would be very private, he said, "We'll go to the cook shack. Rufus has gone to town to buy something or other that he's run out of."

The coffee in the pot was cold, so Chance poured them each a glass of whiskey. When they were sitting at the long table where the cowboys took their meals, Chance came right to the point of his uncle's visit.

"What's worrying you, Uncle George?"

George took a sip of his whiskey, then began. "I've never told anybody about this before, not even your father, because I never thought it was necessary. But I feel I have to tell it now. The thing is, Irene had two children when I married her. Sixteen-year-old Jadine, as you know, and a nineteen-year-old son. Carlin was already bad medicine. Irene hadn't been able to handle him since he was fourteen. She said that he took after his dead father, who was a violent, gun-happy man.

"Me and Carlin didn't hit it off too well, and he didn't want to come with us to Montana. Irene cried because he wasn't even there to tell her good-bye when we left. Now, after all these years, he showed up at the ranch yesterday. He claims that he's been a trapper for four years and only recently set out a line in our mountains. I didn't believe him for a minute. For one thing, his hands are as smooth as a whore's, and another thing, he's too lazy to trap for a living.

"Chance," George said leaning forward, "I bet he's with a gang of outlaws holed up in the mountains. I wouldn't be surprised if they're running from the law. Carlin and Jadine looked mighty nervous when I walked into the kitchen. I know they were trying to hide something, for Jadine was acting real nice toward me. Normally she doesn't even speak to me, let alone act nice and friendly.

"And another thing, Carlin didn't ride in the direction of town, like he said he was going to. I was in my bedroom changing my pants when I saw him through the window riding north toward the mountains. I think that come spring we can expect to have some of our cattle rustled."

The more the old man talked, the more upset he

became. To calm him, Chance said, "We don't have to worry about that now. I'll send some telegrams to different sheriffs in the territory, inquiring if he's wanted by the law. In the meantime, it wouldn't hurt to keep an eye on Jadine as much as you can. See if she ever rides toward the mountains. Her brother is going to need supplies off and on, and if he's running from the law, he won't dare go to town for them. He'll depend on her to bring them to him."

Chance's common-sense advice soothed the old man, and he was calm as he agreed that Chance was right. "I'd better get home and start keeping an eye on Jadine. She wouldn't hesitate for a minute to help her brother steal every head of my cattle."

Chance watched his uncle ride away, worry creasing his forehead. Something seemed to whisper to him that danger lay ahead for the old fellow, his last remaining relative.

Chapter Twelve

"By all signs, it's gonna snow again before the week is out," Cal said as he and Raven and Tory sat at the breakfast table finishing off a meal of ham and eggs and fried potatoes with cups of coffee. "Raven, if you need anything in the line of supplies or women's fripperies, I'd say we'd better go to town today. The next snowfall could snow us in for a couple weeks."

"We are short of flour and sugar," Raven said, then grinned as she added, "and maybe some fripperies. I broke my comb yesterday and I'm getting low on soap."

"No, you're not. There's a lot of soap in that bottom cupboard."

"That's lye soap. I can't use that on my face and hair and bathe with it."

"I don't know why not," Cal snorted. "All the

124

other women around here use the yellow bars."

"Really?" Raven winked at Tory. "How do you know what the neighbor women bathe with? You haven't been peeking through their windows watching them, have you?"

Cal's face blazed red. "Of course not," he snorted in indignation. "I would never do a thing like that! Shame on you for thinkin' that I would."

"Cal, I was only teasing you." Raven reached across the table and laid her hand on his gnarled one. Gently squeezing it, she added, "I know you wouldn't do a thing like that."

The angry light faded from Cal's eyes and he grinned sheepishly. "I laid myself out for that, didn't I? Lettin' on like I know what other women do. My wife used the homemade soap, and I just assumed all the other women around here did the same."

"You could be right," Raven agreed, and looking at her brother she asked, "Don't you think so, Tory? Tory," she repeated when she received no answer from her brother. He was staring out the window, his coffee cup cradled in his hands.

A puzzled sigh feathered through Raven's lips. Tory had been acting strange ever since he came home from his cattle drive. Something had happened to him that he wasn't telling her about. He didn't seem worried or angry. It was more a dreamy quality in his eyes, as though he was remembering something pleasant.

She wondered suddenly if Tory had met a young woman he was attracted to. Women had never figured much in his life on the Nebraska farm. The young, giggly farm girls hadn't appealed to him; he thought they were silly. She knew that on Saturday nights he and his friends went to town to visit the red light district.

Raven remembered that when she and Tory were reunited in Clayton, he hadn't mentioned a woman in his life. So he must have met someone after he had brought his herd into the stockyards.

Tory would tell her in his own good time, she decided. Looking at Cal, she asked, "When do you want to leave for town?"

"I thought around ten, when the sun has warmed up some. I'm gonna go down to the bunkhouse and visit with the men until you are ready to leave."

Raven tried again to start a conversation with Tory, but when he only answered her in monosyllables she gave up and left him to his daydreaming.

In her room she pulled on a two-piece set of woolen underwear, then her Levi's and then a heavy flannel shirt. It was going to be a bitterly cold ride to Bitter Creek. When she left the house at ten sharp, she wore a sheepskin-lined jacket and a heavy scarf tied over her Stetson.

Tory vaguely heard the door close behind his sister. His thoughts were miles away. What did Amy do on cold days like this? he wondered. Did she get lonely in her rustic cabin with only a rough old mountain man who came once in a while to see how she was getting along? Did she ever long for the company of younger people?

A thought came to Tory that made him stir restlessly. Maybe Amy had a male friend who courted her. After all, he had only spent one night in her company.

He had never met a girl like her before, Tory thought. She was shy and soft-spoken. She didn't giggle like most girls her age, and she didn't chatter constantly, or flutter her eyes and play with her hair. She didn't bounce around, but walked gracefully, sedately, almost like she was floating.

Could he wait until spring? he asked himself, to see her again? What if he couldn't find her little spread? He had lost count of the many hidden valleys between here and Clayton.

A burned-out log in the fireplace fell to the grate with a thud, breaking the silence and bringing Tory back to the present. "I've got to stop thinking about her," he muttered. "If I keep it up, I'll be loco before the next cattle drive."

He was debating what to do with himself the rest of the day when there was a rapping on the door. He strode across the floor to answer it, but the door swung inward before he could open it himself. A woman, near his own age, stuck her head around the door.

"Hello." Thin lips smiled at him. "You must be Raven's brother. I'm Jadine Walker. Is Raven home?"

"No, she's not. She and Cal went into town. But come on in and warm up."

"Thank you. It's bitterly cold today." She smiled again at Tory when he helped her off with her jacket, and he didn't miss the invitation in her eyes, nor the way she managed to brush her body against his when he turned to hang her garment on the wall. He knew at that moment how he would be spending the afternoon.

He remembered what Chance had said about Jadine Walker. "I think you'd warm up faster in bed, though," he said with a wicked smile.

"I wouldn't be at all surprised." Jadine smiled back, an avid light in her eyes.

"Well, why don't we find out?" Tory took her elbow and steered her toward his room.

Jadine was out of her clothes first and was waiting for him on the bed, her knees bent and spread. As he came down on top of her, he felt a twinge of guilt, as though he was cheating on Amy. He only paused for a moment before entering the eager Jadine. He had been a long time without a woman, and he was damned tired of pleasuring himself.

Two hours later, Tory was tired of pleasuring Jadine. He finally realized that she was one of those women who were never satisfied, and swinging his feet to the floor, he said, "That's it, Jadine. There ain't no more."

"But, Tory . . ."

"But Tory, nothing," he snapped impatiently. "I'm beat. Why don't you go down to the bunkhouse? Chuck and Rob are there. They'll take care of you."

Jadine jerked on her clothes, her lower lip in a pout. She stamped on her boots and left Tory sitting naked on the edge of his bed. He grinned when he heard the outside door slam, and went to peer out the window to see where the sullen woman would go. As he had thought, she mounted her horse and rode down to the bunkhouse. He watched her knock on the door, then saw big Chuck open it. With a whoop he grabbed her hand and pulled her inside.

Tory shook his head as he filled the washbasin with water from the pitcher. He had never seen anything like that woman. He wondered why she wasn't working in a whorehouse.

After Tory had washed his body, he stripped the bed of sheets and pillowcases and shoved them into the laundry bag Raven kept in the storage room. He remade the bed and looked as if he hadn't moved from his chair all afternoon when Raven and Cal returned. They did notice, however, that his mood had improved considerably.

Cal didn't say anything, but he knew what had happened. He had noticed Jadine's horse tied up alongside the bunkhouse.

Raven's face wore a dark scowl as she went about preparing supper. Tory raised a questioning look at Cal, but the old man shrugged his shoulders as if to say, "Damned if I know."

Raven had a reason to be moody. Or so she thought.

When Cal had pushed open the door of Bitter Creek's sole mercantile and stood aside for her to precede him, a babble of voices greeted her. "Looks like everyone else around here had the same idea I had," Cal said behind her. "They've read the weather signs too."

As Raven untied the scarf she had tied over her

hat and unbuttoned her jacket, Cal took her arm, saying, "Now is as good a time as any to meet your neighbor ladies. It's most likely the only chance you'll have until spring when the snow melts."

Raven met a pleasant-faced woman named Haley Ryan, whom she judged to be in her mid-fifties. A younger woman in her late thirties came next. Grace Morgan, like Haley, warmly welcomed her to Bitter Creek.

After that the rest of the women she met passed in a haze, their names and faces making no dent on her mind. Across the room she had spotted Chance with a group of young women clustered around him. All were trying to get his attention. The big stallion is eating it up too, she thought irritably as Chance stood facing his adoring audience, his elbows propped on the counter.

He turned his head then and saw her. His eyes widened for a split second; then he was looking at her with lazy insolence. The curve of his mouth seemed to mock her as he said, "Good afternoon, Mrs. Spencer."

Raven ground her teeth in outrage. He was acting as though they were mere acquaintances, as if they hadn't lain in each other's arms, made hot, bone-melting love to each other.

She stared at him a moment; then with hurt pride stiffening her spine, she raised her chin and turned her back to him. His amused laughter followed her as she walked toward Cal, but she didn't know if it was directed at her or at something one of the silly girls had said.

Cal broke away from the group of men gathered

around a glowing pot-belly stove when he saw her coming toward him. "Let's get the things you need and head for home. I don't like the looks of them black clouds that are gatherin'."

Raven was more than ready to leave the store and Chance McGruder's smirking face. She quickly purchased what she had come for, then buttoned up her jacket. As she tied the scarf over her hat, Cal had to remind her to say goodbye to the women she had met.

Angry tears gathered in Raven's eyes as she peeled the last potato in the basin, then opened the oven door to place them around a beef roast that was nearly done cooking. She wiped impatiently at her wet eyes and began to set the table. She didn't even like the man, she reminded herself, so why was she jealous of all those young women who had surrounded him at the store?

Supper was almost ready when she heard the sound of spurs trailing across the porch. The cowhands are right on time, she thought and opened the door to their knock.

She gave an angry start and almost closed the door. Chance McGruder stood on the porch, looking at her with amused eyes. "What do you want?" she asked, holding the door.

"I want to visit your brother."

"Hey, Chance," Tory said, turning around in his chair and grinned at the tall rancher. "Come on in and thaw out."

Chance looked down at Raven, who stood barring his way into the house. She stared back at him, wanting to slam the door in his face. She couldn't do that, she knew. How could she explain it to Tory? She reluctantly released the door and stamped back to the stove.

"Mmm, something sure smells good." Chance sniffed the air as he took off his mackinaw and wiped his boots on the rug in front of the door. When Raven made no response to his compliment, only continued to furiously stir the gravy in the roasting pan, his teeth slashed white against his dark skin in a satisfied smile. He walked over to the stove and, standing behind her, leaned over to look at the bubbling mixture of flour and beef juice.

"My mouth is watering just looking at that," he said, and his husky voice made Raven wonder what he was really gazing at.

Again she made no response to his remark. She couldn't. The touch of his shoulder on her back as he leaned over her was sending wave after wave of hot desire through her veins. Her breath came out in a whoosh of relief when Chance turned from her and went to join Tory and Cal in front of the fireplace.

Raven had put the roast and potatoes on the table and was dishing up a bowl of string beans when Chuck and Rob entered the kitchen in a gust of cold air. Tory, Cal and Chance came to the kitchen then and there was a scraping of chairs as the men seated themselves at the table. They waited for her to place a basket of hot biscuits on the table, then seat herself between Tory and Cal. Chance sat on the other side of the table, but near the end where she didn't have to look at him.

The food was passed around and there was the clatter of forks and knives and no conversation as hungry appetites were satisfied.

When at last they were sated and leaning back in their chairs, Raven asked Tory if he would serve the coffee. He gave her a puzzled look but stood up and did as she asked. Raven had no intention of going near Chance McGruder if she could help it.

Once the coffee was finished, Tory and Cal and Chance left the table to resume their seats in front of the fire, and Chuck and Rob returned to the bunkhouse. Raven rose to her feet and hurriedly put the kitchen in order. Then she untied her apron strings and hung it on a peg next to the stove. She said a short good night to the men soaking up the warmth of the fire and went into her room.

It would have pleased her a great deal if she could have seen the look of disappointment on Chance's face as she closed the door behind her. And though Chance managed to keep up his end of the conversation, in the back of his mind he was visualizing Raven curled up in bed, with nothing on her beautiful body but a nightgown. He wished he hadn't acted such a fool at the store today.

His thoughts of Raven were interrupted when Tory said with a chuckle, "Jadine Walker paid me a visit today."

"She did, did she?" Chance's eyes kindled in amusement. "I'm surprised you can still walk."

"Me too. I had to rest for about an hour after

she left. She wore me to a frazzle. I finally had to tell her I was drained." He grinned. "I sent her down to the bunkhouse to entertain Big Chuck and Rob."

"Damn!" Cal spit into the fireplace. "She'll be over here every day now. I hope you don't plan on takin' that whore in your room in front of your sister."

"Of course not, Cal." Tory sounded insulted. "I wouldn't do that to Raven."

"What you can do," Chance laughingly said, "is take her to the bunkhouse, share her with the boys. That way you won't be worn out."

"Now that's a fine idea." Tory grinned as Chance took the makings from his shirt pocket and rolled a cigarette.

The men spoke of unrelated things then, and when Chance finished his smoke, he flipped the butt in the fireplace, stood up and announced that it was time he was getting home. "The wolves will be coming out soon and my stallion will look very tasty to them."

Raven heard the door close behind Chance and stared up in the darkness. She tried to tell herself how much she hated him, but it didn't work. It wasn't hate she felt for the tall, handsome rancher. God help her, what she felt was something much stronger.

Chapter Thirteen

It was nearing dawn when Jadine shoved her feet into a pair of boots, then pulled on a jacket over her nightgown. She slipped quietly out of the house and made her way to the barn.

Just as she walked in, a dark figure stepped out of the shadows and grabbed her arm. "Juan!" she whispered. "You nearly gave me a heart attack, grabbing me like that."

"Where were you last night?" the Mexican demanded, pulling her down on a pile of hay. "I waited until after midnight for you to come to me."

"I don't have to tell you my whereabouts, Juan. You don't own me," she said coolly, but didn't move away from his embrace. "But I'll tell you anyway.

"I was over at our new neighbors' house helping

135

Raven Spencer sew a dress," she lied easily. "Before we knew it, it was midnight and she insisted that I stay the night." Her hand moved down between them to slide under the waistband of his trousers. "I slipped away from her house before daybreak so I could be here with you."

"I'm sorry I spoke harshly to you," Juan apologized, his voice husky as Jadine's fingers began to fondle him. "I'm always so afraid that you are seeing another man when you don't come to me in the evenings. My blood boils at the thought of that."

"You mustn't think like that." Jadine wrapped her fingers firmly around his growing hardness. "Instead, think of the many years we have been lovers."

"I do think about that, and I believe it's time we got married. I long to start a family."

"Get married!" Jadine's fingers fell away from him. Did this Mexican horse wrangler really think he could marry her, the stepdaughter of the second richest rancher in the area?

A sham sigh feathered through her lips before she said, "We can't get married, Juan. George McGruder would disown me, write me out of his will. Where would I go then? You couldn't provide me a home."

"Let him keep his money and his ranch," Juan said earnestly. "I've been saving most of my wages all these years. I have enough put away to buy us a nice little farm in Mexico. We could be so happy there, just you and me and the little ones that would come along."

Jadine wanted to laugh out loud at the notion of her living like a peon, with a stairstep of children clinging to her skirts while Juan sat in the shade of a tree with his friends drinking from a jug of mescal.

She bit back her mirth and spoke none of her thoughts to the man who had loved her since she was seventeen. She wasn't ready yet to break all ties with him. She might want to use him later on. She would have to talk to her brother, learn what his plans were.

As she unbuttoned Juan's fly, she whispered, "I'll think about it. My mind is on something else right now." She hitched up her nightgown and pulled Juan on top of her.

An hour later, just as the sky was turning pink in the east, Jadine slipped back into the house. Good, she thought when she heard George snoring. He's still asleep and none the wiser that I was out of the house.

Walking into her bedroom, she moved across the floor to the window and pulled aside the heavy drapes. She peered up at a tall pine standing alone on top of a knoll about a hundred yards from the house. Carlin had told her to watch the tree, that if he ever needed to talk to her he would fasten a piece of a dry, broken limb on one of its branches. He had added that if anyone else noticed it they would think that the wind had blown it there.

The tree looked no different than usual and Jadine was about to pull the drapes back together when she saw a folded piece of paper on the window ledge. There was a rock holding it in place.

She slowly eased the window up, careful not to make any noise. As she reached out and picked up the white slip, she noticed footprints alongside the house. Her lips stretched in a thin smile. Carlin had been careful not to make a straight path to her window. He had walked close to the building, so as not to draw attention to his boot prints.

Jadine sat down on the edge of the bed and unfolded the note. The written words on it were brief. "Am short on rations. Need same as before. Meet me in the foothills where my path leads. Time for you to meet my friends."

Excitement glittered in her eyes as she tore the note into tiny pieces and hid them in her dresser drawer. Carlin was letting her enter his world, if only for a short time. He must have devised a plan concerning the talk they'd had the last time she saw him.

She looked at the clock on her bedside table. Not quite six. The cook wouldn't be up yet and she would have time to visit the storage shed before he awakened. Everyone slept later these days. There wasn't much to do on a ranch in the wintertime.

Jadine swiftly changed into longjohns, woolen trousers and a heavy shirt. In the kitchen she slipped into her jacket, and slapping her Stetson on her head, she cautiously opened the outside door.

Minutes later she had tied a sack of supplies on her horse. She led the saddled mount outside and climbed onto his back. As she headed in the direction of the mountain, staying in Carlin's tracks, the sun was just peeping over the eastern horizon.

Jadine had ridden close to an hour when she saw a horse and rider standing beneath a bare cottonwood.

"It's about time you got here," Carlin complained when she rode up to him. "I'm damn near frozen. I've been waitin' here for over an hour."

"Don't get so riled up," Jadine snapped, half frozen herself. "I didn't find your note until an hour ago. I hurried as fast as I could."

"Well, come on, let's get up to the shack." Carlin led the way up the mountain, his voice still cross. "The men are waiting for something to eat."

They had climbed the snow-packed trail for about twenty minutes when Carlin drew rein and pointed. "There's where we're holed up."

It took Jadine a minute to spot her brother's winter quarters. The original builder of the shack had chosen his spot well if he wanted passersby to miss it, she thought. It was set low among a jumble of boulders, built with scraps of gray weathered lumber that took on the colors around it. An elbow stovepipe stuck out from one side, and a feathery spiral of smoke rose from it and curled over the roof.

Jadine gave a start when Carlin called a loud hallo. In seconds the sagging door swung open and three men trailed outside. Carlin continued to hold the stallion in until one of the men gave a peculiar-sounding whistle. A signal that everything was alright, Jadine thought, for only then did her brother lift the reins and guide the horse down the narrow, twisting path.

When they drew rein only feet away from the scurvy-looking trio, the men stared at Jadine through narrowed, hungry eyes. Especially one desperado. That's the biggest, tallest man I've ever seen, she thought. He must be at least six and a half feet tall and weigh close to three hundred pounds. And he didn't look very bright. He was loose-lipped and low-browed. However, there was a mean cunning in his pig-like eyes. He was probably a master at inflicting pain on humans and animals. The other two men looked like ordinary cowboys, and she wondered if Carlin would allow her to be friendly with one of them.

"Alright, men"—Carlin slid out of the saddle—"put your eyes back in your heads and get them supplies in the shack. I'm starved."

"Yeah, boss," one of the men said and lifted his arms to help Jadine to dismount. As he slowly slid her down his body, he pressed his hips against hers. She looked up at him and, with invitation in her eyes, pressed back. The man's eyes glittered and he began to buck rapidly against her.

"Curly"—Carlin spoke sharply behind them. "There'll be time for that later. Now bring in the supplies."

As Jadine followed Carlin and the other two men, who had watched with interest the little by-play between her and Curly, she noticed many yellow stains in the snow outside the small building. Her pulses beat a little faster when she visualized the men relieving themselves.

When she stepped inside the dim interior, she wanted to hold her breath against the stench of unwashed bodies, dirty socks and underwear. With the exception of the stove, there was no furniture. Three bedrolls were spread on the dirty floor. She assumed that Carlin's lay behind a blanket that had been strung across one corner of the room, giving him some privacy.

"Come on, Jadine," Carlin said behind her. "Stop your inspection of our mansion and get your coat off so you can start cooking us something to eat."

Jadine was thankful that someone had made an effort to wash the tin plates, cups and flatware and a skillet and battered pan as she rummaged through the pack sack she had filled at the ranch. Taking out a slab of bacon and two cans of beans and a loaf of sourdough, she balanced them in one arm as she picked the skillet off the floor. As she placed it on the hot stove, Curly took the bacon from her, and holding it against his chest he used a long pocket knife to slice off several thick strips.

Jadine smiled her thanks and laid the meat in the now hot skillet. Using the same knife, her helper cut open the cans of beans and dumped them into the pan.

The bacon sizzled and the beans heated up. Ten minutes later the men were filling their plates from the skillet and pan. Carlin, his plate in his hand, motioned Jadine to follow him behind the blanket. "Let me eat," he said, sitting down on one end of his blankets and motioning her to sit on the other end, "then we'll talk."

Jadine waited patiently while he emptied his plate, then rolled a cigarette. He took a long drag on it, and as the smoke curled up and around his face, he said, "When we talked about you being old McGruder's heir when he passes on, I got to thinking. Why not hurry his demise along? He's a tough old bird and could live for another ten years."

Carlin took another drag on his smoke, then looking at Jadine through the smoke, said, "He must have an accident. A clever one that will not arouse any suspicions."

Jadine leaned forward and asked eagerly, "Have you thought of a plan?"

"Maybe. We can't do anything while all this snow is on the ground. One plan I came up with will take place in the spring when the melt water comes rushing down from the mountain, swelling the river and creeks. The old man could get caught in a flood and drown . . . with a little help. Also, there is the spring roundup. Anything can happen during that time. A dangerous river crossing, a stampede; he might be gored to death by a bull. We'll wait until spring to decide which plan will be more feasible."

"In the meantime, though, you've got to get your supplies some other way," Jadine said. "If I keep taking your provisions from the supply shack, the cook is going to notice and start asking questions."

Carlin nodded his head. "I thought of that. I guess I'll have to trust Curly to go into town and buy our supplies. He can pretend to be a trapper. I don't want to show my face in town, have people wonder who I am. After the old man has met his end and you're the owner of the ranch, your long-lost brother can turn up to help you run the place."

"I know this Mexican that works on the ranch. I could get him to help us in whichever plan we decide to use," Jadine said, watching her brother's face for his reaction.

Carlin slid her a knowing look that made her squirm uncomfortably. She remembered his dislike of Mexicans; "greasers" he called them.

But all Carlin said was, "Do you think he can be trusted?"

"Oh yes. He'll do anything I tell him to."

"Let me think on it. The fewer people who know our plans, the better. My men don't even know what I have in mind." Carlin gave Jadine a long, steady look. "When it's done and over, we don't want anyone left alive who might talk, or decide to blackmail you. Do you understand what I'm saying?"

It took Jadine a minute to grasp Carlin's meaning. When she did, she smiled and answered, "There will be no one to say what happened to George McGruder."

Carlin nodded his satisfaction. "Now, you probably won't see me again until spring when the water starts pouring down the mountain. Watch for my signal then on the tree." He stood up, ready to join the men.

Jadine rose beside him and touched his arm. "The man, Curly. I kind of like him. Do you suppose we could spend an hour alone together before I leave?"

Carlin shook his head. "If I should let it be known that I would let Curly come in here, Ox, the big one, would demand that he be allowed to spend time with you. Curly would back off. The men fear Ox's fists."

"You're his boss. Couldn't you stop him?"

"Only with a bullet. I'm not ready to do him in yet. I may need him later on." With his hand on the blanket, ready to push it aside, he said, "I want you to go home now, and don't smile at the men, especially Ox. Don't even look at him."

When they stepped from behind the blanket, Jadine kept her eyes on the floor. As she shrugged into her jacket, she sensed the giant's gaze boring into her. She was grateful when her brother followed her out and stood there until she had mounted her horse. With a wave of her hand and a kick in the animal's flanks, she left the hovel and the mean-eyed Ox. She had never before feared a man.

Chapter Fourteen

I'm a damn fool, Chance told himself as Brutus followed the beaten-down path through the snow. *I'm sure it's going to snow today, and like a lovesick teenager I can't stay away from a woman who wants nothing to do with me.*

Sure, she was eager once he got her into bed, but was that just because he'd gotten her so aroused that any man would do? He wanted to believe that she desired him, only him, but he wasn't at all sure.

After all, he didn't really know Raven very well. He was intimately acquainted with her slender body, but he didn't know if there had been other men before him who knew those soft curves as well.

What if her husband had loaned her out before? He had arranged for her to spend the night with a stranger. A dark frown formed on his forehead. The beauty could have had a dozen men before him.

When Chance reached his new neighbor's ranch house, his reason for being there had changed drastically. Originally, he had planned to try to make peace with Raven, to tell her that those silly girls in the store meant nothing to him.

But he had no intention of doing that now. He'd made a fool of himself over her long enough. It was her turn to feel his indifference.

Tory answered his knock, and a welcoming smile lit up his handsome face. "Come in, Chance, and defrost yourself."

Chance stepped into the warm kitchen, which was filled with the spicy aroma of apple pies baking in the oven. As he took off his hat, unwrapped his scarf and shrugged out of his mackinaw, Tory asked, "What brings you out on such a day, man? The blizzard that's been threatening us for three days is gonna hit before the sun sets."

"I know." Chance held his hands over the cookstove to warm them. "And I don't want to get snowbound at the ranch for a couple or more days. I thought maybe you'd like to ride in to Bitter Creek with me and weather out the storm in the saloon, get a little excitement in our lives."

"Now, that's the best suggestion I've had in a long time." Tory's excitement sounded in his voice. When Cal and Raven walked into the kitchen, he turned to the old man and asked, "Can you take care of things around here for a while, Cal? I want to go into town with Chance."

Before Cal could answer, Raven exclaimed, "The weather is going to change anytime now, Tory. You could get snowed in in town for days."

"I know that, sis. That's why Chance and I want to go to Bitter Creek. Have a little excitement while we wait out the storm."

"I don't have to ask who came up with this idea," Raven said stiffly, finally acknowledging Chance's presence with a cool look.

"And a good morning to you too, Mrs. Spencer," Chance said dryly.

Raven's chin came up a trifle; then she looked back at her brother. "You deserve to kick up your heels a bit, Tory, but don't drink too much of that rotgut whiskey. I don't want you coming home with your stomach all torn up."

"I don't plan on doing much drinking." Tory slid Chance a sly look.

When Raven saw Chance hide a grin behind his hand, she said in a voice that sliced through the air, "And I don't want you coming home smelling like a whore, either."

Tory looked sheepish, Chance gawked in surprise, and Cal's lips spread in a grin as Raven flounced out of the kitchen and slammed her bedroom door behind her.

"Well, you'd better get gettin' if you don't want to be snowed in here," Cal said, breaking the uneasy silence.

"I didn't think she saw me wink at you," Tory said as he and Chance pulled on their jackets, preparing to leave the warmth of the kitchen.

"It was that smirk you tried to hide that gave

away the beans, Chance," Cal said. "It's hard to put anything over on her."

"I'm not going to take the blame for riling her up," Chance said. "I'm sure she knows there will be loose women hanging around the tavern." Chance settled his Stetson on his head and followed Tory outside.

Chance silently argued back and forth with himself all the way to Bitter Creek. He had acted the fool once again in Raven's presence. His spur-of-the-moment idea of asking Tory to go to town with him hadn't softened her feelings toward him. It had only made her dislike him more.

The next minute he told himself that he didn't care how she felt about him. After all, his only interest in her was taking her to bed . . . wasn't it? He'd be getting everything she could offer from the whores in town . . . wouldn't he?

It won't be the same, he realized. *The whores' flabby, worn-out bodies won't feel the same. They won't wrap satin-smooth arms and legs around me, call my name, cry out their pleasure when I bring them release.*

The blizzard struck just as they rode down the single street of the village. "We made it just in time," Chance said, guiding his stallion to the back of the saloon. Baldy, the owner of the establishment had hired someone years ago to erect stables to shelter his customers' mounts from bad weather. There was also hay and blankets for the animals. It was not unusual for some of the owners to be snowbound for a few days. The ranchers and cowboys appreciated this thoughtfulness.

148

When Chance and Tory pushed open the saloon door, they were greeted with raucous noise. A song was being pounded out on an out-of-tune piano, and the shrill laughter of whores and the deeper tones of men as they danced around the room rang out.

A group of scantily clad women gathered around Chance and Tory before they could get their jackets off, shoving and pushing each other, practically fighting over the two handsome men. Tory, his face lit up with wide smiles, joked and laughed with the women enjoying himself tremendously. In just a short while he was making his way up a wide flight of stairs, a saloon girl clinging to each of his arms.

That wasn't so with Chance, however. The dark scowl he turned on the women sent them looking for other men. A sour half-smile lifted the corners of his lips when he heard one of them say, "I don't know what has gotten into Chance. He never takes any of us to bed anymore. Remember the times he'd pick one of the girls and wear her out?"

"Maybe that's what has happened to him. He wore himself out." Their laughter trailed behind them as they walked over to a table where four men were playing cards.

It wasn't a mystery to Chance why he had lost all interest in them. Every time he thought about a woman, a delicately beautiful face framed in long, flowing, raven-black hair swam before him.

Chance walked over to the poker table and when a new game started, he sat down and motioned to the dealer.

The sun sank behind the distant mountains to the west, and the wind-driven snow seeped through the cracks and under the door of the saloon as the blizzard howled like hounds from hell outside.

Baldy lit several hanging kerosene lamps, and everyone carried on as usual, thankful to be in a warm place.

Chance sighed and picked up the fresh hand dealt him. He wished that he was home where the only noise he would hear was the crackling of the fire and the only odor he would smell would be that of wood smoke. He wished it was possible to go upstairs to one of the rooms and crawl into bed and sleep.

His eyes narrowed in thought when he glanced up from his cards and noticed an older whore sitting at a table with a drunk who had passed out. He thought to himself she looked tired and in need of a rest.

When the hand had been played out, he stood up and walked over to the woman, who sat with her chin on the heel of her hand. "How much do you charge for the whole night, Maudie?" he asked.

The surprised woman named a price, and Chance reached into his vest pocket and counted out the money to her. As they climbed the stairs, he posed another question. "Is your bed clean, Maudie?"

"Yes, it is, Chance," she answered. Then the woman added with a short laugh, "I don't get many customers anymore. All the men want the younger girls. You will be my first customer to-night."

In the narrow cell-like room that held only a bed and a small washstand with a basin and a pitcher of water, Chance began to undress. When he saw Maudie doing the same, he said gently, "Put on your nightclothes if you want to, Maudie. I'm only interested in getting a good night's sleep."

"Are you sure, Chance?" The woman tried to keep the relief out of her voice.

"I'm sure," Chance answered as he pulled the bed covers down, then crawled between the blankets. "But it will be our secret, alright?"

"Absolutely, Chance. It's nobody's business what goes on behind locked doors." Maudie walked across the floor and slid home the latch on the door.

Chance was sound asleep when Maudie, in a high-necked flannel gown, slid in beside him.

The wind whistled over the chimney, causing the flames to leap higher in the fireplace. "This storm is worse than the last one, don't you think, Cal?" Raven asked, looking over at the old rancher slumped in his favorite rocking chair.

She smiled when she received no answer. Cal was sound asleep, his mouth slightly open, snoring softly. Half an hour later when the cow lowed painfully from a full udder, she let him sleep on. Cal must have forgotten to milk Sweetie, but she could do it. She needed some fresh air anyway, even if it did nearly freeze her lungs.

Raven bundled herself up until only her eyes

showed above the woolen scarf she had wound around her neck. Her hands in a pair of knitted gloves, she picked up the milk pail and a bucket of warm water with a clean cloth in it, and stepped out into a world of swirling, driving pellets of snow.

The blast of icy wind took away her breath as she checked to make sure the rope leading from the porch to the barn was tied securely at each end. It was taut, and she gripped it with her free hand and guided herself to the barn.

The interior of the sturdy little building was pitch-black. Raven felt her way over to a supporting post where a lantern hung. Setting the buckets on the floor, she took from a crossbeam a jar of tightly capped matches. She took one from the container and, tilting the lantern's glass chimney, struck it and held its flame to the kerosene-soaked wick. She placed the glass globe back in position and carried the light over to where the cow was stabled.

"Sweetie," she said, drawing up a stool and starting to wash the cow's udder before milking her, "don't fool around about letting your milk down. It's too damn cold for you to act coy."

When the udder was empty and the pail half full, Raven pitched some fragrant hay to Cal's horse, and then to her gelding, Sam. She blew out the light then, pulled the scarf back over her mouth, and reached to pick up the pails.

At that moment the barn door flew open and she had to jump aside to keep from being hit by the body that fell inside. Alarmed, she let out a squeak, her hands at her throat. Her eyes sought for something she could protect herself with. She remembered the pitchfork and sprang to grab it. Keeping her eyes on the intruder, she stole toward him, the fork at the ready. When she came within a few feet of the man, she saw that he was lying still, not moving a muscle. She laid her weapon down and hurried back to the lantern to relight it. It took two efforts, her fingers were trembling so.

The man lay face down, but before she managed to turn him over she knew by his black hair and the blanket he wore that he was an Indian.

A rifle was slung over his shoulder.

In the circle of light she studied his face. He was young, in his early thirties maybe. Even in his unconscious state his features were proud and commanding. She had no doubt that he was of great importance to his tribe.

When Raven reached a hand to shake his shoulder, she saw a bullet hole in the blanket. The Indian had been shot. She pulled aside the heavy material that had protected him from the elements. His shirt was soaked with blood. He must get help immediately.

Hurrying outside, Raven cupped her hands around her mouth and shouted for Cal. The wind blew her words back in her mouth. She tried twice more, with the same results. Swearing under her breath, she grasped the rope and started toward the house. She had gone but a few feet when she walked into a little Indian pony. The sturdy animal shook his head, blowing softly.

"Poor fellow," she said softly, "you've had a hard

ride, haven't you?" She took the time to lead him into the barn, out of the blizzard, before again starting to the house.

"Cal! Wake up!" Raven burst through the kitchen door. "There's a wounded Indian in our barn!"

"Are you sure?" Cal jumped to his feet, his eyes wide.

"Of course I'm sure. Get bundled up and help me get him to the house. He's still breathing, but he doesn't look good."

"Why, that's Moon Shadow," Cal exclaimed when they reached the barn and he knelt down to look at the Indian's face.

"You know him?"

"Yes." Cal nodded. "He's the son of Chief Black Cloud. Their village is up in the foothills of the mountain. I wonder who shot him, and what brings him here. We have lived in peace with them for years."

"Maybe one of their own shot him."

"I don't think so. People of a tribe don't shoot each other. If there is trouble between two braves, the chief holds a meeting and settles the argument with very stern words."

"Let's get him to the house before he freezes to death," Raven said.

With much heaving and grunting, Cal and Raven got the Indian to his feet. With one on either side of him, and their arms around his waist, they tugged his dead weight to the house. Cal toted the Indian's rifle. They had to stop and catch their breath before they could get him inside and lay him in front of the fireplace.

When Cal spread open the blanket, they saw that Moon Shadow was wearing a shirt, buckskin trousers and knee-high moccasins. In a pouch at his waist was a fire-stick and a long knife.

Cal broke the breech of the rifle and sniffed it. "It's been fired recently, and I'll wager not at an animal. No one in his right mind would go game hunting on a day like this. Something very serious has brought Moon Shadow out in this weather." ·

He looked up at Raven. "While I examine his wound, get me a basin of warm water and a cloth, and some strips of white cloth. And bring me Tory's bottle of whiskey."

"Do you plan to get him drunk?" Raven looked surprised.

Cal shook his head impatiently. "I'll pour some in his wound and some on my hunting knife." When Raven looked puzzled, he explained, "It's to disinfect the blade. I don't want him getting an infection if I can help it." A worried frown gathered on his face. "The bullet is still in him and I have to dig it out. Dr. Enlow would never make it here from town in this snow."

Raven hurried to get the items he had asked for. When she returned and laid everything out, handy to his reach she asked, "Is there anything else I can do?"

"You can clean off the end of the poker and lay it on a bed of live coals. When I get the slug out, I'm gonna have to cauterize the wound."

Cal cleansed the wound, and when he dribbled

whiskey over it, Moon Shadow came to with a jerk. He peered up at Cal through pain-filled eyes.

"Steady, friend." Cal laid a comforting hand on his shoulder.

"So I did find your place after all, Chadwick."

"You did," Cal said soberly. He had known the brave since he was a child. "Why was you lookin' for me?

Moon Shadow took a deep breath. "A deep sadness has come to our village, Chadwick. Yesterday, when the sun was straight overhead, my sister, whose wedding is to take place next week, went to fetch some wood from our community stockpile. We didn't think much of it when she didn't return immediately, figuring she had met some friends on the same errand and was visiting with them. When an hour passed and the fire was burning low, I went looking for her."

Moon Shadow paused to take another deep breath. "My heart stopped when I came upon a small pile of scattered wood. All around it were a horse's hoofprints and a big man's boot prints. I could tell by my sister's small moccasin tracks that she had struggled with the man, but to no avail. He had put Sky on his horse and ridden away with her.

"I immediately prepared to ride after them and had no trouble tracking the man. Just before the blizzard struck, I came within sight of them. Sky was being held in front of the big man, so I raised my rifle and squeezed the trigger. The way his body jerked, I was sure I had killed him. He reined his horse in, and I recklessly urged my pony toward his tired mount. I discovered too late that he had tricked me. Although badly wounded, he still had the strength to pull a gun from its holster, turn and shoot me point-blank.

"The shot knocked me out of the saddle and I lay there stunned for some minutes before I could get up and pull myself onto the saddle. The blizzard hit then, and I knew the hoofprints would be covered before I could come upon them again. My only consolation was seeing the blood that dripped on the snow. The man was badly wounded.

"My own blood was dripping, too, and I was growing weak. I felt pretty sure your place lay to the right of me, so I turned the pony's head in that direction, praying that I was right and that my mount would sense that a warm barn was nearby. The last I remember was hanging on to the animal's mane and the snow striking me in the face."

"Moon Shadow, this young woman found you in the barn and helped me get you to the house. She has a brother. He and Chance will take out after the bastard as soon as the blizard dies down. In the meantime I have to dig the bullet out of you. I don't know how deep I'll have to dig, and it's gonna hurt like hell."

"Do what you must, friend."

"Well, here goes," Cal said weakly, and pouring whiskey over the blade of his hunting knife, he began to probe for the piece of lead that had to come out if Moon Shadow was to live.

A film of sweat broke out on Moon Shadow's brow and he clenched his teeth and fists against the pain of the blade exploring his wound. He made no sound, however.

It seemed to Raven that Cal had worked on the Indian for hours before he held up a piece of flattened lead for Moon Shadow to see. "I got it!" he exclaimed. "And it didn't hit any vital organ."

"That is good," Moon Shadow whispered weakly, then slumped in a faint.

"It's good that he passed out," Cal said in relief as he went to the fireplace and picked up the poker, whose end was a glowing red. "He won't feel the hell of this thing burning into his flesh."

Raven felt nauseated at the odor of burning flesh and had to walk away for a moment. She stood at the kitchen window, gazing out into the darkness, where the windswept snow was drifting against any object in its way. The forgotten pail of milk must be frozen by now, she was thinking when Cal spoke from his kneeling position beside their patient. "You can come help me bandage him now." He sounded tired.

By turning Moon Shadow back and forth, they managed to wrap him with the strips of cloth Raven had torn from one of her petticoats.

"Do you think we can get him to bed?" Raven asked, panting a bit.

"We won't try," Cal answered, equally out of breath. "Anyway, Indians don't sleep on beds. They use a pile of furs on the floor. Since we don't have any of them, we'll make him a pile of blankets here in front of the fire where he'll keep warm. I don't want him catchin' pneumonia."

Raven found four blankets and two quilts in the

linen cupboard, and together she and Cal folded each one in half and piled them one on top of the other. Cal took hold of their patient's broad shoulders and Raven grasped Moon Shadow's legs, and together they managed to move him. Raven covered him up with a heavy quilt she had held back for that purpose.

"He's a handsome feller, ain't he?" Cal said.

"He certainly is," Raven agreed. "I bet the Indian maidens follow him around all the time."

Cal chuckled. "If they do, they'd better not let his wife see them."

"He's married, then?"

"Yes. And he has two teenage sons that will grow to be as handsome as their father."

Raven stood up and stretched her tired back. "I'm exhausted, what about you?"

"Now that I think about it, I'm beat. It's way past our bedtime. I hope Tory gets back early in the morning, so he can go search for that poor Indian girl. I hate to think what might be happening to her right now."

Sky sat hunched in a corner of the shack, her terrified eyes watching three men work on the giant who had captured her and brought her here. Her midsection still hurt from the powerful grip of his arm holding her on the horse, and her breasts were sore from being squeezed and pinched.

She hoped that the vile man would die. One of the men had said that he had been shot and had lost a lot of blood. One man, evidently their leader, had been angry that the giant had brought her here and had lashed out at him with harsh words. "You damn woman-chasing fool! If her people follow her here, I'll shoot you myself, and it will be a fatal shot."

"I can't stop the bleedin'," one of the men said, jarring Sky back to the present. "There ain't much a person can do with only a pail of water to tend him with."

The leader shrugged, as if to say, "Let him die then."

The man who had spoken pulled a blanket up to the wounded man's chin, then remarked, "I'm starved. When are we gonna eat around here?"

The youngest of the four got up from his bedroll and, shoving more wood into the rusty stove, placed a skillet on the burner next to a pot of beans that had been simmering for a couple hours.

Even though she was fearful of what might happen to her later, Sky's mouth watered as the aroma of frying meat filled the shack. Would they feed her? she wondered, then doubted that they would.

But after the three men had eaten their steak and beans, the one who had done the cooking forked a steak onto his empty plate, dipped some beans beside it and carried it over to her. He had added a spoon, but there was no knife to cut up the meat. He stood a moment, looking down at her, then took a knife from his pocket and dropped it at her feet.

When he reached a hand down and stroked her shiny hair, the leader barked, "Get away from her, Dude, and stay away. If her people come looking for her, it will go easier for us if she's not harmed.

If he's still alive"—he looked at their wounded companion—"we'll turn him over to them."

"What if he's dead?"

"The girl can tell them who abducted her and we'll hope for the best. If there's not too many of them, we'll shoot it out."

Sky's spirits rose. Knowing that she wasn't going to be harmed by the men, she ate her large steak and the helping of beans. The leader walked over to where the wounded man lay on his side. He pulled the blanket down and raised the lantern so that its light shone on the bullet hole. Flipping the blanket back in place, he said, "He's still bleeding. He'll be gone before morning."

No one made any response to the remark, and as far as Sky could tell, no one cared if the man did die.

"Let's get some sleep," he said, "be ready for whatever happens tomorrow." He tossed a blanket in Sky's lap and said, "You sleep behind the curtain. There's a chamber pot of sorts if you need it."

Sky hurried behind the blanket, thankful for some privacy and eager to get away from the men's hungry eyes. As she stretched out on the bedroll, she wondered why they hadn't tied her up. A bitter smile twitched her lips. They knew she wouldn't try to run away. The snow would be up to her waist in some places.

Chapter Fifteen

A faint early dawn shone through the grimy, thin curtain. With one silent motion Chance swung his feet to the edge of the bed and stood up. Moving quietly, he walked to the window and pushed aside its covering.

All was still and pristine white outside. The wind had stopped blowing and sometime during the night the snow had ceased to fall. The blizzard was over and it was time for him to make his way home.

"Has it stopped snowing, Chance?" Maudie's sleepy voice asked from the bed.

"Yes, it's all over until the next storm," Chance answered, sitting down on the bed. "You look nice and refreshed." He smiled at his bed partner as he reached for his denims.

"I feel that way, Chance. Would you like . . ."

"No, Maudie." Chance stopped her as he buttoned up his shirt. "I have to get back to the ranch and see that the men haul hay out to the cattle."

He stood up and shoved his shirt tail into his trousers, then sat back down to pull on his boots. Looking over at the silent, watching whore, he said, "You remember the agreement we had last night, don't you?"

"Oh yes," Maudie answered immediately. "No one is to know that we shared my bed as brother and sister."

"Good. I've, ah . . . I think . . . I've met a woman who appeals to me. My attraction to her is so strong I don't have any desire for any other woman. But I don't want anyone else to know this since the woman in question doesn't know about my feelings for her."

Chance lifted his gaze to Maudie. "Do you understand what I'm trying to say?"

"I understand, Chance."

"I'm glad you do, for I hardly understand it myself. At any rate, from now on when I come to town with my men, or friends, I'd like to spend the night with you." He grinned and added, "As brother and sister, that is."

Maudie smiled back. "I'll look forward to your visits. I can't tell you how nice it was to get a good night's sleep. I feel like a new person this morning."

"You look like it too." Chance studied her thin face. It looked relaxed, and the tired lines around her eyes and mouth were smoothed away. He patted her blanket-covered leg. "Go back to sleep. It will be expected that you stay in bed all day. Right?"

Maudie nodded with a wide smile and said goodbye to Chance as he left the room.

When Chance walked down the narrow, dim hall, he had to knock on three doors before he recognized Tory's gruff "Who is it?"

He found his new friend sprawled out on his stomach, taking up the whole bed. The room reeked of cheap perfume and spent passion. His nostrils twitching, Chance said, "The storm is over. It's time we were getting home."

Tory groaned. "Stop yelling. My head is ready to burst open."

"You'll feel better when you get a cup of coffee in you. And for God's sake, wash that smell off you. You know what your sister said."

"What about you?" Tory sat up and peered at him through bloodshot eyes. "Have you cleaned yourself up?" When Chance answered that he had, Tory asked, "Did you spend the entire night with one whore? Every time I went downstairs to get a drink, you were nowhere around."

"Yes, I did. I have a favorite one I always take to bed for the night."

Tory stood up carefully so as not to jounce his head, walked over to the basin and pitcher of water on a rickety table. "I'll be down in a minute," he said, reaching for the pitcher.

Neither man spoke much on their way home. For one thing, it took most of their attention to guide their horses around drifts and often they had to dismount and help the animals through some of the deeper snow. Tory was pretty much silent because his head and stomach hurt, and a pair of big brown eyes kept swimming in front of him accusingly.

When finally they came within sight of the McGruder ranch, Chance turned toward it, saying, "See you later."

Tory lifted a hand in acknowledgment and rode on.

Just as Tory's tired horse made it to the barn, Cal pushed open the door and stepped outside. He carried a steaming bucket of milk in one hand and in the other a pail of frozen milk.

"You got snowed in at the saloon, did you?" He peered up at Tory's red-rimmed eyes and whisker-stubbled jaw. "From the looks of you, you had a rip-roaring time."

"I guess I did. I can't remember most of it, though." Tory slid out of the saddle. "Is everything alright with you and Raven? No trouble from the storm?"

"We had some excitement last night. A wounded Sioux fell off his horse right here in front of the barn. Raven had milked the cow and was about to return to the house when he landed almost at her feet. Like to have scared the bejeebers out of her."

"What happened to the Indian? Is he alright?" Tory asked as he led the horse into the barn.

"He's up at the house." Cal followed him inside. "He's pretty weak right now. I got the bullet out of him, but he's lost a lot of blood. But with Raven's good cooking, he'll be alright in a few days."

"Did he say who shot him?"

"Only that it was a big man who sneaked into his village and made off with his sister. He took off after the feller, and had no trouble following him until the snow covered up his horse's tracks. They had been shootin' at each other before that. Moon Shadow is sure he hit him, because he saw a trail of blood in the snow."

As they left the barn and began tramping through the snow to the house, Cal continued. "As soon as you have somethin' to eat, go get Chance and track that bastard down what stole that young girl. He was travelin' up the mountain, Moon Shadow said."

"Lord, Cal, do you know what you're asking of me?" Tory gave the old rancher a pained look. "My head aches fit to bust, and my stomach feels like it's on fire. I didn't think I was going to make it home."

"You'll feel better after you've eaten somethin'," Cal replied, brushing aside Tory's complaint.

Tory gave a resigned sigh. "Saddle me Raven's gelding while I go speak to her, will you, Cal?"

"Do you know this Moon Shadow?" Tory asked Chance as they entered the foothills of the mountain.

"Yes, I know him. I know him well. We've hunted together many times. I know his sister too. She's a sweet, innocent young maid. Moon Shadow raised her when their mother died of influenza. It will go hard on him if she's been harmed."

The men lapsed into silence when they had to

give all their attention to the precarious rocky, twisting way up the mountain. The cold air stung their cheeks and pinched their noses. Tory hunched deeper into his jacket, thinking they were on a fool's errand. How were they to find the girl in this trackless, knee-deep snow.

Chance reined his mount in sharply, causing the horse behind him to bump into his hardy little quarter horse. "What is it?" Tory ran a fast glance around the area.

"Smell," Chance answered. "Can't you smell wood smoke?"

Tory sniffed the air. "Yes, by God, I can. Do you suppose we're getting close to the man we're after?"

"Maybe. There are a few trappers who live up here. The smoke could be coming from one of their cabins."

Chance and Tory followed the scent of smoke. After climbing for about twenty minutes, they spotted a stovepipe puffing smoke into the air. They reined in again, and after studying the spot closely, they made out the shack the pipe was attached to. It was almost undetectable, squatting among large boulders with the snow on its roof and drifted around the sides.

"Do you have a plan in mind?" Tory asked in low tones.

"Not really. I don't know who's living in there. It could be honest trappers, and I wouldn't want to burst through the door, guns blazing, killing innocent people."

"What should we do then?"

Chance lifted the reins and started a slow approach to the shack. "I guess we'll keep our guns handy and knock on the door."

Sky was picking at her breakfast. She had awoken that morning to the sound of voices on the other side of the horse blanket.

"Did anyone check on Ox?" She'd heard the leader ask.

"Yeah, I did," the young cook had answered. "He's dead. Stiff as a board."

"What are we gonna do with him, boss?" one of the men asked. "I don't like being with a dead man in these close quarters. It gives me the willies."

When the others agreed, their boss ordered, "Carry him outside and lay him beside the door. If the Indians come along and see him, they'll be more apt to believe we had nothing to do with taking the girl. After all, one of them shot Ox."

Sky listened to the scraping, grunting and swearing as the huge man was tugged outside.

"Damn, but it's cold out there," the cook said when they came stamping back into the shack. "Must be thirty below." She'd heard him putting more wood in the stove, then the clatter of cooking utensils being put on its top. Before long she had smelled salt pork frying.

She had accepted a tin plate of salt pork and fried potatoes, but she was too nervous to eat from worrying about what was going to happen to her now that the giant was dead. What if one of his shots had killed her brother? No one would know then where to look for her.

168

"You know, boss," the cook was saying, "I'm gettin' a little nervous that the girl's people ain't showed up yet. Why do you reckon that is?"

"I don't know about the Indians"—the leader turned from the small window—"but there are two white men approaching the shack."

"Are they trappers?" someone asked, his hand going to the holster strapped around his waist.

"No, they're ranch men, and don't draw your hardware. They're both packing guns and you could get us all killed. Remember, we're not guilty of anything, so don't go acting like we are.

"Now I'm going behind the blanket. Someone might have seen me when I visited Jadine, and I'm not going to chance being recognized. Just tell them straight out what happened and with luck they'll believe you. If they do, they will take the girl and leave."

The squeaking of leather, the jingle of bits, and the crunching of snow under foot was heard by those waiting nervously inside. Sky didn't know what to feel. She was disappointed that the newcomers weren't her people. The two new white men could be as bad, or worse, than those who held her captive.

So she waited, as tense as the men for the knock on the door.

As the minutes dragged by, the men looked at each other with knowing eyes. The two outside were examining Ox's body.

Finally the awaited knock sounded on the door. The oldest member of the gang stood up, wiped damp palms down his hips, and opened the door.

Sky recognized Chance's voice, and her heart leapt joyfully when he asked, "Have you fellows seen a white man with an Indian girl around here?"

"We sure enough have," the tall one said, opening the door wider so that Chance and Tory could step inside. "That dead hombre you seen outside grabbed the girl and brought her here. But I want you to understand up front, the rest of us didn't have a thing to do with it. We're just trappers mindin' our own business. You can ask the girl if that ain't the truth."

"The girl is here then?" Chance asked.

"Chance!" Sky gave a glad cry and, standing up, threw herself in his arms.

"Are you alright, honey?" Chance hugged her to him.

"I am now. I was plenty scared when that awful man grabbed me back in the village."

Chance held Sky away and asked, "Is it true what this man claimed, that he and the others had nothing to do with your being brought here?"

"Yes, he spoke the truth."

"How did they treat you?" Chance looked soberly at her. "They didn't . . ."

Sky shook her head. "They mostly ignored me. But, Chance, I'm worried about Moon Shadow. He followed us until the snow came and wiped out our tracks. My brother and the giant were shooting at each other. I'm afraid that Moon Shadow was hit."

"He was, Sky," Chance said gently, "but he made it to Cal's place. He's lost a lot of blood, but he's going to be alright. Get your wrap and I'll take you to him."

"Would you men like a cup of coffee or a snort of whiskey before you go?" the young cook asked.

"Thank you. I'd like some whiskey," Chance said. "What about you, Tory?" He grinned when Tory shivered and said that he'd like a cup of coffee.

Sky's eagerness to leave showed on her small face, so Chance and Tory didn't linger over their drinks. Chance thanked the men for taking care of Sky, and they left the shack to brave the cold again.

Sky avoided looking at the stiff form of the giant, and in her hurry to leave him behind, they were halfway to the ranch before she remembered to tell Chance that one of the gang had hidden himself behind the blanket when he and Tory arrived.

Chance mulled over what Sky had said. Why would the man want to hide from him and Tory? Was it possible that these men weren't trappers? Were they an outlaw gang hiding from the law?

Chapter Sixteen

Cal had propped Moon Shadow up with pillows behind his back so that he could drink a cup of beef broth. Raven was in the kitchen cutting up meat for a stew when she happened to glance out the window. The blood rushed in her veins. Chance and Tory were approaching the ranch. Her eyes honed in on the female figure sitting behind Chance, her arms wrapped around his waist.

"Chance and Tory are coming," she called over her shoulder, "and I think they have your sister, Moon Shadow."

As Cal hurried to look out the window, Moon Shadow set his almost empty cup on the floor and looked eagerly toward the door.

"It's Sky alright, Moon Shadow," Cal called excitedly. "I knew that Chance would find her even if he had to tear the mountain apart."

Raven frowned. Was the Indian maid that important to Chance? It was possible, she told herself. Actually, she didn't know anything about Chance's private life, his friends, his social affairs. He could very well be in love with the pretty little Indian girl. The only thing she knew for sure about him was that he lusted after Raven Spencer, and that he didn't consider her much better than a whore.

The horses were in the yard now and Raven looked closely at Sky as she slid off the horse and ran up on the porch. The door flew open, and Sky hurried to her brother.

"Oh, Moon Shadow," she cried, grasping his hands. "Are you badly wounded, my brother?" Her gaze ran over his broad, bandaged chest.

"I'm afraid I am, little sister." Moon Shadow gently squeezed her hands. "But our old friend Cal and our new friend Raven Spencer have doctored me and I will be well soon."

"I can't thank you enough, Cal." Sky threw off her blanket. "And you too, Raven Spencer." Her soft brown eyes smiled at Raven, who had left the kitchen to stand in the doorway.

She must not be more than fifteen, Raven thought, scanning the flawless skin of Sky's small oval face, the full red lips and long black hair that rivaled her own. Innocence looked out of the large brown eyes, and Raven's heart sank. Sky was the type of young woman Chance would marry when he decided to settle down. He would never consider marrying a woman he had paid to sleep with him.

Raven forced her lips to smile at the girl and to say, "No thanks are needed, Sky. Cal and I were happy to care for your brother."

Chance brushed past Raven and hunkered down beside Sky. He stroked a hand down her hair as he asked, "How are you feeling, Sky?"

Raven turned away. She wished Chance would show her such tender affection. With her it was always grabbing, fondling, and kisses so hot they scorched her lips.

She looked at her brother, who sat at the table, and said, "I expect you're hungry."

"Yes. We're starved. Will you please fry us up some ham and eggs?"

Ham was sizzling and Raven was cracking half a dozen eggs into a skillet of hot fat when Chance walked into the kitchen. "And how are you this fine day, Mrs. Spencer?" he asked, a mocking look in his eyes as he sat down at the table.

"I'm just fine," Raven answered shortly, her pulses racing at his nearness.

"You're looking fine." His eyes glinted as he watched the sway of her hips while she worked at the stove. "You've taken good care of my friend Moon Shadow."

When Raven made no response, he asked as he watched her closely, "He's right handsome, isn't he?"

"He's very handsome . . . and quite a gentleman too."

"How do you know he's a gentleman?" Chance asked, his voice suddenly harsh. "He couldn't be otherwise with a bullet hole in him."

"A woman can tell."

"Would you say I'm a gentleman?"

Raven's answer was a sharp "Hah!"

"What makes you think I'm not?" Chance demanded.

Before Raven could answer, Cal and Sky walked into the kitchen. Chance pulled out a chair alongside his and said, "Sit here beside me, Sky. Are you hungry?"

Raven gritted her teeth when the Indian girl smiled sweetly at Chance and answered, "Yes, I am. Although those men gave me food, I was too nervous and frightened to eat much."

"Poor little thing." Chance stroked Sky's hair again. "It must have been a frightening experience for you. You must work at putting it behind you."

"I'm trying to, and I'm sure that in time I will forget."

"We'll work on it together," Chance said softly, his hand continuing to stroke her hair as he watched Raven out of the corner of his eye.

Old Cal, looking on, could tell that the rancher was trying to make Raven jealous. And he was doing a good job of it, he thought, judging by the way Raven was holding her back so stiff and keeping a frozen smile on her face.

"Can I set the table for you, Raven?" Chance asked, amusement barely contained in his voice.

"No, thank you," Raven answered coolly. "You're too busy with other things."

"Not really. I'm not doing anything that can't be put off until later," Chance said amiably, a devilish twinkle in his eyes.

Raven ignored his taunt. When breakfast was ready, she took a stack of three plates from a cupboard and slapped them on the table. The platter of ham and eggs and a pan of hot biscuits followed them. "Help yourselves," she said and stalked out of the room.

"What's wrong with Raven?" Tory asked as he helped himself from the platter. "She sure is in a bad mood."

Cal saw the smug look on Chance's face and decided it was time the handsome rancher was taken down a peg or two. He felt no remorse at the lie he was about to tell.

"Raven ain't been feelin' well. I think she caught a cold helpin' me get Moon Shadow to the house. She got chilled, the wind was so cold and fierce. She had a fever this mornin'. I think I'll go tell her to lie down for a while. I don't want her comin' down with pneumonia."

Cal stood up and slid a look at Chance. His thin lips twisted in a slight smile. The big man didn't look so cocky now. He looked as concerned as Tory did.

Chance didn't have much to say after Cal left the kitchen. He removed his hand from Sky's head and left it up to her and Tory to carry on a conversation.

Raven had looked so beautiful, so untouchable, he'd had to rag her, Chance thought. Otherwise he might have grabbed her and kissed her as soon as he walked through the door. He confessed to himself that he was unreasonably angry at her for taking care of his handsome friend. He hadn't missed the tender looks Moon Shadow had given her several times.

As Chance topped his breakfast off with a cup of coffee, he wondered how long Moon Shadow would have to stay with Tory and Raven. Was it possible the Indian could be moved to the Mc-Gruder ranch? He dismissed the thought. With all the deep snow that lay on the ground, it would be a while before Moon Shadow could go anywhere.

When Sky tried to hide a yawn behind her hand, Chance said, "We'd better get you to bed so you can sleep. We'll go as soon as we say goodbye to your brother."

"But won't I be staying here with Moon Shadow?"

"There's no place for you to sleep," Chance explained. "I'll bring you over every day to help take care of Moon Shadow." Chance helped her out of the chair and led her into the parlor.

"I don't have to tell you, Chance, how grateful I am to you for finding Sky and bringing her to me." Moon Shadow paused a moment, then said, "There is one more favor I would ask of you. Would you ride to my village and let my father know that both Sky and I are alright? I'm sure he's very worried."

"I was planning to do that as soon as I got Sky settled in at my ranch," Chance said, wondering why Moon Shadow hadn't mentioned his wife. Was he so smitten with Raven that he'd forgotten he had a mate and family?

* * *

Raven sneezed twice in rapid succession. Her lips twisted wryly. Was Cal's lie going to come true? she wondered, feeling a chill creep over her. She wished that Chance would take his precious little Indian princess and leave so that she could go in by the fireplace and warm up. The bedroom doors were always left open so that some of the heat would filter in from the parlor. But she had pulled her door shut when she entered the bedroom this time.

At last she heard Chance and Sky say goodbye to Moon Shadow. They would ride to Chance's ranch now and sit in front of the fire, exchanging kisses and caresses. Chance wouldn't try to make love to Sky, though, she thought. With a woman he intended to marry, he would wait for their wedding night.

She pictured them in bed together, Chance doing the same things to Sky that he had done to her. She almost groaned aloud her mental pain.

When Raven heard the kitchen door open, then close, she scooted off the bed and hurried into the kitchen. Tory and Cal still sat at the table, and after another sneeze, she ordered, "You two go sit with Moon Shadow. I don't want you underfoot while I'm getting my stew together. The cowhands will be here in a couple hours expecting their supper."

"Didn't I hear you sneeze in your room before?" Tory asked, coming to stand beside Raven as she dredged the pieces of meat with flour. Before she could answer, he laid his palm on her forehead. "You're running a slight fever," he said, frowning.

"I want you to go to bed right now. Cal and I will make supper."

"Yes, go ahead, Raven," Cal urged. "I'm gonna feel awful bad if my lie comes true."

"Well, if you're sure, I think I will. Maybe I can warm up in bed."

"I'll check on you in a little while, see if you have enough covers," Tory said, worry creasing his forehead. It wasn't like Raven to give in to a case of sniffles.

Moon Shadow was sleeping when Raven passed through the parlor, for which she was thankful. She didn't feel like talking, she thought as she disrobed and pulled a high-necked flannel gown over her head.

When she slipped between the cold covers, she immediately started shivering. When Tory entered the room a short time later, her body was shaking so hard the covers were moving.

"Are you all right, Raven?" He laid a hand on her shoulder.

"I'm just cold," Raven mumbled. "I'll be alright as soon as I get warm."

But three hours later she was burning up with fever and had developed a rasping cough. Tory and Cal were helpless to know what to do for her, and Moon Shadow chastised them both for not having anything in the house to doctor her with. When Raven's cough worsened, he said impatiently, "I know you have lard. Do you by any chance have turpentine?"

Cal nodded his head eagerly. "I got a bottle of

that, but do you think it's all right for her to drink it?"

"Of course she can't drink it. You mix it with lard, then spread it on a cloth and lay it on Raven's chest. It might ease her cough some. Bring me the two items and I will make the poultice."

In seconds, it seemed, Cal was placing next to Moon Shadow a small bowl with a spoon in it, a cup of lard, and a dusty bottle of clear liquid. His and Tory's eyes watered as the sharp odor of the turpentine spilled into the room when Moon Shadow uncapped the bottle. They watched as the Indian mixed the two ingredients, then spread the paste on a piece of wool cloth Cal had found.

"Put it on her chest now." Moon Shadow handed it to Tory. "And pray to your white God that it will help Raven some. Continue to bathe her face and hands with cold water."

Although the Indian's remedy helped Raven somewhat, the next morning when Chance and Sky arrived, she was out of her mind with delirium.

"What's wrong?" Chance asked when Tory opened the door to them, his face pale and harassed looking.

"It's Raven. I'm afraid she has pneumonia, and I don't know what to do for her."

Chance was hurrying to Raven's room when Moon Shadow called to him, "Chance, you must go talk to our medicine man in the village. Tell him Raven's condition and he will give you a mixture of roots and barks and tell you how to use it. You must go now! Raven is very ill."

Chance wanted to see Raven first, but the urgency in the Indian's voice told him that every hour counted. He wheeled around and hurriedly left the house.

"I will continue to bathe her in cold water, Tory." Sky wrung out the cloth that lay in a basin of snow water.

When Tory saw Chance riding toward the house, he felt he had just passed the longest two hours of his life. "How is she?" Chance asked as he flung open the door, a deerskin pouch in his hand.

Tory shook his head. "No better."

Dumping the contents of the pouch into a large kettle, then filling it with water, he said to Tory, "Stoke up the fire. We've got to get this steaming hot. Then we've got to make a tent of sorts over Raven's bed to trap the steam inside it. The old medicine man claims it will loosen Raven's congestion.

"If you'll keep an eye on the kettle, I'll go ask Sky to help me get some contraption rigged over Raven's bed."

When Chance looked down on Raven's small, flushed face he swore that never again would he taunt or torment her. It wasn't her fault that she didn't return his love. After all, what reason had he ever given her to do so?

And it's not my fault that I love her so, that she never leaves my mind. A man can't help whom he loves.

The bed with its high posts made it easy to fasten blankets over the top and the sides, creating a tight little tent. They had just finished when Tory came in with the kettle, whose steaming water gave off a piney odor that stung the nose. Chance lifted the blanket at the foot of the bed and Tory placed it some distance from Raven's feet.

She began to fuss and thrash about when the sharp tang of roots and bark hit her face. Chance parted the two blankets by her head and grabbed her hands, while Tory hurried to do the same thing with her feet. She could be scalded badly if she kicked over the steaming water.

"You must lie still, honey," Chance soothed, hoping that he wasn't bruising her tender flesh. "I know it smells awful, but it will help you. It will draw the poison from your lungs."

The tone of the man's voice was reassuring to Raven, and vaguely familiar. She peered through fevered eyes and asked haltingly, "Is that . . . that you, Chance?"

"Yes, it is, honey." He stroked her cheek. "Now lie still and let the steam do its work."

Raven smiled and turned her cheek and nestled it into his palm. Chance's heart thudded. Would she remember that affectionate act when her mind was clear?

Half an hour later Raven's cough was loose enough to begin clearing her lungs. "Tory," Chance said, "you and Cal go get some sleep." He pulled a chair up beside the bed. "I'll sit with Raven."

It was around noon when Raven's breathing became easy and she fell into a deep, natural sleep. "I think we can take the blankets down now," Sky said, walking into the bedroom. "Raven will be all right now. She'll be up and about in a couple days."

"Thanks to your medicine man, her cold didn't go into pneumonia."

"He will be pleased to hear that." Sky smiled. "I will watch over Raven while you're gone."

Once again Chance shrugged into his jacket and went outside to brave the freezing weather.

Chapter Seventeen

Raven sat staring into the red coals of the fire-place. Several weeks had passed since her illness; Moon Shadow and Sky had returned to their village, and Christmas had come and gone. It was now mid-January.

Sometimes she felt as if she had what Cal called cabin fever. The old man spent most of his time puttering around in the barn, and Troy often went with Chance to Bitter Creek. Most times he stayed overnight, playing cards, so he claimed. Perhaps he did play some poker, but she was no fool. It was the tavern women that drew him to town.

And Chance—it was the same with that long-legged wolf. That one had his favorite whore, Maudie. While Raven was recuperating she had overheard their cowhands and Tory talking about it. One of them had said that every time Chance

184

went to town he took Maudie to her room and wasn't seen again until the next morning.

Raven jumped to her feet and, grabbing up the poker, unnecessarily jabbed it into the fire, scattering coals and ashes. When she realized she had almost put out the flames, she sat back down, thankful that no one had seen her angry outburst.

As she set the rocker in motion with a push of her foot, she wondered if Sky knew about all the time Chance spent with Maudie. And if she did, did she care? Undoubtedly she did. Women were the same, no matter their race. But where most white women would raise hell with their man for visiting a whore, she suspected Indian women pretended ignorance.

Raven's lips formed a tight line. If Chance was her man, he'd damn well better not stray. She would give that rooster a kick that would cool him off real quick.

But Chance wasn't her man, and all she could do was stand back and suffer when she heard stories of how he had his favorite whore.

Raven gave a start when the kitchen door was flung open. She didn't have to look around to know that it was Tory. She didn't know of anyone else who entered a house with such energy. "How would you like to take a ride into town?" he asked, striding into the parlor and flinging himself into a chair next to hers. "The sun is bright and the air dry. I think it would be safe for you to venture out, and good for you too; it would put some color in your cheeks."

Raven's face brightened. "I'd love to get out of

here for a while. See some different faces."

"So you're tired of looking at your brother and poor old Cal, are you?" Tory retaliated by giving one of her curls a yank.

"Speaking of Cal, I thought the reason he wanted to sell the ranch was because he was going to move into Bitter Creek. I wonder when he intends to go."

"He doesn't seem to be in any hurry, does he?" Tory grinned. "You know what I think, I think he wanted to move to town because he's been lonesome since losing his wife. But now that we're here to keep him company, he has no desire to leave the place."

"You're probably right."

"You don't mind his being here, do you?"

"Heavens, no. He's become like family. I'd miss him if he ever decided to leave us."

"Me too, even though he sometimes acts like the ranch is still his," Tory said in amusement.

"When do you want to go to town?" Raven changed the subject, eager to get out of the house.

"Any time you're ready. Should I go saddle the horses now?"

"Yes. All I have to do is brush my hair."

Fifteen minutes later as they rode away from the house, Cal called, "Pick me up some makin's. I'm about out of tobacco."

The air was crisp, heavy with the smell of pine and wood smoke. Raven breathed deep, filling her lungs with air. It felt so good to be outdoors, to feel her old self again.

She wondered if Moon Shadow was faring as

well as she. He was a healthy specimen and in all likelihood completely healed. She knew he'd been attracted to her, and hoped that once he was home with his family, all thoughts of her had left him.

And Sky. Even though she resented the girl, was jealous of her, the Indian maiden was so sweet she couldn't help liking her.

Halfway to Bitter Creek, six cowboys from the McGruder ranch caught up with Raven and Tory and rode along on either side of them. "Howdy, men," Tory greeted them. "Is Chance coming into town later?" When he received no answer, he glanced around and saw that they hadn't even heard him. They were too busy ogling Raven.

"Ahem," he said. When the men, blushing, pulled their attention away from Raven, he repeated his question.

One of the cowhands answered, "He's already in town. He rode in yesterday and stayed all night." This was said with a thinly veiled snicker.

"Why don't you men ride on ahead?" Tory said before the men could add more about Chance. "My stallion is beginning to act up. He doesn't like to be crowded."

With a last lingering look at Raven, the cowboys guided their mounts onto the snow-packed trail and cantered ahead.

The excitement of going to town left Raven. Chance had spent the night with his favorite whore. If she should run into him, she didn't know what her reaction might be. She could possibly start crying, or just as bad, rail at him bitterly.

Raven realized suddenly that it would be impossible for her to live in the same area with Chance. It would be too painful always hearing about him and the woman Maudie, and when he got around to marrying Sky, that would be her undoing. When the snow melted, she must leave all that had become dear to her.

Where she would go, she had no idea.

She left off her morose thoughts when in the distance she saw smoke rising like feathery ribbons from a group of chimneys. Bitter Creek lay just ahead.

As she and Tory rode down the wide rutted street, Raven was amazed at the number of men in town. On the wooden sidewalks hunters clad in buckskin shirts jostled with surly teamsters wearing slouch hats and cowhide boots. There were stage drivers, their faces deeply wrinkled by hardship and exposure to all kinds of weather. There were also a few Indians, wrapped in blankets, their faces stolid, unemotional. She recognized a couple of gamblers by the black suits they wore.

And there were several mountain men who stepped aside for no man.

"There certainly are a lot of people in town today," Raven said.

"That's because it was announced last week that a couple of freight wagons would be arriving today, so most of the men are here for supplies. I'm sorry I brought you here today. I forgot about the freighters coming in. You notice there are no women on the street. Not even the whores will venture out today."

"What are we going to do?" Raven was growing

uneasy at the hungry looks sent her way.

"I don't know. Let me think a minute, decide what . . ."

"What in the hell were you thinking, Tory, bringing Raven to Bitter Creek today?" An angry and upset Chance was suddenly beside Tory, grasping his horse's bridle and bringing him to a halt.

"Dammit, Chance, I forgot about the supplies coming in today. I know I have to get her out of here, but we're short on rations."

"What all do you need? I'll pick them up for you."

Tory fished his list out of a vest pocket and handed it to Chance.

The irate rancher folded the piece of paper and shoved it in his jacket pocket, then said, "I'll follow you to the edge of town. I don't like the looks of some of those men." And without looking at Raven once, he swung onto his horse's back and waited for Tory to rein around and head back out of town. Raven choked back tears as she heard Chance's horse plodding along behind them.

When she and Tory reached the end of the street, Chance said as he turned his horse around, "I'll bring your supplies to you this afternoon."

Raven and Tory didn't have much to say to each other as they rode along. Raven was afraid she would break into tears if she spoke too much, and Tory was too busy silently berating himself for exposing her to danger. Neither noticed the rider who had dropped in behind them, trailing them at a distance.

They were several miles out of Bitter Creek when a shot rang out and Tory fell out of the saddle. With an alarmed cry Raven started to dismount, but before she could get out of the saddle, the strange rider was upon her. In seconds he was off his horse and swinging up behind her. Spurs were applied to Sam as the stranger grabbed the reins from her and raced down the trail cut into the snow. She tried to look over her shoulder to see if Tory had risen to his feet, but the man's shoulder blocked her view. She tried screaming then, but every time she opened her mouth, the frigid wind bit into her face, strangling the words in her throat.

Raven grew more alarmed when her captor left the beaten trail and struck off toward the mountain. The horse's progress slowed considerably as it fought its way through snow a foot past its fetlocks. Who was this man, and where was he taking her? Was her brother dead or alive? Her mind raced with the frightening questions.

The horse's pace was slow enough now for her to throw herself out of the saddle, but Raven knew she wouldn't get far before the man would be upon her. So far he hadn't harmed her, but if she made him angry he might.

When they reached the foothills and began to climb, Raven's mind raced with ways to get out of her dilemma. Nothing came to mind, and she was overwhelmed with despair. Nothing good waited for her at the end of this ride, she was sure.

Her shoulders sagged and her chin dropped in defeat. In her mind's eye she again saw her brother sprawled in the snow, blood running down his face. Whether he was dead or alive, she would never see him again.

And Chance, she would never see him again either. Not that it would matter to him. He would be too busy with Sky and his whore, Maudie, to give her any thought.

Just then they rounded a bend in the trail and the man sitting behind her swore and jerked the gelding to a halt.

A big gray horse stood in their path, and on his back was a fierce-looking mountain man, staring at them out of narrowed eyes. His voice was deep and rough when he demanded, "What are you doin' in these mountains, stranger?"

"Why, I'm a trapper, the same as you." The friendliness in her abductor's voice didn't ring true.

Raven realized suddenly that this might be her only chance of getting free of the stranger whose arms had tightened around her. She also realized she might be exchanging one brute for another.

Deciding she would chance it, she cried out, "That's not true. He just shot my brother and kidnapped me."

"That right, mister?" The mountain man moved his hand to rest on the hilt of a knife strapped to his waist.

Then, in an effort to pull his gun, the man who had held her so tight knocked her out of the saddle.

As she tumbled to the ground she heard a gunshot; then everything went black as her head came up against a rock.

Chapter Eighteen

It was nearing sundown when Chance managed to escape his friends and left Bitter Creek, with Tory's sack of supplies tied to his saddle. As the stallion moved along at a fast clip, his thoughts were on Raven, which wasn't unusual. Half of his daylight hours were spent thinking of her.

It had been all he could do not to grab and kiss her today. That was why he had acted an ass, thinking it was best to ignore her. Realizing now that he had acted like an insecure teenager, he hoped that when he reached her house he could make her forget his callous behavior.

Chance hadn't ridden far when he recognized Tory riding toward him. He thought with a grin that his friend had gotten rid of his sister and was now returning to town to kick up his heels a little.

When Tory came closer, however, he saw the

blood covering his face and he kicked his mount into a gallop. "Good Lord, what's happened to you?" he exclaimed as he approached. "You look like you've been shot."

"I was bushwhacked, Chance," he said weakly, clinging to the saddle horn, "and I guess the bastard made off with Raven. When I came to, they were gone."

Chance's face paled to the color of the snow on the ground. "Did you see the man, recognize him?"

"I didn't see him, or hear him. All I knew was that suddenly it seemed like my head was exploding."

"Do you think you can make it to the tavern? Someone there will take care of your wound."

"I'll make it. Are you going after Raven?"

"I'm on my way right now." Chance lifted the stallion's reins and nudged him with his knees.

It didn't take Chance long to come upon the spot where Tory had been shot and Raven abducted. The snow was trampled with hooves and boot prints. His searching look found where Tory had fallen from his saddle, the blood on the snow. When he saw fresh tacks leading off, he headed the stallion in the same direction.

Chance swore savagely when dark clouds began to gather and an early dusk settled in. If it snowed, the tracks he was following would be covered up. He pressed on, entering the foothills and climbing upward. After about half a mile he rounded a bend in the trail and sharply reined the stallion in.

A man, a stranger, lay on the ground, his sightless eyes staring up at the sky. The front of his jacket was soaked in blood. Chance climbed out of the saddle and knelt down beside the dead man. A slit in his mackinaw just over his heart told its story. The stranger had been knifed in the heart. A pistol lay in his hand, his forefinger frozen on the trigger. Had he wounded the man who had wielded the knife with such accuracy? And who had Raven now?

Chance climbed back in the saddle and rode on, following two sets of hoofprints. One was from a large horse whose prints were deep in the trail as though carrying the weight of two people. The shallower prints of the other horse told him that this mount was riderless.

As Chance had feared, he hadn't gone far when snow began to fall. He shouted his rage to the sky. Within minutes the tracks he followed would be covered.

His broad shoulders sagged in frustration. There was nothing he could do now but turn around and head back to the ranch while he could still see how to get there. He swung to the ground, and taking the kerchief from around his neck, he tore it into strips. He tied one to the branch of a pine. As he rode back down the mountain, he stopped at strategic spots to tie one of the strips to branches.

The last one he fastened was on a tree at the beginning of the foothills. Tomorrow he would know where to start his search for Raven.

As Chance turned the stallion's head in the direction of his ranch, it occurred to him that old

Cal knew nothing of what had happened to Tory and Raven. He would inform the old rancher what had befallen the brother and sister before riding on home.

While Chance was telling the worried Cal everything that had transpired, farther up the mountain, in the outlaw shack, Carlin Walker paced the floor, mumbling curses and threats about the man he had sent to Bitter Creek to buy supplies. "He's getting drunk and wallowing around with some whore. He'll be running off at the mouth, telling her all about us, all our plans."

Jadine watched her brother, careful to stay out of his way. When Carlin Walker was in a rage he was very dangerous to be around. He could, without warning, suddenly pull his gun and shoot someone.

Jadine had spent the past week with her brother and his outlaw gang and she had come to realize that Carlin was often of unsound mind. He could be quite pleasant one minute, then turn on a person with the swiftness of a killer wolf. When it stopped snowing, she was going home and staying there until spring, when it would be time to do away with her stepfather.

And Carlin, she thought, dangerous and undependable, might just as well go the same way as George when the time came. She didn't want to have a crazy man around when the ranch became hers. She could talk Juan into taking care of that.

Isaac Hunt watched the girl stir and waited for her to open her eyes. She had lain in an unconscious state for over two hours. As soon as he got her to his cabin, he had felt her limbs and found no breaks in them. He had come to the conclusion that it was the knot on the right side of her head that kept her lying so still.

The girl's eyelids fluttered, then opened, and Isaac leaned forward to catch any word she might utter. When her eyes widened in alarm, he sat back. "Don't be alarmed, miss," he said softly. "You've been hurt. I ran into you and a man that you was tryin' to get away from. When I interfered, he knocked you out of the saddle and went for his gun." Isaac left the story there. He didn't know how the girl might take the fact that he had killed her companion. "I guess you've got a headache. You've got a big knot on the back of your head."

When the young woman made no answer, only looked at him in confusion, Isaac asked, "What's your name and where do you come from?"

When her bewilderment grew, Isaac said, a little impatiently. "I've got to know all that so's I can get you home. There must be somebody who is very worried about you."

Frustration in her voice, the girl finally choked out, "I don't know the answers to your questions."

"You don't know your name?" Isaac asked incredulously. "Everybody knows his own name. Even my old hound knows his name."

When the only answer he received was a look of helplessness, Isaac scratched his head and said with a nervous laugh, "Do you think that maybe you have what they call amnesie? You know, a memory gap. I've heard of people havin' it, but I ain't never seen a body with it."

"I guess that's what I have." The girl looked ready to cry. "I can't remember anything."

"Well, I reckon you ain't married. I don't see no ring on your finger, and I reckon that means you ain't got no young'uns. But you must have family around here. Probably down on the flats in the Bitter Creek area. Soon as it stops snowin', I'll ride down there and make some inquiries, find out what I can about you and the man that was takin' you somewhere against your will."

Isaac stood up and laid two small logs on the fire. "Are you hungry?" he asked as he lit the kerosene lamp on the mantel.

The girl nodded eagerly. She didn't remember when she had eaten last, but her stomach said it was some time ago.

While Isaac dished up steaming bowls of venison stew, Raven, lying on a narrow bunk bed, let her gaze wander over the room. The log walls had not been paneled over with wood, but the chinking between the logs had been applied in a neat fashion. And though the room was rustic-looking, she thought it attractive.

She turned her head to look at a huge fireplace that took up a good portion of one wall. On one side of the high, wide hearth the mountain man kept his cooking and eating utensils. Positioned in front of it were two rocking chairs, each padded with sheepskin.

Directly across from the bunk bed where she was lying was a fair-sized window above a table with a bench on either side of it. There was a door, half open, adjacent to the fireplace. She could see the footboard of a bed and assumed that was where the mountain man slept.

Everything in the room was hand-crafted, plain and sturdy. Raven couldn't envision the big mountain man having anything different.

Her eyes smiled her thanks when her host pulled a stool up beside the bed and placed a bowl of stew and a thick slice of sourdough on it. "Do you think that if I ease you up real slow and gentle like and prop pillows behind you, it would make your head hurt worse?" Isaac asked.

When Raven answered that she'd like to try, he put a hand under each of her arms and slowly and carefully raised her almost upright. "How's your head?" he asked anxiously as he propped the pillows behind her. "Is it hurtin' worse?"

"I don't think so. I was a little dizzy at first, but I feel alright now."

"Good." Isaac smiled at her and walked into a part of the room she could not see. He returned shortly with a clean fustian towel which he laid across her lap. "There now," he said, placing the bowl on the towel, "you can enjoy your supper more than if I was spoonin' it into you. And if you don't mind, I'll sit on the stool and we'll eat together."

As the wind roared across the prairie and whirled through the mountains, Isaac and Raven ate in silence. They didn't talk until their hunger was sated and Isaac poured them each a cup of dark, strong coffee.

When Raven took a sip of hers, then grimaced, Isaac grinned and again went into that part of the room Raven couldn't see. He returned carrying a tin of canned milk and a cup of sugar.

"You must be a city girl." He grinned down at her. "Men and women in cow country like their coffee strong."

"Does that really mean I'm from a city?" Raven questioned, her tone serious.

"Naw. That's just my observation. I make a lot of them and mostly I'm wrong. You probably just don't like the bitter taste."

There was a lengthy pause, then Isaac tried to jar her memory again by saying, "I feel sorry for the line camp men tonight."

When Raven asked, "What are line camp men?" he held back a disappointed sigh. The girl just didn't remember any of her past. But since she had questioned him, he had to go on and tell her about line camp men.

"Line camp men are cowboys who live in one-room cabins a long way from the ranch. They have to be out in all kinds of weather, keeping an eye on the cattle, bein' especially watchful during storms. There are usually two men to a camp. A big ranch may have three or four line camps, around twenty miles apart.

"Of course, in the worst storms, like this one that is raisin' hell now, it's impossible for any man to be out."

A gale of wind whistled around the cabin and Raven shivered. "I wouldn't want my worst enemy to be out in this weather."

"Do you have enemies?" Isaac asked, watching her face closely.

Raven shrugged. "I don't know, but you said that man was holding me against my will. I imagine he must be an enemy."

Isaac gave up. Maybe tomorrow after a night's sleep the girl would have regained her memory. He yawned, then said, "I'm sleepy. What about you? If it has stopped snowin' in the mornin', I have to run my traps."

Raven agreed that she was sleepy, too, and as the mountain man helped her to lie back down, he said, "My name is Isaac. I'll just call you Honey until you remember your name."

"Do you think I ever will, Isaac?" she asked in a small voice. "It's scary not knowing your name, where you come from, if you have parents."

"I reckon it is." Isaac awkwardly patted her shoulder. "But I got a feelin' everything will come back to you in good time. But you know, once your memory comes back, there might be things that you'd just as soon not recall. The way it is now, you're like a new baby just starting out in life. Think about that, think about a new future, what you'd like to do with it.

"I'm gonna get more covers for you. It gets real cold in here after midnight. I'll be sleepin' in there"—he jerked a thumb in the direction of the partly opened door—"so if you need me during the night, just sing out. I'll hear you, and my old hound Sampson here, will sleep in front of the hearth. I'll leave him here with you tomorrow if the weather permits me to run my line."

Although Isaac had piled on enough wood to keep the fire burning all night, Raven was thankful for the extra covers that had been spread over her, even though she could hardly move under their weight.

She was wondering where she was and where she came from as she fell asleep.

Chapter Nineteen

Dawn came dimly through the snow, but the blizzard seemed to blow harder. A long sigh escaped Chance as he turned away from the window. How was Raven this morning? Where was she? What was happening to her right now? He didn't dare dwell on that last question.

An unfamiliar tightness threatened to close his throat and moisture gathered in his eyes. If he lost her, life wouldn't mean anything to him anymore.

Chance thought of Tory as he poured himself another cup of coffee and carried it into the main room. Tory, too, must be half out of his mind with worry about his sister. He and Raven were very close. Tory had raised his sister since she was a little girl. He wondered if Tory had recovered enough to get home.

The clock began to strike eight, and on its last

gong bright sun broke through the clouds, bathing the area with its warmth. Chance set his coffee cup down and hurried to look out the window again.

A wide smile brightened his face. The wind had died down and snow no longer whipped through the air. It was still early, he could get in a full day looking for Raven. "Mary," he called as he pulled on his boots, "I'm heading for the mountains."

"Dress warm," his housekeeper said, bustling into the room, a woolen scarf in her hand. "It might have stopped snowing, but it's bitterly cold out there, and you have no idea how long you'll have to be tramping around the mountain looking for Raven."

"I just pray that I can find her no matter how long it takes me." Chance reached for the scarf.

He was ready to pull on his mackinaw when his uncle George arrived. "I was just about to leave, uncle," he said apologetically. "I can't talk very long."

"That's alright, nephew." The gray-haired man smiled pleasantly. "I can't stay long anyhow. I just wanted to ask you if you'd seen Jadine recently. She's not been home for a week. As far as I'm concerned, she can stay away forever. But in memory of her mother I feel obligated to make some inquiries about her."

"I haven't seen her for over a month, and that was at a distance. She was riding with some man. Maybe she's up in the mountains with her brother."

"I thought of that and I don't like the idea. Jadine is bad enough on her own. I hate to think what the two of them together might get up to."

"I'll ask around," Chance said, thinking that when he found the time he would ask Juan what he knew of Jadine's disappearance.

"Thanks, nephew. Go on about your business now. I'll stay a bit and have a cup of coffee with Mary."

The snow was up to the stallion's chest in some places, forcing Chance to dismount and help the animal break through the drifts. However, there were many windswept patches where he made good time.

It took Chance an hour to reach the foothills and find the piece of cloth he had tied to a branch. Another hour found him at the spot where he had been forced to turn back.

He struck out in an easterly direction where the tracks had been leading. After about fifteen minutes, Chance reminded himself how the mountain trails twisted and turned as they led to individual cabins. By now the snow-covered tracks could be heading westward.

He pulled the stallion in while he thought for a minute. As he stared around, his gaze lit on a tall crag rising out of a rock mass. It rose about thirty feet in the air and had a flat top large enough for a man to stand on. If he could scale it, he would have a clear view of any smoke rising out of chimneys.

Chance nudged the stallion with his heels and rode up to the towering rock. After studying it a minute, he decided that it would be difficult to climb, but it could be done.

It was a tedious climb because each step had to be studied before going onward. The higher he climbed, the colder it became. When he finally reached the top, his eyes were tearing so much he couldn't see. Wiping away the wetness with his gloved hand, he peered down from his perch. He was rewarded for his effort. He saw three thin spirals of smoke lifting from chimneys and disappearing among the tall pines. They looked about a mile apart, staggered in their positions. He wanted to shout aloud his joyous relief. He felt sure that he would find Raven in one of those cabins.

When he was on the ground once again, he decided to ride to the nearest cabin. If Raven wasn't there, he'd move on to the other two.

It didn't take him too long to come within hailing distance of a sturdy little cabin. A large man was wielding a shovel, making the snow fly. He must have been at it for some time, Chance thought, for he had cleared a path from the cabin halfway to a barn shed. Chance pulled the stallion in when a big hound spotted him and began barking. The man put down his shovel and ordered the dog to quiet down as he walked up the path he had shoveled.

"What can I do for you, stranger?" he asked gruffly. "Are you lost?"

"Not quite," Chance answered in genial tones, although his right hand hovered close to the holster strapped around his waist. "I'm looking for a young woman who disappeared up here in the mountains yesterday."

Isaac studied Chance a moment, then asked, "What makes you think she's up here?"

"I followed two set of hooves leading from a dead man yesterday. I had to turn back when it began to get dark and to snow."

"What does the girl look like? . . . in case I should see a strange woman up here."

"She's about five foot, six inches tall, slender and has raven black hair. And she's the prettiest woman you'll ever lay eyes on."

"Is she related to you?"

"No, but I hope she will be some day."

Isaac studied Chance's face again, then asked, "Are you that big rancher by the name of Mc-Gruder?"

"Yes, I am." Chance dismounted, and they exchanged names as they shook hands.

"I think I've got your young woman," Isaac said, and added quickly when he saw the relief jump into Chance's eyes, "but there's somethin' I have to tell you before you see her."

Alarm replaced Chance's elation. "Is she hurt? Did that bastard harm her?"

"Quiet down now and listen to me. Her body is fine. It's her mind."

"What do you mean, her mind?" Chance asked. "Do you mean she's gone mad?"

"No, not that." Isaac shook his head. "She has all her faculties. The thing is, she can't remember her past. She doesn't even know her name."

"She'll remember me," Chance said confidently and started toward the cabin.

"Hold on!" Isaac grabbed his arm and swung him around. "I don't want you bargin' in there and upsettin' her. If she remembers you on her own, that will be good. But don't go tryin' to force her, get her all confused. Do you savvy what I'm sayin'?"

"Yes, I understand." Chance jerked his arm free. "I'll let you lead."

Chance spotted Raven as soon as he walked into the cabin. She sat motionless before the fire, her hands folded in her lap. She had never looked so lovely, and it was all he could do not to rush to her side and gather her in his arms.

"Honey," Isaac said quietly, "we have a vistor."

She turned her head to look at them, and Chance was struck by the soft innocence in her eyes. *She looks like an untouched maiden,* he thought.

His heart plummeted. There was no recognition of him in her deep blue eyes. Her serene expression told him that he was a stranger to her.

"Honey"—Isaac laid a gentle hand on her shoulder—"this is Chance McGruder. He knows you. He can tell you all about yourself."

When Raven stiffened and looked a little frightened, Isaac said softly, "You can trust him, honey. He's a well-respected rancher. Maybe he'll tell you something that will jar your memory."

"I certainly hope that happens." Raven's body relaxed. "It's awful, not knowing who you are." She looked at Chance and waited for him to begin.

"Your first name is Raven," Chance began. "Raven Spencer. You were recently widowed. You live on a ranch with your brother, Tory McCloud. He's not with me today because he was wounded by the man who kidnapped you.

"I expect Isaac has told you what happened after that, how you happened to end up here."

All the time Chance talked, Raven was wondering if the handsome rancher was married, and why it was that he had come looking for her.

"Did any of that help you, Raven?" Isaac asked. "Make you remember anything?"

Raven shook her head and sadly answered, "No." She looked at Chance and asked, "Why did you, in particular, come looking for me?"

Chance stared down at the floor, asking himself if he dared say what he was thinking. It would work if she never recovered her memory, but what if she did? He decided he would take that chance, and looking up at Raven, he made her and Isaac gasp when he said, "I'm your intended."

"She can't marry you, man." Isaac regained his speech first. "She don't know you anymore."

"I know that," Chance answered impatiently. "I intend to court her. I hope the new Raven will fall in love with me also." He smiled at the wide-eyed Raven.

"I guess that makes sense." Isaac looked at Raven to get her opinion. When she only stared back at him, confused and upset, he said gently, "It will be entirely up to you, honey. Nobody is gonna force you to get married if you don't want to.

"But for now you must leave with him and return to your brother. Maybe seeing him, and being in familiar surroundings will bring everything back to you."

Raven looked at Isaac. "I don't suppose I could stay here with you until my memory returns."

"Raven girl," Isaac scoffed gently, "you don't want to live with an old mountain man in a two-room cabin. And you got to remember there's a chance you may never recall your past life. Besides, your brother will want you to be home with him."

"I suppose you're right," Raven agreed reluctantly.

"That's the ticket. Now let's get you bundled up. McGruder wants to get off the mountain before dark sets in." He turned to Chance. "Her horse is in the shed."

Raven rose to her feet and stood like an obedient child as Isaac helped her into her sheepsin-lined mackinaw, then wound a red scarf over her head and neck. "Here's your gloves." He pulled them out of her jacket pocket.

She had just pulled them on when Chance returned and smilingly asked if she was ready to ride?

Raven nodded, and Isaac followed them outside. As Chance helped Raven to mount, Isaac said, "I'll come down to see you once the weather warms up a little."

"Don't forget." Raven's eyes brightened a little. "I'll be looking for you."

"I won't forget, girl. I'll be droppin' in to see how

Norah Hess

you're farin'." Isaac stepped back into the cabin then and closed the door behind him.

Chance led off, and after one lingering look at the cabin door, Raven kneed her mount and followed him. She wondered what kind of man this handsome Chance McGruder was. He must be a decent sort if she had loved him once. He had said that he was going to court her and, blushing, she thought to herself that she would like that. She had felt a ripple of excitement rush through her when his two hands grasped her waist and lifted her into the saddle.

Chance was feeling the same excitement, only double in his case. He had experienced the bliss of making love to Raven and he was on fire to do it again. He wondered how long it would be before he knew that pleasure again, and fretted that it would be much longer than he would like.

Half an hour later Chance led them into the foothills, and once clear of them they rode out onto the plains. He looked over his shoulder and smiled at Raven. "Does any of this look familar?"

He wasn't disappointed when she answered, "I'm sorry, but it means nothing to me."

As the horses plodded on, Chance felt guilt that he didn't want Raven to remember the past. Her amnesia must be very frightening to her. But he desperately wanted the time to make a new start with her, a time when there would be no insults flung at each other, no more retributions, trying to get even with each other. He wanted them to start out with a clean slate, so that Raven would grow to trust and love him in such a way that if she did regain her memory the past wouldn't matter.

When he smelled wood smoke he said to Raven, "Look to your right and you'll see your ranch buildings."

They were only specks on the snow-covered land, but Raven could make out several buildings. As the horse brought her closer, each one took on a definite shape.

There was a house, a barn and stables, a corral and three other shed-like buildings. She stared hard at them, hoping to jar her memory. She felt like crying when even her home couldn't bring the past back to her.

When she and Chance rode up to the house, its door opened and an elderly man stepped out onto the porch. He was smiling widely as he said, "You found her! I knew you would!" He waited eagerly for Chance to help Raven dismount so that he could hug her.

Cal's smile died when Raven stepped up on the porch and looked at him without recognition. He looked at Chance for an explanation.

"She's lost her memory for a while, Cal. We've all got to help her recover it."

"Well, I'll be doggone." The old man stared at Raven, making her feel like a freak. But when he took her arm and patted her hand as he led her into the house, she realized that he was a very kind man.

"Everythin' will come back to you, Raven," Cal promised as he helped her out of her mackinaw. "Me and Tory and Chance will see to that." He ushered her to the fireplace where flames leapt and danced. "Now you sit down here and thaw out. Would you like a cup of coffee?"

"I'd appreciate that, Cal." Raven smiled her thanks.

"What about you, Chance? I guess a glass of whiskey would suit you better. While you sip it you can tell me how you found Raven."

"Thanks, Cal, but I'm going to ride on into town and give Tory the good news. Maybe he's coming along well enough that he can come home tomorrow."

"That's a good idea. I'm sure he's been worried sick about Raven.

"He's more than that. He was half out of his mind with worry when I left him." Chance pulled on his gloves and said, "I'll leave you two to get reacquainted. I want to reach town before dark." He smiled and winked at Raven. "I'll see you tomorrow."

She blushed and returned his smile, and Chance felt warm all over as he stepped outside and mounted the stallion.

Chance reached Bitter Creek and swung out of the saddle just as the sun dipped behind the mountain. He led the tired horse to the back of the tavern where the stables were. He unsaddled him and gave him a forkful of hay. When he had draped a blanket over him, he entered the tavern through the back door.

The fat cook turned from the kitchen range, where he had been stirring a pot of chili. "Howdy,

McGruder," he greeted. "Did you find Tory's sister?"

"I found her. How's Tory coming along?"

The cook grinned and turned back to his pot. "The way the girls have been fetchin' and carryin' for him, I'd say he's well on the way to recovery."

"I'll go upstairs and tell him that his sister is alright, then I'll have a bowl of chili."

Chance took the stairs two at a time and without knocking opened the first door to his right. "Oops, I didn't know you had company." He grinned as one of the tavern women removed her hand from beneath the blanket that covered Tory to the waist. As she left the room she gave Chance an inviting smile.

"Did you find her?" Tory asked as Chance pulled a chair up to the bed.

"She's waiting for you at the ranch." Chance smiled.

"She is! How is she? Did that bastard harm her?"

"He didn't have time to. A mountain man came along and put his knife through the no-good's heart. We owe Isaac Hunt a lot. He took Raven home with him, calmed her down and fed her."

"As soon as I'm able, I'll ride up there and thank him."

"Do you think you'll be able to ride home tomorrow?"

"I'll do it if it half kills me."

"There's one thing I haven't told you, Tory," Chance said solemnly. "Raven can't remember anything of her past. She won't know you."

"You're crazy!" Tory came up on his elbows. "She'll remember her brother!"

"Don't count on it. She doesn't remember me or Cal."

"That's different. She's closer to me than she is to you and old Cal. She only recently met you two fellows."

Chance nodded, thinking to himself that Raven knew him better than her brother thought. They had made long, sweet love to each other. "Maybe you're right," he said, and added, "I'm going back downstairs to have a bite to eat; then I'm going to bed. I'm beat. I rode all over those mountains today."

"You do that, and I'll be ready to ride with you in the morning. And, Chance," Tory added just before Chance closed the door behind him. "Send Myrt back in here, will you? She's got a job to finish."

Chance shook his head in amusement. Now that his friend knew his sister was back home, he'd keep the whores busy. As for himself, as soon as he ate he would go to Maudie's room and go to bed.

Chapter Twenty

Raven, her sleeves rolled up and a clean white dish towel tied around her waist, was kneading a large ball of sourdough. She had been home for three weeks and still didn't remember her past. The first week had been spent at odds with herself, not knowing how to spend what seemed like endless hours. Then Cal had mentioned that she used to cook for him and Tory and the two cowhands. Without knowing why she knew that she would be able to cook, she had said she would take over that chore.

"I couldn't do any worse than you and Tory do at making meals," she had laughingly tacked on.

Cal had laughed with her and she had gone to the kitchen. And as if someone were whispering instructions in her ears, that evening at supper she served Tory and Cal a perfect beef roast, mashed potatoes and baked squash. Her biscuits were light and fluffy and her coffee clear and strong.

That she could prepare good, healthy meals for the menfolk meant so much to her. She no longer felt like a parasite, living off Tory, doing nothing useful in return.

But how she wished she could remember Tory. He was so good to her, so sweet. He did everything he could think of to put her back in the past. Nothing had worked, and she always felt like crying at the disappointment that flickered in his eyes.

And old Cal, bless his heart, asked her a dozen times a day if he could do something for her. He had told her that he couldn't help her much with her past life because he hadn't known her and Tory all that long. He said he knew their parents were dead and that Tory had raised her.

Then there was Chance McGruder, handsome, with eyes that sometimes stripped the clothes off her when he thought she wouldn't notice. But she always noticed him. From the time he stepped into the house, her gaze was seldom off his person. And every time she looked at him, he was looking at her. Most times his eyes were soft and yearning, but there were instances when she would surprise a smoldering fire in the depths of his eyes that stirred a throbbing deep in her woman's core. She always lowered her lids to hide the heat his looks kindled inside her.

He claimed that they had been engaged to be married, and she often wondered how far they had gone in their courtship. The way his slightest touch sent her pulses to racing, she couldn't help thinking that they had made love to each other.

Whatever had happened between them before, she found herself looking forward to his visits, their long talks in front of the fire, the light kiss he planted on her cheek when they said good night. She wondered what would happen if one time she turned her head and his kiss landed on her lips. She wished she had the nerve to do it.

But what about the man she had been married to for two years? The one shot and killed for cheating at cards. She must have loved him or she wouldn't have married him. Had they had a good marriage? She sighed. There was so much she couldn't recall. Old Cal told her not to fret about it.

"You're too young to have had much happen to you. Just take up your new life and go on. So what if you don't know about things that happened to you before, that you don't remember Tory and Chance being in your life then? You know them now. It's easy to see that you love your brother, and that Tory loves you. As for that long-legged McGruder, I can see that you're beginnin' to cotton to him. If you loved him before, you'll love him again."

"What about you, Cal?" she had teased, "Do I love you?"

"Course you do. How could you not love a handsome feller like me?" he had teased back.

Still smiling over Cal's retort, Raven shaped three loaves of bread and slipped them into long, narrow pans. She had just covered them with a cloth, to keep them warm so they would rise to double their size before going into the oven to bake, when a knock sounded at the door.

Chance! she thought, and hurriedly wiped her hands.

When she opened the door, a stranger stood before her. Too late she remembered Tory and Cal cautioning her never to open the door until she knew who was on the other side of it.

As she stood staring at the stranger, his eyes kindled and he said, "Either my pard went and got married on me or you're Raven, the sister he was always talking about."

Raven immediately liked the tall, rough-looking man with the sunny smile. "Tory's not married," she said with a smile, "so I must be Raven."

"I suspected that you were." He grinned, stepping into the kitchen when Raven opened the door wider.

"My handle is Rock Booker," he said, wiping his feet on the small rug before stepping further into the kitchen.

Raven reached for the coffee pot that always sat at the back of the stove, keeping warm. "Take off your hat and jacket," she invited. "Then tell me how you come to know Tory while we have some coffee."

"Well," Rock said, as he watched Raven fill two cups "for the past two years Tory and I traveled around together, finding jobs at the same ranches. Tory always had this dream of owning his own spread someday and saved practically every penny he made. I mean to tell you, he went around in rags with big holes in the soles of his boots.

"About six months ago he started corresponding with an old rancher who wanted to sell his ranch. This one, I guess." He looked questioningly at Raven. When she nodded, he continued. "I guess they came to some kind of understanding, for three months ago Tory said he was going to Montana, but was stopping first in Clayton to visit with his sister for a few days. When I finished a cattle drive for the rancher Tory and I had been working for, I decided to try to find Tory and spend a few days with him before returning to the ranch next spring."

"He'll certainly be glad to see you," Raven said when Rock finished his story. "As you see, he's not here now. He and the old man we bought the ranch from have gone into Bitter Creek for some supplies. They usually try to get home before dark."

"It's almost sundown now." Rock looked out the window, then exclaimed, "Here comes that son-of-a-gun right now. Man, is he going to be surprised to see me."

Surprise hardly described what Tory felt when he came into the kitchen. Stunned would have been a more apt word. "Rock Booker, you hellion, where did you come from?" he exclaimed as he threw himself at his friend.

After they had pummeled each other's arms and slapped each other's backs, Rock's teeth flashed in a smile. "Like I told your sister, when I finished a late cattle drive, I decided that before returning to the ranch I'd look up my old partner and spend a few days with him."

"I've thought about you a lot," Tory said as he took off his coat and hat. "I wondered if you had stayed on at the ranch after I left."

"I may stay there for a while." Rock followed Tory into the parlor. "I kinda like the big Anger there."

When Raven's eyes questioned Cal, who had been standing by silently, the old man explained, "Anger means the boss of the outfit."

Remembering his manners, Tory said to Rock, "Meet my friend Cal, He's the man I bought the ranch from."

The two men shook hands, and Tory smiled at Raven. "Could you please bring me my bottle and three glasses?"

When each man had a whiskey in his hand, and his feet were propped upon the hearth, Tory asked, "Did you run into any bad weather on your trip?"

Rock smiled wryly. "I got hit with every damn blizzard as I came along. I got caught in one blizzard where I made a lean-to out of branches to keep the wind off me. It sheltered me fairly well until the storm lost most of its power. My horse fared pretty well. I covered him with a couple horse blankets.

"Then there was one storm in which I got completely turned around. If this mountain man hadn't run into me, I think I would have frozen to death. He took me to a cabin he shared with the prettiest little girl-woman I'd seen in a long time." Rock's eyes took on a dreamy look. "Her name was Amy. I would have liked to stay longer, get to know her, but the next morning when the storm let up, the crusty old mountain man lost no time in pointing me in the direction I should go." Rock's eyes twinkled. "I don't think he trusted me to be around Amy too long."

Tory had straightened up and listened intently when Rock spoke the name Amy. He leaned forward now and asked, "What did this girl look like, besides being pretty?"

"Well, let me think. She's tall. About five feet and a half, I'd say. She's slender, but has curves in all the right places. She's got long, reddish brown hair and green eyes that kinda tilt at the corners."

Rock gave Tory a curious look. "Why are you interested in how she looks?"

"I met a girl named Amy on my last cattle drive. She had a small ranch in one of those hidden valleys."

"It must be the same young woman, then. This Amy had a small ragtag ranch she was trying to build up. And it was certainly in a hidden valley. I doubt that I could find it on my own."

Tory leaned back in his chair, crossed his wrists behind his neck and gazed into the fire. As if from a distance, Tory heard Cal and Rock talking, heard Raven say that she was going to put supper on the table. He was picturing Amy Mitchel's green eyes and shy smile. He was still daydreaming about her when Raven called them to the table.

Much talk and laughter went on during the meal, Rock complimenting Raven on her stew, he and Tory telling stories about some of the men with whom they had punched cows.

Tory asked about one in particular. "Whatever became of Jones, that man we always kept downwind of because of his stench? The one who never took a bath or washed his clothes."

Rock thought a minute, then grinned. "Hell, he finally died of dirt."

Everyone was laughing uproariously when Chance walked into the kitchen. "I knocked," he said, "but everyone was laughing so hard I guess you didn't hear me."

Although he made his remark to everyone, Chance's eyes were fastened on Raven.

"Hiya, Chance," Tory greeted him. "You're just in time for supper. I'll get you a plate."

"Thanks, but I've already eaten." Chance shrugged out of his jacket and removed his Stetson. "But I'll have a cup of coffee. It's freezing out there."

While Raven rose to fill another cup, Tory said, "Chance, I want you to meet Rock Booker, an old friend of mine,"

After the men shook hands, the conversation was resumed. Chance took small part in it; his attention was on Raven, who had made room for him next to her. As usual, her nearness made him tremble inside, he hungered for her so desperately. How much longer, he wondered, could he control himself?

For the present he'd better restrain his hunger or he was going to embarrass himself with the bulge that was growing in his trousers. He stood up and announced that he'd better be getting home. Raven rose and stood beside him as he said, "Rock, it's nice to know you. I'll probably see you tomorrow."

When Chance had left, and the clock struck nine, Tory said with a yawn, "Rock, we're a little cramped for sleeping quarters. Would you mind sleeping with the boys in·the bunkhouse?"

"Not at all. I've been missing my bunkmate's snoring." Rock laughed.

When Rock said good night and left, Raven commented, "Your friend seems awfully nice."

"He is. He makes a great sidekick. But don't go getting interested in him. He's a mover. He never settles down anywhere too long."

"That's a shame. What's going to become of him when he gets too old to herd cattle and has no wife or children to take care of him?"

Tory shook his head somberly. "I've seen a lot of old cowpokes down on their luck. They hang around saloons hoping someone will give them a quarter. Some become crotchety old cooks on some ranch. But sometimes those who have worked on the same ranch all their lives will get a little house and grub, a gift from the rancher." Tory sighed and shrugged. "In Rock's case, I guess I'll have to give him a home."

"You're a good man, Tory McCloud," Raven said, squeezing his shoulder on her way to bed.

A full moon shone on Chance with his chin and mouth muffled in his collar, and the reins loose in his hands, as he continued to dwell on Raven. In her memory loss, she was like a young virgin now, unaware of the passion that slumbered inside her. He knew how to awaken it, had done so before. But did he dare do it now? When Raven was aroused an iron man couldn't resist her. And resist her he must until they were married.

Marrying Raven was his driving ambition. The fear that she might regain her memory before they were wed chilled him to the bone. If that happened, she would remember every insult he had flung in her face, recall the times he had seduced her against her will. It would be all over between them then.

But if they were already married when everything came back to her, they could still have a good life together. By then she would be sure of his love for her and would forgive the past.

I would ask her to marry me tomorrow, Chance thought, *but I know she's not ready yet. She's still getting to know me. Maybe I should do a little more than kiss her cheek every night when I leave her. Move things along a little faster.* Surely a few kisses wouldn't hurt if he kept control of himself and didn't ravish her mouth, scare her away.

I'm going to do it, he decided. *At the rate we're going, I'll be still kissing her cheek a year from now.*

The trick would be getting her alone. Old Cal was always underfoot.

The stallion came to a sudden snorting halt, jolting Chance back to the present. A horse and rider stood in his path. "Dammit, Jadine," he swore. "Don't you watch where you're going?"

"You've got eyes too," she snapped back at him.

224

Chance let her answer pass. He hadn't been paying attention to the trail either. "Where have you been for the last week?" he said instead. "Uncle George stopped by at the ranch the other day to ask if I knew anything of your whereabouts."

"I took a little vacation."

"So he got tired of you and kicked you out, huh?"

"Who said I was with a man?" Jadine asked in sham indignation.

"You sure as hell weren't with a woman. You don't have any women friends."

"Bah, women friends! Women bore me to death. The single girls giggling and simpering, the married ones always talking about their brats, a new recipe they have."

"Where are you going at this hour?"

"I thought I'd visit with Tory a bit. I haven't seen him for a while."

"Hell, woman, he's in bed by now. Besides, you should know by now that he's not going to fool around under his sister's nose."

"Ah yes, the precious Raven. How is she these days?"

"She's alright, considering she had a run-in with a stranger who was trying to abduct her."

Eager to get away from the immoral woman, Chance didn't see her stiffen when he mentioned the stranger. "Did the man get away?" Jadine asked.

"Not likely. A mountain man came upon him and Raven and when the stranger tried to shoot him, he put his knife through the bastard's heart."

"Did Raven learn anything about the man before he was killed?"

"We don't know. She's had a loss of memory ever since the incident."

"Well I'll be dammed. Ain't that something?"

Chance thought he must be mistaken in thinking there was a sound of relief in Jadine's tone. Why should she care one way or the other if Raven had learned anything about her abductor?

When Jadine saw that Chance wasn't going to move out of the deeply trodden path so that she could get around him without forcing her mount into snow up to his chest, she turned the horse around.

"You'll have to make do with Juan tonight," Chance called after her as she turned the stallion on to the snow-packed trail leading back to her stepfather's ranch.

"Go to hell," she called back, her tone sour and aggravated.

Chapter Twenty-one

Jadine favored her left side, leaning to the right as she rode toward home. When she had suggested yesterday that they wait until the river was in full flood before doing away with her stepfather, Carlin had gone into one of his mad fits, and for the first time laid angry hands on her. He had knocked her all over the one-room shack, calling her every scornful name that could be put on a woman. She felt positive that she had at least three broken ribs.

When her brother had drunk himself unconscious, and his two friends had done the same, she had pulled on her jacket, tied a scarf over her head and around her shoulders, and slipped outside to the lean-to where the horses were kept.

Using only one hand and arm, it had taken her some time to saddle and ready her stallion. Then it took two attempts before she managed to mount the animal.

Jadine admitted to herself as the horse plodded along that her brother was mad. When crossed or angered, he became deranged. She understood now why the others always went along with him, no matter how crazy some of his plans were.

"When the time comes for old George to go, Carlin must go with him," she muttered. "I will not have a crazy man dictating to me, maybe kill me in one of his mad fits."

The ranch buildings took shape and Jadine reined the stallion in. The house was dark. The old man had gone to bed. She looked toward the barn. A dim light shone from Juan's quarters. She nudged the mount and rode toward the big building. It did not bother her that she would have to listen to the Mexican's angry admonishments, his jealous accusations. All she had to do was sit quietly until he ran out of words, or breath; then he would want to make love to her.

When Jadine pushed open the door to the room built in one corner of the barn, where Juan had resided as horse wrangler since he was a young teenager, it happened as she had known it would.

First a look of gladness and relief passed across Juan's face, followed by a spate of angry Spanish. Then, as though he remembered that she wouldn't understand half of what he was saying, he switched to English and the room rang with angry questions. As he ranted on, she removed her jacket and scarf and sat down on the bed and closed her ears to his shouting.

Finally silence descended on the room and Juan sat down beside her. He put an arm around her shoulders and said softly, "Why do you torture me like this? I thought you had found a new man and had left me forever. Where have you been? Are my thoughts true?"

"No, Juan, your thoughts were wrong. I went to visit my brother and got snowed in. I have been so miserable." She forced a couple tears to roll down her cheeks as she took Juan's hands and gazed deep into his eyes. "When the time comes, my brother must die with my stepfather."

When Juan drew back, his eyes widening, Jadine begged, "You must do it, Juan. My brother is mad. I thought he was going to kill me yesterday, the way he knocked me around. I'm sure I have some broken ribs. I want you to bind them up."

Jadine took off her shirt, the only article of clothing she wore above her waist. The Mexican shook his head at seeing the ugly bruise along her left ribcage and gently stroked his fingers over it.

"I would kill him now if he was here," he said, leaning forward to kiss the red discoloration.

Jadine wasn't surprised when his mouth moved to settle on her breast. She moved his head and said huskily, "You can do that after you've bound my ribs."

She watched him tear a sheet into strips and thought that she was going to miss her longtime lover when he was gone. But he, like her brother, was to be disposed of. Both would be a hindrance in her new life. Come spring, when the melt water flooded the river, she would inherit the second largest ranch in the territory.

"Is it my imagination, or has the snow melted a little?" Chance asked as his housekeeper placed a plate of ham and eggs in front of him.

"I think you're right. We're in mid-February and it's time it starts melting," Mary said, taking up her own breakfast plate and carrying it to the table. "The paths to the outbuildings are all muddy now."

"I'll be glad to see it go, even though we'll be walking in mud up to our ankles for a while."

"What are you going to do with yourself today?" Mary asked when Chance pushed aside his empty plate and took a pouch of tobacco and a packet of thin papers from his vest pocket.

"I don't know." Chance tapped the makings into the paper he held between finger and thumb. "Probably ride over to Tory's place and shoot the breeze with him and his friend Rock."

"Of course, you won't have anything to say to the young woman you plan to marry," Mary teased.

"Naw. I won't even look at her." Chance grinned.

"Is she coming any nearer to regaining her memory?"

"No." Chance shook his head. "Everything is strange to her, everybody's a stranger. But she's developed a strong liking for Tory. Love is maybe the right word, I guess."

"It's said that blood will tell, and I expect that it's true." After a moment, Mary said, "I don't mean to pry, but is Raven showing any signs of growing to care for you the way she used to?"

Chance took a long drag on his cigarette. It was at times like this he wished he hadn't lied about him and Raven being engaged. How could he tell this nice woman that Raven had never loved him? Hated and despised him was more like it.

He exhaled tobacco smoke and said, "I think I'm making a little progress with her. She always seems to be glad when I show up."

"Just be patient. In time she will either remember her past or fall in love with you again." Mary gathered up the dishes and took them to the dry-sink, and Chance stood up and went to his room.

There he went through the ritual of removing the stubble that had grown overnight: stropping the razor, working up a lather on a bar of soap, then spreading it over his face.

Drawing the straight blade over the hard planes of his face, he toyed with the idea of asking Raven to ride into Bitter Creek with him. They never had a chance to be alone. She could wander about the town's one store, purchasing the things that delighted women: fancy combs, earbobs, a bottle of rose scent to dab behind her ears.

He remembered the first time they'd made love. Her body had smelled of roses. Especially her arms when she wound them around his shoulders while her soft body cradled his hard one.

A ragged sigh feathered through his lips as he rinsed the soap off his face, then cleaned the razor. If only he had it to do all over again he wouldn't act such an ass. By now they would be married with maybe a babe on the way.

Chance was about to lead Brutus outside when he stopped in the doorway. Riding down the trail from the McCloud ranch were Tory, his friend Rock and old Cal. Chance waited to see if they were coming to visit him, and sighed in relief when they rode on past. He couldn't believe his good fortune. The men would spend at least half the day in Bitter Creek. Finally he could spend some time alone with Raven.

And I've got to make the most of it, he told himself, climbing into the saddle.

Raven had just finished sweeping the parlor and the kitchen. As nice as Rock was and as much as she liked him, the cowboy was careless about tracking mud into the house. She had complained to Tory, but her brother had answered, "Never mind, sis. He's leaving today. Cal and I are going to ride down to Bitter Creek to see him off."

She propped the broom in a corner of the kitchen. She was rinsing her hands in a basin of water in the dry-sink and gazing out the window. Her heart gave a little leap. Coming toward the house was Chance, astride his handsome stallion. She felt nervous, yet excited. It would be the first time they'd been alone together since she'd bumped her head.

Raven opened the door as soon as she heard his footsteps on the porch. They gazed silently at each other with hungry eyes. Chance thought Raven had never looked lovelier or more desirable.

Her hair hung loose, the curls tousled the way they had been after he had made love to her. Her bodice was open three buttons down, showing much of her firm, round cleavage. His eyes fastened there, and he remembered with a growing hardness how her breasts had felt against his lips.

Raven sensed his intent gaze there and felt her nipples puckering. She wondered what it would feel like to have his mouth on them. A stirring in her woman's core told her it would feel wonderful.

When Chance stepped inside, she said breathlessly, "The men aren't here."

"I know," Chance answered huskily, and reached for her as he closed the door with a backward kick of his foot.

She went willingly into his arms and leaned into him as his lips came down on hers.

When he broke the long kiss Chance whispered, "I can't stand it much longer, not being able to make love to you. Don't you ever think about it, want it?"

"Oh yes, I do," she whispered. "I pray every night that my memory will come back so that we can get married."

Chance began planting small kisses down her throat, stopping when he came to the half-revealed breasts. He slid a hand into her chemise, freeing a breast then bent his head and closed his mouth over it.

Raven gasped her pleasure, and when his lips drew the aching nipple between his teeth, a smoldering heat ran through her veins. As she strained closer to him, damning his heavy jacket that kept

233

her from feeling his hard length against her softness, he whispered, "Why wait for your memory to return? We love each other. Why waste time waiting for that to happen? What if your past never comes back? I can't wait forever to make love to you again."

Chance swore softly under his breath as soon as the words left his mouth. He had forgotten caution. How would Raven react to what he had let slip out?

Raven's body was stiff for a moment, then she lifted his chin so she could look into his eyes. "You said *again*. Does that mean we have made love already?"

"Yes, Raven, it does," he answered huskily, unbuttoning his jacket and pulling her close to his body. "And it was wonderful between us." He put his hands on her bottom and pulled her tight against his throbbing hardness. "Please, Raven, I want you, need you," he whispered, pumping his maleness against her. "Don't you want me, just a little?"

Raven whispered, "I do, Chance, but as things stand now, this is all new to me. I'm half afraid."

"Don't be, honey. I'll go slow and be very gentle with you."

When he read acceptance in her eyes, Chance shrugged out of his jacket and laid his hat on the floor before sweeping her up in his arms. As he carried her toward her bedroom, he kept his mouth on her breast, suckling the nipple. He must keep her desiring him until he could get her in her room. Once there, their clothes discarded, he knew exactly how to keep the heat burning through her veins.

Chance set Raven on her feet and kicked off his boots. They tore at each other's clothes, and in a minute's time everything lay scattered on the floor.

They stood bare before each other, each staring hungrily at the other. Chance swallowed hard as he ran his gaze over Raven's body, starting at her proudly jutting breasts. He remembered vividly her narrow ribcage, the rounded hips, the mat of black hair between her thighs. And her long legs. He repressed a groan, remembering how they had wrapped themselves around his waist as she cradled his body.

And Raven, she was thrilling at the sight of his broad shoulders, rippling muscles, flat stomach and narrow hips. Her eyes widened as her gaze fastened on the thatch of hair between his legs; his engorged manhood, jutting out of it, was long and throbbing.

She couldn't believe that she had felt that length inside her and couldn't remember it now. She lifted her gaze to Chance, and a thrilling wave rushed through him when he saw in her eyes the same desire that was threatening to bring him to his knees. He led her to the bed and pulled her down with him. When she lay down on her back, he positioned himself on top of her, and with desperate urgency, gently spread her legs apart. He waited a moment, then slowly entered her.

When he had sheathed himself deep inside her, Raven stiffened and whispered a protest. "It's all right, honey," he whispered, and bent his head to open his mouth over her breast.

The rigidness left Raven's body, and Chance slid his hands under her bottom and began to slowly thrust in and out of her. "God, you feel so good," he groaned as his body rose and fell on her. "You feel just like velvet. Tighten yourself around me like you used to," he begged.

For long minutes out of time the bedsprings creaked and the headboard thumped against the wall, and Chance's chest was bathed in perspiration. Then, when he felt Raven's femininity tightening around him, he increased the pace of his plunging manhood so that he could climax with her.

Raven moaned her satisfaction, and Chance gave an exultant cry when they found release together.

Raven lay quietly, listening to Chance's heavy breathing, feeling his damp hair on her chin and shoulder. Finally he rolled off her, and looked into her eyes. He began to tell her how wonderful it was to make love to her again, then caught his breath. Her eyes were like glacial ice.

"What's wrong, Raven?" He raised a hand to smooth the damp hair off her forehead.

She knocked his hand away and said in a voice that matched her eyes, "My memory has returned. As soon as you entered me, my past came rushing back. I remembered clearly all that had gone on between us before. I recalled all the insults you hurled at me, the times you were able to seduce me against my will. Just like this time. I haven't figured out yet why you claimed we were engaged, but I will."

Chance sat up, cursing himself for a fool. Why hadn't he waited until they were married, however long it might have taken? Raven would probably have been just as angry with him as she was now, but they would have been husband and wife and they could have worked things out.

He laid his head back down on the pillow and, staring up at the ceiling, said dispiritedly, "I won't bother you again."

"See that you don't," Raven said coolly. "I want you to know that my husband forced me to sleep with you that first time. I'd never done such a thing before, and I never plan to make love to you again," she declared. Then they both stiffened and listened. Someone was in the house.

Tory and the two other men hadn't gone far when Tory's horse began limping. He reined in and swung to the ground. Lifting the horse's left front leg, he swore under his breath. "He's thrown a shoe," he said to the waiting Cal and Rock. "You two go on in to Bitter Creek and I'll meet you there as soon as I get a new shoe on him. It won't take long."

His companions nodded. As they rode on, Tory turned his mount around and led him in the direction of the ranch.

As he rode past the house, he saw Chance's stallion tied up at the porch. His lips curved in a crooked grin. His friend and sister were probably enjoying some time together without him, Rock and Cal underfoot.

As he had promised, it didn't take long to reshoe the horse. He led him up to the porch and tied him a good distance from the stallion. The mean devil always wanted to fight.

Tory stepped up on the porch, anticipating a hot cup of coffee before taking off for Bitter Creek again. Walking into the kitchen, he frowned. The room was empty. He walked into the parlor and found it empty, too. Where could they be? he was asking himself when he heard their voices coming from Raven's room. What were they doing in there? Raven's voice sounded angry.

In three long strides he was at her bedroom door and flinging it open. He took a step into the room, then stopped short, his eyes raking over the naked pair in disbelief.

"What in the hell is going on here?" he demanded as Raven fumbled the quilt over her bare body. When neither one answered, only stared guiltily at him, he said, "As if I have to ask. An idiot would know what's been going on."

When neither tried to defend themselves, Tory ordered, "Get dressed. We're making a little visit to the preacher's house."

"What are you talking about?" Raven scooted up in bed, almost dislodging the cover that hid most of her bareness.

"I'm talking about your wedding, sister. Yours and my supposed friend's."

"You're crazy!" Raven cried incredulously. "I've

regained my memory now and I know that we don't love one another."

"That makes it all the worse. You went to bed together out of pure lust."

"It wasn't that way." Chance tried to intervene, to explain. When he found himself staring down the barrel of a gun, he snapped his mouth shut. After all, things were working out the way he wanted them to. But he didn't like the word "lust" to describe what he and Raven had just done, and he didn't like the idea of a shotgun wedding.

"I'm not going to do it," Raven said, challenging her brother. "You can't make me."

"I won't have to if you calm down and think a minute. Think how you'll feel if nine months from now you give birth to a baby who will have no father."

Raven grew still, her face pale. He might be right. Chance hadn't withdrawn when he found his release. She had felt his hot seed exploding inside her.

Her shoulders sagged in defeat. "Turn your head so I can get dressed."

The only sound in the room then was the rustling of clothing as Raven and Chance got into their clothes. When they had hurriedly combed their hair, their eyes avoiding each other, they followed Tory into the kitchen and donned their jackets and Stetsons.

No word was spoken as they made the trip to Reverend Ralph Manus's small house outside Bitter Creek.

As the surprised preacher led them through the

marriage rites, Raven's mind continued to race with the questions that had nagged her on the ride over here. Would Tory expect her to live with Chance? If so, would Chance expect to share her bed? If that was what he had in mind, he was in for a big surprise. She had her wits about her now and she would never again sleep with a man who didn't love her.

There was an awkward moment near the end of the ceremony when Reverend Manus told Chance to put his ring on her finger and he had none. "Here," Tory said and withdrew his mother's wedding band from his little finger.

His hand shaking a bit, Chance slipped the circle of gold on Raven's wedding finger. When he would have held her hand, she snatched it away. And when the preacher said, "You may now kiss your bride, Chance," she turned her head so that his lips only touched her cheek.

The last step was signing the marriage certificate. As Raven wrote her name beneath Chance's, she wondered how long she would carry the McGruder name. If she was lucky it wouldn't be long, but the way her luck had run over the last few years, she'd probably be stuck with the new title for the rest of her life. A love wasted in a union with a man who didn't love her. With a sigh she laid the pen down and wordlessly walked outside.

Tory was right behind Raven, and before she could stop him, he lifted her onto Chance's stallion. When he looked up at her and said gently, "Someday you'll forgive me for this," she felt like kicking him in the mouth. She would never in a hundred years forgive him.

Chance was climbing up behind her then, and as they rode away, Tory called out, "I'll send Cal over with your clothes and your gelding." When she made no answer, he added, "I'll drop in on you in a couple weeks to see how you're getting along."

Chapter Twenty-two

When Chance drew rein at the wide porch of a rambling white house, Raven slid off the stallion before he could help her dismount. She waited for him at the steps as he handed the horse over to an old man who gave her a wide, toothless smile. She smiled back. It wasn't his fault that his boss was a down-and-dirty dog.

When Chance would have taken her arm to lead her up the two steps, she jerked free of him. His face flushed an angry red, but he didn't express what was on the tip of his tongue.

When he pushed open the door and stood aside for her to enter ahead of him, a thin woman with graying hair looked up, then tried to hide her surprise as she dropped a potato she was peeling.

"Mary"—Chance smiled at her—"this is Raven. We just got married."

"Holy moley, you don't say." The housekeeper's eyes widened at the startling announcement. Then she regained her composure and, drying her hands on her apron, offered one to Raven. "Does this mean you've got your memory back?" she asked as Raven shook her hand.

"Yes, I have," Raven answered wryly.

"Well, don't that beat all. I'm real happy for you, honey. You look a little peaked. Take off your jacket and hat and sit down. I'll pour both of you a cup of coffee."

"How about a piece of that apple pie that smells so good," Chance asked as he took off his jacket, not daring to try helping Raven off with hers. She would only jerk away from him and make Mary curious.

"I guess a small slice wouldn't spoil your appetite for supper." Mary picked up a knife and walking to a counter sliced into the still warm pie.

"What are we having for supper?" Chance sat down across from Raven.

"It's hardly anything fancy enough for a wedding feast," Mary apologized. "Just beef stew."

"Stew will be fine, Mary," Raven said, her tone suggesting that there wasn't anything special to celebrate.

When Mary gave Chance a curious look, he asked, "Do you know if the mare had her foal yet?"

Mary blinked at the sudden change of topic. ". . . I uh . . . I don't really know. I haven't seen any of the men today." She started to add that she hadn't known they had a mare ready to foal, but something told her that Chance didn't either. He only wanted to get off the subject of his hurried marriage. She wished he'd go to the barn or someplace, so that she could pump the beautiful bride who didn't seem to be all that enthusiastic about her union with Chance.

But it was different with her boss. He hardly took his eyes off his new wife. He, at least, was well pleased with his marriage. And drat it, he didn't show any intention of leaving Raven alone with her.

"I've been thinking, Chance," Mary said as she added potatoes to the stew pot, "maybe I'll move into town and live with my married daughter. You don't need me now that you've got a wife to take care of you."

"That's not necessary, Mary!" Raven exclaimed as soon as the older woman got the words out of her mouth. "I'll be glad to have your company and your help. I'm not used to taking care of such a large house."

"Well . . ." Mary looked at Chance for direction.

After a slight hesitation he said, "If Raven wants you to, you can stay on for a while." Chance was wishing, however, that his housekeeper would leave today. How were he and Raven ever to straighten out misunderstandings, disagreements, with an audience to overhear them?

It was nearing time for Mary to put supper on the table when Cal rode up to the house. Raven's gelding followed him on a lead rope, her clothes and personal items tied to his back.

As Raven watched Chance help the old rancher unload her horse, she grew tense. The time had arrived when she must take a stand, making it clear to Chance that she was not sharing a room with him. When a few minutes later he entered the house carrying a large carpetbag and started walking down a hall, she hurried after him. When he stopped in front of a door and reached for the knob, she asked sharply, "Whose room is this?"

"Mine, of course," he answered, not looking at her as he started pushing the door open.

"Well, it's not mine." Raven grabbed at the piece of luggage and yanked on it. "I'll have my own room, if you don't mind."

"I do mind." Chance yanked back. "I'm not going to have all of Bitter Creek snickering that Chance McGruder's wife won't sleep with him."

"I don't care what they think or say." Raven tugged at the carpetbag again. "Tell them that I don't satisfy you as well as your whores do."

"I don't have any whores." Chance's voice rose. When Raven continued to glare at him, he realized that he'd have to use force to pry her fingers off the luggage, so he released his hold on it.

"You can have the room next to mine," he said, and, his back stiff, he flung open the door he had indicated and stamped down the hall.

Raven stepped into a room that was icy cold. She set the bag down and in the semi-gloom walked to where a lamp sat on a table beside the bed. A box of matches lay beside the kerosene lamp and striking one, she lifted the glass chimney and touched the flame to the wick. In its soft glow she took stock of the room.

The first thing that caught Raven's eye was a

small wood-burning stove in a corner. A full wood-box sat next to it. She picked up the box of matches and walked over to the stove. When she opened the door to the fire box, she discovered that the makings of a fire had been laid inside it. All she had to do was strike a match and hold its flame to the dry wood shavings.

When the fire was started, she let her gaze drift over the room. *By the time I hang my pictures on the walls and place my porcelain figurines around, it will be quite cozy in here,* she thought. *A nice little place I can escape to when I can no longer bear to be in the presence of my husband.*

"My *husband*. What a laugh," she muttered, picking up her bag and laying it on the bright quilt.

When she had hung up her dresses and two coats in the narrow wardrobe next to a window, she placed the remaining clothes in the dresser. After she had set out her comb and brush, powder jar and a bottle of rose scent on its top, she sat down in a padded rocker close to the woodstove. With a push of her foot she sent it rocking slowly, and waited for what would happen next.

Chance was in a thunderous mood as he walked toward the bunkhouse. Even in the presence of others, his wife wasn't going to pretend that theirs was a love match.

At last he had what he had wanted for a long time, he thought sourly, but he had to admit that Raven was going to make his life hell. Could he endure her coldness, her silence? It would be almost impossible. Every time he looked at her he wanted to carry her off to bed.

Before she regained her memory, he had done everything in his power to show her how much he loved her. She had responded to that treatment, had begun to return his love. She remembered everything now; why couldn't she remember that? Why couldn't they carry on in the same way?

She doesn't trust me, that's why, Chance thought grimly as he pushed open the bunkhouse door. Not only did she remember his previous insults, but she must also have heard the talk that he had a favorite whore he always visited.

As he stepped into the long building, he was thinking that if Raven ever met poor old Maudie she would know what a foolish rumor it was.

"Hey, boss—" One of the men looked up from a book he was reading. "We hear tell you've taken the plunge. That you're an old married man now."

Chance barked a short laugh. "I see old Cal stopped in to spread the news."

"Yeah. He was as pleased as a rooster that's just caught a hen. Claimed you had captured the sweetest, most beautiful woman in the territory for a wife."

"Is it true, Chance?" another man asked. "Or was Cal telling one of his tall tales?"

"It's true." Chance nodded. "And she is beautiful. But sweet? I don't know about that. I've discovered that she has claws when angered."

The men laughed, and one of them remarked, "You wouldn't want a tame wife, now, would you, boss?"

"No. I like a woman with spirit, and this one has plenty of it."

"I guess you won't be ridin' into town with us anymore."

"The hell I won't." Chance forced a careless smile to his lips. "When is the next time you fellows are going into Bitter Creek?"

"Actually, we're goin' into town tonight." The young cowhand gave him a sly grin. "I don't expect you'll want to join us, it being your wedding night and all."

"What's so special about that?" Chance pretended a nonchalance he was far from feeling. He had looked forward to this night for so long, but he knew from Raven's demeanor that he wouldn't be spending it with her, after all.

"I've got a lifetime of nights to spend with the little woman," Chance said. "I feel like raising a little hell. Count me in."

There was a surprised silence for a second. Then one of the men said, "You've got the right idea, boss. Let her know from the start that you ain't changin' your ways for her. It's my opinion that every newly wedded man should do that. I've seen too many new husbands hen-pecked into giving up all their fun."

Chance looked at the opinionated man and mentally shook his head. He was loud-mouthed, lantern-jawed, and going bald. If that one ever convinced a woman to marry him he'd be lucky.

The conversation turned to ranch business, and after about half an hour Chance stood up and remarked, "I reckon it's supper time. What time are you men leaving for town?"

When someone announced it would be around seven, he said, "I'll see you then."

"Where's Raven?" Chance asked when he walked into the kitchen and found Mary alone.

"I haven't seen her since you took her to your room." Mary carried a large bowl of steaming stew to the table. "Maybe she's taking a nap. She looked a little tired."

"Probably." Chance took off his jacket and hung it up. As he removed his Stetson and hung it on a peg, Mary said slowly, choosing her words, "I know it's none of my business, but things don't seem quite right between you and your bride. Am I right or wrong?"

"You're right," Chance sighed. "We've gotten off to a rocky start, but things will straighten out in time."

His terse words let Mary know that he wasn't going to say any more on the subject of his marriage. She nodded when he said, "I'll go call Raven to the table."

When Chance left the kitchen, Mary thought to herself that the time he spoke of would be long in coming.

Chance strode down the hall, rapped twice on Raven's door, announced that supper was on the table, then walked back to the kitchen.

Raven listened to the thump of his heels, the jingle of his spurs receding. "If I wasn't half starved I'd ignore his hateful summons," Raven muttered as she left her room, head held high.

From beneath lowered lids Chance watched Raven walk into the kitchen and sit down at the table. And though he often shot quick glances at her, not once did he catch her looking at him. What really bothered him was that, though she ignored her husband, she chatted brightly with Mary. She congratulated the housekeeper on her stew and asked if she would teach her how to make the delicious bread that was served with the meal.

Flattered, Mary went into great detail on how to make the dough. She explained how much flour to use, how to add the other ingredients, and how long to let it rise before popping it into a properly heated oven. When the genial housekeeper finally finished, Chance felt that he could also make a fine loaf of bread if he was so inclined.

His lips twisted in a bitter smile when Raven switched to talking about the house. She began with the changes she intended to make. "I noticed as I passed through the main room that the window hangings are old and faded. I shall want to get rid of them and purchase new, bright ones. I detest things dark and drab. And that scruffy leather furniture must go. It has outlived its useful life a long time ago. And those bare wooden floors could use some bright throw rugs to liven them up."

She ran her gaze around the kitchen. "That stove has seen better days. We need to replace it with one of those new large ones in the stores these days. Their tops have more cooking space and are twice as large as that ancient thing." She gave the old one a scornful look. "They also have a water reservoir on the side, giving the cook an instant supply of warm water to clean up the kitchen and for bathing."

Raven looked down at the scarred table top, the cracked china off which they were eating supper. "I think it's time we get a new table and chairs, and these dishes are dangerous to eat off of. All kinds of dirt could be hiding in the cracks."

Mary was too astounded to vocally interject the thoughts that were running through her mind. Her eyes were also getting good excerise as they shifted from the young wife to the dark-browed husband.

When Raven asked, "What do you think, Mary? Aren't those good ideas?" the housekeeper looked at Chance as if for an answer, but received only silence from him.

"Never ask a man his opinion on decorating a house, Mary." Raven shook her head at the house-keeper. "They couldn't care less what their homes look like. After all, they don't spend all that much time at home. But," she added laughingly, "they can tell you every crack the town's saloon has in its floor, and how many stair steps it takes to reach a certain bedroom."

Mary's mouth flew open, and when Raven smiled sweetly at Chance, he threw down his fork and pushed back his chair with a loud scraping sound. Yanking his jacket and hat off the wall, he flung open the door. When he slammed it behind him, the whole door frame shuddered.

"My, oh my." Raven pretended surprise. "I wonder what set him off?"

"Now, Raven, you know very well what set him off," Mary replied gently. "Chance spends a lot of time at home. The thing is, he grew up with most of this furniture, and even these awful dishes, but man-like he's never noticed how run-down things were becoming.

"For years he's taken naps on that beat-up old couch, and the chair holds the shape of his body. They're like old friends to him. But that's not to say he'd mind you changing things if you didn't belittle all his favorite belongings. I'm sure you've heard the old saying about honey and vinegar.

"As for the stair steps in the saloon, don't put much faith in the gossiping you may have heard. I admit he drinks and brawls too much, but as to women, he's no better or worse than any of the other single men around here." Mary reached across the table and patted Raven's hand. "Now that he's married, Chance won't even look at another woman. He's a very honorable man."

"Time will tell." Raven pushed away from the table. "You go sit down, Mary. I'm going to do the dishes."

The cowhands were finishing their evening meal with a cup of coffee and a cigarette when Mel the foreman came into the cookshack after visiting the privy. "I guess the boss is in a big hurry to get to town. He just went racin' by like the devil had him by the tail."

"Chance ain't got half a brain in his head," Rufus

the cook said. "Goin' off and leavin' a pretty little thing like his wife alone on their weddin' night."

"It does seem mighty strange, but I guess the boss knows what he's doin'," the youngest cowhand said. "I guess we might as well get goin' too."

Chance beat his men into Bitter Creek by fifteen minutes. He had just enough time to order a bottle from the bartender and climb the stairs to Maudie's room. There, he discarded his jacket and hat, kicked off his boots and sat down on the edge of the bed. He swung his legs up, propped the pillows behind his back and uncorked the bottle. As he lifted it to his lips, he said sardonically, "Here's to you, my sweet little vicious bride."

Two hours and a half bottle later, Chance slid off the pillows and fell into a drunken sleep. When Maudie entered the room later, she shook her head sorrowfully as she took the bottle out of his hand and spread a blanket over him. "My friend, you're never gonna win her actin' this way," she said softly, then disrobed and climbed into the cot she occupied when Chance spent the night with her.

Chapter Twenty-three

Raven sat rocking by the fire, reliving one of the worst evenings of her life.

She had been quite satisfied with herself at first as she poured hot water over the pan of dirty dishes. She had riled Chance so, he had escaped to the bunkhouse. He could stew in the company of his men.

She had just dropped a bar of yellow lye soap into the water when galloping hooves had drawn her attention to the window. She'd been just in time to see Chance flash by on his stallion. Her jubilation had faded away with her next breath.

Her newly wedded husband was going to spend the night in his usual carousing fashion. With a sinking heart, she'd wondered if a woman would be included in his pleasurable diversions.

No doubt there would be. A tear slipped down

her cheek as she began to wash the dishes.

Raven took her time drying and putting everything away. She was in no hurry to join Mary, to see the pity that would be in her eyes.

She was taken aback when she took a seat in a matching rocker beside Mary. There was no pity in the look the housekeeper shot her. There was reproach.

"What? What did I do?" Raven squirmed uncomfortably. "I didn't tell him to ride off to the saloon."

"You might as well have. Chance will let you get away with a lot, but he has a limit. If you truly don't want your marriage to work, keep on doing like you did tonight. I promise you, it will work."

Before Raven could make excuses for her bad behavior, Mary had said a brisk good night and went to her room.

Now Raven fumed as she sat alone. Mary didn't know the whole story about her and Chance. She didn't know that brother Tory had forced Chance to marry her. She didn't know how that could shame a woman.

Maybe I did go too far, picking on his home. I wouldn't have done it if I didn't want to make him so mad he wouldn't want to share my bed. He might not love me, but he lusts for me, and I'm not about to let him use me, married or not. Her first husband, Milo Spencer, had used her, though not for his own pleasure. He kept her sitting beside him to draw men to his poker table.

"I won't dwell on that," Raven thought out loud.

"That's how I met Chance. And fell in love with him."

The clock struck ten and she realized that she had unconsciously been waiting for Chance to return home. With a long sigh she stood up. He wouldn't be coming home tonight.

Nevertheless, she laid a couple small logs on the fire and left the lamp in the kitchen burning just in case.

Chance awakened to a hard shaking of his shoulder. "Wake up, Chance." Maudie shook him again. "It's nine o'clock. You've got to get home."

Chance rolled over on his back and peered up at the aging whore out of red-rimmed eyes. He tried to speak but his mouth and throat were too dry. He started to sit up, then groaned and grabbed his head. It felt as if there were a hundred little hammers pounding inside it.

"Good Lord," he croaked, "how much did I drink last night?"

Maudie picked the whiskey bottle off the floor and held it up for him to see. "Half a quart," she said grimly. "I hope the lady is worth the suffering your stomach is goin' to experience today."

Placing the bottle on the table, she grabbed hold of Chance's hands and slowly pulled him up into an upright position. When he stopped groaning, she handed him a cup of coffee. "I put a lot of sugar in it to help sweeten your gut a little. Drink it down; then we must get you lookin' a little more presentable. If your wife could see and smell you now, she'd never want to lay eyes on you again."

"Hah!" Chance snorted. "I could look and smell like a fancy banker and she'd still never want to set eyes on me again."

"I don't believe that. The trouble with you two is you're both too proud and stubborn. If each of you would just give an inch, your marriage might have a chance."

"That's all you know," Chance grunted as he finished drinking the coffee. "This marriage was doomed before it started."

"Then why in the hell did you marry her?" Maudie demanded, her hands on her hips.

"Look, Maudie, I don't want you to spread around what I'm going to tell you," Chance said as he swung his feet to the floor. "The thing is, Raven's brother, Tory, caught us in bed together and marched us off to the preacher."

Surprise flashed in Maudie's eyes, then was quickly replaced by disbelief. "That's a bunch of hogwash if ever I heard it. Chance McGruder don't do anything he don't want to. It's not like you seduced a young virgin. From what I hear, your wife has been married before. So it was none of her brother's business if she wanted to go to bed with you."

"He did have a gun on me," Chance said lamely.

"As if that would make you marry a woman you didn't love. You know damn well you could have bluffed him out. Didn't your bed partner have anything to say?"

Chance grinned. "She was too busy trying to cover up her nakedness."

"She could have said something after she got her clothes on. Did she?"

Chance thought a minute, then said, "She told Tory that we couldn't get married because we didn't love each other. That made him all the more angry. He said that our lust might have put a baby inside Raven, and that there had never been any bastards in their family."

"Might she be carryin' your seed?"

Chance's face flushed a dark red. Looking away from Maudie, he mumbled, "It's possible."

"Yeah, I just bet," Maudie said wryly. "You lost control, didn't you, big man?" The aging whore sighed. "I guess what can't be remedied must be endured. Let's get you cleaned up so that you look half human when you get home. There's a basin of hot water on the washstand and a clean shirt I borrowed from the bartender."

"And, Chance," Maudie said before closing the door behind her, "work at making your marriage a success. You know damn well that you're crazy about her."

Chance kept the stallion at a leisurely walk as he rode homeward. Each step the animal took jarred his brain unmercifully. Even so, the cold, brisk air was chasing the cobwebs out of his head, allowing him to remember more clearly what an ass he had made of himself. He had acted like a pouting teenager, staying away from home all night. After all, it was his wedding night, regardless of whether he was going to share his wife's bed. He had shamed her badly, spending the night in a whore's bed.

Only he and Maudie knew that nothing went on between them; everyone else thought different. There would be a lot of talk, and eventually it would get back to Raven.

If that happens, he thought at the end of a long sigh, *the chance of a happy marriage between us will be nil.*

Chance left off thinking about Raven when his attention was caught by a distant horse and rider. They were traveling in the direction of the mountain. Cupping his hand against the sun and peering hard, he recognized the sorrel. The horse belonged to Jadine.

I expect she's going to visit that no-good brother of hers, he thought. *She must have a yen for one of his men . . . or the whole bunch, however many are holed up there.*

He'd be glad when the snow melted and they pulled out, he thought, taking the fork that led to his ranch. According to Uncle George, his stepson was bad medicine. The ranchers in the area would have to keep a sharp eye on their stock. His lips firmed in a tight line. If Carlin messed with Chance McGruder's herd, he would be one sorry man.

The ranch house came in view, and the closer Chance got to it, the more nervous he became. What kind of greeting would he receive from Raven? he asked himself. Would she give him one of those looks that set his teeth on edge? He had never before known a woman who could, with one look, make him feel like a mangy dog.

I probably look like one this morning, he thought,

rubbing a hand across his whisker-stubbled jaw.

The ranch house loomed in front of him, and with a sigh that came from the pit of his stomach, he swung out of the saddle and stepped up on the porch.

He tried to keep his eyes from kindling as he walked into the kitchen and Raven looked up from a pan of dishes she was washing. Her eyes swept over his scruffy appearance and he received one of the looks he had dreaded.

"Well, good mornin', Chance." Mary walked into the kitchen and gave him a crooked grin that said he was in trouble. "Have you had breakfast?"

"Yes," Chance lied, hoping that the women couldn't hear his empty stomach grumbling and rolling. He couldn't wait to get to the cookshack and have old Rufus fry him up a mess of eggs and bacon.

"How are you this morning, Raven?" Chance ventured to ask.

"I'm just fine," Raven answered coolly, not sparing him a glance.

"What about a cup of coffee?" Mary pressed. "It's still hot."

Chance shook his head, his eyes still on Raven's back. "I've got to go have a word with the men. I just stopped in to tell Raven that the next time she goes to town, she can buy anything she wants to spruce up the house. If the store doesn't have what she wants, it can be ordered for her."

"Now ain't that nice, Raven?" Mary went and stood beside Raven and gave her a coaxing smile.

Her only answer was an indifferent shrug of her shoulders.

Chance stood a moment, an angry flush coloring his face. He muttered something under his breath, then spun around and slammed out of the kitchen.

"Don't you agree that it's right nice of Chance to let you buy whatever you want?" Mary picked up a towel and began drying the dishes. "I don't know of any other man around here who would let his wife do that."

Raven gave Mary a look that said the housekeeper must be simpleminded, and retorted, "Do you know a single woman around here who would forgive her husband for sleeping with a whore on her wedding night?"

"Chance didn't do that." Mary looked appalled that Raven would think such a thing.

"Don't look so shocked, Mary. Your boss is no saint. This morning when I went to the cookshack to borrow a cup of sugar, I overheard the men inside talking about what happened in town last night. Even they were surprised that my new husband spent his wedding night with his favorite whore."

Annie pulled a chair away from the table and sat down, the dish towel lying limp in her lap. "I can't believe that," she said dazedly. "The men must be mistaken."

"How could they be mistaken? They were there when he went to this Maudie person's room and didn't leave it all night.

"Now you know why you didn't have any sugar

for your coffee this morning. After hearing the men talk about Chance, I couldn't bring myself to go inside and ask the cook for some."

"Just wait until I see him." Mary's face was flushed with anger. "He's going to get a tongue-lashing he won't forget for a long time."

"I'd rather you didn't say anything to him, Mary. I'd only listen to a pack of lies as he tried to deny everything. I want to live as peacefully as I can until the snow has melted and I can leave everything behind me . . . the pain, the disappointments, the shame."

"I hate to see you go, Raven." Mary's hands twisted the dish towel. "Do you have to leave the area? Can't you go back to your brother?"

Raven wished she could tell the nice woman that she was almost as mad at her brother as she was at her husband. It was Tory's fault that she was in this predicament. He had been so sure that she was carrying Chance's seed. She gave an inward laugh. Her menses had started this morning.

Raven looked at Mary, who was waiting for her answer, and said quietly, "No, I won't be going back to Tory. I want to get so far away from here I'll never see Chance McGruder again."

Mary gave Raven a pitying look. She had heard the underlying pain in her voice.

Chapter Twenty-four

When Jadine came to the foothills and the stallion began to climb, excitement grew inside her. Half an hour from now she would reach the outlaw shack, where the younger of her brother's men, Brady Clayton, was waiting for her. He had only recently turned eighteen and had the stamina of a young bull.

When Jadine arrived at the hideout and stepped inside the shack, she was shocked at the change in her brother's appearance. His face was bloated and hadn't been shaved for several days. But it was his eyes that held her attention. They had the look of a wild animal about to spring at a man's throat.

He's mad, she thought. Totally mad. She slid a glance at Brady and the other outlaw. She saw that they knew it also, and the wary look in their eyes said that they were afraid of Carlin.

Why? she wondered. They could always shoot him if he tried to kill them in one of his rages.

But they have no guns, she realized. She stared with shocked eyes at the men's empty holsters. Somehow Carlin had taken possession of their guns. The men were at his mercy.

The weight of her own gun in her skirt pocket felt very good.

"Jadine," Carlin barked her name, "have you been laying the groundwork for the job we're gonna pull off?"

"Yes, it's all set," she hurried to answer. "The Mexican knows what he must do. We're only waiting for the melt water to start flowing."

"Is George suspicious of anything? Did you stay home and butter him up like I told you to do?"

"I never set foot off the ranch until I rode up here today."

"That's good." Carlin nodded and seemed to relax a little. "The thaw should start in about three weeks." He turned to the older man and ordered, "Charley, make us some supper."

Charley jumped to obey the order, and soon the odor of beans heating and saltpork sizzling in a frying pan filled the shack. Jadine's nerves grew tight as Carlin drank freely from a bottle of whiskey. She wished she could go home tonight. But there would only be a sickle moon, not enough light to show her the way to the ranch.

Jadine's eyes narrowed in thought. Carlin, unstable as he was, could ruin the plans they had made. She had planned on getting rid of him after the ranch was hers, but it was clear that it had to happen sooner. She did not want him involved when they got rid of her stepfather. She would slip her gun to Brady and tell him what he must do.

As soon as the simple meal was eaten, Jadine and Brady went to the place behind the blanket. When they had hurried out of their clothes, Jadine held Brady off her until she explained what she wanted him to do. When she handed him the gun, the young outlaw gave her a wolfish grin.

"Nothing would please me more than putting a bullet in that crazy bastard's heart."

Raven swept the snow off her boots before entering the kitchen. "The snow has shrunk another couple inches," she called to Mary, who sat in front of the fireplace mending a shirt of Chance's. "Another three weeks or so and it will all be gone."

"I suppose you'll be gone too." Mary dropped the shirt in her lap.

"Yes." Raven hung up her jacket and hat, then joined the housekeeper. "And I can hardly wait. Each day it gets harder to stay on here."

"Have you decided yet where you will go?"

"No." Raven shook her head. "I know it's not logical, but I'd like to find a cave, crawl inside it and let the world pass me by for a few months."

Mary laughed. "You'd soon get tired of that."

"I know. I told you it wasn't logical." Raven stood up. "I have some mending to do, too."

She was on her way to her bedroom when a knock sounded on the kitchen door. "I'll get it," Mary said and laid aside Chance's shirt.

In her room, Raven stiffened when she heard

her brother greeting the housekeeper. She remembered he had said he would stop by in a couple weeks to see how she was faring.

Well, she wasn't faring well at all and she was going to tell him so.

Tory's eyes lit up when his sister walked into the room, her mending folded over her arm. "How are you, sis?" he asked. "I've missed you."

"Well, I haven't missed you," Raven said coolly as she resumed her seat and started rummaging around in Mary's sewing basket, looking for a needle and thread.

"You're still mad at me, aren't you?"

"Yes, I am. I have never been so miserable in my life. As soon as the snow is gone, I'm leaving here."

"I did what I thought best," Tory said in defense of himself. "I still think that you will thank me for it someday."

"Thank you for forcing me to marry a man who doesn't love me or want me? I don't think so."

Mary interrupted them by rising and leaving the room. When the door clicked shut behind her, Tory said, "I feel sure that Chance loves you. Maybe he doesn't let on because you don't give him any encouragement."

When Raven made no answer, only sat in stony silence, her brother added, "And I think that you care for him, but for some reason you're too stubborn to let it show."

Raven laughed hysterically. "So you think we are in love with each other. Explain to me then why my new husband preferred sleeping with a whore on our wedding night."

"You're crazy. Chance would never do that," Tory declared.

"Wouldn't he? Go to Bitter Creek and ask whose bed he slept in that night."

"I'll just do that," Tory replied.

"I hope you beat the hell out of each other," Raven muttered as she heard Tory say goodbye to Mary, then close the door behind him.

"Where will I go?" she asked herself, staring into the fire. Perhaps she should return to Clayton. At least she knew several people there; knew the owner of the saloon where her husband had dealt poker. As much as she had hated being a lure to her husband's poker table, she felt that for the time being she would have to do that again. She felt confident that if she approached one of her late husband's competitors, he would pay her well to lure customers to his table.

And it would only be a job. She'd make sure he understood that.

Raven laid her mending aside and walked into her bedroom. She lifted the lid of the large trunk at the foot of her bed. Kneeling on the floor, she began lifting the fancy dresses she had worn a lifetime ago, or so it seemed.

She examined each frock of satin, silk or sheer muslin and found them in excellent condition. She then carefully folded them back into the trunk, on top of her jewelry, silk stockings and high-heeled shoes. She closed the lid on the past, wishing it need not be resurrected in the not too distant future.

* * *

Tory's face was grim as he rode toward Bitter Creek. He usually kept a tight rein on his emotions and seldom lost complete control of his temper. But if today he found out that Raven's accusation against Chance was true, he'd beat the bastard into a pulp.

Tory was relieved to see only two horses tied up to the hitching rail in front of the saloon. He didn't want a large audience when he started making inquiries about Chance and the whore.

But how discreet could he be? he asked himself as he pushed open the saloon door. If what Raven said was true, everyone knew about it already.

He stood a moment in the dimness, glancing around the room. No one stood at the bar, but off to his right two men were playing cards; three tavern women were hovering around them. He crossed the floor to the bar, knowing that the whores would follow him.

In the time it took to order a drink he knew how he could get the information he sought. The bartender was pouring him a glass of whiskey when the trio moved in on him.

"How are you, Tory?" A chesty redhead purred as she leaned into him. "You must be cold after such a long ride. Would you like for Flossie to warm you up?"

When the woman ran light fingers over his fly, Tory knew who was going to give him the information he wanted. Besides, he hadn't had a woman for a week and he felt himself growing hard.

"That sounds real good, Flossie." He grinned

down at her. "Let's go see what you can do."

The other two women watched them climb the stairs with envious eyes. Tory McCloud was a close second to Chance McGruder in the bed department.

When the lusty Flossie had seen to his pleasure twice, Tory sat up and asked casually, "Who was the lucky one who slept with Chance the night of his wedding?"

Flossie gave a disgruntled laugh and said, "Maudie, of course. For some reason we girls can't figure out, that worn-out old hag has become Chance's favorite."

Flossie was too busy counting the money Tory had laid on the table next to her bed to notice how stiff Tory's back had become. Neither did she wonder at his abrupt leavetaking. She merely shrugged and put the money in the drawer of her nightstand.

Tory's horse was almost winded when he drew rein in front of the McGruder barn. As he swung to the ground, Chance came walking up from the corral where he kept his prize mares. "Hiya, Tory." His white teeth flashed in a welcoming smile. "Come on up to the house and warm up with a glass of whiskey."

"I don't have time." Tory walked toward him. "I only want to ask you one question."

Chance's face took on a wary expression. His brother-in-law wore a look of unbending resolve, as though he was ready to beard a lion in its den. "Ask away," he said, guessing what the question would pertain to.

"Did you shame my sister by sleeping with a whore on your wedding night?"

Chance prepared himself for the onslaught of Tory's fists as he answered, "Yes, I did, but it's not what you—"

Tory charged him then, much like a mad bull. Just as the hard fist was ready to land on his chin, Chance jumped to one side.

The momentum of Tory's mad rush carried him past Chance, and he went sprawling in the snow, face down. With the speed and agility of a cat, Chance was on top of him. He had no trouble grabbing Tory's right arm and pulling it behind his back.

"You're going to let me have my say." Chance jerked the arm up between Tory's shoulder blades. "Now," he panted. "It goes against the grain to tell you this, but I see no way of getting out of it.

"You know what a sharp tongue your sister has when she is angry. When we argued she made me feel like a low-down mangy dog. I was so mad I knew I had to get away from her, so I rode into town.

"Now, this is the part you will probably find hard to believe. First though, I want to tell you that I love Raven with every breath I draw, and that I haven't slept with a whore since I met her. But to save my foolish pride, I made a pact with Maudie. I would pay her for her time, but all I asked was to spend the night in her room, without touching her."

From the way Tory had stopped straining against him, Chance knew he was listening to his explanation. "When I rode into town that night, rage muddling my brain, I didn't stop to think how it would look when I bought a bottle of whiskey and went to Maudie's room." He paused, then added, "That's the size of it."

Chance waited for Tory to make a response, to say something, but he didn't utter a sound. After a moment his shaking shoulders said that he was laughing. "What's so funny?" Chance demanded.

"The idea of you humpin' old Maudie is the funniest thing I ever heard. You can let me up now, you big buffalo."

"Are you sure you're not going to swing at me again?"

"Yes, I'm sure. I guess I understand why you did something so foolish. A woman can drive a man crazy."

When Tory stood up, he rubbed his arm to get the blood circulating in it again, then brushed the snow off his clothes. "Do you know Raven plans to leave you as soon as the snow melts?"

Chance's face paled. "No, I didn't know, but I'm not surprised." He gazed out over the snow-covered land. "I can't let her go, but I don't know how to stop her."

"You've got less than three weeks to do something about her leaving here."

"I've run out of ideas how to win her over," Chance admitted, hopelessness in his voice. "I've tried courting her and making her jealous. I even told her she could buy all new furniture when she said she didn't like what was in the house. But anything I say or do seems to backfire."

"Did it ever enter your mind to tell her that you love her?"

"It has, but she would only laugh in my face. I hate to think what she'd do if she should learn about Maudie."

"She already knows about Maudie."

"Oh, God," Chance groaned.

"It's too bad she can't meet your favorite whore. That would convince her of your innocence more than a thousand words or acts."

A couple cowboys came from the bunkhouse and walked toward them. "I've got to get home," Tory said, swinging onto his mount's back. "Give some serious thought to what we talked about."

Chance's face was a picture of gloom as he watched his brother-in-law ride away.

Chapter Twenty-five

Raven gazed through the window at the muddy yard. It had rained steadily all day yesterday, and today a misty rain shrouded the valley. The grayness of everything seemed to reflect her feelings. All the snow was gone now, and it was time she was gone also.

She dreaded the solitary three-week trip ahead of her. She wondered if she would fool anybody, camouflaged as a young teenage boy. What if she should run into a bunch of outlaws and they decided to examine what the packhorse carried? What would they think of a trunk full of fancy dresses? How could she explain them away? Would they believe her if she said she had stolen them?

I'm just borrowing trouble, she told herself.

Chances are I won't run into anybody. But to be on the safe side, I'll keep my pistol handy.

Raven's thoughts moved to the supplies she had secretly prepared to load onto the packhorse. There were a small bag of coffee, cans of beans, a slab of salt pork, hardtack, clean underclothing, a bar of soap, washcloth and towel, a coffee pot, a pan to heat the beans in and a tightly sealed jar of matches. And last, her trunk and bedroll.

Everything was hidden in the barn under a pile of hay. She knew Mary would say nothing of her plans, but she didn't want Chance to know she would soon be gone. He was so unpredictable, she couldn't begin to imagine what his reaction would be.

Surprisingly, she hadn't had to worry about fighting chance off. Her husband now slept in the bunkhouse. He still took his meals with her and Mary, but he had little to say, speaking mostly to the housekeeper.

Like last night when Mary asked him if he had lost many cattle to the weather. He had answered, "Surprisingly, I only lost a few head. They wintered on the thickly wooded bottoms." He had looked at Raven when he added, "Tory's cattle have done the same thing. It will take us a week to separate them."

"Have you started yet?" Mary asked.

"We did a few yesterday. It was hard, with the rain and all. You have to go slow, be careful not to spook them. The mud is so deep and slick that if they ran, many of them would go down with broken legs. We'd have to shoot them then. I don't want to lose any more than necessary, and Tory can't afford to."

I must see Tory before I leave, Raven thought now. *There's no telling when we'll see each other again. He won't know, of course, that I am saying goodbye. Since I haven't said any more to him about leaving, he probably thinks I have given up the idea.*

Raven wondered how Chance felt about her. She couldn't tell by his face. His expression never showed what was on his mind. Even when she caught him giving her those fast glances, she could never read anything in his eyes. She was aware that he hadn't been to town in the last few weeks.

Raven suddenly had the urgent desire to be held and kissed by Chance once more before she went out of his life forever. How that might come about, she couldn't imagine. Mary was always with them.

A knock on the door brought Raven back to the present. She turned from the window and walked into the kitchen to open the door.

Jadine was in high spirits as she stood on Chance's porch, waiting for someone to answer her knock.

It was almost time to act on the plans made over the winter. Would everything go as plotted? she wondered. She knew that young Brady Clayton would take care of his assignment. He would delight in putting a bullet between her brother's eyes. As for Charley, the other outlaw, Brady would probably shoot him, too.

She was a little uneasy about Juan taking care of her stepfather. He had reluctantly agreed to drown George in the flooding river once she had lured the old rancher there. She would claim that a cow was caught in the branches of a tree that had been swept down the river. As for Brady, Juan wouldn't hesitate to shoot him. She had told Juan that the young outlaw had raped her.

So, she thought, with no expression of regret in her eyes, it would be up to her to do away with the man she had made love with so many times over the years. He was no longer any use to her. In fact, he would be a hindrance, so he must go. Nothing or nobody was going to keep her from achieving what she'd wanted for years. To marry Chance McGruder and combine their two ranches.

A malignant darkness clouded her eyes. There was one last thing that had to be taken care of. The woman Chance had foolishly married had to have an accident.

She would arrange for that later. Right now, she wanted to rile Chance's pretty wife, encourage her to leave his protection.

"Why, hello, Jadine," Raven said when she saw her caller.

"Hello," Jadine returned with a smile that did not reach her eyes.

"Come on in and get rid of your slicker, then sit by the fire and warm up."

When Jadine stepped into the kitchen, Raven helped her out of the rain slick coat and hung it on the coatrack beside the door.

Goodness, but she is thin, Raven thought, following her neighbor to the fireplace. She's got a shape like a gangly teenage boy. "Would you like some coffee?" she asked when Jadine seated herself in one of the leather chairs.

"I'd rather have a glass of Chance's good whiskey. I haven't enjoyed a snort of it in ages. You'll find it over there in that cabinet beneath the window."

"Yes, I know," Raven said, an irritated frown furrowing her forehead as she went to bring a bottle and glass from Chance's private stock. Her caller acted as though Chance's wife wouldn't know where her husband kept his spirits.

She had a sudden feeling that this wasn't a neighborly call from Jadine Walker.

She placed the whiskey and glass on the table beside Jadine's chair. Jadine lost no time uncorking the bottle and filling the short tumbler with amber liquor. After she had taken a long swallow, half emptying the glass, she swiped the back of her hand across her mouth and said, "I can't count the times Chance and I have sat here and got sloshed." She paused and looked at Raven, who sat quietly, her hands folded in her lap. "Chance and I go a long way back, you know."

"So you said. Actually, he has never mentioned you to me. Fact is, I know very little about Chance's past." Raven paused a moment, then boldly told her lie. "We only talk about our future together."

Raven knew she had hit a sore spot by the angry flush that spread over Jadine's face, and it pleased her that she had scored one for herself.

Retaliation came quickly. After giving a harsh laugh, Jadine said pityingly "You foolish woman.

You and Chance will never have a life together. Any day now he'll send you packing and dissolve this marriage he was pressured into." She took another long swallow from the glass, and then with a cruel twist of her lips, she said, "Chance must despise the sight of you. He and I planned on getting married come spring."

Raven wondered if Jadine's words could possibly be true. They seemed to explain so many things. Why Chance had never said he loved her. Why he used her as a paid whore, someone to spend his lust on until he could marry the woman he loved.

She knew that hearts didn't break, but she felt that hers was shattering, falling apart in little pieces. It had never entered her mind that there was another woman besides Sky in Chance's life, one that he planned on marrying. No wonder he always looked so angry.

While Raven searched her mind for something to say to this woman who plainly hated her, Mary came stomping into the room. With a furious look on her face, she grabbed Jadine by the arm and jerked her out of the chair. As she practically ran the woman to the door, she grated out, "Don't you ever come back here, you little troublemaker." She opened the door and gave the frightened Jadine a shove that sent her sliding across the icy porch. She grabbed Jadine's slicker and hat off the rack and flung them outside. When she had slammed the door shut, she panted, "Wait until Chance hears about this. He'll strip the hide off her."

"No, Mary, please don't say anything to Chance.

Don't even tell him she was here. I don't want to cause him more trouble."

Mary looked into her pleading eyes, then said reluctantly, "All right, if that's how you want it. But it's gonna gripe hell out of me, keeping my mouth shut."

"Thank you, Mary."

Mary nodded, stood a moment, her face showing that she wanted to say more, then with a sigh walked back into the kitchen.

Raven resumed her seat. When she saw the whiskey bottle and glass, she snatched them up and threw them into the fire. As the glass broke and the alcohol splashed on the fire, sending flames leaping up the chimney, she couldn't help comparing the shattered remains to her life.

She went into her bedroom, flung herself on the bed and let her pent-up tears soak the pillow. She could not put it off any longer. Tomorrow morning as soon as the gray dawn arrived, she would leave.

For the past three mornings Chance and his men had been up at dawn to hunt out the cattle that had hidden themselves all over the plains. It had been twice the work, having to separate his brother-in-law's cattle from his, and then keep them apart. Tory's steers wanted to drift back to the ones they had spent the winter with.

The animals had drifted into a large area heavily thicketed with chaparral and mesquite. The steers were wild as deer by now, and the men would have a devil's time chasing them out of the thorny protection they had found.

The men had encircled the dense thicket, a half mile long and a quarter mile wide. Shooting into the air and yelling at the top of their lungs, the men began to cautiously move into the herd's hiding spots. Angry and frightened, the animals bawled their distress and fought for every foot they had to give up.

It was noon by the time the mud-splattered, thorn-scratched men drove the last steer out into the open. Chance called to two of his men, "Tex, you and Rabbit keep them critters milling while the rest of us have lunch. You'll be relieved as soon as possible."

The cook had a hot meal and coffee waiting for the men. He had pulled down the tailgate of his cook wagon and built his fire under it. The fine drizzle of rain hadn't stopped for a moment. On top of the makeshift table, tin plates, flatware and cups waited to be used.

The first act of the men was a rush for the coffee pot. They curled their chilled fingers around the hot tin cups and sipped cautiously at the steaming brew. Meantime the cook was heaping beans and crisp salt pork onto the plates. Hard work meant hearty appetites, and he was generous with the food he dished out.

Within minutes the only sound to be heard was the scraping of spoons against the tin plates.

Their bellies full, the men built themselves cigarettes, taking long, satisfied draws. When Tory saw his two cowhands flip their smokes into the mud, where the drizzle soon put them out, he signaled to them to relieve the men watching the cattle.

A minute later, with heavy sighs the men remounted and rode out to find more cattle.

It was nearing sundown when, soaked and exhausted, Chance and Tory and their men turned their horses toward home. "A good long, hot bath sure will feel good," Tory said to Chance.

"I don't know if I have enough energy left to climb into a tub of water."

Tory grinned at the remark, and spurred his mount away from the others. "Say hello to Raven for me, will you, Chance," he called back over his shoulder.

Chance gave a dry grunt. It was next to impossible to say anything to his wife these days. She never even looked at him, let alone spoke to him.

Chance had ridden but a short distance when he heard several voices yell, "McCloud! There's a maddened devil of a bull charging your horse!" He left off thinking about Raven and looked ahead to see an old steer, with a set of horns that had a spread of at least six feet, galloping toward Tory's little quarter horse. He put spurs to his mount, but before the animal could surge ahead, the bull was upon its chosen victim.

Even as Tory pulled his gun, a long, sharp horn sliced across the racing horse's belly. The animal screamed in agony as it went down. Tory went down with it, but was immediately on his feet, his gun aimed at the spot between the bull's glaring, beady eyes. He squeezed the trigger. Nothing happened. The gun was wet and had jammed.

The bull was upon Tory then, a deadly horn ripping into his thigh as he was tossed into the air like a rag doll. When he slammed back onto the ground, a shot rang out and the bull dropped in its tracks. Through a haze of pain Tory saw Chance reholster his Colt, then come running up to him.

"The bastard got me good, Chance," he gasped painfully.

"He sure as hell did," Chance agreed, looking at the torn pants leg, which was already soaked with blood. Kneeling beside his brother-in-law, he said, "I'm going to use my belt as a tourniquet until we can get a doctor to stop the bleeding."

By now all the men were gathered around the downed man, and someone put a bullet through the little horse's head, ending his suffering. Just as Chance finished wrapping his belt around the wounded leg, the cook came running up with the wagon's tailgate under his arm.

"Get him onto this, Chance, then put him in the chuck wagon. I'll get him home in no time."

"I'll ride to town and fetch the doctor," one of Tory's cowhands said, and took off running toward his horse.

As several pairs of hands lifted Tory onto the board, he looked at Chance and said, "Bring Raven to my place. I want her to tend me."

Chance nodded, and the cook slapped the reins on the horses' steaming bumps. The wagon rolled slowly away, the cook taking as much care as he could to avoid ruts and gopher holes.

With a spring, Chance was in the saddle and the quarter horse's hooves sliced the sod and mud in chunks as he raced away.

Raven heard the thudding hooves approaching the house before she saw the horse galloping through the mud and water. She didn't recognize the horse, but the man urging him on she knew immediately. Those broad shoulders could only belong to Chance McGruder.

She set aside the broom she had been wielding against the clumps of mud on the porch and went inside moments before her husband brought the horse to a plunging halt in front of the porch.

Raven had barely closed the door behind her when Chance burst through it, almost knocking her over.

"Will you watch what you're doing?" Her eyes blazed at him. "You almost knocked me down, barging in here like that. Weren't you taught how to enter a house?"

"We have no time to discuss my upbringing," Chance shot back, his jaw tightening, his eyes glaring at her. "Tory's been gored by a bull. Get some clothes together while I go saddle your horse."

All color left her face as Raven choked out, "Is he badly hurt?"

Chance turned from the door and, looking at her pale, frightened face, said gently, "Yes, he is, but he's going to be all right."

Raven rushed around in her bedroom, hardly aware of what she was throwing into the large satchel. Her mind was on the brother who had mainly raised her. He had taught her how to read and write and do sums. He had taught her how to ride and fish and had even given her his vision of God. He explained that there was a Greater Being whom she would meet someday, and that He would judge her by her actions on earth.

And now it's my turn to take care of him for a change, she thought, forgetting at the moment the plans she had made for leaving Montana Territory.

She was waiting on the porch for Chance when he rode up, the reins of her gelding gripped in his hand. He reached down and took the bag from her, but before he could take her arm and assist her onto her mount's back, she had already swung into the saddle.

With a jab from their heels the two horses lunged away. Mary called from the porch, "I'll pray for Tory, Raven."

Raven and Chance arrived at the McCloud ranch only minutes before the doctor's buggy pulled into the muddy yard.

Dr. James Enlow, a no-nonsense man, nodded to the men standing around on the porch and stepped inside the house. Chance, standing in the bedroom doorway, turned and jerked his head over his shoulder. Enlow took one look at Tory's pale face and said to Cal and Raven, "You two can leave now."

"But he's my brother," Raven protested. "I want to stay with him."

"You'll just be a hindrance. I don't need a female fainting on me. Now skedaddle."

"I don't see why I can't—"

"Listen to the doctor, Raven." Chance took her by the arm and led her, still protesting, into the parlor. "He's right about you. You look faint. As soon as Tory is resting easy, you can go sit with him."

When Raven would have argued further, Chance walked back into the bedroom and closed the door behind him. Cal came to her and helped her out of the wet slicker, then led her to the fireplace. "Sit down and warm up, honey," he said gently. "Tory is going to be alright."

"But, Cal," Raven wailed as the old man pressed her down into a rocker, "didn't you see all the blood on his pants leg?"

"I saw it, but Doc will patch him up real good. He's a fine—"

Cal was interrupted when Chance opened the bedroom door again. "Cal," he said, "Doc needs a basin, a bottle of whiskey and a kettle of warm water. Right away."

When Raven started to stand up, Chance shook his head at her and closed the door.

She watched Cal carry the basin and whiskey into Tory's room, then the kettle of water. When he returned and sat down in the other rocker, they both stared at the door from which came the low murmur of voices. Chance passed through the parlor twice to empty the basin of bloody water.

The last trip through he said, "Everything is coming along fine. Doc is sewing him up now."

Raven wanted to ask him how badly Tory was hurt, whether he was in a lot of pain, but Chance had already gone back into the bedroom.

Cal rose to put more wood on the fire. When he sat back down he said, "Chance must have sent the men away. At any rate, they're gone. Including our two hands. The bunkhouse is dark, so I guess they'll be taking supper with Chance's men." After a while he said, "I know you're not hungry, but would you like a cup of coffee?"

"I'd appreciate that, Cal." Raven gave the old man a wan smile.

When the coffee was brought to her on a small tin tray, Cal had also made a beef sandwich and placed it alongside the cup. He hid a grin when Raven picked up the sandwich and bit hungrily into it.

She had just finished drinking the last of her coffee when Dr. Enlow came out of Tory's room, followed by Chance. "How is Tory?" she asked, leaning forward anxiously. "Was he badly gored?"

"Answering your first question, your brother is doing fine. I gave him some laudanum and he'll sleep for two or three hours. As for your last question, yes, the bull did quite a job on him. The beast's horn ripped him from just above the knee to midway up his thigh. It took twenty-four stitches to close the gash. Luckily, the wound wasn't deep, so he won't have to worry about infection.

"I left a bottle of medicine for the pain he is going to have for a couple days. Mix a spoonful in a glass of water and give it to him when he needs it."

"May I go see him now?" Raven asked.

Enlow nodded. "He won't know you're there, though." He scrutinized Raven's face, then said, "You look a little peaked. Why don't you go lie down and catch a nap while your brother is sleeping?"

Raven nodded that she would, but had no intention of doing so. She stood up and offered her hand to the doctor. "Thank you for coming out in this miserable weather to take care of my brother."

Chance watched Raven and the doctor shake hands and was struck by how thin she had grown. He hadn't looked closely at her for weeks, had only given her quick surreptitious glances. How unhappy she must be, he thought. As he walked the doctor to the door, he wanted to go into Tory's room and beat the hell out of him. Raven wouldn't look so unhappy now if her brother hadn't forced her into marrying a man she despised, even though she was drawn to him sexually.

Chance closed the door behind the doctor, and then with a heavy sigh he went to tell Raven that he was leaving, and that if she needed anything during Tory's convalescence she could send Cal to fetch him.

Raven was standing alongside the bed, gazing down at her sleeping brother, when Chance reached Tory's room. He stood in the open doorway gazing at her. His fingers were clenched in fists. He loved her, and wanted her with a passion that rocked his mind.

Raven became aware of his presence and turned around to face him. "I must thank you for all you've done today," she said stiffly.

Chance grinned ruefully. "No thanks are necessary. After all, he is my brother-in-law."

Raven gave a quiet, short laugh and said, "Only because he held a gun on you."

Chance stepped into the room and stood beside Raven. "It's time Tory realizes that his sister is a grown woman who can make up her own mind about what she does with her life." He gave he a wry grin.

"Thank you, Chance." Raven looked at him in surprise. "I couldn't have said that any better. I think, though, that Tory has learned a lesson. He won't be so fast to stick his nose into my business anymore. He knows he made a big mistake insisting that we get married."

"Was it such a big mistake, Raven?" Chance asked softly, taking her arm and turning her around to face him again.

"Well, of—" She got no further. Chance had grabbed her to him and covered her lips in a hot, searing kiss.

As usual, Raven's body heated to a fever pitch of passion and she pressed herself into him, returning his kiss with wild abandon.

Her arms were sliding up around his shoulders when he raised his head and said huskily, "I want you so, Raven. I need you so badly."

Raven stiffened, all the passion draining out of her. Love hadn't been mentioned in his passionate words. She braced her hands against his chest and

288

gave him a push that sent him stumbling backwards. As he gaped at her, stunned, she gritted out, "Take your lust to the woman you intend to marry as soon as you can get rid of me."

"What in the hell are you talking about?" Chance came toward her again.

"Don't act the innocent with me, Chance McGruder." Raven backed away from him. "Now get out of my house and never come near me again."

"You're crazy, do you know that?" Chance glowered at her. "Stark, raving mad. Don't worry about me ever coming near you again."

He was gone then, and Raven sat down on the edge of the bed, bitter tears running down her cheeks.

Chapter Twenty-six

Ten days had passed since Tory's injury by the bull. The doctor had removed his stitches two days ago, leaving a long, angry-looking scar. He was up, hobbling around, growling at everyone in sight. Being an outdoor type of man, he felt penned in like a wild animal in a cage.

Melt water formed streams that rushed down from the mountains, promising the worst flooding in history, according to old Cal. Tory wanted to be out with his men, checking on his cattle and the swollen river. He wanted to judge for himself if the rising water would endanger his herd, how much of the range would be submerged beneath it.

Raven's nerves were on edge also. Now that Tory was recovered, her thoughts returned to her plans of leaving the territory. She was all the more anxious to get away now, and as soon as possible. Dr. Enlow had dropped a stick of dynamite in her lap when he visited Tory last.

Luckily she'd been alone in the kitchen when the gruff man stopped to have a few words with her.

"How are you feeling, Mrs. McGruder?" he had begun the conversation.

"I'm just fine." Raven smiled at him and added, "Now that I know my brother is going to be alright. At first I was so nervous and afraid for him I actually vomited every day."

"My dear woman," Dr. Enlow said with wry amusement, "I doubt you lost your meals from worrying about your brother. It's only natural that in your condition you would do that."

"My condition? What do you mean, my condition?" Raven frowned at the doctor.

"Dammit, woman, you're a newlywed wife. It's very probable that you are with child."

"No, I'm not. I had my menses after . . . after the . . . the last time I had . . . had relations with my husband."

"Did it last long? Was it a regular menstrual flow?"

"Well, no." Raven thought back. "It only lasted a couple days, but . . . ."

"It's not unusual for that to happen," the doctor interrupted. "I'd lay odds you are with child," he said. "I wondered if you might be the night I came to tend your brother."

Raven, her face drained of color, reached blindly for a chair and sat down. The doctor said something to her before he left, but none of his words registered. *You are with child, you are with child*, kept ringing in her ears.

Now, as she prepared the evening meal, Raven plotted what excuse she could give for returning to the McGruder ranch. She had to retrieve the trail provisions she had stashed away in the barn.

A plan came to Raven as she was dishing up a large bowl of stew to place on the table. Around two o'clock this coming morning she would ride to the McGruder place, get everything strapped onto the packhorse and head out from there.

The two cowboys came in for their supper, smiling shyly at Raven. Tory and Cal joined them shortly at the table and started passing the food around. Raven sat quietly at the foot of the table, half listening to them talk about the condition of the flooding river.

"The Old Missouri is deceitful and treacherous, like a bad woman," Cal said. "Give it half a chance and it will grab you, drag you down to its muddy bottom and never let you go."

As Raven picked at the food on her plate she remembered that she and Tory had crossed the river on the way to Cal's ranch. But that had been downstream a ways. She hoped it wasn't flooded down there.

The men continued to talk long after they had finished eating. Tory wanted to know every little detail about his cattle, and swore more than once because he wasn't able to ride a horse and see things for himself. The doctor had said he wasn't to ride for at least two weeks, that the stitches might break and he would start bleeding again.

Raven didn't care how long the men discussed business. She took the opportunity to brew another pot of coffee. She would need several cups to keep her awake until it was time to ride to the McGruder ranch.

The cowboys finally left, and Tory and Cal went into the parlor. Sitting in front of the fire, they continued to talk cattle and flooding water. Raven gave the kitchen a good cleaning, thinking it would be the last one it would get for a while. Not until Tory got married, if he ever did.

Before she joined her brother and the old man for the last time, Raven went to her room and laid out the clothing she would change into in the next few hours. A ladies' union suit was spread on the bed, woolen trousers and a heavy flannel shirt. She added last a pair of gray woolen socks.

The men were hardly aware of her coming into the parlor and sitting down on the raised hearth. She gazed at her brother through lowered lashes, thinking how much she would miss him, how much she loved him even though he was the cause of her dilemma. When at last he and the old man stood up, ready to go to bed, she gave Tory such a hug, he grunted. He grinned and said, "You haven't given me a squeeze like that since you were a pesky little girl dogging my footsteps." She even kissed Cal on the cheek, making him duck his head in embarrassed pleasure.

Raven sat down in her brother's rocker to watch the clock. She had said her goodbyes.

* * *

Raven gave thanks for the full moon as she led Sam out of the barn. It was so bright outdoors, the house and outbuildings stood out in bold relief. Even the branches on the three tall pines at the corner of the house were plainly discernible.

She led the gelding several yards from the barn before mounting and urging him into a canter with a jab of her heels. Riding across the range, she thought of her brother peacefully asleep, and of the note she had left propped against the kitchen lamp. It was brief, telling him only that now that he was on the mend, she was going on with her plan of leaving. She wrote that he shouldn't worry about her, that she would be alright.

When the McGruder ranch buildings came in view, Raven steered the stallion to the right and pulled up behind the barn. All was quiet as she dismounted and tied him to a tree.

Inside the barn, Raven bridled the packhorse, then struggled her belongings onto his back. When it was all tied down securely, she quietly led the sturdy horse outside to where Sam waited for her.

According to the position of the moon, it was about three o'clock when she quietly rode away, leaving the moonlit yard empty once more.

Jadine awoke to the roar of rapidly moving water. "Melt water!" she whispered hoarsely as she sat up. "And very close." She grabbed Brady's naked hip and shook it hard. He turned over on his back and reached for her.

"No, you damn fool," she whispered. "Don't you hear that roaring sound? It's flood water and it's nearby. We've got to get out of here, and fast." She got up on her knees and began feeling around for her clothes.

Brady was wide awake now and very aware of their danger as he, too, began groping for his clothes where he had laid them at the foot of the pallet. He hurried into his clothes and was strapping on his holster when Jadine, shrugging into her jacket, said in a low voice, "You know what you have to do before we leave."

Brady nodded and drew his pistol. He jerked the blanket aside, and in the shaft of moonlight striking through the small window, walked over to the sleeping men he had ridden with for four years. Their rest wasn't a natural one, it was more like a drunken stupor. Her brother and Charley were in the habit of drinking themselves to sleep every night.

As they lay there, mouths open and snoring, Brady got off two quick, deadly shots.

"Come on, let's get out of here." Jadine had to raise her voice to be heard over the increasing roar of the water rushing down the mountain.

The four horses tethered behind the shack were terrorized by the danger they sensed and were whinnying and lunging against the strong ropes that kept them prisoners.

Although Brady hadn't shown any compassion for the men he had killed in cold blood, he drew his knife and freed the dead men's horses so that they could escape the raging waters.

It took ten nerve-wrecking minutes for Jadine and Brady to get saddles on their rearing mounts, climb onto their backs, then lean over and free them from the tree. The animals needed no urging to run madly down the mountain trail, the raging water almost at their heels.

"This way," Jadine yelled, turning her stallion off the beaten track. She knew the mountains well. She had climbed all over this area with Chance when they were teenagers. She led the race to a gap in the mountain where the snow had long since melted. She shuddered when she heard the cracking up of the shack as it was swept away in the angry, rushing water.

When she and Brady reached the foothills, they reined in and watched the water spreading out over the range, rushing toward the river. "What do we do now?" Brady looked at Jadine for guidance. "Our plans have been knocked cockeyed."

"Let me think a minute," Jadine said impatiently, her eyes narrowed in thought as she looked down at her stepfather's holdings.

Her gaze lit on an old two-room log cabin a quarter mile away from the big house George McGruder called home. In his younger years, while he was getting started, he and his first wife had made the small place their home. Over the years it had been the catch-all for discards of every kind. Jadine's lips twisted in a half smile. It was the perfect place for Brady to hide until she set her plan in action.

"See that log house sitting off by itself?" She turned to Brady. "You can hole up there until we're ready to set everything in motion."

"How long will that be?" Brady frowned, not at all happy with the idea of having only his own company to pass the time.

"It won't be long. The river is out of its bounds already. I need to talk to the Mexican, make sure he understands what he has to do. You keep an eye on the house and barn, and when you see me and the old man ride out and head for the river, follow us."

Jadine watched Brady's face closely as she said, "Tell me what it is that you're to do after that."

"I am to hide in the willows at the bend of the river, and after this Juan drowns the old man, I'll put a bullet in the Mex's head."

"Good." Jadine smiled. "I'll get some food and blankets to you as soon as possible." She reached across to stroke the bulge in his crotch. "Of course I'll spend the nights with you." She licked her tongue across her lips suggestively.

"You damn well better," Brady growled, and with a laugh Jadine kicked her heels into the stallion and raced away.

It was daylight when Jadine rode up to the barn and drew rein. There was no one around as she unsaddled her horse and led him into one of the stalls. She was not surprised at the absence of all the cowhands. Everyone would be out on the range, keeping an eye on the cattle and the flooding water.

She was relieved to find the house empty also. She needed to take a hot, soaking bath before she ran into Juan. If he smelled Brady's spent passion on her, she'd have a devil of a time explaining the stench. He might even refuse to take part in doing away with her stepfather. He was already reluctant to do it.

A sly smile twisted the corners of her lips. She knew just what to say to him. Words that would make him do anything for her.

The remnants of a hurriedly eaten breakfast remained on the table, and as Jadine heated water on the stove, she filled a plate with cold bacon and scrambled eggs. By the time she had sated her hunger, the two big pots of water were sending off steam. She dragged the wooden tub out of the storage room and placed it near the stove. She emptied the hot water into the tub, then tempered it with a bucket of cold water. Dropping a washcloth and a bar of yellow lye soap into her bath, she stripped off her soiled clothes and stepped into the tub.

"Juan," George McGruder called to his horse wrangler, "bring us some fresh horses, will you?"

The Mexican gathered the horses that were spent from chasing cattle away from the dangerous waters, and led them into the barn for a rest and a feedbag of oats. As he was taking care of the animals, his gaze lit on Jadine's stallion in its stall. His brown eyes sparkled. His love was home from visiting her brother. He was soon approaching the ranch house at a half run, eager to make love to Jadine.

He burst into the kitchen just as Jadine stood up in the tub. She opened her arms as he rushed to her. He kissed her lips, then knelt and, heedless of the water running down her body, kissed her throat, nuzzled her wet breasts, drawing the nipples into his mouth, sucking and nipping at them.

He stood up at last, a glazed look in his eyes as he scooped Jadine up in his arms and carried her into her bedroom.

Half an hour passed, and Juan rolled off Jadine for the second time. When his breathing had returned to near normal, she asked, "What is the condition of the river?"

"It's bad and getting worse by the hour." He gave a disgusted snort. "I think cattle are the dumbest animals in the world. The men spent hours keeping them out of the flooding river."

"I suppose there's a lot debris floating down."

"There sure is. Everything from small uprooted trees to parts of an old log cabin. I'm not sure, but I thought I saw the body of a man in the broken-up building as it floated by."

Jadine thought briefly, uncaring, that the dead man was probably Charley or Carlin. She moved closer to Juan and laid her head on his shoulder. "The time is near for what we must do. You know that, don't you?" she asked, stroking her fingers through the hairy patch on his chest.

"I've been thinking on that, Jadine." Juan frowned up at the ceiling. "Mr. McGruder has always been good to me. He's been a friend. I just don't know if I could bring myself to drown him."

"Of course, he's been good to you, you fool," Jadine snapped in angry impatience. "You've worked like a dog for him most of your life. Has he given you your own little house like he has some of the older white hands? He has not," she answered her own question. "You're still living in the same room in the barn as when you first came here."

"That's not quite true. I've stayed in the barn because it made it easier to see you."

"Look, Juan"—Jadine tried to keep her voice calm as she rolled over on her back—"if you've decided that you don't want to marry me after all, just come right out and say so."

"Jadine, my love," Juan said, leaning over her, "you know I want that more than anything in the world."

Jadine took his hand and laid it on her stomach. "I'm glad to hear you say that, for lying beneath your hand is your son or daughter. I want more for it than a three-walled shack in Mexico. I want it to be brought up here on this ranch the same way I was. I want my sons to inherit it when we're gone. And, Juan, none of this can happen if George McGruder isn't done away with. He would disown me if I should marry you while he's still alive."

The adoration he felt as he gazed down at Jadine blinded him to the calculation in her eyes, the lie she had just told him. "You are right, my love," he whispered, and bending his head, he kissed her stomach. "Our children must have much more than I have ever had. But is this the only way?"

Jadine forced back an impatient sigh and thought quickly. She would have to rearrange her plans. "One of my brother's men can do the actual killing. Once he has taken care of George, all you'll have to do is shoot him. He must die. He wants part of the ranch and will blackmail us if we don't give it to him."

Juan was so busy trying to remember all that Jadine was saying, it didn't enter his mind to wonder why the stranger would feel that he should have a part of the ranch.

"We'll do it tomorrow morning, early, when the men are out on the range. And now you'd better get the fresh horses to the men before they come looking for you."

Jadine sighed when she heard the kitchen door close behind Juan. She'd had serious doubts about his following her orders to do away with her stepfather. But the story about her carrying his child had done the trick, as she had thought it would. There was no end to the things he would do for her now.

She slid off the bed, pulled open a dresser drawer, and took clean underclothing from it. She must get dressed and take a bedroll and some grub to Brady.

It seemed a shame to waste food on him, she thought as she stepped into her riding skirt. He wouldn't be needing any food after tonight. But knowing that she had to keep up a pretense of caring for him, she made some thick beef sandwiches and wrapped them up, then measured coffee grounds into a cloth bag. In the storage room she unearthed the battered coffee pot George always took with him when he went on one of his hunting trips with Chance. His bedroll was lying on the floor and she picked that up too. Her lips twisted wryly. He wouldn't be needing either one anymore.

The one thing Jadine did regret as she headed her stallion in the direction of the old cabin was that tonight would be the last time she could wear herself out with Brady. She was going to miss him in that respect. He was the best she'd ever had.

As she neared the cabin where Brady was waiting, Jadine remembered the new cowboy her stepfather had hired recently. He was young and virile and would probably replace Brady quite nicely.

Chapter Twenty-seven

A knock on the door awakened Cal. He rolled over on his back and listened for Raven to answer the caller. As he waited he sniffed the air and thought it was strange that there was no aroma of brewing coffee and frying bacon.

When the rapping came again, this time a little louder, Cal crawled out of bed, grumbling, "Hold your horses." Walking into the kitchen he was struck with the fact that not only had Raven not started breakfast, she hadn't even made a fire in the big black range.

He opened the door and muttered to the two cowboys who had come for their breakfast, "Come on in. I guess Raven has overslept. I'll get a fire started, then go wake her up."

The two cowhands sat down at the table, and the one called Chuck picked up the slip of paper propped against the lamp. He ran a brief glance over the note and said, "I think you'd better take this to Tory, Cal."

Cal read Raven's letter twice, then, shaking his head, hurried out of the kitchen. "Read this, Tory," he said, bursting into Tory's room.

Tory took the sheet of paper thrust at him. "Damn," he exclaimed, sitting up and crushing the message in his fist after reading it. "I thought she had given up on that crazy notion."

"Are we gonna go after her?"

"I'm dammed if I know what to do." Tory carefully swung his injured leg to the floor. "I interfered with her life before, which was a big mistake. If I'd minded my own business, Raven wouldn't be running away now. Besides, I wouldn't even know where to begin looking for her, even if I was able. And let's say that I was lucky enough to find her. I couldn't make her return home with me. I've realized that she's not a little girl anymore and she can do as she pleases."

"You gonna tell Chance that she's gone?"

"I don't think so," Tory said after a thoughtful pause. "He might think that I expect him to go after her."

"Of course, if you should run into him and the occasion arises, you can mention it."

"I think you're wrong not to tell him," Cal said. "He might track her down and we'd know where she is, and if she's all right."

"I feel in my heart that she'll be alright. Raven always had good common sense. I'm the one who is a dunderhead. I guess you'll have to be cook again," Tory said, switching the subject, letting it be known that he would say no more about his sister.

But when Cal left the room to start breakfast, Tory sat for a long time staring down at the floor. Where had his unhappy sister gone? He hoped she hadn't gone back to Clayton where he had found her. There was only one way she could make a living there, and Raven had hated being bait to draw men to a poker table.

Tory cursed the leg that kept him from saddling up and riding off to find his sister. He cursed Chance McGruder then for not being a good husband. And last, he cursed himself for putting her in this predicament.

The odor of burning bacon drifted into his room, and shaking his head, Tory began to get dressed. He might as well get used to old Cal's cooking.

Raven pulled Sam in and looked down into a valley, a wild and lonely place. The only movement was a soft breeze stirring the tall grass and early wildflowers.

She turned around in the saddle and looked behind her. The towering mountains of Montana, wild and remote, brooded in silent majesty. Although it was too far away for her to see it, she knew that east of the mountains there was lush prairie grassland where herds of cattle grazed. Her brother's cattle, as well as her husband's.

Raven looked up at the sun that would set in another hour and visualized Tory and Chance and their cowhands coming in from the range, hungry as bears. She felt a jab of guilt when she thought of the supper Tory and his men would have to eat. Neither her brother nor old Cal could cook worth spit.

Chance's men would eat well; they had a cook. And of course Mary would see to it that Chance had a hearty meal. What had he felt when he learned that she was gone? she wondered.

A bitter sigh escaped her. If he felt anything, it was probably relief. He could divorce her for desertion and be free to marry Jadine.

She still couldn't believe that a woman like Miss Walker would appeal to Chance. She looked so used up. Of course, a person couldn't help whom they loved. She should know that. Hadn't she fallen in love with a man who was the worst kind of husband material?

The sun had sunk a little lower when Raven heard the rush and roar of the Missouri. She grew uneasy. She had thought, had hoped, the river would be safe to cross down here.

Fifteen minutes later, Sam and the packhorse topped a knoll and Raven caught her breath as she gazed down on the muddy, turbulent waters of the Missouri. With a sigh she lifted the reins, gave the pack horse's lead rope a jerk and sent both animals down the slight hill toward the roiling water. The river had to be crossed if she was to get to Clayton.

Sam seemed to sense her uneasiness as he nervously picked his way over the debris thrown up on the bank. "I know you don't like it any better

306

than I do." Raven patted the horse's quivering neck. "I want to find the best possible spot for us to cross."

She found none. As far as she could see down the river there was no change in the width of the water, or its strength. She sighed again and with a shiver of dread prodded the reluctant Sam into the river. The current bore in on them and the horses fought it. Step by step they moved over the slippery bottom before they were forced to begin swimming.

Raven began to breathe more easily. They were more than halfway across the river and both animals were swimming smoothly. It happened then. Swirling around a bend in the river came an uprooted tree, its branches black and bare as though they were reaching out for her. Sam whistled a frightened whinny and strained against the reins held tightly by his white-lipped mistress.

Raven leaned forward to pat his quivering neck and to speak soothingly, "We're almost on the other side, boy. We're doing just fine." But when the tree was almost upon them, the terrified gelding reared up on his haunches and the reins tore loose from her grip. At the same time, the packhorse jerked the lead rope out of her hand.

Raven slid down over Sam's rump, grabbing at his tail. She missed, and as she floundered in the water both animals struggled out of the river and tore off across the prairre. The tree was only feet away now and she swam frantically to get out of its way. She only partially succeeded. A limb caught her left arm, tearing the sleeve off her jacket, and a larger one rammed into her hip. The cottonwood swept on by then, leaving her to fight the turbulent waters as she strained to get to the opposite shore.

Her arms became leaden, and for every foot she gained she was pushed back two.

"I'll never make it," she panted. "I'm going to drown in these muddy waters. I'll never again see my brother's laughing eyes, never again feel my husband's arms around me."

Raven was ready to give up, to let the river have her, when she heard a feminine voice shouting, "Stay clear of that rapids!"

She hadn't heard the rapids before as she concentrated on reaching the opposite bank, but she heard its roar now. Realizing there was another human being nearby gave her the determination to hang on, to keep pulling with her arms and kicking with her feet.

"You're not going to make it," the voice called. "I'm going to throw you a rope. Tie it around your waist and my horse will pull you out."

Amy Mitchel twirled the loop in the air a couple times, then sent it sailing toward the bobbing head. It landed short of the fingers reaching for it. But the second throw was successful. The woman was just a few yards from the rapids when she caught the lasso and fastened it around her waist. Amy spoke a command to her pinto and he began to slowly walk backward, pulling the almost limp body from the water as he moved.

Amy swung out of the saddle and hurried to the

woman who lay so still. Squatting on her heels, she pushed the wet strands of hair off the pale face and felt for a pulse in the limp wrist. She nodded her head thankfully when she felt a steady throb beneath her fingers. "Let's get the water out of you now," she said and rolled the woman over on her stomach. She coughed and river water spewed out of her mouth and onto the grass.

"Are you alright?" Amy asked when the slim body no longer heaved.

"Yes." The word came weakly. "Just worn out."

"I'm not surprised," Amy said, helping her to roll over on her back. "Do you think you can stand and get on my horse? You must get out of those wet clothes as soon as possible."

"I'll make it." Amy took hold of her hands and tugged her to her feet. As they moved slowly to the pinto, the woman asked, "I don't suppose you saw my gelding and packhorse?"

"No, I haven't." Amy boosted her into the saddle, then climbed up behind her. Gathering the reins and nudging the pinto into motion, she said, "My name is Amy Mitchel. I have a small spread a couple miles from here. Maybe they'll wander over there. I caught a wild mare a couple months ago and she's in heat now. Grit here wants to get to her in the worst way," she added with a laugh.

"I'm Raven . . . Raven Spencer." She hesitated over her last name. "I was on my way to Clayton when Sam spooked at a tree sweeping down the river while we were crossing."

"So you're from Clayton. Were you visiting friends or relatives around here?"

"Yes. My brother. He has a ranch in the Bitter Creek area," Raven answered, becoming uneasy at the young woman's questions. She didn't want to leave any clues behind her in case Tory came looking for her in Clayton.

But Amy, as though sensing that Raven was reluctant to talk about herself, didn't ask any more questions.

By the time they reached the small cabin sitting snugly in a stand of pines, Raven's body was shaking uncontrollably. Raven slid off the horse and practically fell into the girl's arms. "Ike, come help me!" Amy yelled, about to fall down from the dead weight.

"What's wrong?" Ike burst through the door. "Yellin' and screechin' like somebody was beatin' your hound."

"Can't you see I've got a half-dead woman hanging on to me?"

"Danged if you don't." Ike came down the two steps as fast as his heavy weight would allow. "Where did you find her?" He scooped Raven into his arms and stepped back up on the porch.

"I pulled her out of the river." Amy followed him inside, then led the way to her bedroom. When she began to undo the buttons on the wet clothing, Ike turned and left the room. "Pour a cup of coffee and put a good-sized slug of whisky in it," Amy called after him.

By the time Amy had helped Raven into one of her flannel nightgowns and tucked her into bed, Ike returned with the whiskey-laced coffee.

"I put a couple spoonsful of sugar in it," he said,

setting the cup on the bedside table. "Something sweet is good for shock."

Amy looked at the steam rising from the drink and said, "While it cools a bit, I'll towel some of the water out of her hair."

"Who is she? Did she say?"

"Her name is Raven Spencer. She's been visiting a brother."

Raven was aware that her hair was being combed and rubbed with a towel, but she didn't let on. She was too tired to talk, and her body was one big ache.

As she lay there, giving herself over to Amy's ministrations, she worried about the baby she was carrying. Was it still lying beneath her heart, or had she lost it in her battle with the river? She had no way of knowing. She grasped at the thought that she wasn't bleeding and that there was no pain in her lower regions. Wouldn't there be if she had suffered a miscarriage?

Raven said a silent prayer that she hadn't lost Chance's child. It was so important that she have a piece of him through the years ahead.

"Raven, that's about as dry as I can get your hair for the time being," Amy said, breaking in on her somber thoughts as she laid aside the comb and towel. "Anyhow, I think your coffee has cooled enough for you to drink."

Raven pushed herself up in bed and took the proffered cup. The dark liquid was sweet and bracing, and a relaxing warmth spread through her body. By the time the cup was empty, she was yawning. Amy took the cup from her and suggested, "Why don't you lie back and get some sleep, rest your body. We'll talk more in the morning."

Amy barely finished talking before Raven was snuggled under the covers and nodding off to sleep.

"She's awfully pretty, isn't she?" Amy said to Ike, who had entered the bedroom and stood beside her.

"She is that. Now that you've cleaned her up and combed her hair, I recollect that I've seen her before. I seen her once in Bitter Creek. She was buyin' some gee-gaws in the general store there."

"Let's let her sleep now. Her body needs rest," Amy said and led the way out of the room.

Chapter Twenty-eight

Jadine awoke early, her nerves already tingling. If everything went as planned today, her life would take a dramatic turn. Not only would she be the richest woman in Montana Territory, she would also see the fulfilment of a dream she'd had since she was seventeen. Chance McGruder would be her husband. They would combine the two ranches and control thousands of acres. The area women would no longer curl their lips at her, draw aside their skirts when they met her on the sidewalk. They wouldn't dare do that to Mrs. Chance McGruder.

When Brady turned over on his side, facing her, and placed his hand between her legs, Jadine slapped it away. She had spent the night in the two-room cabin pleasuring herself with the young outlaw, but she had no patience for him now.

313

"There's no time for that this morning," she said firmly. "We've got to be alert." She didn't say that she had to get to the barn to make sure that Juan wasn't weakening.

As she untangled herself from the blanket that was wrapped around her legs, she said to the disgruntled Brady, "Remember, you're not to take your eyes off the ranch house. As soon as you see me and George ride out, you follow us."

"How could I forget it?" Brady flung an arm over his head. "You've told me often enough."

"I know," Jadine softened her voice, "but our whole future together hinges on everything going right today."

Fifteen minutes later she was entering Juan's room, which always smelled slightly of the stables. She undressed and crawled into bed with him. When he continued to snore she laid her hand on his limp sex. Her fondling fingers brought him awake immediately. Unlike her rejection of Brady earlier, Jadine didn't object when Juan covered her body with his. She had to handle her long-time lover in a different way. He had to be brought to a white heat and kept there to make sure he didn't back out at the last minute.

She allowed him only one release to make sure she left him wanting more. For good measure, she said as she got back into her clothes. "Make sure everything goes right, Juan. Our children's future depends on what you do today."

Jadine didn't go directly to the house when she left Juan. Instead, she rode along the swollen river looking for the best spot to lure George McGruder to his death.

She found it. A perfect place about half a mile from the ranch house. A patch of young willows were half submerged under water. If a cow was driven among them, it could easily be caught among the branches and held fast.

She looked up at the old log cabin, then at the small window in Juan's room. She hoped that both her henchmen were doing as she had ordered them. Her gaze ranged over the nearby area. When she saw a young yearling, she spurred the horse toward the animal. Cutting it away from its companions, he soon had the frightened animal floundering among the branches, bawling its distress.

That taken care of, Jadine raced toward the house, frantically calling George's name.

"What in tarnation are you screeching about?" George stepped out on the porch.

"There's a yearling caught in the willows at the river," Jadine answered in an agitated voice. "I tried to free her but I couldn't. You'd better hurry, the water is rising fast."

George reached into the kitchen and took his jacket off the wall, saying, "Come on, let's go."

Jadine cast a fast glance at the cabin as she and George thundered toward the river. Her lips curled in satisfaction. Brady, at a slower pace, was riding toward the willows also.

Everything is going as planned, she gloated to herself when from the corner of her eye she saw

Juan leave the barn and ride toward the willow copse.

Reaching the river, Jadine and George leapt off their mounts. They waded into the water together, making their way to the bellowing yearling. From the corner of her eye Jadine saw Brady ride up to the riverbank about fifteen yards downstream. She saw him raise his rifle and aim it across the water at George. But before he could squeeze the trigger, a shot rang out. His body jerked, then fell from the saddle and into the river.

As Jadine watched the river grab Brady and sweep his lifeless body downstream, she raged helplessly at Juan. The idiot had shot too soon.

"Who was that?" George grunted as he wrestled with the yearling.

"I-I don't know," Jadine stammered. Everything was going wrong. She scanned the bank for Juan.

She saw him ride up then, but instead of dismounting he sat looking apologetically at her. *The bastard,* she inwardly raged. *He shot early on purpose. He didn't want George to die. He has lost his nerve just I should have known he would.*

"By God, I can do it myself," she muttered with a swelling strength inside her. She bent over and thrust a hand into the water, feeling its muddy bottom. Her fingers touched a rock. It was large, and she needed both hands to free it of the mud. She grappled it free, and with ruthless determination moved in on her stepfather, whose whole attention was on the yearling.

She stood a moment in the thigh-high water,

then, oblivious to Juan's protests, she brought the rock down on the gray head.

Jadine couldn't believe that she had only stunned George. She had hit him hard enough to kill him. As he stumbled toward the bank, she jumped on his back and brought him face down in the water. In his weakened condition, it wasn't hard for Jadine to hold his head under water until he stopped struggling.

Juan was openly crying and making the sign of the cross as he prayed when Jadine released the rancher. She gave Juan a cold, scathing look, then before his terrified eyes she drew her pistol and shot him in the head. She shoved the gun back in its holster and watched the river grab Juan's body and carry it downstream until it was swept out of sight.

Jadine waded out of the water and climbed onto her stallion's back. She spurred him in the direction where she knew Chance was holding his cattle.

Chance saw Jadine racing toward him and rode out to meet her. "What's wrong?" he asked as they both pulled their mounts in.

"It's your uncle," Jadine panted. "He was trying to free a yearling caught in a willow patch and it trampled him so badly, I'm afraid he's dead."

Chance's face paled beneath his tan. "Take me to him," he said hoarsly.

It took but a short time to reach the place in the river where the yearling bawled and George's body was caught up against it.

As Chance waded toward his uncle, he knew he was dead before he reached him. The old gray head was too smashed in for him to still be alive. He pulled a knife from its sheath on his boot and cut away the branches that held the yearling. When it went splashing up onto the bank, he gathered the limp body of his uncle in his arms and waded ashore with it.

"Ride and tell Uncle George's men what has happened to their boss. Tell them I am taking his body to my place."

"But shouldn't he be taken to his own home?" Jadine started to protest.

"No. I want him with me," was Chance's terse reply. He warned Jadine not to argue further. But displeasure was on her thin face as she rode to tell the cowhands the sad news. She should be taking care of the funeral arrangements, she told herself. After all, she was the boss of the ranch now.

That thought brought a wide, satisfied smile to her lips. *Let Chance handle things for now*, she told herself. *Everything will go my way once old George is put in the ground.*

When Jadine approached the cowhands out on the range, it took an effort to wipe the smug smile off her face. But she managed and even squeezed a few tears out of her eyes as she told the men that their boss was dead. As they stared at her, stunned and saddened, she ordered in an authoritative voice, "Keep on with your work. Chance has taken George's body to his house. You can come view his body after you've eaten supper tonight."

Lifting the reins, she galloped away. The men

stared after her. They had all liked and respected George McGruder, and the last thing they felt like doing was nursing a herd of steers that weren't going anywhere anyhow.

"Is that whorin' bitch gonna be our boss now?" one of the men asked.

"It looks like she's given us our first order, so I guess she is," the foreman answered.

"I'll quit before I let the likes of her order me around," a young cowhand vowed, and was seconded by others.

"Settle down, men," the foreman advised. "We won't do anything until after George's funeral."

Chapter Twenty-nine

Half of Montana Territory must be here, Chance thought, standing at the head of the open grave and staring down at the pine coffin. Every rancher within fifty miles was there. Also cowboys from surrounding ranches had come to pay their respects to the well-liked and respected man. Most of the people from Bitter Creek were in attendance as well. Chance had even spotted several older cowpunchers who had at one time worked for his uncle before getting the wanderlust and moving on.

Chance felt Jadine's arm brush against his and he frowned. The bitch had stuck to him like a cockle burr caught in a horse's tail. He knew what she was up to. She wanted them to pose as a united front, so she could get a little symapthy as the grieving stepdaughter.

No one there would buy that, though. Chance moved a few inches away from Jadine. There wasn't a man, woman or child who didn't know that she was the biggest whore on the range, and that she never cared diddly for George McGruder. The corners of his lips twitched. Wait until she heard the reading of his uncle's will.

The Reverend Ralph Manus was closing his Bible. The sermon was over. He nodded to Chance to pick up a handful of dirt and toss it onto the coffin. After the others had followed suit, they paused to shake Chance's hand as they walked past him. Still standing beside Chance, her body stiff, Jadine seethed inside. Not one word of condolence had been offered her.

Finally, only Chance, Jadine and the lawyer were left staring at the mounded grave. When they turned around and walked toward their tethered horses beneath a large cottonwood, the lawyer, Tom Woodman, said, "I might as well read George's will to you now. It will save you a trip into town later."

"What will?" Jadine's eyes narrowed to slits. "Why would my stepfather have a will? Naturally, I will inherit the ranch."

"Let's wait and see what George had in mind," Woodman said as he swung onto his horse's back.

Chance slid a look at Jadine and chuckled to himself. He had never seen her so angry and upset.

The three reached George McGruder's ranch house and walked through the rooms to the deceased man's office. Jadine, as though it was her right, hurried to sit in the large leather chair behind the equally large desk.

In the hush that fell over the room, the rustle of papers in the lawyer's hand seemed unusually loud. As Chance and Jadine waited and watched, Woodman picked up a sheet of paper. He adjusted his glasses, cleared his voice and began to read:

Having no children, or any other blood relatives other than my nephew, Chance McGruder, I leave everthing I own to him, with one exception. The old cabin and the two acres it sits on, I will to my stepdaughter, Jadine Walker.

Chance almost felt sorry for the woman, she looked so angry and stunned. But when she turned into a raving maniac and called his uncle every vile name known to man, he wanted to reach across the desk and slap her as hard as he could. When she stopped long enough to catch her breath, he said coldly, "I'll expect you out of here this time tomorrow. And don't take anything but your clothes."

Chance and the lawyer rose, and in the scraping of their chairs neither heard the desk drawer being pulled open. As they walked away from the sullen-faced Jadine, a shot rang out and Chance felt the breeze of the bullet that struck the door frame only inches from his head. He spun around and crossed the room in several large strides. He snatched the gun from Jadine's hand and gritted out, "Tomorrow. And take only your clothes with you."

"You'd better watch that one," Woodman said as they mounted their horses. "I wouldn't be surprised if she takes another shot at you."

"Me either." Chance lifted the reins. "From now on, I'll have one of my men keep an eye on what she's up to."

Chance was nearing home when Tory and Cal overtook him. "There sure were a lot of people who turned out for your uncle's funeral," Tory said, riding alongside Chance. "He must have been well liked."

Chance nodded. "He was. I don't think he ever had an enemy."

After a moment Tory said, "I don't say that Jadine was the old man's enemy, but she sure didn't like him. I wanted to slap those crocodile tears off her face at the grave site."

"It's a shame the likes of her is getting my old friend's property," Cal said gloomily. "She don't deserve it."

"She's not getting it." Chance reined in when they came to the fork in the trail that would take him home. "All she's getting is that old cabin Uncle George and his first wife lived in for a while. With the exception of the two acres it sits on, everything else was left to me. I just finished giving her until tomorrow to get out."

"Man, I bet she threw a fit when she learned about that." Tory grinned.

"The bitch tried to shoot me in the back. Missed me by inches."

"You'd better watch your back trail from now on," old Cal warned. "She might not miss you the next time."

"Don't I know it. The back of my neck is gonna prickle every time I step out of the house."

Chance abruptly changed the subject. "I don't mind telling you that I was a little surprised and put out that Raven didn't come to Uncle George's funeral. I'm sure the neighbors thought it strange that she wasn't there."

Tory and Cal looked at each other, baffled. Each was waiting for the other to tell the husband that his wife had left the valley. When neither spoke, Chance asked a little anxiously, "She's not sick, is she?"

"Look, Chance," Tory said, uneasiness coming over him, "I should have told you right away, but what with the flood and your uncle dying, I never seemed to get the chance."

"To tell me what?" Chance gripped the reins so hard his knuckles turned white.

"She's gone, Chance. She left me a note saying not to worry about her, that she'll write to me when she gets settled."

Chance almost visibly wilted in the saddle. "Do you have any idea where she might have gone?" he finally managed to ask.

"Not a clue."

"Maybe she went back to Clayton."

Tory shook his head. "I doubt it. She hated that town and the life she spent there with her husband. I'm pretty sure that would be the last place she would go."

"Dammit, man, are you just gonna sit back and do nothing? Doesn't it bother you that she could have run into Indians, rustlers, wild animals?"

"Of course it does, Chance. She's my baby sister. I raised her. But I don't know where in the hell to look for her, and it's driving me crazy."

I'm sorry I spoke so sharply, Tory. I know you're worried. But I think you're mistaken about her not returning to Clayton. Whether she likes the town or not, it's the only place she is familiar with. I think she's either gone there or to where she grew up."

Chance turned the stallion's head toward home. "I'm heading out for Clayton as soon I change clothes and pack some grub."

"I'll go with you."

"I think it's best you stay here and keep an eye on things. Especially that bitch, Jadine. I wouldn't put it past her to set fire to Uncle George's place. Besides, you're in no condition to travel, and I don't know how long I'll be gone."

Tory nodded, and Chance dug his heels into the stallion, sending him racing for home.

Chapter Thirty

It was Chance's second day on the trail when he reined in the tired stallion and gazed down at the swollen Missouri. He reached forward and patted Brutus's sweat-slick neck. "I'm sorry I've pushed you so hard, boy," he apologized, "but I've got to find that foolish wife of mine before she gets herself into trouble."

He could tell by the debris washed up on the bank that the river had been much higher than it was now. If Raven had come this way, she would have found it difficult to ford the muddy water.

As he sat resting the stallion, he asked himself where he would look next if he didn't find her in Clayton. *I feel sure she is there, though,* he thought, and lifting the reins of the tired horse, he urged him into the river.

The water had lost most of its force and the big

stallion had no problem swimming across it. When he waded ashore with water streaming down his haunches, twilight was near. Chance studied the landscape, looking for a likely place to camp. He decided on a knoll of scrubby pine. The trees would shelter him from the cool night air.

After unsaddling Brutus and hobbling him in a patch of grass at the edge of the trees, Chance built a fire from dry broken limbs and started a pot of coffee brewing. He unfolded his bedroll, then dug into the grub pack and pulled out a couple strips of dried beef.

The dancing flames of the fire cast long black shadows as he chewed his supper and drank strong black coffee from a tin cup. Then, bone-tired and weary from worrying about Raven, he rolled up in his blankets when the first stars began to appear in the sky. His last thought before falling asleep was, Where is Raven tonight?

When dawn broke over the range the next morning, Chance rolled out of the blankets. He folded them up and tossed them down beside the saddle before rekindling the fire and putting the coffee-pot on the flames. When he had made a necessary trip deeper into the pines, the coffee was ready to drink. He pulled another strip of beef from the grub bag and chewed on it as he saddled the horse. When he had washed down the cured meat with the leftover coffee, he poured the grounds on the fire, extinguishing it. When that was done, he freed the stallion's legs and swung into the saddle.

Chance had ridden about five miles when he saw a horseman up ahead. His eyes narrowed on the horse the man was riding. The animal looked very familiar. He'd almost swear it looked like Raven's gelding, Sam. He kicked Brutus into a gallop and overtook the rider in a short time.

"Hey!" he yelled as he thundered up beside the rider. "Where did you get that horse?"

Chance's eyes widened in surprise when he got a close look at the startled man. He was old. Very old. His beard was white, as was his shoulder-length hair. His weathered face was criss-crossed with deep wrinkles. But the blue eyes that stared back at him were clear and sharp, and defiant.

"I didn't steal him, if that's what you think." The voice was cracked but unafraid.

"How do you come to have him? He belongs to my wife."

"I'm right sorry to hear that, young feller." Softness had replaced his defiant tone.

"Why?" Chance demanded, a strange sensation gathering in his chest.

After a slight hesitation, the old man replied, "I'm afraid the river got her, son."

His jaw clenched and tight, Chance denied the old man's words in a tortured whisper. "I would know it if she had drowned. I would feel it in my heart."

Pity shadowed the gray one's eyes. "I saw the horse escape the woman's grip. She was left fighting the swollen river. I was too far away to get to her, to help her in her struggle as she was swept downstream. After I caught the horse, I rode for miles down the river to see if she had made it to shore. There was no sign of her. I came to a patch of mean rapids and found this caught on a rock."

Chance gasped when he saw the red kerchief held out to him. He had seen it around Raven's neck so many times. When the old man said, "It was the rapids that got her," Chance ran his hands through his hair, a groan issuing from his throat.

With tears blurring his vision, Chance took the reins thrust at him. Looking drained, he turned his horse around, and leading Sam, he headed toward home and the sad duty of telling Tory that his sister was dead.

Chance made the long journey home by rote alone. He made camp wherever he was when the sun went down. He stared unseeing into his campfire as he drank a cup of coffee and chewed a supper of beef strips. He spread his bedroll, and cried out often in his sleep. When dawn broke over the land, he rose, saddled up and rode off.

The afternoon he looked down on the ranch buildings, he was but a shadow of the man who had started out looking for his wife. His face was gaunt from the weight he had lost, and his eyes were dead.

Mary saw Chance and the two horses approaching the house and knew by the slump of his shoulders that all had not gone well. She hurried out onto the porch when he rode up.

Looking at his drawn face with concern, she exclaimed, "You look half dead, Chance." When he climbed tiredly out of the saddle, she said in a hushed voice, "You didn't find her, did you?"

Chance didn't answer right away as he climbed the three steps, then in a voice thick with grief, he said, "She's gone, Mary. The river took her."

"Oh, Chance I'm so sorry." His housekeeper and friend took his arm and led him inside. Pulling a chair away from the table, she pressed him into it. "You look worn out, and hungry, too. I was just getting ready to fry some fish one of the hands caught this morning. While I'm fixing them, do you want to tell me about it?" she asked, glancing out the window and seeing the young horse wrangler leading the two weary horses away.

"There's not much to tell," Chance said woodenly. "From what an old man told me, he saw her swimming Sam across the flooding Missouri when the gelding spooked. He dumped Raven into the water." He paused and took a long breath. "According to the old-timer, she was swept away in some rapids. All he found of her was her red neckerchief caught on a jagged rock."

When he grew silent, Mary gave his shoulder a sympathetic squeeze, but didn't say anything. What could she say that would comfort a man's suffering at losing his wife?

Chance was practically asleep by the time he finished eating the crispy fried fish and hoe cakes. He left the table and went to his room. Removing only his boots, he plopped face down on the bed and fell asleep instantly.

He had been sleeping an hour when Tory came riding up at a gallop. He pulled the horse to a rearing stop and was out of the saddle before the animal's hooves hit the ground. Bounding up on the porch, he burst into the kitchen. He looked at Mary, his eyes wild. "Where's Chance?" he demanded. "One of your men rode over to tell me that he was back, that he had Raven's horse, but that she wasn't with him."

"Sit down, Tory," Mary said gently, pulling out a chair for him. Chance got in about an hour and a half ago. He was worn out and is asleep now." She sat down at the table, and laying a hand on the young rancher's arm, she said softly, "Your sister didn't return with him. I'm so sorry to say this, but your sister is gone." She paused a moment, then added, compassionately, "She drowned in the flooded Missouri."

Tory sat stunned a moment before he denied savagely, "No! No! Not my little Raven!"

Mary reached out to him but he had already stumbled to his feet and was heading blindly toward the door. She followed him and stood on the porch watching him gallop across the range.

She shook her head sorrowfully as she turned back into the kitchen. Because of Raven's death, two men would never be the same.

Chapter Thirty-one

The spring sun shone hot on Chance's thighs as he rode toward his uncle's ranch. It was the first time he had left his ranch since coming home from searching for Raven.

Two weeks had passed since his return from his fruitless search for her. Her gelding had been returned to Tory, for Chance couldn't bear to see the horse grazing in the fenced-in pasture behind his barn. He had kept her red kerchief, however. He had folded it into a square and placed it in a vest pocket where it lay next to his heart.

He and Tory hadn't talked much. Each man knew the grief the other was feeling, so words weren't necessary between them. A few days back they had spoken about a cattle drive they would make together to Clayton later in the spring when the steers had fattened up some.

Both men still suffered keenly. Sometimes Tory was overcome with an appalling sense of loss and loneliness when he thought of his sister. And Chance went around with dead eyes, seldom showing any emotion. Sometimes his mind reeled under the loss of his wife.

But Mary had said to Chance this morning, "Things don't always shape up the way a man thinks they will. As hard as it is going to be for you, you have to carry on without her. You have the ranch to run, as well as your uncle's spread.

"You don't even know if that Jadine has moved out of his house. I think you should go over there and see if the foreman is running the place the way he should. The loss of your wife will be a little easier to bear if you keep your brain busy on something else. You'll sleep better, too, if you tire yourself during the day."

Chance hoped his housekeeper was right as he reined the black stallion to a stop in front of his uncle's barn. He had to do something, for he was slowly going out of his mind. Not only with grief, but guilt also. As he walked toward the big building, he caught a glimpse of Jadine disappearing around its corner.

"What was that bitch doing here?" he asked the horse wrangler and the big smith standing in the semi-gloom. "Never mind telling me," he growled, noting the men fastening their trousers. "I know what she was doing here."

He pinned the men with a glacial glower. "If I ever hear of her being here again and that any of the men were with her, they are fired on the spot.

You can pass that around to the cowhands."

The men nodded, then the young wrangler asked, "Is it alright if the men go up to her cabin?"

"It's her property. She can take on all of you if she wants to. She's just not going to do it here." Chance started to walk away, then turned back to ask, "Is she charging the men?"

"Yeah. Some," the young man answered. "She claims she has to in order to make a livin'."

Chance said no more, but he was thinking contemptuously that Jadine, with her stamina, would be a wealthy woman in a short time.

He asked himself why someone so depraved as Jadine Walker should live on, enjoying a day such as this, while his beautiful and decent Raven would never see the sun again.

When Chance left the barn and entered the house, he checked every room. Everything seemed in order. If Jadine had taken anything, it hadn't been any furniture. As for jewelry and such, he didn't know how much of that had been in the house. Some day when he had more time, he would inspect everything more carefully. Right now he wanted to look over the cattle he had inherited.

He heard the animals lowing about fifteen minutes before he came upon the site where young yearlings were milling about in a holding pen. Nearby a small fire burned with branding irons heating on its red coals. He watched as one by one the animals were roped and pulled to the fire. There they were thrown on their sides and a hot iron was applied to their rumps. Then they were released to run bawling out onto the range.

Chance made a mental note that next spring his newly acquired cattle would wear his brand. He had been too immersed in grief to remember to bring his irons to the branding pen today.

He rolled a cigarette and sat watching the men continue with the branding. He fought hard to keep Raven from entering his mind, but lost the battle.

He gave up after a while, and pinching out his smoke, he turned the horse's head toward home. Maybe tomorrow would be better.

Chance was riding past the clump of willows where his uncle had drowned when he heard his name called. The voice was so weak he barely heard it. He reined in and dismounted, cautiously parting the ground-sweeping branches.

"Over here," the low voice directed him.

By peering, Chance made out the dim figure of a man, his back propped up against a tree trunk.

At first he didn't recognize the man with the whisker-stubbled face, untended hair full of twigs and dried leaves, and rumpled clothing. Then he asked in startled surprise, "Is that you, Juan? Everyone thought you drowned in the river." He squatted down beside the Mexican.

"Who told you that, Señor McGruder?" Juan asked bitterly. "Was it Jadine?"

"Why, yes, it was. She said the water had grabbed you and swept you away."

Juan's lips lips pulled back, baring his teeth like those of a wolf. "That one is the devil's own daughter, I sadly discovered. After making love to her

335

for years, I only recently discovered the evil inside her.

"It sickened me when she began to make plans with her brother to kill Señor McGruder so that she could inherit his ranch. When her brother started acting crazy, she plotted with one of his men to kill Carlin. When the deed was done, she told me that the outlaw had raped her, which I now doubt, and that I should shoot and kill him after he had murdered my old boss.

"I went along with her plan because I loved her with all my being." A shudder ran through Juan's slight body. "But when it was time for the outlaw to kill my boss, I couldn't let him do it. The old man had always been good to me, treated me like everyone else who worked for him. I shot the outlaw before he could get your uncle.

"Jadine was enraged. She grabbed up a big rock from the shore, and with both hands holding it she kept hitting Señor McGruder on the head until he sank under the water. She gave me a terrible look, then drew her gun and shot me in the head. The bullet only grazed me, but the force of the shot knocked me into the river, where the water swept me away.

"But unknown to her, I managed to grab onto a log floating by and worked myself to the bank. I have been hiding here ever since. If she knew I was still alive, she would hunt me down and make sure she killed me the second time."

Chance was struck dumb. His uncle had been murdered. Murdered by the woman he had raised since she was seventeen. Somehow, he wasn't surprised by Juan's revelation. He had learned a long time ago that Jadine had no conscience. She was quite capable of murder to get something she wanted badly.

"Juan," he said, "after I have her arrested, will you swear in court that she killed my uncle?"

"Sí," Juan answered immediately. "The love I had for her turned to hate the day she tried to kill me. I know now she never cared for me. She only wanted the use of my body. She is worse than the lowest *puta*."

"Good man." Chance squeezed Juan's shoulder. "When it gets dark, I'll slip you into Uncle George's house. You can shave and have a bath, then get into the clean clothes I'll bring you." Before he left, he asked, "What have you been doing for eats?"

"At night when everyone is asleep, I sneak into the cookshack and eat whatever I can find."

"I'll bring you food, too—around midnight," Chance said and left the willows. As he rode home he laid his plans.

It was just before midnight when Chance left the house and saddled his stallion. A half moon shone dimly as he rode toward his uncle's holdings. Arriving there, he found all the buildings in darkness. But in the two-room cabin nearby a dim light shone through a window. His lips curled.

As he approached the log building, he kept the stallion in the grass to muffle the thuds of its hoofs. When he reined in among a stand of pines at the corner of the building, he saw a horse hitched at the porch. Jadine had company. How long had the man been there? he wondered. How long would it take him to finish with Jadine?

He had to wait only about five minutes before the door opened and a man stepped outside and mounted his horse. Chance waited until the hoofbeats faded, then he dismounted and walked to the cabin. Pushing open the door, he found that the light he had seen came from a lamp in the kitchen. The bedroom beyond was in darkness except for a sliver of light from the moon shining through the window.

He paused a moment. Then, taking two pieces of rope from his pocket, he walked into the room. He wanted to hold his breath against the rank odor.

There was a stirring in the bed, and Jadine said in a raspy voice, "Put your money on the table, big man, then come join me."

His eyes glittering with hatred and contempt, Chance walked over to the bed and quickly straddled her hips. When she raised eager arms to him, he grasped her wrists, and before she knew what he was about, he had them securely tied together.

"Hey," Jadine cried out, "I don't go for rough stuff. If you get your jollies by inflicting pain forget it. Just untie me and get out."

Chance ran his hands down her bare, skinny legs. When he felt her ankles, he whipped the second piece of rope around them. In seconds they were bound as tightly as her wrists.

"Dammit, who are you?" Jadine cried out, fear creeping into her voice. "Turn me loose this minute."

Chance climbed off the bed and, taking a match

from his vest pocket, struck it against the bedside table and put its flame to a lamp sitting there.

"Chance," Jadine gasped, able to see his face now. "Why have you tied me up? You know I would willingly give myself to you. I wouldn't even want money from you."

"You're doing pretty well in that department, aren't you?" Chance looked at the bills scattered on the table. "There must be fifty dollars there."

"I have to make a living," Jadine whined. "It's not been easy for me since you kicked me out. I hate this little old hovel and I can't wait to get away from it. That money is going to help me do it."

"Oh, you're going to get away from here," Chance said harshly as he sat down in a chair across from the bed. "And it won't cost you a dime."

"What are you talking about?" Jadine looked at him, growing fear darkening her eyes.

"I'm talking about turning you over to the law for murdering my uncle."

"What in the hell are you talking about? I told everyone what happened to George. It was none of my fault."

"You might as well shut up, Jadine. Juan has told me the whole story and it's quite different from your version of how my uncle died."

"Juan couldn't tell you anything." There was relief in Jadine's eyes. "He drowned that day. I saw the river take him away."

"No." Chance shook his head. "You just thought he was dead. Your bullet only grazed him. He's been hiding from you ever since. He can't wait to tell the judge the whole truth about what happened that day."

"Hah! No judge will take the word of a Mexican over that of a white woman."

"He will when I and some of the other white men tell what we know about you."

"You wouldn't do that . . . would you?"

"In a heartbeat. You murdered a fine old man who never harmed anyone in his life."

Chance rose and left the room. Jadine was calling him every vile name she had ever heard.

Chance found Juan sitting in the dark in George's house waiting for him when he got back from a trip to his ranch. "Light the lamp, Juan," he said.

There came the scratch of a match, the sound of a chimney being lifted, then light glowed on the table. Chance laid some clothes and a sack of food on the table and said, "We'll start for Clayton before dawn tomorrow morning. If the cowhands saw us leading her away, her hands tied behind her back, they would want to know why. They could get ugly if they found out that she killed their boss."

Chance opened the sack and dipped his hand into it. He had told Mary Juan's story, and that the Mexican was half starved. The horrified housekeeper had made four thick beef sandwiches and two slices of apple pie for them.

"Eat up," Chance said, "then heat some water and take a bath. And here's some clean clothes you can change into."

The way Juan bit into the sandwich told Chance that food had been a skimpy item in the Mexican's stomach for some time. He knew that the man wanted to really wolf the food down but was holding back because of his presence. To give him some privacy, he said, "I'm spending the night here, too, so that we can get an early start in the morning. Blow out the light when you go to bed. I'll be in the second room off the hall."

The blackness of night had turned to gray when Chance awoke. He pulled on his clothes and walked next door to awaken Juan. He gave a start when he looked into the room. The bed had been slept in, but Juan was gone.

"Damn," he swore under his breath. Had the Mexican had second thoughts about testifying against Jadine? She could get off if he wasn't there to tell what had happened.

Chance smelled coffee then, and when he walked into the kitchen, Juan was sitting at the table drinking a cup of the freshly made brew.

"That sure smells good." Chance smiled as he filled himself a cup. "Let's drink up and get started before the ranch starts waking up."

Juan waited outside the cabin while Chance went inside to bring Jadine out. When he entered the bedroom and pulled her upright, she said sullenly, "It's about time you got here. I'm dying to use the outhouse."

Chance hesitated. He hated to untie her, yet nature probably did need to be attended to. Besides,

341

she was a skinny woman who couldn't possibly get away from two men.

He untied Jadine's wrists and ankles, then handed her her clothes. "Make it quick," he said when they stepped outside.

He followed her to within eight feet of the tall, narrow outhouse, then leaned against a tree waiting for her to come out. As he rolled a cigarette, Juan joined him, a smoke between his lips.

"It's taking her a while," Juan said when a few minutes had passed.

Chance gave a short laugh and remarked, "I guess she had a pretty full bladder."

Juan was laughing with him when Jadine burst through the privy door; the pistol in her hand was blazing. "Damn," Chance swore as he ducked behind a tree. "I forgot that Uncle George kept a gun in there in case of an emergency." His hand was going for his Colt when Juan grabbed it from its holster.

"Hold on, Juan," he cried out, but the wrangler was already exchanging fire with Jadine.

Chance never knew whose bullet killed first because the man and woman seemed to wilt to the ground at the same time. He knew by the limp sprawl of their bodies that both were dead before he knelt to examine them. He felt sympathy for the man who had loved so long, so unwisely. He gently smoothed his palm over Juan's eyelids, closing the brown eyes. As for Jadine, he walked away in the rosy glow of first light, leaving her to stare sightlessly at the sky.

Chapter Thirty-two

When Raven reached the crest of a slight rise, she reined in and looked down on a shallow valley. Amy's small herd was grazing peacefully on the new green grass. They were the young woman's pride and joy. She almost envied Amy. She had a purpose in life, something that made her eagerly greet each new day.

Unlike myself, Raven thought. She awoke each morning knowing that the new day held nothing for her. She would follow the same routine she had fallen into three weeks ago. While Amy went about the business of ranching, Raven made up beds, cleaned the kitchen and swept out the snug little cabin. She prepared lunch at noontime; then the long afternoon stretched before her until it was time to start the evening meal. In the hours before then she took long rides, trying to figure a way out of her dilemma. As sweet as Amy was and as much as she liked and admired the girl, Raven couldn't stay in the valley forever. She had to make a new life for herself and her baby.

A soft sigh escaped Raven. How much longer could she keep her secret from Amy? A pregnancy could only be hidden so long. When she started showing, Amy would be curious, and Raven would have to tell her about Chance; that she was running away from a husband. She wanted that part of her life to be kept secret.

Her shoulders sagged in frustration. She had no money, no clothes of her own, and no horse. She should be thankful that she had a roof over her head and three meals a day. And two good friends in Amy and Ike.

When Raven returned to the cabin to start supper, her spirits lifted somewhat. The old mountaineer was sitting on the porch. A couple weeks ago he had gone back up the mountain to spend some time with his friends. He was back now to check on Amy, to see if she was alright. She and Amy enjoyed his company and had missed him. He was always full of stories, and his unique outlook on life was thought-provoking.

She waved at Ike and continued on to the small fenced-in pasture to one side of the barn. When she had unsaddled the old plow horse, she opened the gate so that he could crop the tall grass in the enclosure.

"How are you this fine day?" Ike asked as Raven stepped up on the porch and sat down in a chair beside him.

"It is a fine day, isn't it?" She neglected to tell him how low her spirits were. If he even caught a hint that she was in the doldrums he would chisel away at her until she told him more than she wanted to.

"And how are you?" She smiled at him.

"I'm fair to middlin'. I always feel rejuvenated after I've been up in the mountains."

"Amy and I have missed you."

"How is the girl? What's she up to today?"

"She's fine. She rode down to the river right after lunch to see if there's any sign of a cattle drive coming through."

"They should start showing up any day now. The range has dried out and the river is almost back to normal. If Amy can get a few more calves from the ranch foremen, plus the ones her cows have dropped, she'll be takin' her own herd to market in the fall."

Sudden excitement washed over Raven. She asked herself why she hadn't thought of it before. She could masquerade as a young teen and wait at the river for a herd to come through. She could be a cook's helper, a dishwasher or she could assist the wrangler. And even if she was turned down, she would be allowed to ride along with the herd, be allowed to eat three squares a day. Once in Clayton she had a couple friends who would help her get on her feet until she could find a job luring customers to the gambling tables. She could put aside enough money to live on before the baby arrived.

"I won't think beyond that," she silently told herself.

Her hope for the future grew. When Amy arrived home around sundown and the three of them were eating venison stew and freshly baked bread, Amy remarked on her animated face and the sparkle in her eyes. "You're certainly in high spirits tonight, Raven," she said. "When I left you this afternoon you looked down in the mouth."

"She perked right up when she saw me sittin' on the porch," Ike remarked with a grin as he helped himself to another slice of bread. "She ain't stopped talkin' since I got here."

Raven winked at Amy. "You can take that with a grain of salt. You can imagine how many words I could get in with this one."

Everyone laughed, including Ike.

"Did you see any sign of a herd crossin' the river?" Ike looked at Amy.

"I saw where a small one had crossed. I won't be able to pick up any dogies from little herds like my own. I have to wait for big ones to come through. Like the one Chance McGruder crosses the river with. Sometimes I get as many as eight calves from his trail boss."

Raven's body went still. It hadn't occurred to her that Chance would be driving a herd to market. And so would her brother. They might even drive together. She must be very careful when approaching the trail bosses about work.

She idly stirred the sugar in her coffee. If she should run into Tory, he would insist that she return home with him. As for Chance, she had no idea what his reaction would be.

In any case, she didn't want to see him. She might somehow reveal that she loved him. That might make him feel sorry for her, and that would be unbearable. She didn't want his pity, she wanted his love.

Raven came back to the present when she heard Ike teasing Amy. "I betcha you're hopin' that young feller Tory McCloud drives a herd through." The old man's eyes twinkled devilishly.

"I am not!" Amy blushed.

"Tell the truth now, girl. You and him got kinda sweet on each other when he was here."

"You're crazy. We did no such thing."

"I seen them calf eyes you two made at each other," Ike continued.

"You're a hateful old man!" Amy jumped to her feet and ran outside; Ike's laughter followed her.

Raven turned her head from Ike so that he wouldn't see the shock on her face. So this was the cabin where Tory had recuperated. Amy had taken care of him. Had there been tender feelings between them? If there were, Tory could very well come looking for Amy.

Chance watched his cowhands from his perch on top of the corral fence. They were in good spirits despite the long day of branding cattle. The air pulsed with their talk and horseplay as they washed their dust-stained faces from the tin washbasins on the bench outside the cookshack.

For days they had been rounding up cattle,

branding them, preparing them for the long trek to Clayton. He was actually looking forward to the tiring drive. He welcomed anything that would take his mind off the loss of Raven. Instead of his pain lessening, it seemed to grow worse. There were times when he would awaken in the middle of the night, calling her name. He couldn't wait to throw himself into the long drive that would leave him so exhausted at the end of the day he could be sure of dreamless sleep.

Chance reminded himself that after supper he must ride over to his uncle's place to see how the roundup was coming along there. The combined cattle from the two ranches would set a record for the largest drive in Montana history. And he mustn't forget that Tory McCloud's cattle would be among the herd.

He had only seen the young rancher a few times since they learned of his sister's death. To be around Tory only intensified his grief at losing Raven.

The men were trailing into the cookshack and Chance followed them. There were a couple moments of scraping chairs as everyone settled around the table. Good-natured bantering went on as platters and bowls of food were passed around. After that it grew quiet; the only sound was that of knives and forks being put to use.

Out of habit, cowboys never had a leisurely meal. There was almost always something waiting for their attention. Consequently, it was but a short time before Rufus, the cook, was moving around the table filling cups with strong coffee.

Some of the men had a second helping of the dark brew, but the majority left the table, pulling a cloth sack of cigarette makings from a vest pocket. One of the remaining men swallowed his coffee and hurried after his departing friends. "Any of you fellers want to come with me to town?" he called out. "I'm gonna get me a poke. Once we start the cattle drive we won't see a woman for three weeks."

Chance shook his head. He couldn't believe that there had been a time when he would have ridden with the men, with the same purpose in mind. But that seemed eons ago. Since Raven, no other woman had stirred him.

When the cook asked, "You want another cup of coffee, boss?" Chance realized that he sat at the table alone. He shook his head at Rufus and walked out onto the narrow porch. Leaning on a supporting post, he gazed at the far reaches westward where a misty veil hung over the land. This hour of the day had always been his favorite time. A time to relax after a hard day's work, and plan for tomorrow.

He had lost that drive. Now he only dreaded all the tomorrows that stretched ahead.

When the gray dusk that precedes darkness began to settle on the land, he ground out his smoke and walked toward the barn. It was time to saddle up and ride to his new property. No matter how beaten down a man might feel, there were always obligations he must attend to.

Chapter Thirty-three

All day a thick mist had enveloped Amy's valley, making it eerie looking, yet somehow serene. When the time came, Raven was going to hate leaving this place. She was going to miss Amy, and Ike too. Maybe after she had her baby she would come for a visit. She would also like to manage somehow to make Amy godmother to her little one. A child couldn't be entrusted to anyone better than the young woman sitting next to her, her feet swinging over the edge of the porch.

Raven looked up and smiled at Ike when he stepped outside and sat between her and Amy. "I like that sound," he said when along a distant creek, frogs began tuning up. "It always reminds me of when I was a young'un and I'd sit with my ma and pa of an evenin' listenin' to them croakin'"

"Where was that, Ike?" Amy asked. "I don't recall you ever talking about your youth."

"That was back in the Tennessee mountains. Me and my pa and three brothers worked like slaves, grubbin' a livin' out of that rocky soil." Ike grew silent, as though remembering those days of his youth. After a while he said, "When the old folks passed away I lit out, heading west. My brothers, older than me, stayed on at the farm. I reckon they're dead by now."

"You never went back for a visit?" Raven asked.

"No. I always meant to, but never got around to it. I was always busy trampin' around new mountains, lookin' for new places to lay my traps."

All three grew silent then, each engrossed with the thoughts going through their minds. Ike half wished that he had settled down when he was young, married a good woman and had children. Sons and daughters who would look after him in his old age.

Amy dreamed of the young rancher whose kisses had thrilled her to her toes, and she wondered if she would ever see him again.

And Raven's thoughts were on Chance. Was he with Jadine tonight? Had he started divorce proceedings against his wife yet? Probably. He'd be in a hurry to do that.

The night darkened and the moon rose behind the mountains. Ike yawned and knocked out his pipe. "I'm going to bed, girls," he said, his bones creaking as he stood up. "I don't want to hear any giggling between you when you come to bed."

"As if you'd hear us with that snoring of yours," Amy laughed.

When Ike muttered something about smart-mouthed girls and entered the cabin, Raven asked, "Did any big herds go through today, Amy?"

"I didn't see any. I expect the drives will be picking up pretty soon."

There was a hint of dejection and weariness in the young woman's voice. Raven gave her a sharp look, then asked kindly, "What are your dreams of the future, Amy, besides enlarging your herd? I imagine a husband and children figure in them."

"I've never really thought that far ahead," Amy answered after a moment. She gave a short laugh then and added, "Stuck back here in this valley, I'm not likely to get to know any men that would be good husband material."

"What about the men passing through on their way to the stockyards? Some of the young cowboys would make fine husbands."

Amy looked out into the darkness. "Like you said, they're just passing through. You see them once and probably never again."

"You'll see," Raven said jokingly. "A man will cross the river one day who'll see you and follow you home."

"You are a dreamer, Raven." Amy laughed, then shifted the subject to Raven. "What are your plans for the future? You're welcome to stay here as long as you want to, but you're too smart and beautiful to vegetate here in this lonesome valley."

"I've been giving some thought to that. As you know, I was on my way to Clayton when you found me half drowned. But after losing my horse and trunk of clothing, I haven't been able to figure out how to get there or what kind of job I could get wearing men's clothing. However, I may have come up with a plan. I'll tell you about it when I've got it all figured out."

Amy yawned and got to her feet. Laying a hand on Raven's shoulder, she said wryly, "We're a couple of sorry women, aren't we? We don't seem to know which way to turn, which way to go."

Raven's answer was a short, bitter laugh.

It was barely dawn as the cowhands on the McGruder ranch waited for the foreman to give the signal to start the herd on their long trek.

Chance had made a last inspection of the chuck wagon, checking out the supplies neatly stacked on shelves and floor. He'd had to have a new cook, but the man seemed to have everything in order. Outside the awkward vehicle a full grease bucket swung from the side of the high seat, and the attached water barrel was full.

Next came the hoodlum wagon. It was packed with bedrolls and wood for a cookfire in case they made camp where there were no trees.

Last, he checked out the horses in the remuda. The wrangler, a seasoned worker, had chosen young, healthy stock.

All was in readiness. The ranch foreman snapped his whip, and with a loud "Yooeee!" stirred the herd into motion. A herd that stretched half a mile in length and width.

Chance touched spurs to his stallion and loped along the edge of the moving cattle to where the point man led the way. Names had been drawn from a hat to see who would be the point man. It was very desirable position for those who didn't want to eat dust. The man who drew a blank slip of paper would do that; he would ride drag, bringing up the rear, almost smothered in the dust stirred up by thousands of hooves.

Every morning, however, the drawing was held again by the men, with the exception of the two who had held those best and worst positions the previous day.

"Nice day, huh, boss?" A middle-aged cowhand grinned at Chance.

Chance nodded and answered shortly, "I hope we'll be blessed with the same weather to the end of our drive. I don't look forward to a thunderstorm that might cause a stampede."

"Yeah, they're hell," the cowhand agreed and said no more. Lately there had been a cool constraint in Chance's manner that barred the men from drawing him into conversation.

Two miles away, Tory was waiting with his much smaller herd when Chance bawling, complaining steers topped a rise that looked down on the McCloud ranch. When all the McGruder cattle had finally moved on, Tory drove his herd in behind them.

Ahead of the combined herds stretched green grass as far as the eye could see. Tory was thankful that for the time being there would be a plentiful supply of grazing land.

It was with mixed emotions that he had prepared for the drive this morning. When the hope of finding the small ranch tucked away in a hidden valley, and the young woman running it, excitement fluttered through him. Then he would remember that they would have to cross the river that had taken his sister, and a deep sadness would overtake him.

The noon hour arrived and the cattle were allowed to stop and graze. The men ate their lunch in shifts, and within an hour the drive was resumed. It was an hour before twilight when they crossed over into Wyoming and the point man spotted a wide creek. As he turned the lead steers in that direction, he stood up in the stirrups and waved his hat to Rufus. When he had the cook's attention, he pointed to his left. He was answered with an understanding lift of the man's whip.

There was no problem turning the herd and driving them to the creek. They had smelled the water and headed for it on their own. The men, tired, dusty and hungry, washed up in shifts before heading toward the chuck wagon, where a fire burned with bean pot and coffee pot nestled on red glowing coals on one side and steaks sizzled in a large skillet. Those men who had washed up grabbed tin plates and piled them with meat and beans. The other half of the men, waiting their turn, settled the cattle in for the night. When the first group had finished eating, they would take their turn at keeping the cattle quiet and contented as they circled them, singing lonesome songs to them. By the time the midnight group came on, the cattle would be lying down, peacefully chewing their cud.

When everyone had eaten and Rufus had

scrubbed the dishes, pots and skillets, stars were beginning to twinkle in the black sky. Those men who were idle dug their bedrolls from the hoodlum wagon and spread them on the ground. In minutes there rose an ungodly melody of snores breaking the calm of the evening.

Chance picked up his blankets and walked until he couldn't hear the concert before unfolding them on the ground.

Raven and Amy stood on the porch waving goodbye to Ike. They wouldn't see him again for a couple weeks. "Well," Amy said when the old mountaineer disappeared from sight, "I might as well get on with my chores so that I can ride down the valley and keep my eyes peeled for some herds coming along." She looked at Raven and asked, "What are you going to do today?"

Raven shrugged. "I don't know. Maybe I'll bake a peach cobbler."

Amy's eyes sparkled. "Will you, Raven? I love your peach cobblers."

"Why don't I teach you how to bake them?"

"Another day maybe. After I've checked out all the herds on their way to the stockyard."

"Amy," Raven said, her tone serious, "you should take the time to learn more about housekeeping. You will marry some day, and your husband will expect a comfortable home to come to at the end of a hard day's work, and some well-cooked meals."

"If that ever happens, then I'll learn how to do all those things. In the meantime I've got a ranch, such as it is, to run." Amy stepped off the porch and, walking toward the barn, called back, "I'll see you at lunch."

Raven shook her head, wondering if her new friend would ever become completely feminine. She was afraid that the young woman had led a man's life too long. She walked into the cabin and halfheartedly began preparing the dough for the pastry. At least that would give her an hour's occupation. After that the day would drag.

She had rolled out the dough and lined a baking tin with it and was preparing to open a can of peaches when she heard the thunder of hooves. Glancing out the window, she saw Amy racing her horse toward the cabin. She hurried outside when the little pinto came to a rearing halt.

"What's wrong, Amy?" she asked anxiously.

"Nothing is wrong," Amy answered, her face beaming with excitement. "I just spotted the biggest herd I've ever seen coming along the cattle trail. I wanted to tell you that I don't know when I'll be home. From the size of that drive, I'm guessing there will be a lot of little dogies given to me." She wheeled the little horse around then, heading him back down the valley.

Excitement began to grow inside Raven too. This was probably her best chance of carrying out her plan. She rushed back inside and stood a moment in the bedroom deciding what to do. She would tackle her hair first. She would braid it and fasten it securely on top of her head. One of Amy's old battered hats would completely cover her head.

Her hair taken care of, Raven fretted about the shirt she wore. It was one of Amy's and did not hide the fact that she was female. With her pregnancy, her breasts were fuller than before. She remembered washing clothes yesterday and scrubbing a couple shirts for Ike. She had forgotten to take the wash off the line after they dried. They were still pinned to the rope strung between two trees. She rushed outside, yanked everything free of the pegs and carried the laundry inside, dumping it all on the bed.

She laid aside Ike's gray flannel shirt, then freed a sheet from beneath the pile. She hoped that Amy would forgive her as she tore two strips from it. Even with the old man's large shirt, she thought it wise to bind her breasts.

When she had buttoned herself into the large garment, she found to her relief that it fell well below her hips, hiding her womanly curves. After giving the sleeves a double roll, she walked into the other room and bent over the fireplace. Scooping up a handful of ashes, she carried them to the scrap of a mirror that hung on the wall beside the door. She had learned to paint her face while married to her first husband and the skill came in handy now. It enabled her to smear ashes over her features so that when she finished she looked like a dirty-faced teenager.

And now she must write a note to Amy. She took a pad of paper and a stub of a pencil off the mantel and carried them to the kitchen table. She stared out the window for a few seconds, planning what to write before she put pencil to paper.

"Dear, Amy," she began. "I hate leaving you this way, as though sneaking off, but if I'm to put my plan in action I must act the ingrate and ride away. I intend to ask the trail boss of that big herd you saw if he will hire me on as a cook's helper, dishwasher and so forth. If I am successful I will turn your horse loose. I am sure he will return to you right away. If I fail to get employment, then I'll return.

"I would very much appreciate it, Amy, if you never speak of Raven Spencer to anyone. As you might have guessed, I am running away from a man. I will write to you as soon as I get settled. I will always be thankful to you for saving my life and giving me shelter when I so desperately needed it. I hope that you amass a lot of little dogies in the next few weeks. Say a little prayer for me, Amy. Love, Raven."

She propped the note against the coffee pot, the first place Amy went to on coming home. She pulled the borrowed, misshapen hat over her head, tugging it low on her forehead, and closing the cabin door behind her, walked to the barn to saddle the old plow horse.

Chapter Thirty-four

"Dammit, Chance!" Rufus threw a wooden spoon up against the chuck wagon. "What am I gonna do for some help around here? I never cooked for such a large drive as this before."

When the cook continued to swear and stomp around, Chance tried to pacify him by saying, "If it gets too much for you to handle, I'll pitch in and give you a hand."

"Oh, sure," Rufus grouched, "that would look real good, wouldn't it? The biggest rancher in the state dishing up grub for his help, scrubbing pots and skillets."

"That wouldn't bother me in the least," Chance said as he mounted the little quarter horse he always used when working cattle. "I'll stop by later to see how you're making out."

"Hah," Rufus muttered as he began gathering

up the tins the men had used half an hour ago. He knew that his boss meant what he said, but he also knew that Chance would get caught up in seeing that the drive was going as it should and probably wouldn't think about anything else until it was time to eat again.

The irritated man was making so much noise as he scraped the remains of breakfast off the plates, then tossed them into a pan of hot, soapy water, he didn't hear the lone horseman ride up. His hands were submerged in suds up to his elbows when the voice of a teenager said shyly, "Howdy, mister."

Rufus looked up with a dark frown. "Look, kid," he said, "I'm sorry, but the cowhands just ate up all the grub and drank all the coffee. I might be able to find you a slice of sourdough, though."

"That's alright, mister. I'm not lookin' for anything to eat. I was wonderin' if you might need some help. I thought maybe you would hire me on."

Interest leapt into Rufus's eyes. He took his hands out of the dishwater, and as he dried them on a rough fustian towel, he asked, "Do you know your way around a cookfire?"

"I can cook, if that's what you mean," the teenager answered. "And I know how to wash dishes." White teeth flashed in the dirty face.

"Well, climb down, kid. A storm last night scattered the herd, so the men are rounding them up. By the time they come in for lunch, I'll know your worth and decide whether or not to take you on." He squinted an eye at the lad climbing off his horse. "You look kinda familiar. Are you from these parts?"

Raven jerked a hand toward the mountains. "I'm from up there."

"I wouldn't know you then. You can take your nag over there where the horses in the remuda are grazing. When you turn him in with the others, you can get back here and finish these dishes."

Raven grinned at Rufus, acknowledging her gratitude. She didn't, however, take the "nag," as the grouchy cook had called the plodding plow horse, to the remuda. As soon as he was out of sight, she slapped the old animal on the rump, sending him running toward home.

Raven had never worked so hard in her life as she did the following hours, not stopping for an instant until the men started riding in for the noon meal. As soon as she had finished washing the mountain of dishes and pots and skillets, Rufus had set her to peeling and cubing a pail of potatoes. She was ordered then to cut a half slab of beef into bite-size pieces, salt and pepper them, then dredge them in flour. When she had finished doing that, he directed her to drop the pieces into a large pot of hot fat and to stir them around until they were light brown on all sides. When everything met her boss's satisfaction, he poured enough water into the pot to cover the meat. After adding some herbs to the beginning of the stew, he clamped a lid on the iron pot.

"Now keep a low fire burning so the water only simmers," he ordered. "And stir the meat once in a while. And maybe you'd better fetch a couple pails of water up from the creek over there. About an hour before noon, add the potatoes and a couple onions. Around that same time start a pot of coffee to brewin'."

Raven was ready to drop by the time the first group of cowhands started drifting into camp. "I'll dish up the grub," Rufus said, "bein' as how you're new and the men will try to rattle you. You can pour the coffee after the hogs have filled their bellies. You look a mite tired. Go sit down and rest a bit."

Raven gladly found a tree and plopped down beneath its shade. With her back propped against the cottonwood trunk, she listened to the cowboys ragging the cook and the snappy replies he gave back. She could tell it was all in good fun. The men actually liked and respected the grumpy man.

She leaned her head back and watched the high, thin clouds through the new, clean leaves of the cottonwood, and in the serene silence her eyes began to close and her head to nod. Then her eyes snapped open and she became alert. One of the men had asked, "Where's Tory? I ain't seen him in the last couple hours."

Another man laughed and said, "He met up with a pretty little gal lookin' for any dogies who might not be able to keep up with their mamas. I think he knew her. They were awfully glad to see each other. Anyhow, he rode off with her."

Raven sat forward, her nerves tightening. There could only be one Tory in the vicinity. The name was too unusual. She had wandered into her husband's camp and had been hired by his cook. She remembered that Chance and Tory had been making plans to drive their cattle to Clayton together.

Dear Lord, what am I going to do? she wondered. Chance was probably sitting with his men right now, eating the stew that she had helped make. Soon he would be finished and looking for a cup of coffee. Coffee that she was supposed to serve.

She jumped to her feet in panic and struck out running. She would never be able to get that close to Chance without giving herself away.

Raven followed the creek until she came to a large willow whose branches hung out over the water. As she crawled beneath it, she could barely hear the men's voices. The crabby old cook would be put out at her for disappearing, she thought, catching her breath, but she felt pretty sure he wouldn't fire her. Who else could he get to help him out here in the middle of nowhere?

"I'll tell him I fell asleep," she thought out loud.

That might work this one time, but what would she do about all the other meals to be served? She couldn't disappear at every mealtime.

Curling up in a ball, she told herself she would think of something. She had to.

"I've thought about you a lot, Amy," Tory said with a smile as they drove six calves toward her small ranch. "I hoped that I would see you along the trail, because I was afraid I would never find your place."

"I've thought about you too," Amy said shyly.

"How's your friend Ike?"

"He's the same. Still full of stories. He went back up to the mountain this morning after a two-week visit. He'll be back in a couple weeks. Maybe you can stop by on your way home to see him. He'd be happy to visit with you again."

"I'll look forward to that."

Amy's holdings were suddenly before them and she rode ahead to open the gate to a small pasture where the orphan calves would be kept until they were hand-weaned. When Tory had them safely penned up, Amy asked, "Would you care to have lunch with me?"

"I was hoping you would ask me." Tory smiled.

Her eyes shining, Amy nodded toward the horse trough. "You can wash up over there while I set something out to eat."

The cabin was oddly silent when Amy stepped inside. "Raven," she called out, a happy lilt to her voice. "Where are you? We're having a guest for lunch."

That's strange, she thought when she received no answer. And stranger yet, the stove was cold and the beginnings of a peach cobbler were on the table. She noticed then the slip of paper propped against the coffee pot. She grabbed it up, scanning it quickly.

Stunned, she crumpled the note in her hand, whispering, "Raven, you fool." She lifted the stove lid and dropped the wadded paper inside the stove. She would honor her friend's wish and never speak of Raven Spencer.

Still upset by her friend's departure, Amy cleared the table of the dough and the can of peaches and set out the remains of the beef roast they'd had for supper last night. When Tory stepped into the kitchen, his face clean and his hair slicked back, she had put out two plates and cups and had placed a platter of sliced beef in the center of the table.

"Sit down," Amy invited as she picked up a knife and began slicing a loaf of bread. "Make yourself a sandwich."

When Tory had placed several slices of meat on a piece of bread, then covered it with another piece, she filled their cups with the coffee she had reheated.

Although Amy chewed and swallowed her meat and bread, she could have been eating the inner sole of her boot for all she tasted. She was only conscious of the man sitting across from her. His eyes were saying things that thrilled her to her toes.

"So how is your herd coming along?" Tory dragged his gaze off Amy's lips. "Did your cows fare all right over the winter?"

"They did fine. We're pretty well protected from the weather here in the valley," Amy answered, but she didn't want to talk about cattle. She wanted to talk about them, to have Tory kiss her again.

"I lost a few," Tory said, his gaze back on her lips as he wondered how he could kiss her. He couldn't just grab her.

He shook his head. He couldn't believe that he was sitting here like a greenhorn teenager, unsure of himself. He had lost count and memory of the many women he had kissed. Never before had he felt awkward about doing it. He had even kissed Amy before, so why was he sitting here now, trying to figure out how to approach her again?

Tory was a very disgruntled man when a short time later they were heading back to his herd to cut out more calves for Amy. "I'll damn well kiss her on my way home," he muttered.

Raven paused to wipe an arm across her sweaty brow. Before plunging her hands back into the dishpan of water, she gazed out across the range. It had been unusually hot the past few days. Days in which she had lived in suspense.

So far she had managed not to have direct contact with the men, had avoided speaking to any of them. She longed to speak to Tory, to let him in on her secret. They would have a good laugh about it. But then he would turn serious and insist that she stop her charade and return home with him once the drive was over.

Breakfast and supper had been easy enough to get through. The men were so tired, they noticed little. It was the noontime meal that required ingenuity. Chance had unknowingly come to her rescue. He had told Rufus that the kid should relieve the horse wrangler at lunch so that none of the men would have to waste time keeping an eye on the horses. He said that a wild bunch of horses had been following them at a distance and that the stallion might come in and drive away the mares in the remuda.

The wrangler, Rudy, was around her age, friendly and full of talk about his conquests of the young girls of Bitter Creek. He was very explicit in discussing what went on in his rendezvous with them. Raven was thankful for the dirt on her face that hid her fiery blushes.

It would all end before long, Raven thought as she scrubbed the last pot. According to Rufus they should arrive in Clayton in another two weeks. That wouldn't be soon enough for her. She longed for a long, soaking bath in hot, scented water. What a relief it would be to unbind her breasts and scrub away the sweat and dust, to wash her hair. She prayed that when she was paid her wages at the end of the drive, she would have enough money to buy a dress and some underclothing.

"I swear I'll never put on another pair of trousers again," she silently promised herself as she carried the basin of dishwater to the edge of camp and emptied it onto the grass.

"You can start peelin' the potatoes now." Rufus puffed on his pipe from his perch on a camp stool. "The men will probably raise hell at gettin' stew again, but I've got to use up the beef before it spoils."

"What about supper tonight?"

"Oh, they're really gonna raise cain then. It's gonna be salt pork and pinto beans. I set a pot of them to soakin' last night. After lunch I'll put them on a slow fire to cook."

Raven had placed the pail of potatoes on the wagon tailgate and picked up the paring knife when she heard the thud of hoofs. She looked up, and the knife fell from her suddenly nerveless fingers. Chance was approaching the camp.

"I've gotta go relieve myself," she muttered, and struck off in the direction of a large cottonwood fifty yards or so from camp.

"Where's the kid going?" Chance asked as he dismounted and dropped the reins over the quarter horse's head.

"He had to go empty his bladder."

"You know, I've never met him. I don't even know his name. Is he a good worker?" Chance asked as he lifted the coffee pot out of the coals and filled one of the cups that Raven had just washed.

"He calls himself Tom. He sure ain't afraid of work. I'd like to take him back with us to the ranch once we finish with the drive."

"Doesn't he have any folks?"

"I don't know. I never asked. The kid is kinda close-mouthed. I got the feelin' he might be an orphan."

Chance hunkered down on his heels and gazed in the direction where Rufus's helper had disappeared. Something about the boy bothered him. Whenever he saw him, watched the young man, a warm sensation stole over him. Even in the baggy clothes the teenager wore, he moved with a grace Chance had only seen once before. In his wife.

As he recalled how Raven seemed to float rather than walk, he was plunged into deep despair. Without a word to his cook, he left his unfinished coffee sitting on the ground and remounted his horse. He rode away telling himself that there was no way the kid was going home with them. He didn't need additional reminders of his dead wife every time he saw the teenager.

369

Chapter Thirty-five

The day arrived when the Missouri had to be crossed again. Thirsty men and cattle rushed toward it. The steers hadn't had water in two days and the cowhands' canteens were near empty.

"Tom," Rufus said when he brought the chuck wagon to a halt at the river's edge, "Chance wants you to help Rudy across with the horses."

Raven sat her horse, frozen in place, staring with panic-filled eyes at the swiftly flowing water. She was remembering in detail how this river had caught her in its grip. If not for Amy, she would have drowned.

She was only vaguely aware that the chuck wagon and hoodlum wagon had moved into the water, and that Rudy was yelling at the horses to follow them. "Come on, Tom!" the young man yelled. "I need your help!"

She could only sit and shake her head dumbly.

"What's going on here?" a rough and impatient voice demanded.

Raven recognized Chance's voice, but she was so terror-stricken, it didn't penetrate her mind that she was in danger of being recognized by him.

"Come on, kid, get a move on," she was ordered just before a hat whacked her horse on its rump. With a plunging rush the animal was in the water, and with a terrified scream Raven was sailing over its head. She landed amid the swimming cattle, and as she swallowed a mouthful of the churning water, a long horn hooked into the back of her shirt, ripping the material down the back.

"That damn kid is going to be killed." Chance swore loudly, riding his horse into the river and steering him into the melee of wild-eyed cattle. He was risking the quarter horse's life; one swipe of the deadly pointed horns could rip the horse's belly open.

But never in his life had he been so determined as he was now to save the teenager's life.

The boy was thrashing around with no apparent destination in mind. Chance knew the boy was past thinking logically; only instinct kept his arms and legs moving.

At last Chance was able to lean forward and, by stretching his arm as far as he could, grab hold of the rope that kept the boy's pants secured to his narrow waist. Chance laid the slight body across his thighs, then slowly and carefully made his way through the herd to the opposite bank. He quickly dismounted, dragged the cook's helper from the saddle and laid him on his stomach in the grass. Straddling his waist, he placed his hands on the narrow back and began to push his palms against the lungs.

Chance grunted his satisfaction when the boy began to cough and brown river water flowed out of his mouth.

He was thinking that the young man was awfully slight in build and was wondering if he had been getting enough to eat when he saw through the ripped shirt a wide bandage that was wrapped across his back, extending all the way around to his chest.

His eyes narrowing suspiciously, he whipped away the floppy, water-soaked hat and stared as if he had seen an apparition. Her face was washed clean now, and her long black braid was lying across one shoulder; there was no mistaking the face of his wife.

The wondrous look of gladness that flashed into Chance's eyes lasted but a moment. Anger such as he had never experienced before gripped him. "Damn you, woman," he grated out, "I should throw you back in the river."

"But why?" Raven croaked in confusion, her voice raw from the river water she had swallowed.

"Why?" he half shouted, climbing off her. "Only you would be selfish enough to let people, especially your brother, think that you had drowned in the river."

"Why would you think that?" Raven sat up.

"Because after Tory read your note, I went looking for you. I met an old man who was riding your horse. When I asked him how he came to have the horse, he said that its owner had drowned in the rapids downstream. He said he had searched up and down the river and that the only thing he found was a red neckerchief snagged on a rock."

"I'm sorry people grieved for me, but I had no idea they thought me dead. A young woman came along just when I was ready to give up and let the river have me. She tossed me a rope and dragged me on land. Besides losing Sam, I lost my trunk of clothes, and the ones I had on were torn to rags. These clothes belong to my friend."

"Why aren't you still with her?"

"Because my plans were to get to Clayton, and they are still the same. I have no money so I thought this would be a good way to get there. I hated fooling Rufus, but I didn't know who he was until after he had taken me on as his helper."

"You could have stopped your charade when you discovered you were working for my outfit."

"And have Tory dragging me back home? I don't think so."

"If you're that determined to go back to Clayton, I doubt that he'd drag you go back to a life you disliked so much that you sneaked away from it."

"I didn't sneak exactly. I knew it was the only way I could leave without a big argument." *Also*, Raven thought to herself, *it was the only way I could leave without telling Tory that you were the reason I was going away.*

Knowing that the time for pretense was gone, she asked, "What do you want me to do now?

Should I continue to help Rufus? Should I still pass myself off as a teenage boy?"

"The first thing we're going to do is let Tory know that you are alive. He'll decide what to do about you. I'll go get him."

Shivering in her wet clothes, Raven hugged her knees to her chest and gazed after Chance's rangy figure as he strode toward a knot of men a few yards away. Of course, she thought, near tears, he would leave it up to her brother what was to be done with her. He wouldn't bother making such a decision.

Raven recognized her brother when he broke away from the group and joined Chance. She saw his body jerk, saw his head turn to look in her direction. A second later he was loping toward her, a joyous look on his face.

"Oh, Raven," he cried, his eyes wet as he dropped to his knees and hugged her fiercely to his chest. "If you only knew the hell I've been through."

Raven was openly sobbing as she hugged her brother back. "I didn't know, Tory. I swear I didn't."

"I know. Chance told me."

Chance walked away from the rejoicing brother and sister. Neither knew that he had nearly gone crazy with his suffering. He swung into the saddle and cantered the horse away from the herd that now was spread out over the landscape, peacefully grazing on the lush green grass.

He rode with two thoughts on his mind. A deep happiness that Raven still lived, and an equally deep sadness that she had run away from him—from their marriage. He had mistakenly thought that since they shared a deep desire for each other's bodies, their feelings would deepen to love.

Apparently it had only happened to him, he thought, his shoulders sagging. But could he really and truly blame Raven for not feeling the way he did? God knew he hadn't given her much cause to. He had never told her that he loved her. Like a fool, he had thought that his body would tell her how he felt.

What decision would the brother and sister come to? he wondered, reining in on top of a grassy knoll and gazing unseeingly at the unending stretch of rangeland.

"How is Cal, and everyone?" Raven asked, pulling away from Tory and wiping her eyes. "I guess they all think I'm dead."

"Yes, they do. Old Cal feels very bad, and of course Chance had everybody's sympathy."

Raven wanted to ask how Chance had taken the news of her death but was afraid of the answer she would get. Besides, she didn't want to let on that she cared. "Anything new happen while I've been gone?" she asked instead.

"Yes. Quite a bit has gone on. The river flooded the worst anyone can remember. Chance's uncle lost his life in it."

"How dreadful!" Raven exclaimed. "Chance must feel awful."

"He does that, not only because of the loss of his relative, but because of the way he died."

"You mean because he drowned?"

"That's just it. George didn't drown accidentally. Jadine lured him into the river, then pounded him on the head with a rock until he was helpless, then held his head under the water. Juan, old George's wrangler, saw her do it."

"Oh, my heaven, why did she do that?"

"She wanted the ranch. She thought she would inherit it at his death." Tory gave a short, bitter laugh. "She killed the old fellow for nothing. She didn't know that in his will George left everything to Chance."

"What happened to her then? The law must have punished her."

"It didn't get a chance. She and Juan had a gun battle. They killed each other."

"Chance must feel dreadful. The woman he planned on marrying killed his uncle."

Tory gave Raven a startled look. "What are you talking about, Chance planned to marry that whore? How could he when he's already married to you?"

"That's what Jadine told me. She said that as soon as Chance divorced me, she and Chance were going to get married."

"I can't believe that you believed that hogwash. It's an insult to Chance that you would think he would ever consider marrying a woman who would lie down with any man who came along."

He gave Raven a searching look. "That's why you ran away, isn't it?"

Raven nodded. "I know how foolish I was now, but yes, that's why I left." Tears gathered in her eyes again. "What am I going to do, Tory? I've ruined everything."

"Not necessarily. First off, you must never let Chance know that you thought he was interested in Jadine. I don't know if he would ever forgive you for thinking that. I know that you two love each other, and that if you'd stop knocking your heads together, you'll both realize it and have a fine life together."

"I think you're wrong, Tory. Chance has never shown me the least hint that he feels anything for me except contempt. You did force him to marry me."

"You're the one who's wrong, Raven, but let's drop the subject. What should we do about you now? I wish you would come home where you belong. Give it another couple months, then if nothing happens between you and Chance, I'll take you to Clayton, I'll stay with you until you're settled. Does that sound fair?"

"I'd try anything to make our marriage work," Raven admitted. If only Chance would say he loved her before he found out about the baby, she thought. She would never leave him then.

"Let me go talk to Chance," Tory suggested, giving her braid a tug before he climbed into the saddle and lifted the reins. "Stay where you are. I should be back shortly."

As Tory sent his mount up the knoll where Chance still sat his horse, he went over in his mind what to say to his brother-in-law.

Chance turned in the saddle and looked at Tory

when he rode up. "How is she?" he asked.

"She's feeling better. What are we gonna do about her?"

"Are you asking me what to do about a woman who has run away from me?"

"Yes, I am. You're still her husband, and I think you should express your opinion on what she should do now."

"You must know that what I'd like for her to do is to turn around and go back home with me. If not to my ranch, at least to your place. I don't like the idea of her living alone in Clayton. Too many things could happen to her."

"I don't like the idea of her living alone there either, but she's so strong-minded."

"Stubborn is more like it," Chance said.

"She is that," Tory agreed. He lifted the reins. "I'm going to go talk to her now, tell her what we wish she would do."

"You'd better tell her that it is what you wish she would do. If you tell her it's my wish too, she definitely won't go along with it."

Tory only laughed as he nudged the horse into motion.

"Well, sister," he said when he rode up to where Raven still waited. "Chance and I talked it over, and what we both would like is for you and him to turn around and ride back to Bitter Creek."

"Why Chance?" Raven was quick to object. "Why can't you ride with me?"

"Because, little sister, I ran into the young woman who found me half dead in that blizzard after my first cattle drive. I've thought about her a lot since then, and after I've been paid for my herd, I intend to do some courting before I return home.

"Besides, I think it will be a good thing for you and Chance to spend a couple weeks together. You'll either decide to stay married, or kill each other."

"Most likely the latter," Raven said. She looked up at Tory with a thoughtful frown. "What about Rufus? The old man needs help."

"We've only got about another couple days before we reach Clayton. He can manage alone for that short time. If need be, I'll help him."

"Well, I guess that pretty much takes care of everything." Raven returned her gaze to the river. "When do we leave?"

"Within the hour, I think. There's still several hours of daylight left. I'll borrow some clean clothes for you from the wrangler." Tory grinned and added, "He's not much bigger than you. I'll get a bar of soap and a towel from my saddlebag and keep watch while you take a bath and scrub your hair. I don't mind telling you that you're a sorry-looking sight."

He laughingly avoided the stick Raven threw at him, and rode away.

A short time later as Raven lathered her hair out of sight of the men in the bend of the river, she wondered if Tory had found it hard to convince Chance to take her back to their ranch. She couldn't imagine that he would be anxious to spend a couple weeks with her.

As she soaped a washcloth and moved it over her body, her eyes softened when she came to the

379

slight rounding of her stomach. Her baby lay there, the reason she had left everyone she knew and loved. Her plans had been to go to a place where she could make a new life for herself and her child. Now she was retracing her steps in the hope that she might be able to make a new life with the father of her baby.

Raven was dressed in her clean borrowed clothes and had her hair combed and almost dry when Chance and Tory rode up. Chance was leading a pretty little roan mare for her to ride.

Chance tried not to stare at his wife's loveliness, her hair tumbling about her shoulders, Rudy's smaller-sized shirt showing the shape of her breasts. He didn't remember their being that large. They looked like more than a handful now.

He managed to look away before making eye contact with Raven, and sat quietly while brother and sister said their goodbyes. When Tory helped Raven to mount the little mare, he lifted a hand to his neighbor and led off.

They rode for an hour with no words between them. The only sound to be heard was the thud of hooves in the sod and the creaking of leather and the jingle of bridles.

Raven passed the time gazing at the easy swing of Chance's whip-lean body in the saddle. The only time she looked away from him was when the memory of their bodies joined together became too much to bear.

The lush prairie grasslands attracted buffalos in large numbers. It was near sunset when some distance away Chance spotted what looked like a wide band of rolling smoke. He reined in, an anxious look on his face. Were they going to be caught in a racing brush fire?

He was trying to decide in which direction to ride when Raven cried out, "It's a herd of buffalo!"

That discovery didn't lessen Chance's concern. To be caught in the middle of four thousand thundering cloven hoofs was just as dangerous as a raging fire.

Half a mile away Chance's anxious gaze made out a small stand of cottonwood.

"What are we going to do Chance?" Raven asked, an anxious tremor in her voice.

"Ride as fast as you can toward those trees to your right." He tried to speak calmly. "The beasts won't try to run through them."

Raven's little mare was fast and ran only a length behind Chance's quarter horse as maddened buffalos swept toward them like a black cloud. With a quick glance Chance judged the distance between them and the safety of the trees.

Turning in the saddle, he shouted over the deafening roar coming nearer and nearer, "Lay on the whip!"

Raven had never taken a whip to a horse, but in this instance she knew her life might depend on it. She grabbed the quirt out of its sheath and brought it down sharply on the mare's rump.

As they reached the edge of the trees in a dead heat with the buffalos, the little mare almost went down when a large, shaggy head rammed her in the rump.

"Are you all right?" Chance shouted, dismounting and hurrying to help Raven dismount.

"I think so." Raven clung to him, her voice shaky and her body trembling.

"We'll be all right now." Chance knew he should release Raven. "I don't know how long we'll have to stay here until they've passed us by. I can't see the end of the herd. One time my men and I were caught by a stampeding herd and had to perch on a mesa for three hours before they all passed by."

"In that case we might as well make night camp here." Raven stepped out of Chance's arms.

"We might as well. I'm hungry anyhow. Why don't you look through the grub bag and see what Rufus packed for us while I make a fire. A cup of coffee would sure hit the spot."

This is the first normal conversation we've ever had, Raven thought, opening the canvas bag and peering inside it.

On the very top of the items stored inside was a cloth bag of ground coffee. It was as though the old man knew a pot of brew would be the first thing they would want. When Chance had a fire going, she poured half the water from her canteen into the battered coffee pot. After tossing a handful of grounds into it, she placed the pot on a bed of red coals. While Chance unsaddled their mounts and hobbled them nearby, she dug into the grub bag again.

She found a slab of salt pork, a bag of hardtack, several cans of beans and an equal amount of canned tomatoes. She was aware that the cowhands carried cans of tomatoes in their saddlebags; if watering holes were scarce, the tomatoes would refresh them.

Thanks to what she had learned from helping Rufus around a cook fire, Raven soon had salt pork frying and beans heating in a pan.

Chance lounged against a tree watching the graceful movements of his wife as she turned meat and stirred beans. His blood boiled almost as hot as the fire that cooked their supper. He didn't know how in the world he was going to keep his hands off those shapely curves. But he knew he had to. He must prove to Raven that, although he lusted after her all the time, he loved her even more.

Just as Raven called that it was time to eat, the last straggling remnants of the buffalos passed by. It seemed eerily quiet after so long a time having their eardrums blasted with the deafening racket of a thousand buffalos.

By the time the last of the meal had been eaten, the dust had settled and the red ball of the sun was low on the horizon. Chance joined Raven at the edge of the small woods and watched with her as a soft twilight began to descend.

"It's a glorious country, isn't it?" she said softly.

"It sure is. God must have run out of ugly when he made Montana. As far as I'm concerned, Montana is the best of all places to live in, to work in, to die in."

Raven silently nodded agreement.

When the sun was halfway hidden, Chance said, "Since you cooked the grub, I'll clean up after us." He grinned and jerked his thumb over his shoulder. "There's a big tree back there that you might want to take advantage of."

Raven smiled and said, "You read my mind."

When she returned to the fire, Chance had opened up her bedroll. As soon as he went to use the tree, she hurried out of her shirt and trousers. When Chance returned to the fire he was disappointed to see her sleeping soundly between the blankets.

A pattern developed as Chance and Raven rode homeward. They rose in the pink dawn, drank two cups of coffee each, with a chunk of hardtack dunked in the brew. They were on the trail then, kicking their mounts into a moderate gallop for an hour or so before slowing them down to a walk. This was done for the benefit of the horses. They were refreshed, and in the cool of the morning they wanted to run. Later, when the sun grew hot they were ready for a slower pace.

When Raven and Chance made noon camp for a cup of coffee and to chew on a strip of pemmican, Chance always shaved after the short meal was finished.

One day as Raven sat watching him she remarked, "Your hair is so long, soon you'll have to tie it back, or braid it."

"Do you want to cut it?" Chance challenged with a grin, offering her his straight razor.

To his surprise and dismay, Raven stood up and answered, "I've never cut hair before, but I'd like to try." She took the sharp blade and stepped behind him.

"Now, don't go cutting off too much," Chance

said, a little nervous. "I don't like it too short."

"I won't," Raven said soberly but with a twinkle in her eyes that Chance couldn't see. "I'll just take off six or eight inches."

"Six or eight inches?" Chance exclaimed, alarmed. "I think I'll just wait until I get back to Bitter Creek and let the barber do it."

"Nonsense. I'm sure I can do it as well as he can." Raven walked behind Chance and picked up a strand of his hair. As it curled intimately around her fingers, she almost gave Chance back his razor. She gritted her teeth in determination and gave a slice of the blade.

Chance flinched every time he felt the hair falling on his back. He could not see what Raven was doing and had no idea how much hair she was cutting away. However, when she got to the sides of his head, he drew a relieved breath. He saw she was only cutting away a couple inches from the length.

"You like to rile me, don't you?" he half growled, half laughed.

"That's because you're so easy to rile." Raven grinned as she handed him back his razor.

When they made night camp they almost always had fresh meat to go with their coffee and hardtack. It might be a rabbit or a prairie chicken Chance had shot as they rode along. At night, sitting in front of the campfire, they got into the habit of speaking about the years in which they grew up. They found that they had many fond memories of those days. Gradually they began to relax in each other's company and to look forward to the evenings of easy conversation.

They weren't always relaxed around each other, though. Each burned with the desire of the relationship they'd had before. They both longed to satisfy the ache that was always with them, day and night. Every time Raven detected an expression in Chance's eyes that plainly said he hungered for her, it was all she could do not to cry out, "For God's sake, Chance take me to bed." She kept her silence. She did not want his lust. She wanted his love.

Then came a night that Raven sought her bed early. Before going to sleep she came to the conclusion that she could not go on, that she would settle for his lust. She would go home with him, and if nothing else, she would have his lovemaking every night. Maybe it wasn't in Chance to love a woman.

Chance sat before the fire long after his wife had fallen asleep. The moon rose, so bright he could see in detail Raven's body curled up in her bedroll. He rose and walked in his stocking feet to where she lay. Kneeling at her side, he gazed longingly at her sleeping face.

The covers had fallen off Raven's shoulders, and in her sleep she felt a cool breeze against her arms and face. She pulled the blanket back up around her, then suddenly came awake. She opened her eyes and looked into Chance's hungry ones. With a soft cry of consent, she lifted her arms to him.

With a moan almost of pain, Chance swept back the blanket that covered Raven and took her in his arms. For a long moment all he did was hold her tightly, rocking back and forth. Then slowly his head came down to fasten his lips on her waiting ones.

The kiss was tender at first, but rapidly grew hungry and demanding.

Their hands were busy as the kiss went on and on. When at last Chance raised his head, all they had on was the socks on their feet. In the moon's rays they gazed at each other's bodies, lingering on spots they most wanted. A warm feeling came over Raven and she slid a hand under each of her breasts and raised them invitingly to Chance. He lowered his head to them instantly, taking one in his mouth while his hand fondled the other. As his teeth nibbled and pulled on the nipple in his mouth, he rolled the matching one between his fingers.

Raven slid a hand across his flat stomach, then cupped her palm around his rock-hard arousal. He moaned low in his throat when she began to slide her hand up and down his length. It throbbed and jerked like a live thing, and she couldn't wait for it to do its dance inside her.

When Chance's hand left her breast and moved between her thighs, she squirmed in delight. He parted the crisp curls there and slid his finger inside her. As he rubbed the little pebble-hard nub he found, Raven's breath came fast and harsh.

Chance knew it was time to stop the foreplay. He removed his hand and took hers away from him. When he opened her legs to receive him, she took his rigid manhood in both hands and guided it inside her warmth.

Chance slid his hands under her small rear and slowly shoved his entire long length deep inside her. They lay quietly for a moment, savoring the feel of each other. Then Chance lifted her legs high around his waist, and holding her hips steady, he began to pump slowly in and out, making her sigh happily with each heavenly thrust.

She braced her feet on the ground and raised her body so that she could get every inch of him. "Make it last, Chance," she begged. "Make it go on forever."

But she was asking the impossible. Chance had waited too long, wanted her too much. "I'm sorry, honey," he whispered, "I can't make it last any longer. I promise you, though, that before the night is over you'll be well pleased."

Raven couldn't hold back any longer either, and in the soft night they cried out in joyous release together.

Both were left so limp they couldn't so much as lift a hand for a minute. Then, still joined together, Chance braced himself on his elbows and, stroking the damp hair off Raven's forehead, asked, "Was it as wonderful for you as it was for me?"

She raised a hand to rest against his cheek and teased, "You did real good for an old man."

Chance smiled wickedly into her eyes, luminous in the moonlight. "Didn't you know that old dogs know the best tricks?"

Raven's eyes grew serious. "I expect you've had enough women to know all about that."

"There haven't been so many. But there's no comparing bedding them and making love to a wife you love."

Raven's body grew still. "Chance," she whispered, "are you saying that you love me?"

"Of course I love you. What makes you think that I don't?"

"You never said so before."

"I didn't know you wanted the words. Every time I made love to you my body said it." He bucked his hips at her. "I don't recall you ever saying that you love me. Do you?"

Raven wound her arms around his shoulders and said, "Remember the words you said about Montana? Well, that's how much I love you."

A smile deepened the crease in Chance's cheeks. "That much, huh?"

"Yes, that much," Raven whispered. She looked at him from under heavy lids. "Do you want to show me some more of your tricks, old dog?"

Chance gave a throaty laugh and placed his hands under her hips. "I've been waiting ten minutes to do that."

"But gently, Chance." Raven laid her hands over his. "In fact, it must be slow and easy for the next few months."

"I don't understand." Chance looked down at her. "Why for the next few months?"

"Because, dear husband, come winter you are going to be a daddy."

Raven felt his manhood go limp, but the rest of his body seemed to vibrate from her news.

"Are you sure, Raven?" he asked in wonderment, his eyes shining in the moonlight.

"I'm sure, Chance. Are you happy about it?"

"That's hardly the word that describes what I'm feeling." He grinned crookedly. "Even Montana has never made me this happy."

After a moment Raven traced her finger around his firm lips and asked, "Weren't you about to show me some of your tricks?"

Raven felt him quicken inside her as he laughingly said, "I guess I'll have to learn some new ones from now on."

As the night wore on, both found that the slow, leisurely pace Chance set was more satisfactory than the almost frantic way they used to come together.

The moon was quite low when finally, wrapped in each other's arms, they fell into a deep sleep.

The sun had fully risen when Chance kissed his wife awake. "Good morning, husband," she said, smiling up at him.

"How are you feeling?" Chance asked a little anxiously as he took her arms and pulled her up to sit before him.

"I feel lazy and content," she answered softly before adding with a wry smile, "I'm not sure, though, if my legs will ever come together again."

"Maybe this will help." Chance handed her the cup of coffee he had set on the ground.

"Oh, that smells delicious," Raven sighed happily, bringing the strong liquid to her lips. "You're going to spoil me."

"That's my intention," Chance said huskily as he watched her lips close over the rim of the tin cup.

He determinedly ignored the stirring in his loins. As he stood up he said teasingly, "When you think you can get your legs together, we'll break camp."

The rest of the trip was like being on the honeymoon they had never had.

And so it continued after they reached home. Mary soon felt like excess baggage and left to live with her sister. Even old Cal felt himself in the way on the evening he dropped by to welcome them and ask about Tory. When his questions were answered in monosyllables, he threw up his hands and, scarcely noticed, stomped out of the house. In his opinion, the pair were a couple of loony birds.

Summer passed and fall was upon the range. The baby Raven carried was clearly outlined in her slender body and there was a radiance about her that people remarked upon.

And Chance thought there was nothing so fine on earth as reaching his home in the gathering darkness after coming up from a windswept valley and seeing lamplight shining through the ranch window and knowing that his wife was waiting to greet him with a long kiss.

Wild Fire

NORAH HESS

The Yankees killed her sweetheart, imprisoned her brother, and drove her from her home, but beautiful golden-haired Serena Bain faces the future boldly as the wagon trains roll out. But all the peril in the world won't change her bitter resentment of the darkly handsome Yankee wagon master Josh Quade. Soon, however, her heart betrays her will. His strong, rippling, buckskin-clad body sets her senses on fire. But pride and fate continue to tear them apart as the wagon trains roll west—until one night, in the soft, secret darkness of a bordello, Serena and Josh unleash their wildest passion and open their souls to the sweetest raptures of love.

___52331-0 $5.50 US/$6.50 CAN

Lark — Norah Hess

Trapped in a loveless marriage, Lark Elliot longs to lead a normal life like the pretty women she sees in town, to wear new clothes and be courted by young suitors. But she has married Cletus Gibb, a man twice her age, so her elderly aunt and uncle can stay through the long Colorado winter in the mountain cabin he owns. Resigned to backbreaking labor on Gibb's ranch, Lark finds one person who makes the days bearable: Ace Brandon. But when her husband pays the rugged cowhand to father him an heir, at first Lark thinks she has been wrong about Ace's kindness. It isn't long, however, before she is looking forward to the warmth of his tender kiss, to the feel of his strong body. And as the heat of their desire melts away the cold winter nights, Lark knows she's found the haven she's always dreamed of in the circle of his loving arms.

___4522-2 $5.99 US/$6.99 CAN

Dorchester Publishing Co., Inc.
P.O. Box 6640
Wayne, PA 19087-8640

Please add $1.75 for shipping and handling for the first book and $.50 for each book thereafter. NY, NYC, and PA residents, please add appropriate sales tax. No cash, stamps, or C.O.D.s. All orders shipped within 6 weeks via postal service book rate. Canadian orders require $2.00 extra postage and must be paid in U.S. dollars through a U.S. banking facility.

Name_____
Address_____
City_____State_____Zip_____
I have enclosed $_____ in payment for the checked book(s).
Payment <u>must</u> accompany all orders. ❑ Please send a free catalog.
CHECK OUT OUR WEBSITE! www.dorchesterpub.com

KENTUCKY BRIDE

NORAH HESS

Fleeing her abusive uncle, young D'lise Alexander trusts no man...until she is rescued by virile trapper Kane Devlin. His rugged strength and tender concern convinces D'lise she'll find a safe haven in his backwoods homestead. There, amid the simple pleasures of cornhuskings and barn raisings, she discovers that Kane kindles a blaze of desire that burns even hotter than the flames in his rugged stone hearth. Beneath his soul-stirring kisses she forgets her fears, forgets everything except her longing to become his sweet Kentucky bride.

___52270-5 $5.50 US/$6.50 CAN

Dorchester Publishing Co., Inc.
P.O. Box 6640
Wayne, PA 19087-8640

TANNER

Norah Hess

Roxy Bartel needs a husband. More important, her son needs a father. But the lonely saloon owner cannot forget Tanner Graylord, the man who, eight years before, gave her love and a child, then walked out of her life. And now he is back, hoping she can believe that he has never stopped loving her, hoping for a chance that they might still live a life in each other's arms.

___4424-2 $5.99 US/$6.99 CAN

Dorchester Publishing Co., Inc.
P.O. Box 6640
Wayne, PA 19087-8640

Please add $1.75 for shipping and handling for the first book and $.50 for each book thereafter. NY, NYC, and PA residents, please add appropriate sales tax. No cash, stamps, or C.O.D.s. All orders shipped within 6 weeks via postal service book rate. Canadian orders require $2.00 extra postage and must be paid in U.S. dollars through a U.S. banking facility.

Name_____
Address_____
City_____State_____Zip_____
I have enclosed $_____ in payment for the checked book(s).
Payment <u>must</u> accompany all orders. ❑ Please send a free catalog.
CHECK OUT OUR WEBSITE! www.dorchesterpub.com

DEVIL IN SPURS

NORAH HESS

Raised in a bawdy house, Jonty Rand posed as a boy all her life to escape the notice of the rowdy cowboys who frequented the place. And to Jonty's way of thinking, the most notorious womanizer of the bunch is Cord McBain. So when her granny's dying wish makes Cord Jonty's guardian, she despairs of ever revealing her true identity. In the rugged solitude of the Wyoming wilderness he assigns Jonty all the hardest tasks on his horse ranch, making her life a torment. Then one stormy night, Cord discovers that Jonty will never be a man, only the wildest, most willing woman he's ever taken in his arms, the one woman who can claim his heart.

___52294-2 $5.50 US/$6.50 CAN

NORAH HESS

After her father's accidental death, it is up to young Fancy Cranson to keep her small family together. But to survive in the pristine woodlands of the Pacific Northwest, she has to use her brains or her body. With no other choice, Fancy vows she'll work herself to the bone before selling herself to any timberman—even one as handsome, virile, and arrogant as Chance Dawson.

From the moment Chance Dawson lays eyes on Fancy, he wants to claim her for himself. But the mighty woodsman has felled forests less stubborn than the beautiful orphan. To win her hand he has to trade his roughhewn ways for tender caresses, and brazen curses for soft words of desire. Only then will he be able to share with her a love that unites them in passionate splendor.

_3783-1 $5.99 US/$6.99 CAN